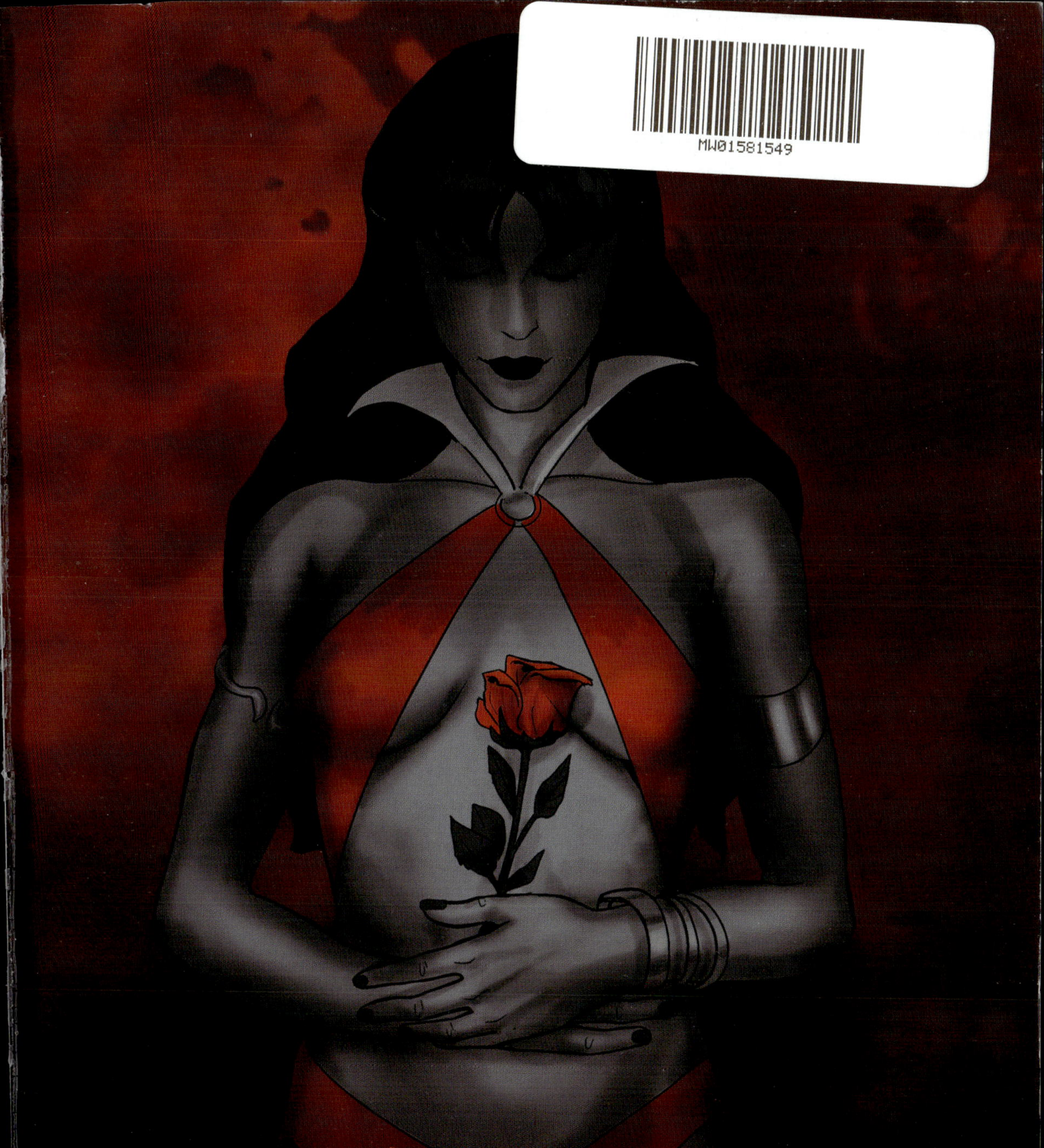

VAMPIRELLA®
INQUISITION

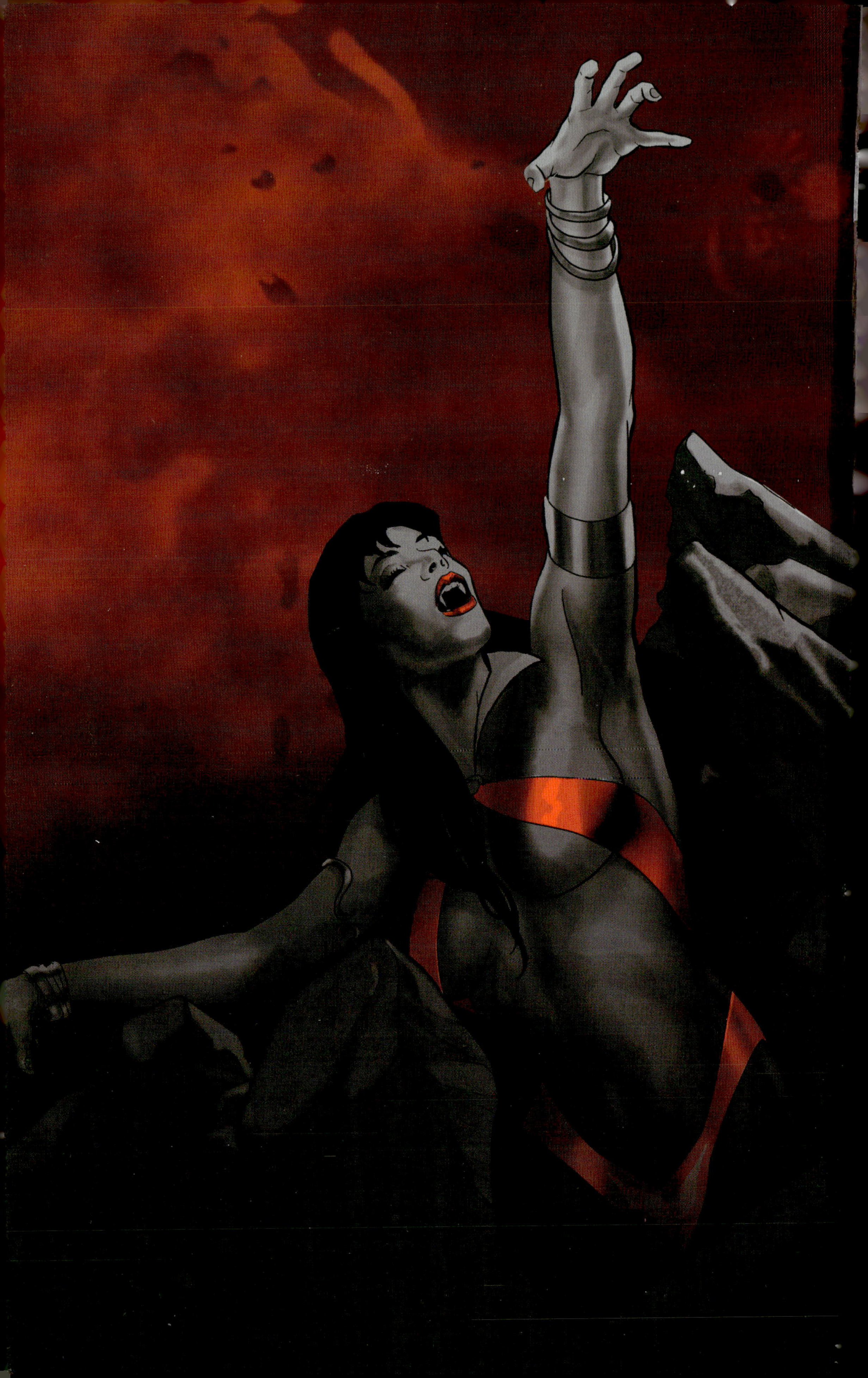

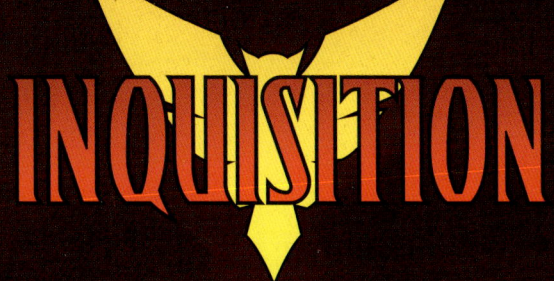

INQUISITION

WRITTEN BY
Brandon Jerwa

ILLUSTRATED BY
Heubert Khan Michael

LETTERED BY
Marshall Dillon

COLORS BY
Mat Lopes issues 21-24, 26
Peter Alves issue 25

COLLECTION COVER BY
Paul Renaud

COLLECTION DESIGN BY
Katie Hidalgo

SPECIAL THANKS TO RICH AMTOWER, CAROLINE CHAVIER, JULIAN CHUNOVIC, GEKKO HOPMAN, ISAO KATO, AND REIKO NINOMIYA.

Nick Barrucci, CEO / Publisher
Juan Collado, President / COO
Rich Young, Director Business Development
Keith Davidsen, Marketing Manager

Joe Rybandt, Senior Editor
Sarah Litt, Digital Editor
Josh Green, Traffic Coordinator

Josh Johnson, Art Director
Jason Ullmeyer, Senior Graphic Designer
Katie Hidalgo, Graphic Designer
Chris Caniano, Production Assistant

Visit us online at www.DYNAMITE.com
Follow us on Twitter @dynamitecomics
Like us on Facebook /Dynamitecomics
Watch us on YouTube /Dynamitecomics

ISBN-10: 1-60690-424-8
ISBN-13: 978-1-60690-424-4
First Printing 10 9 8 7 6 5 4 3 2 1

VAMPIRELLA®, VOL. 4: INQUISITION. This volume collects material originally published in Vampirella #21-26. Published by Dynamite Entertainment. 113 Gaither Dr., STE 205, Mt. Laurel, NJ 08054. Vampirella is trademark and copyright of Dynamite. All Rights Reserved. DYNAMITE, DYNAMITE ENTERTAINMENT and its logo are © & ® 2013 Dynamite. All rights reserved. All names, characters, events, and locales in this publication are entirely fictional. Any resemblance to actual persons (living or dead), events or places, without satiric intent, is coincidental. No portion of this book may be reproduced by any means (digital or print) without the written permission of Dynamite Entertainment except for review purposes. The scanning, uploading and distribution of this book via the Internet or via any other means without the permission of the publisher is illegal and punishable by law. Please purchase only authorized electronic editions, and do not participate in or encourage electronic piracy of copyrighted materials. **Printed in China**

For information regarding press, media rights, foreign rights, licensing, promotions, and advertising e-mail: marketing@dynamite.com

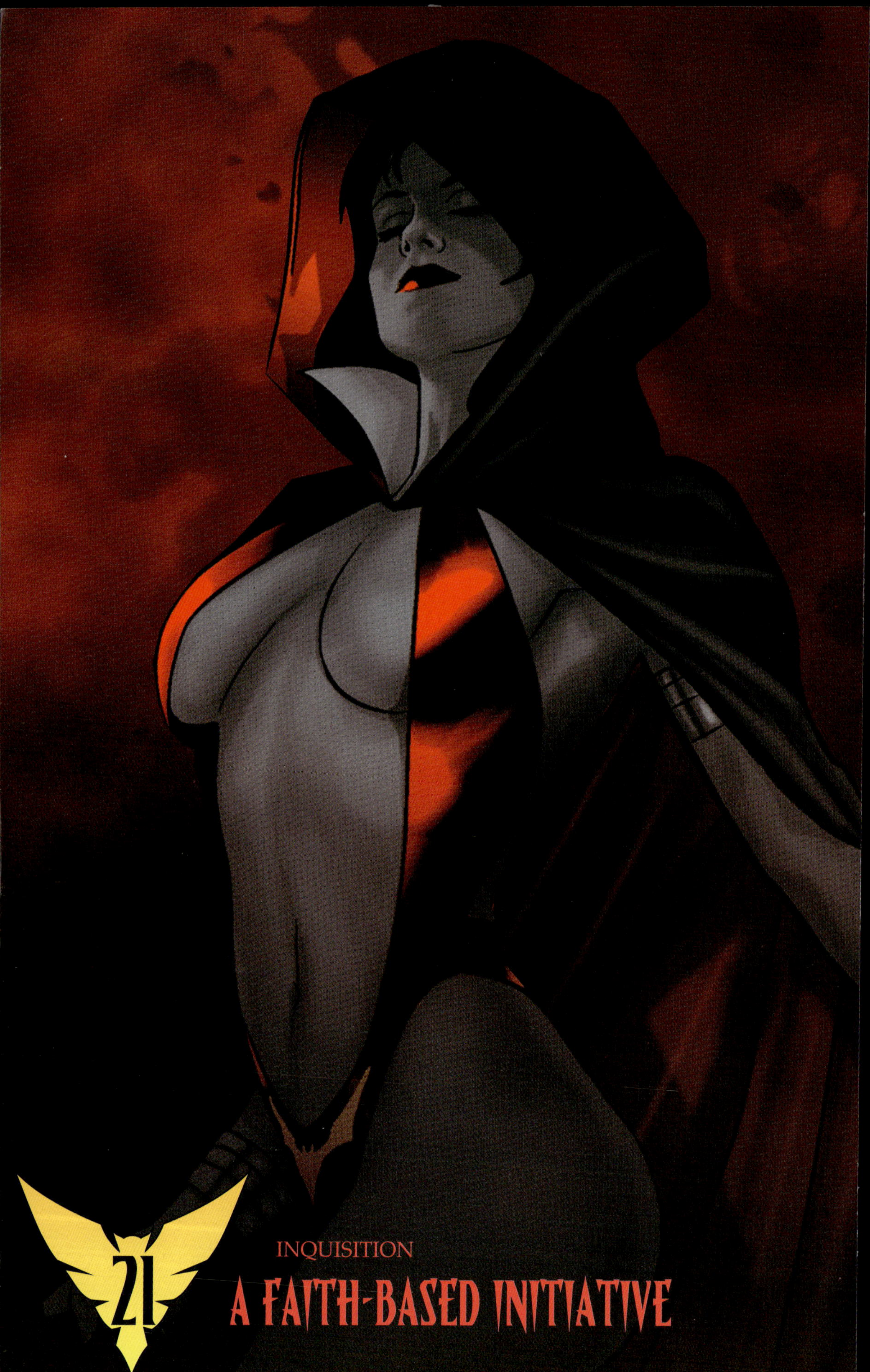
21
INQUISITION
A FAITH-BASED INITIATIVE

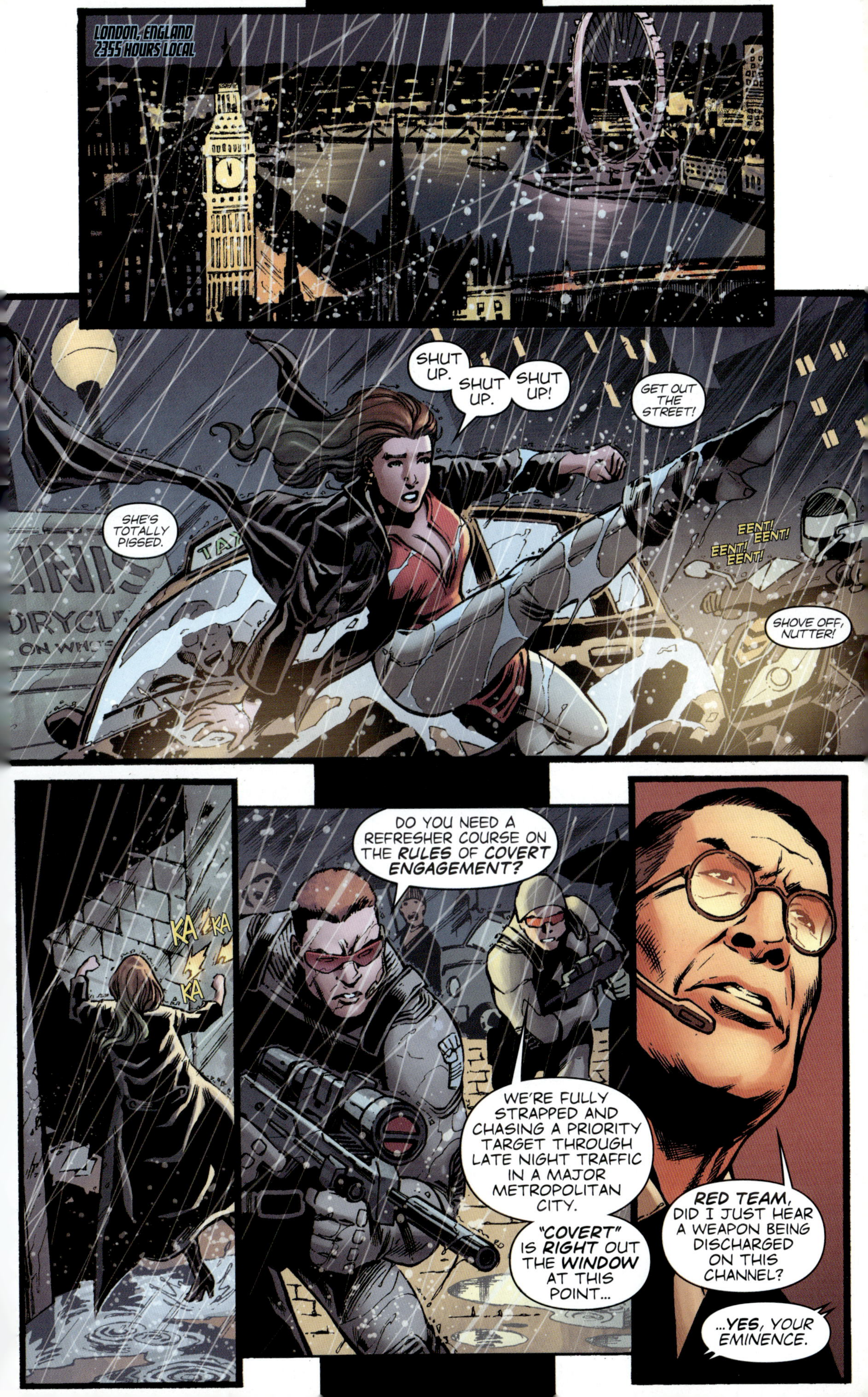
LONDON, ENGLAND 2355 HOURS LOCAL
SHUT UP.
SHUT UP.
SHUT UP!
GET OUT THE STREET!
SHE'S TOTALLY PISSED.
EENT! EENT! EENT! EENT!
SHOVE OFF, NUTTER!
KA KA KA
DO YOU NEED A REFRESHER COURSE ON THE RULES OF COVERT ENGAGEMENT?
WE'RE FULLY STRAPPED AND CHASING A PRIORITY TARGET THROUGH LATE NIGHT TRAFFIC IN A MAJOR METROPOLITAN CITY.
"COVERT" IS RIGHT OUT THE WINDOW AT THIS POINT...
RED TEAM, DID I JUST HEAR A WEAPON BEING DISCHARGED ON THIS CHANNEL?
...YES, YOUR EMINENCE.

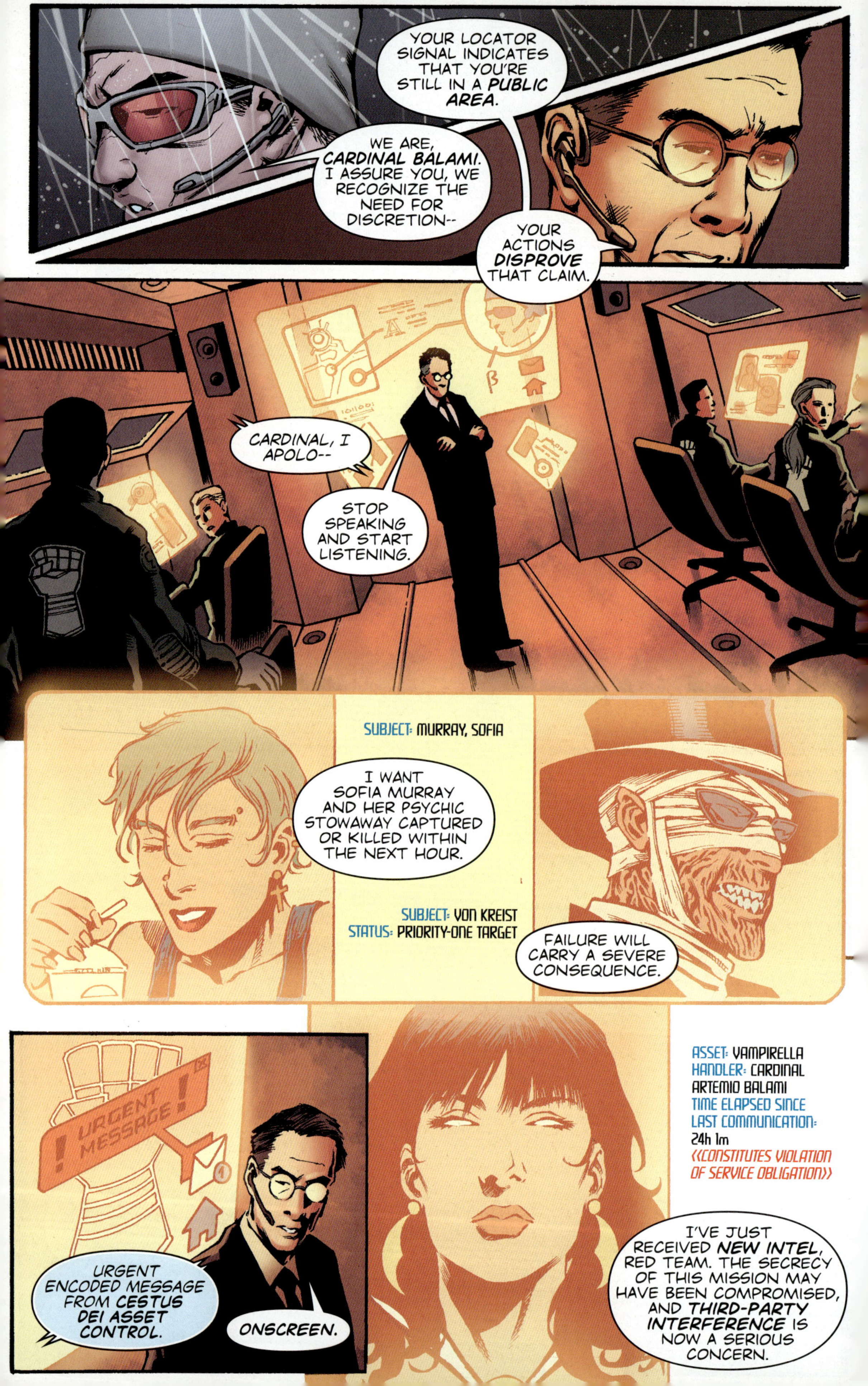
YOUR LOCATOR SIGNAL INDICATES THAT YOU'RE STILL IN A PUBLIC AREA.
WE ARE, CARDINAL BALAMI. I ASSURE YOU, WE RECOGNIZE THE NEED FOR DISCRETION--
YOUR ACTIONS DISPROVE THAT CLAIM.
CARDINAL, I APOLO--
STOP SPEAKING AND START LISTENING.
SUBJECT: MURRAY, SOFIA
I WANT SOFIA MURRAY AND HER PSYCHIC STOWAWAY CAPTURED OR KILLED WITHIN THE NEXT HOUR.
SUBJECT: VON KREIST
STATUS: PRIORITY-ONE TARGET
FAILURE WILL CARRY A SEVERE CONSEQUENCE.
URGENT MESSAGE
URGENT ENCODED MESSAGE FROM CESTUS DEI ASSET CONTROL.
ONSCREEN.
ASSET: VAMPIRELLA
HANDLER: CARDINAL ARTEMIO BALAMI
TIME ELAPSED SINCE LAST COMMUNICATION: 24h 1m
((CONSTITUTES VIOLATION OF SERVICE OBLIGATION))
I'VE JUST RECEIVED NEW INTEL, RED TEAM. THE SECRECY OF THIS MISSION MAY HAVE BEEN COMPROMISED, AND THIRD-PARTY INTERFERENCE IS NOW A SERIOUS CONCERN.

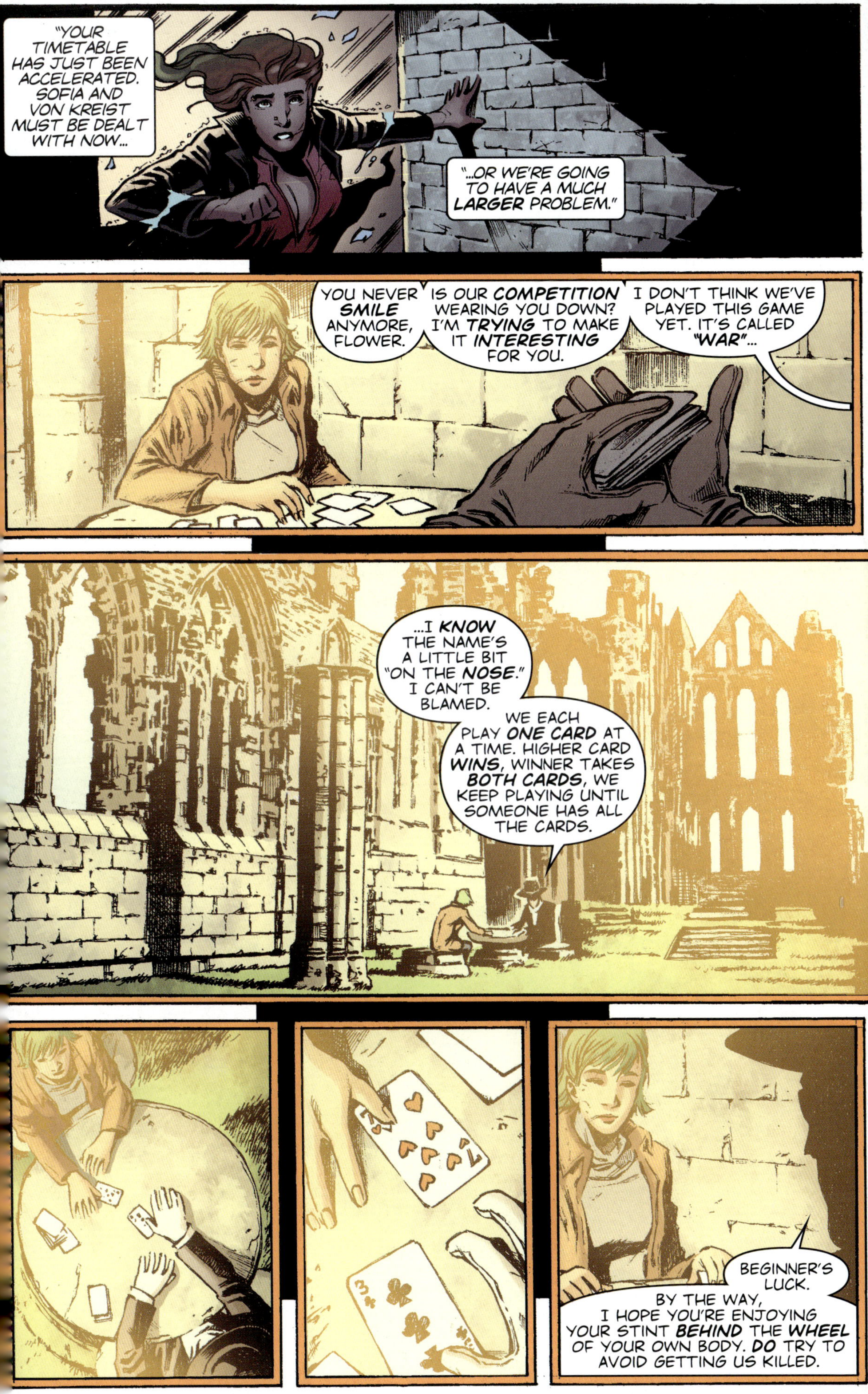
"YOUR TIMETABLE HAS JUST BEEN ACCELERATED. SOFIA AND VON KREIST MUST BE DEALT WITH NOW...
"...OR WE'RE GOING TO HAVE A MUCH LARGER PROBLEM."
YOU NEVER SMILE ANYMORE, FLOWER.
IS OUR COMPETITION WEARING YOU DOWN? I'M TRYING TO MAKE IT INTERESTING FOR YOU.
I DON'T THINK WE'VE PLAYED THIS GAME YET. IT'S CALLED "WAR"...
...I KNOW THE NAME'S A LITTLE BIT "ON THE NOSE." I CAN'T BE BLAMED.
WE EACH PLAY ONE CARD AT A TIME. HIGHER CARD WINS, WINNER TAKES BOTH CARDS, WE KEEP PLAYING UNTIL SOMEONE HAS ALL THE CARDS.
BEGINNER'S LUCK.
BY THE WAY, I HOPE YOU'RE ENJOYING YOUR STINT BEHIND THE WHEEL OF YOUR OWN BODY. DO TRY TO AVOID GETTING US KILLED.

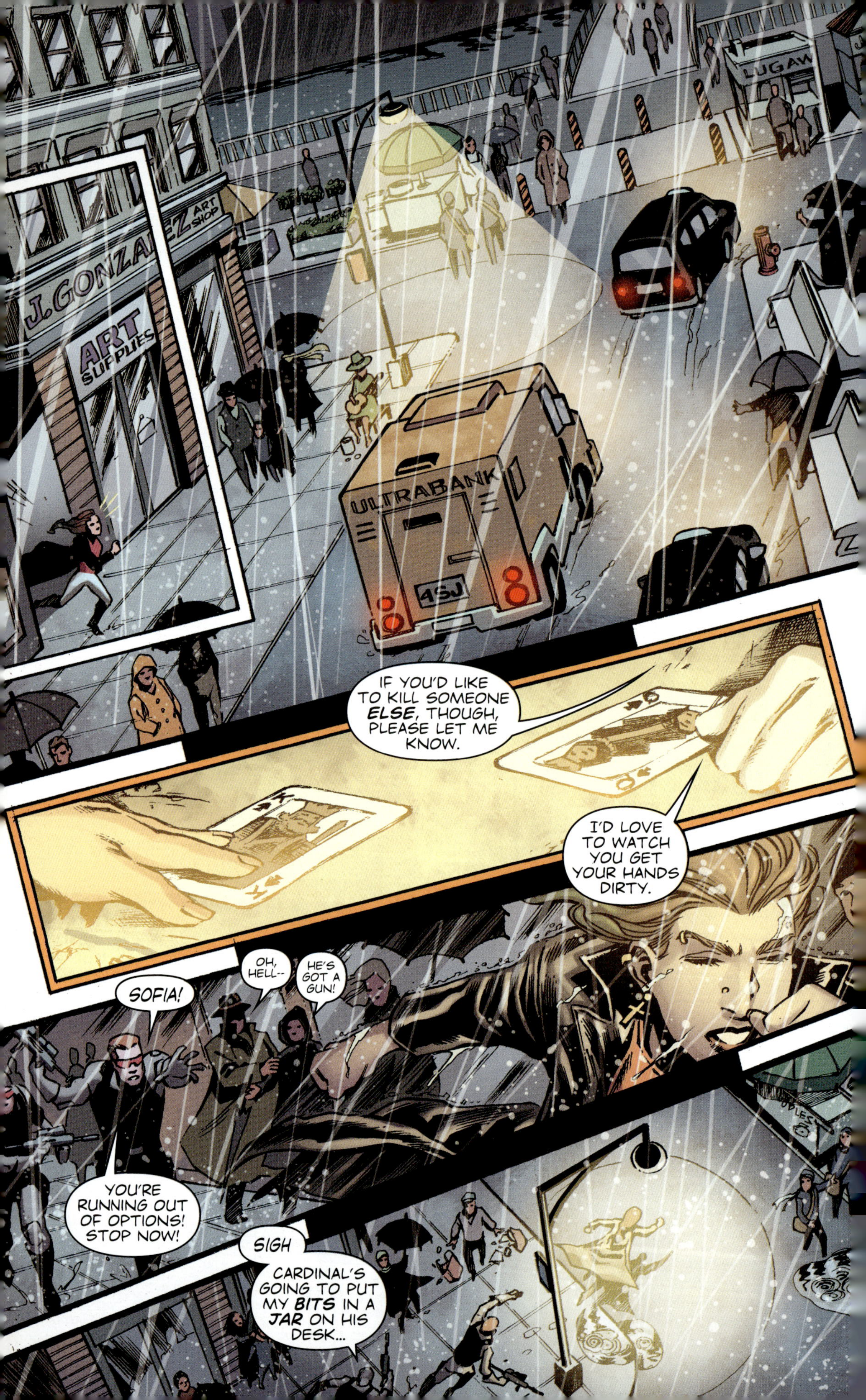
J. GONZALEZ ART SHOP
ART SUPPLIES
ULTRABANK
4SJ
IF YOU'D LIKE TO KILL SOMEONE ELSE, THOUGH, PLEASE LET ME KNOW.
I'D LOVE TO WATCH YOU GET YOUR HANDS DIRTY.
SOFIA!
OH, HELL--
HE'S GOT A GUN!
YOU'RE RUNNING OUT OF OPTIONS! STOP NOW!
SIGH
CARDINAL'S GOING TO PUT MY BITS IN A JAR ON HIS DESK...

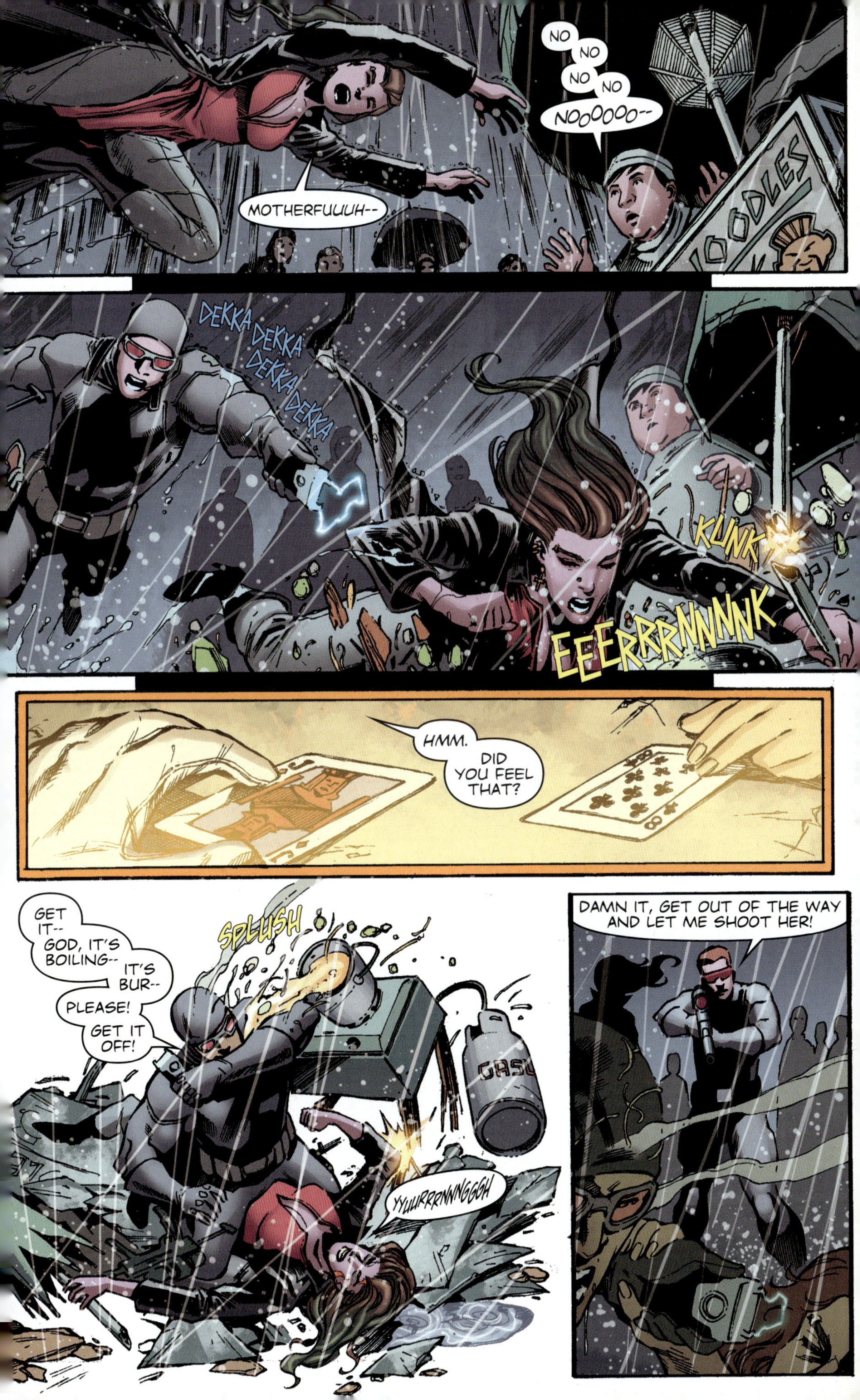
NO NO NO NO NOOOOOO--
MOTHERFUUUH--
NOODLES
DEKKA DEKKA DEKKA DEKKA
KUNK
EEERRRNNNNK
HMM.
DID YOU FEEL THAT?
GET IT-- GOD, IT'S BOILING-- IT'S BUR-- PLEASE! GET IT OFF!
SPLUSH
GASU
YYUURRNNNGGGH
DAMN IT, GET OUT OF THE WAY AND LET ME SHOOT HER!

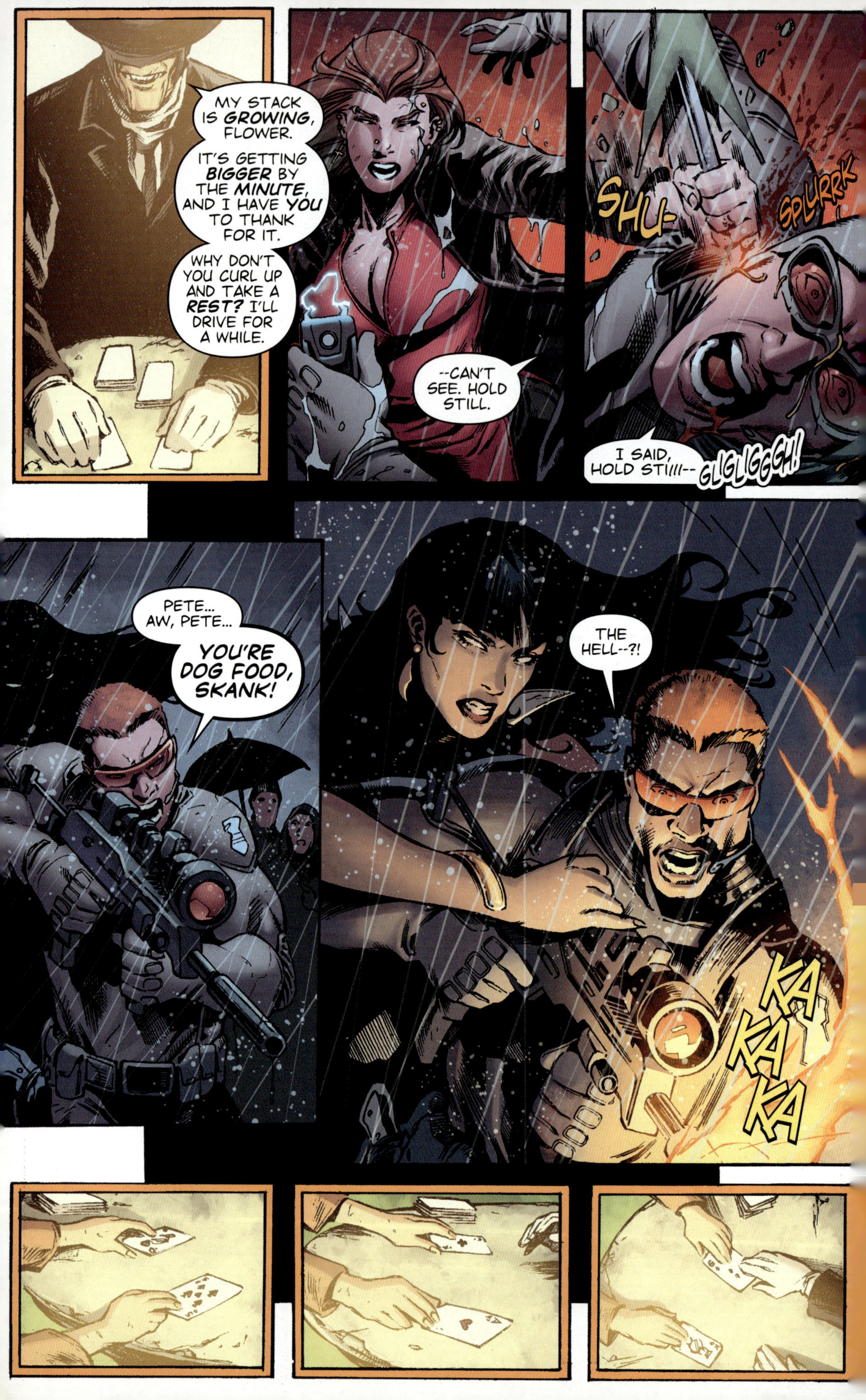
MY STACK IS GROWING, FLOWER.
IT'S GETTING BIGGER BY THE MINUTE, AND I HAVE YOU TO THANK FOR IT.
WHY DON'T YOU CURL UP AND TAKE A REST? I'LL DRIVE FOR A WHILE.
--CAN'T SEE. HOLD STILL.
SHU-
SPLURRK
I SAID, HOLD STI///--
GLGLGGGH!
PETE... AW, PETE...
YOU'RE DOG FOOD, SKANK!
THE HELL--?!
KA KA KA

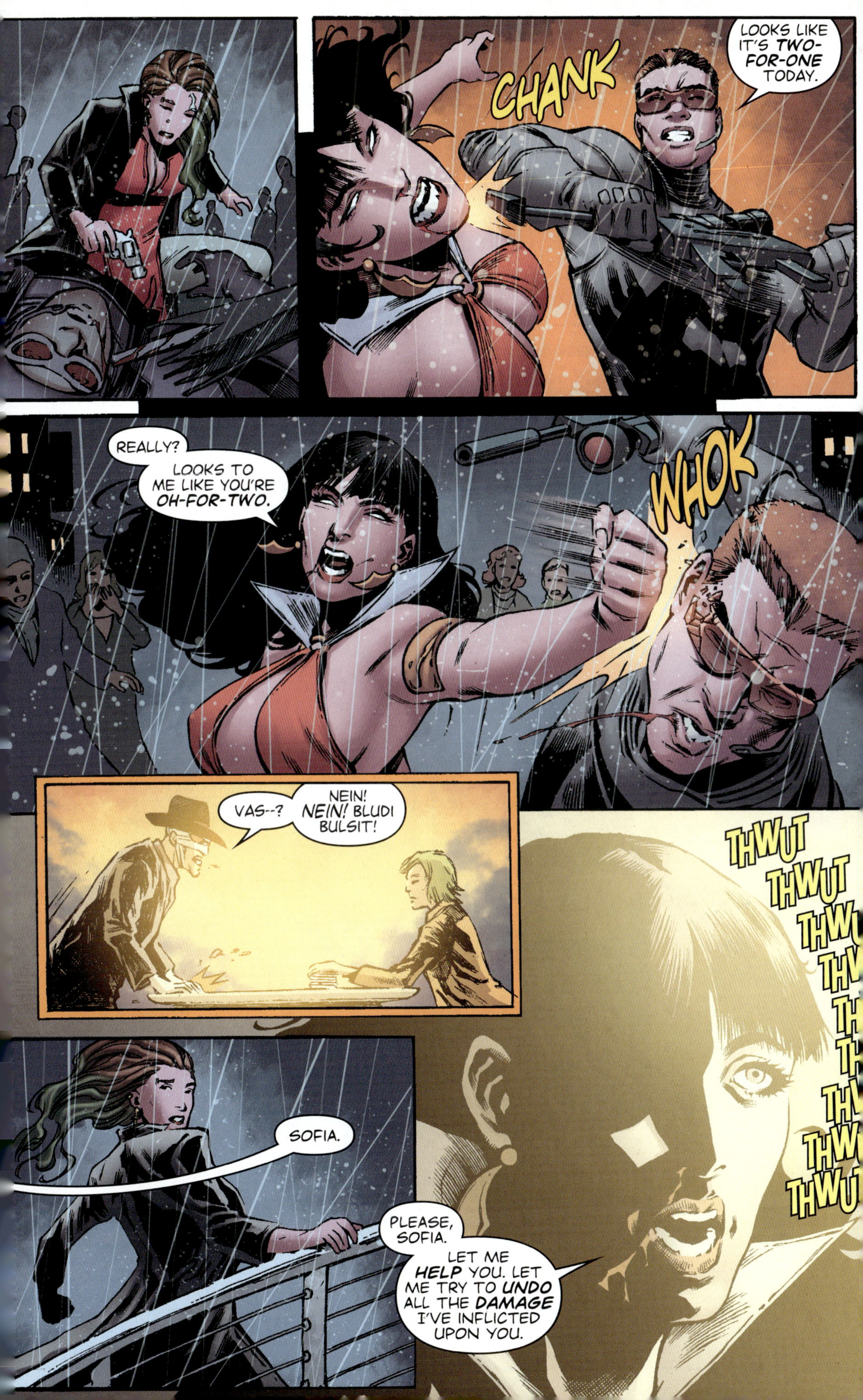
CHANK
LOOKS LIKE IT'S TWO-FOR-ONE TODAY.
REALLY?
LOOKS TO ME LIKE YOU'RE OH-FOR-TWO.
WHOK
VAS--?
NEIN! NEIN! BLUDI BULSIT!
THWUT
THWUT
SOFIA.
PLEASE, SOFIA.
LET ME HELP YOU. LET ME TRY TO UNDO ALL THE DAMAGE I'VE INFLICTED UPON YOU.

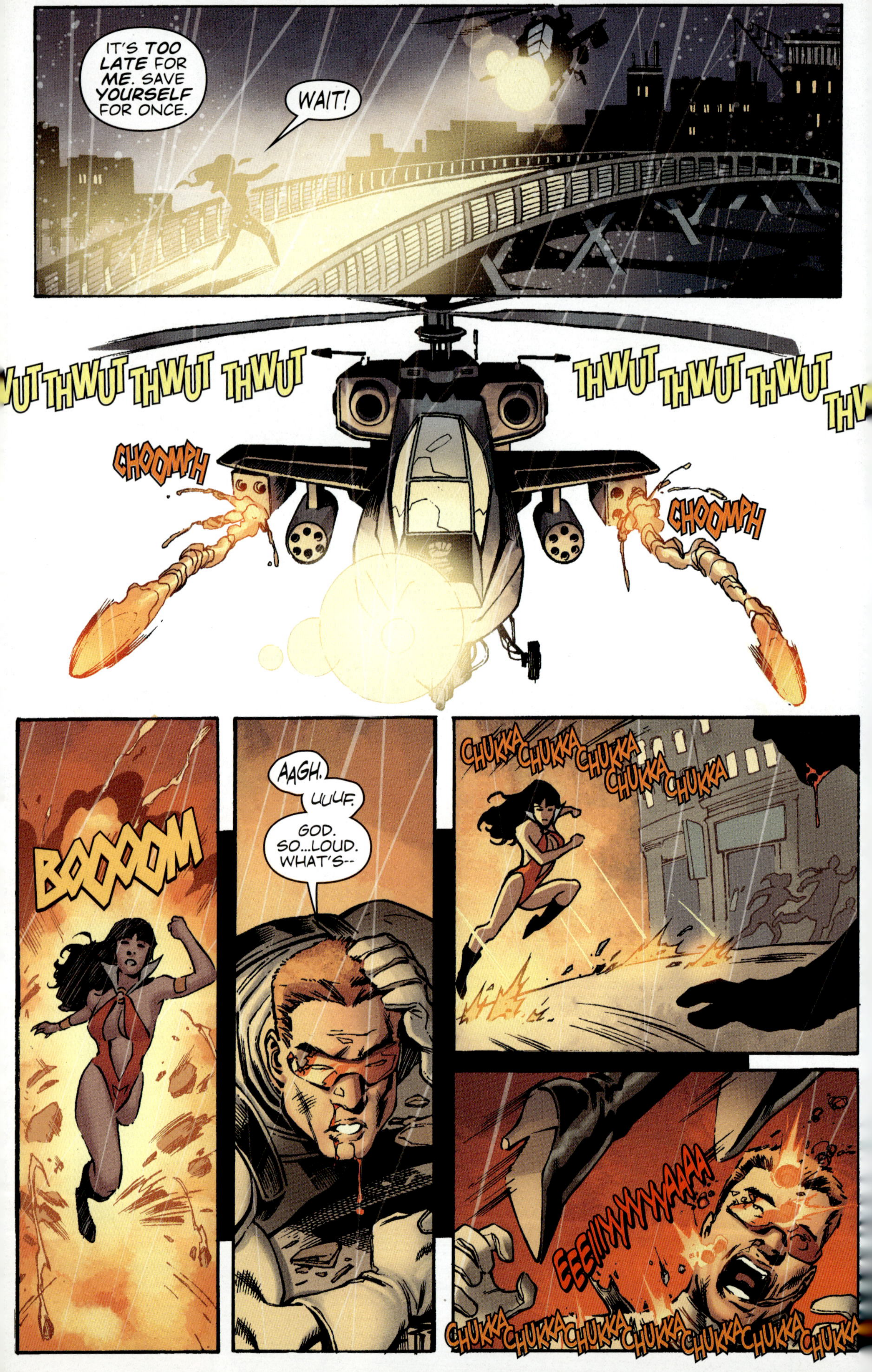
IT'S TOO LATE FOR ME. SAVE YOURSELF FOR ONCE.
WAIT!
THWUT THWUT THWUT
THWUT THWUT THWUT
CHOOMPH
CHOOMPH
BOOOOM
AAGH.
UUUF.
GOD. SO...LOUD. WHAT'S--
CHUKKA CHUKKA CHUKKA CHUKKA CHUKKA
EEEIIIYYYYAAAA
CHUKKA CHUKKA CHUKKA CHUKKA CHUKKA CHUKKA CHUKKA

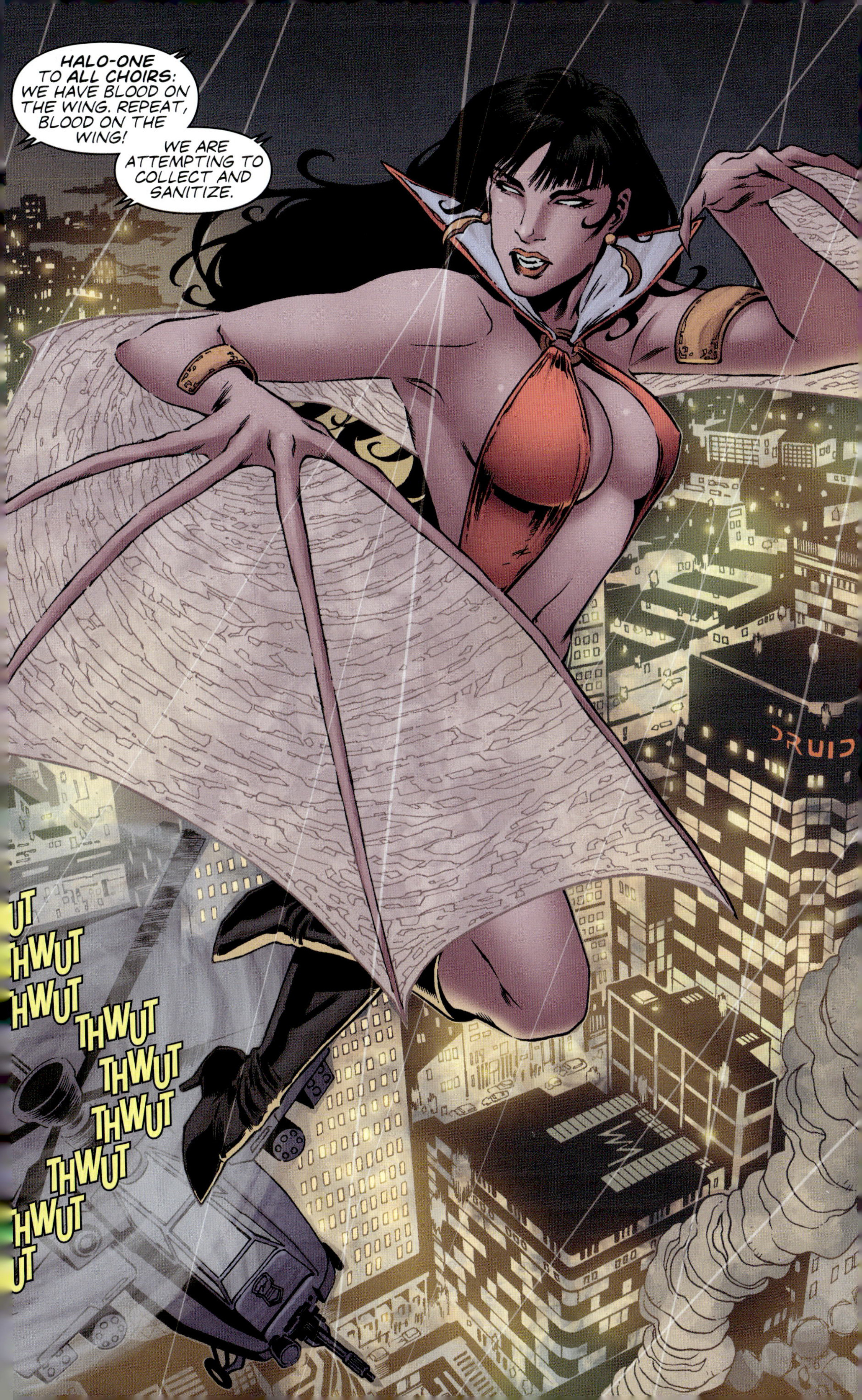
HALO-ONE TO ALL CHOIRS: WE HAVE BLOOD ON THE WING. REPEAT, BLOOD ON THE WING!
WE ARE ATTEMPTING TO COLLECT AND SANITIZE.
DRUID
UT THWUT THWUT THWUT THWUT THWUT THWUT THWUT UT

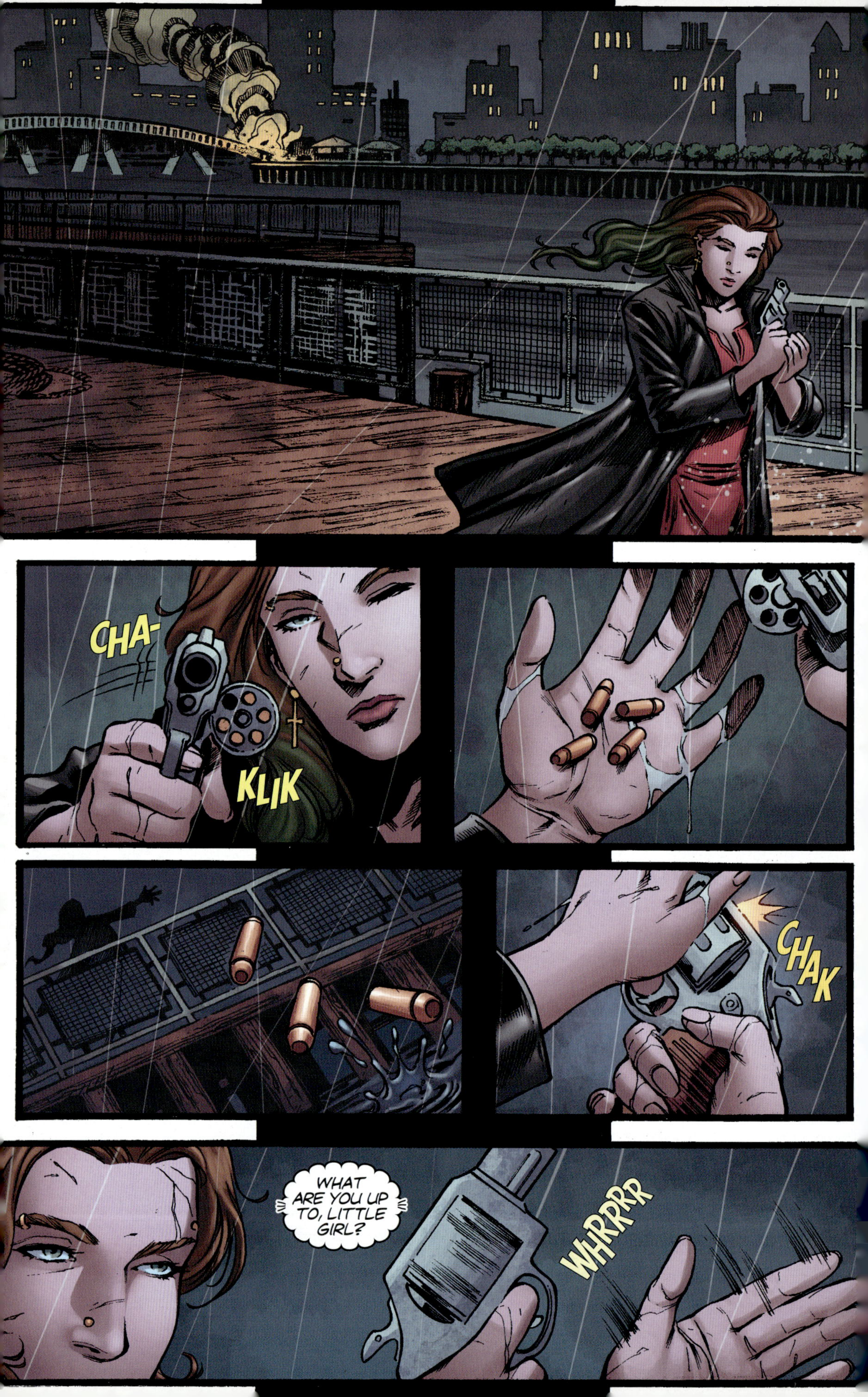
CHA-
KLIK
CHAK
WHAT ARE YOU UP TO, LITTLE GIRL?
WHRRRR

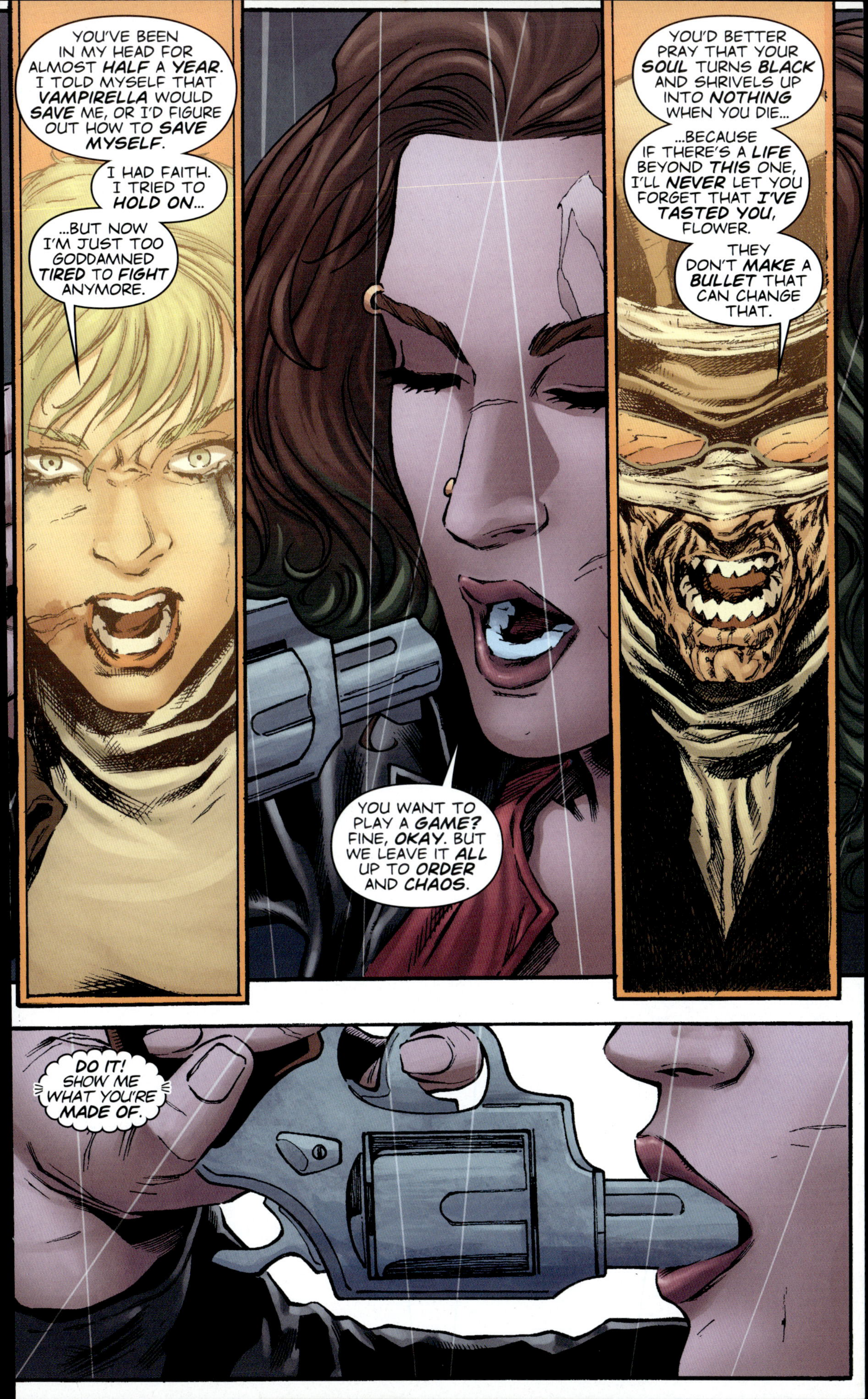

YOU'VE BEEN IN MY HEAD FOR ALMOST HALF A YEAR. I TOLD MYSELF THAT VAMPIRELLA WOULD SAVE ME, OR I'D FIGURE OUT HOW TO SAVE MYSELF.
I HAD FAITH. I TRIED TO HOLD ON...
...BUT NOW I'M JUST TOO GODDAMNED TIRED TO FIGHT ANYMORE.
YOU WANT TO PLAY A GAME? FINE, OKAY. BUT WE LEAVE IT ALL UP TO ORDER AND CHAOS.
YOU'D BETTER PRAY THAT YOUR SOUL TURNS BLACK AND SHRIVELS UP INTO NOTHING WHEN YOU DIE...
...BECAUSE IF THERE'S A LIFE BEYOND THIS ONE, I'LL NEVER LET YOU FORGET THAT I'VE TASTED YOU, FLOWER.
THEY DON'T MAKE A BULLET THAT CAN CHANGE THAT.
DO IT! SHOW ME WHAT YOU'RE MADE OF.

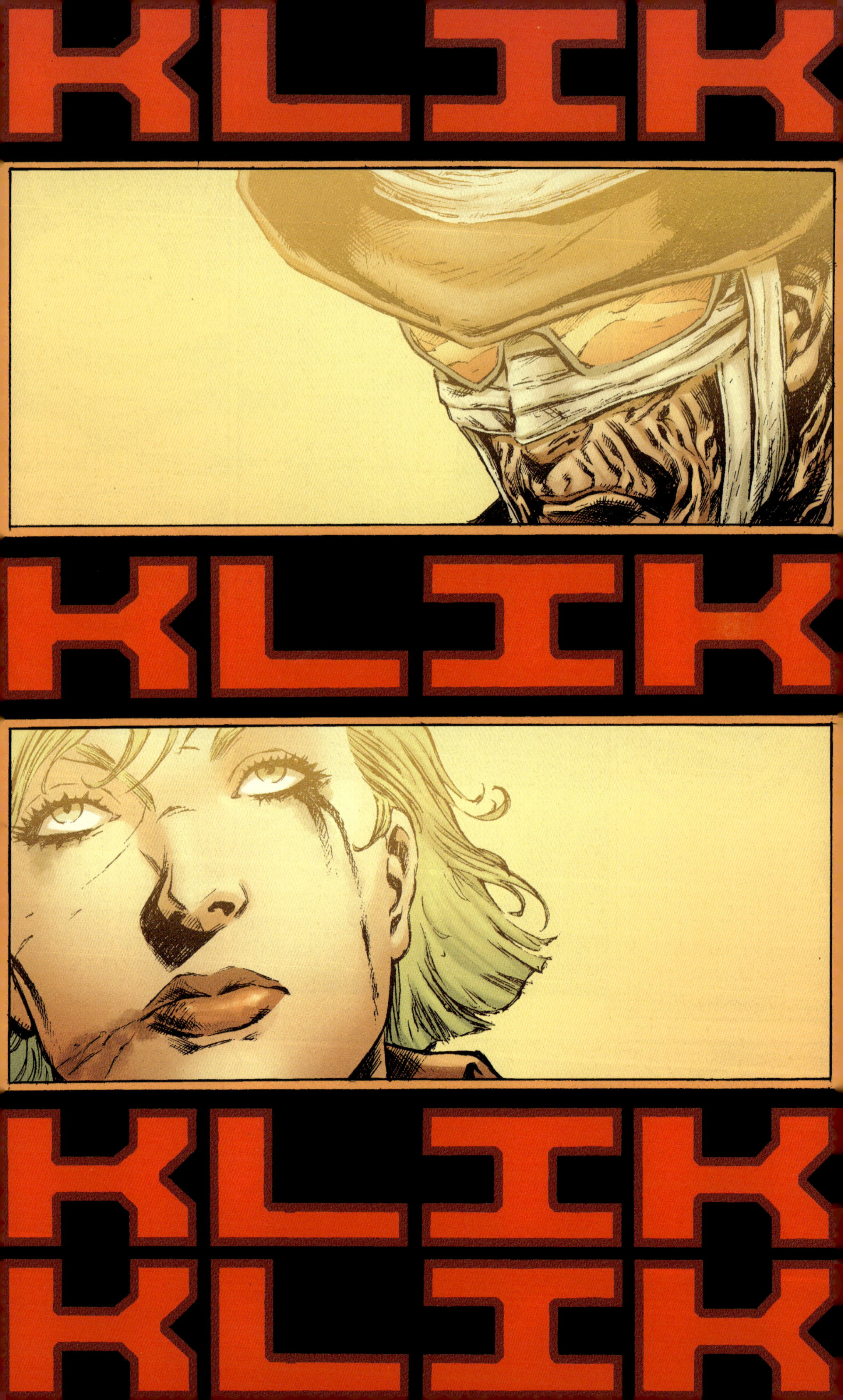
KLIK
KLIK
KLIK
KLIK

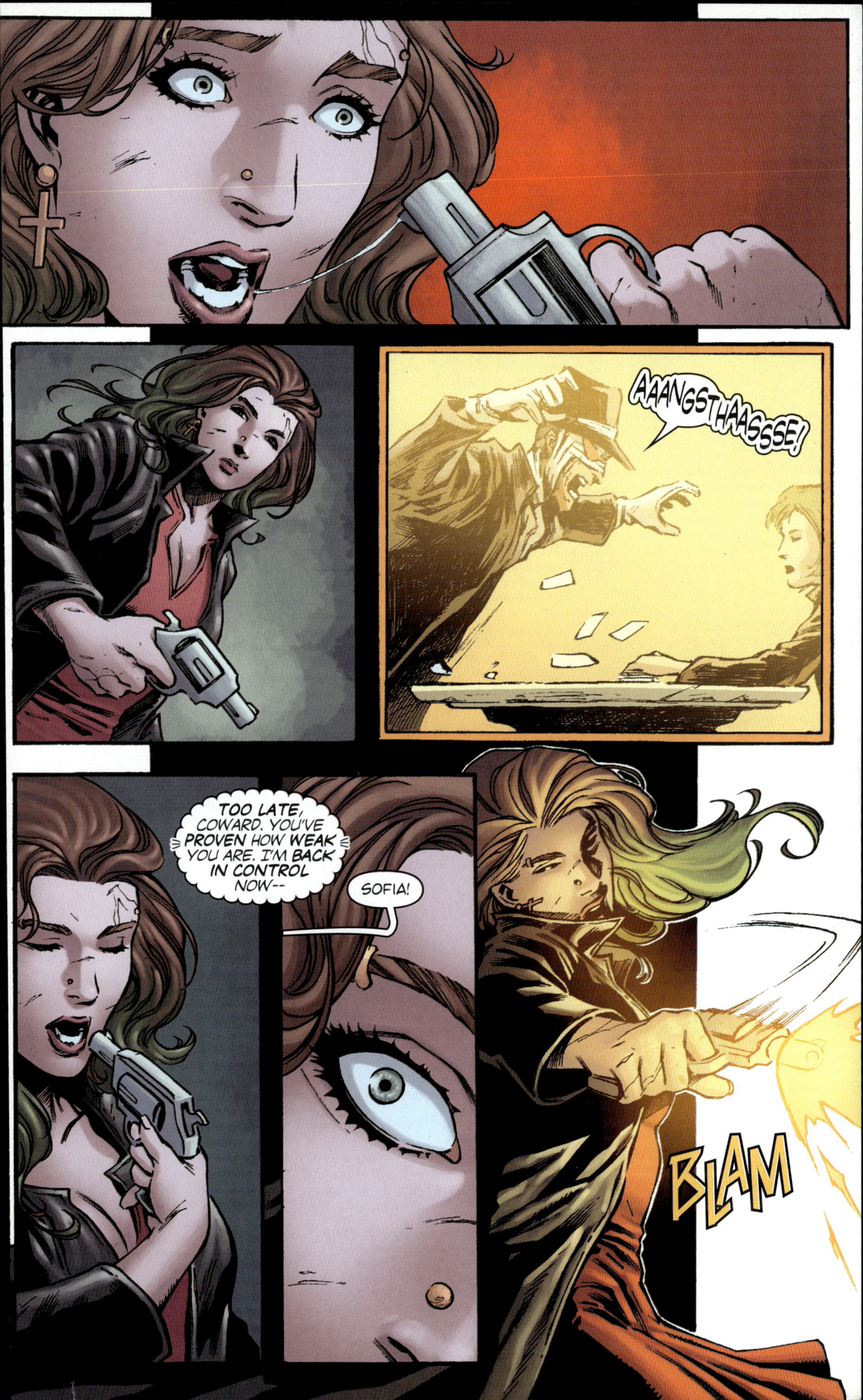
AAANGSTHAASSSE!
TOO LATE, COWARD. YOU'VE PROVEN HOW WEAK YOU ARE. I'M BACK IN CONTROL NOW--
SOFIA!
BLAM

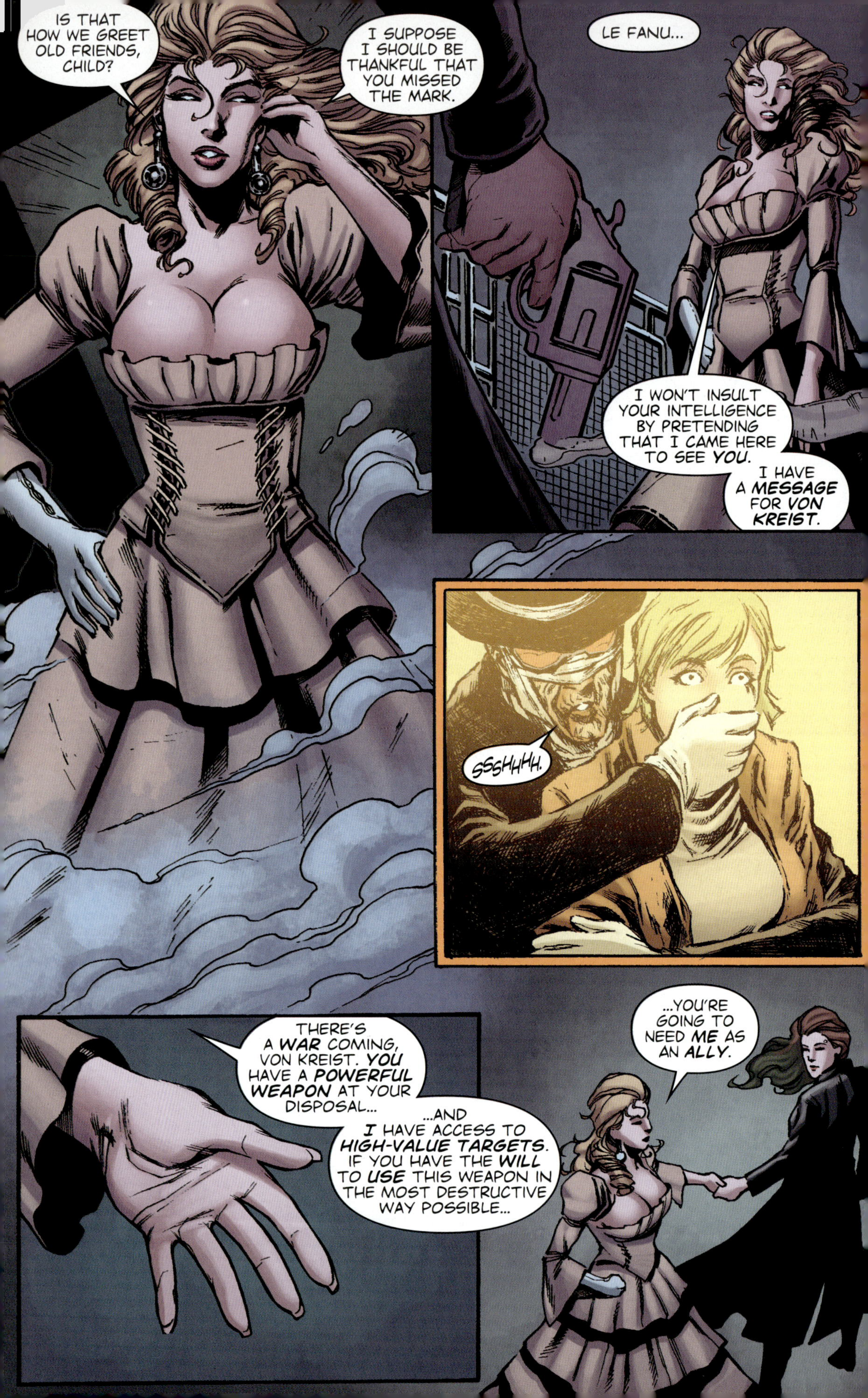
IS THAT HOW WE GREET OLD FRIENDS, CHILD?
I SUPPOSE I SHOULD BE THANKFUL THAT YOU MISSED THE MARK.
LE FANU...
I WON'T INSULT YOUR INTELLIGENCE BY PRETENDING THAT I CAME HERE TO SEE YOU.
I HAVE A MESSAGE FOR VON KREIST.
SSSHHHH.
THERE'S A WAR COMING, VON KREIST. YOU HAVE A POWERFUL WEAPON AT YOUR DISPOSAL...
...AND I HAVE ACCESS TO HIGH-VALUE TARGETS. IF YOU HAVE THE WILL TO USE THIS WEAPON IN THE MOST DESTRUCTIVE WAY POSSIBLE...
...YOU'RE GOING TO NEED ME AS AN ALLY.

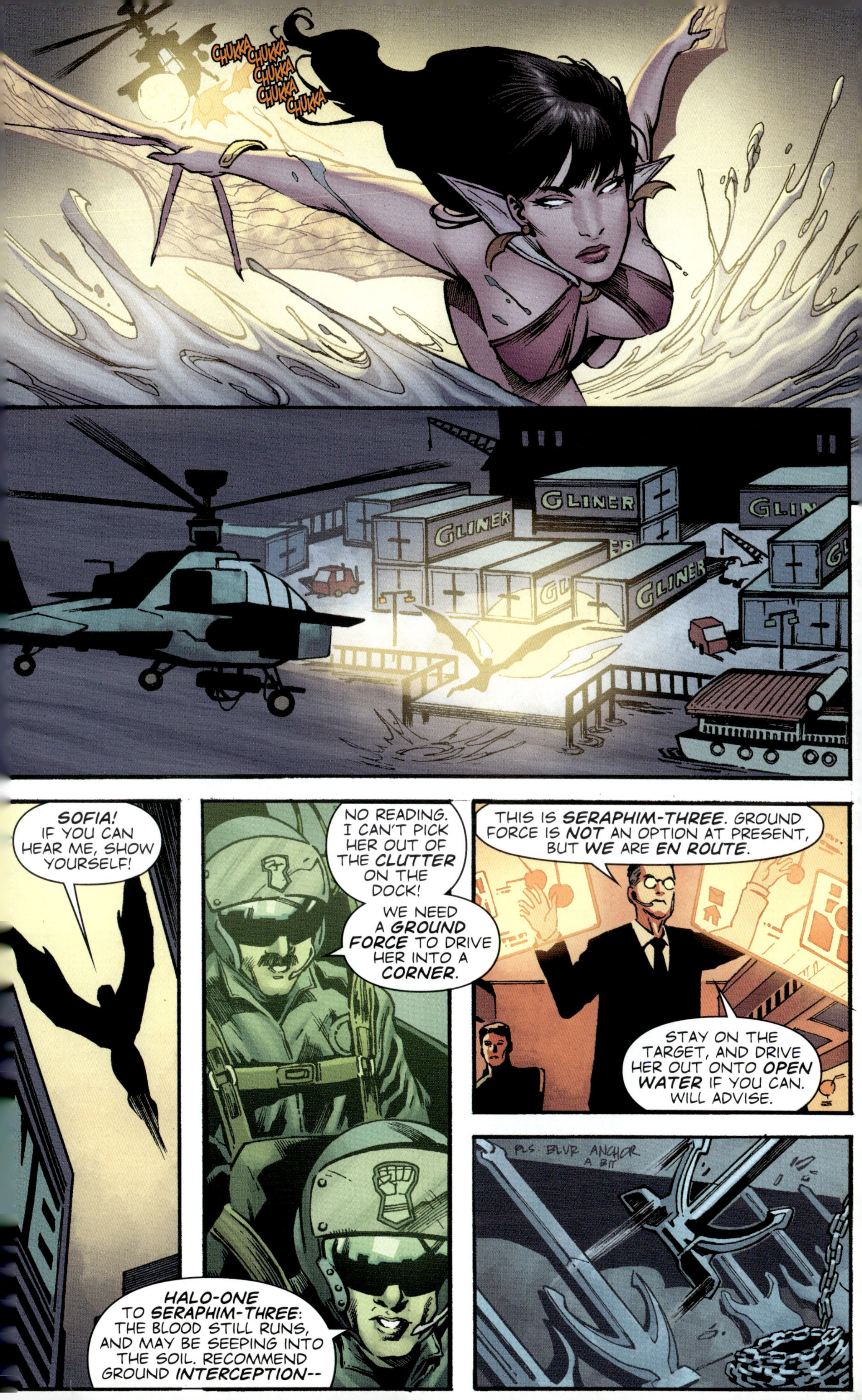
CHUKKA CHUKKA CHUKKA CHUKKA CHUKKA
GLINER
GLINER
GLINER
SOFIA! IF YOU CAN HEAR ME, SHOW YOURSELF!
NO READING. I CAN'T PICK HER OUT OF THE CLUTTER ON THE DOCK!
WE NEED A GROUND FORCE TO DRIVE HER INTO A CORNER.
HALO-ONE TO SERAPHIM-THREE: THE BLOOD STILL RUNS, AND MAY BE SEEPING INTO THE SOIL. RECOMMEND GROUND INTERCEPTION--
THIS IS SERAPHIM-THREE. GROUND FORCE IS NOT AN OPTION AT PRESENT, BUT WE ARE EN ROUTE.
STAY ON THE TARGET, AND DRIVE HER OUT ONTO OPEN WATER IF YOU CAN. WILL ADVISE.
PLS. BLUR ANCHOR A BIT

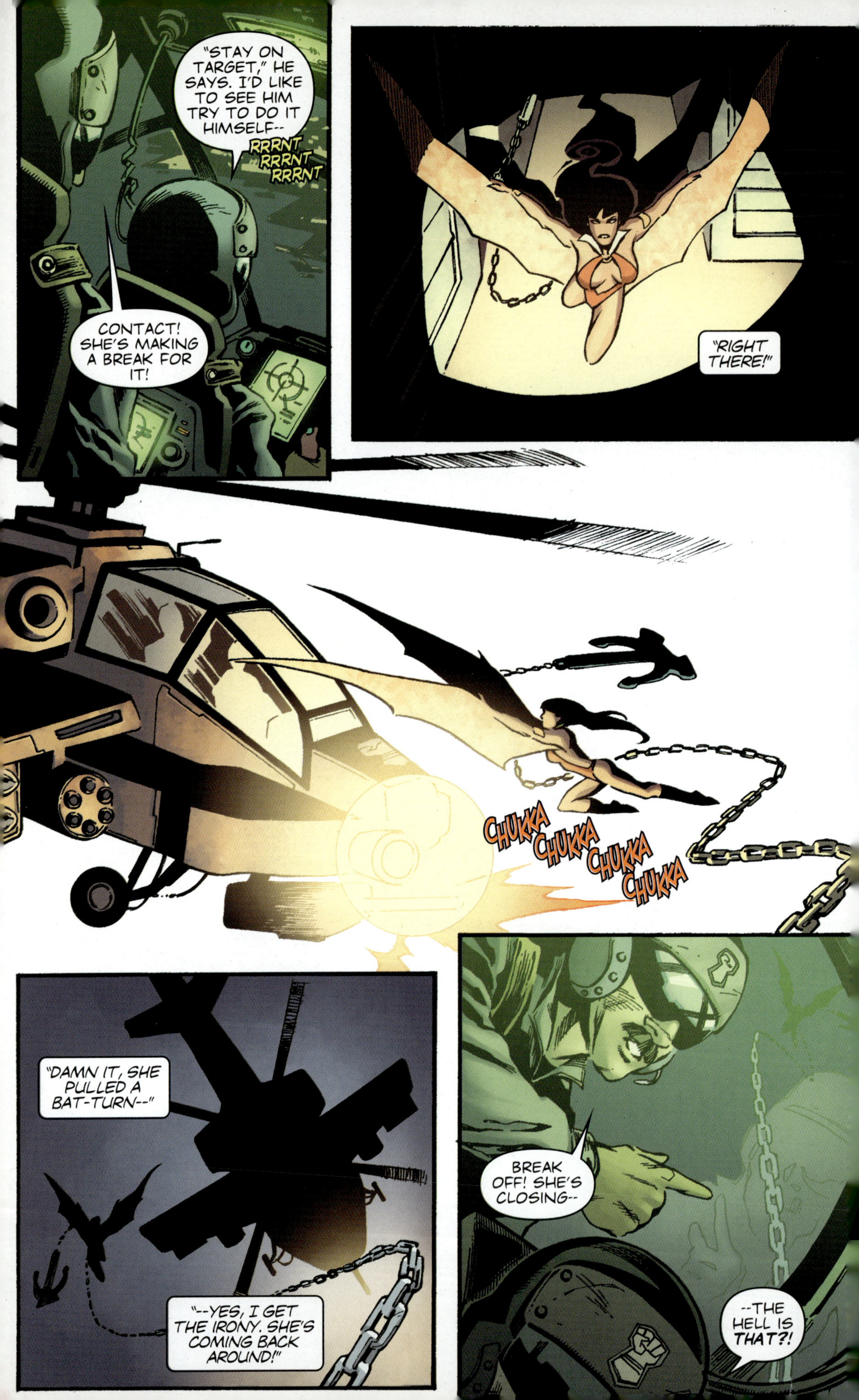
"STAY ON TARGET," HE SAYS. I'D LIKE TO SEE HIM TRY TO DO IT HIMSELF--
RRRNT RRRNT RRRNT
CONTACT! SHE'S MAKING A BREAK FOR IT!
"RIGHT THERE!"
CHUKKA CHUKKA CHUKKA CHUKKA
"DAMN IT, SHE PULLED A BAT-TURN--"
"--YES, I GET THE IRONY. SHE'S COMING BACK AROUND!"
BREAK OFF! SHE'S CLOSING--
--THE HELL IS THAT?!

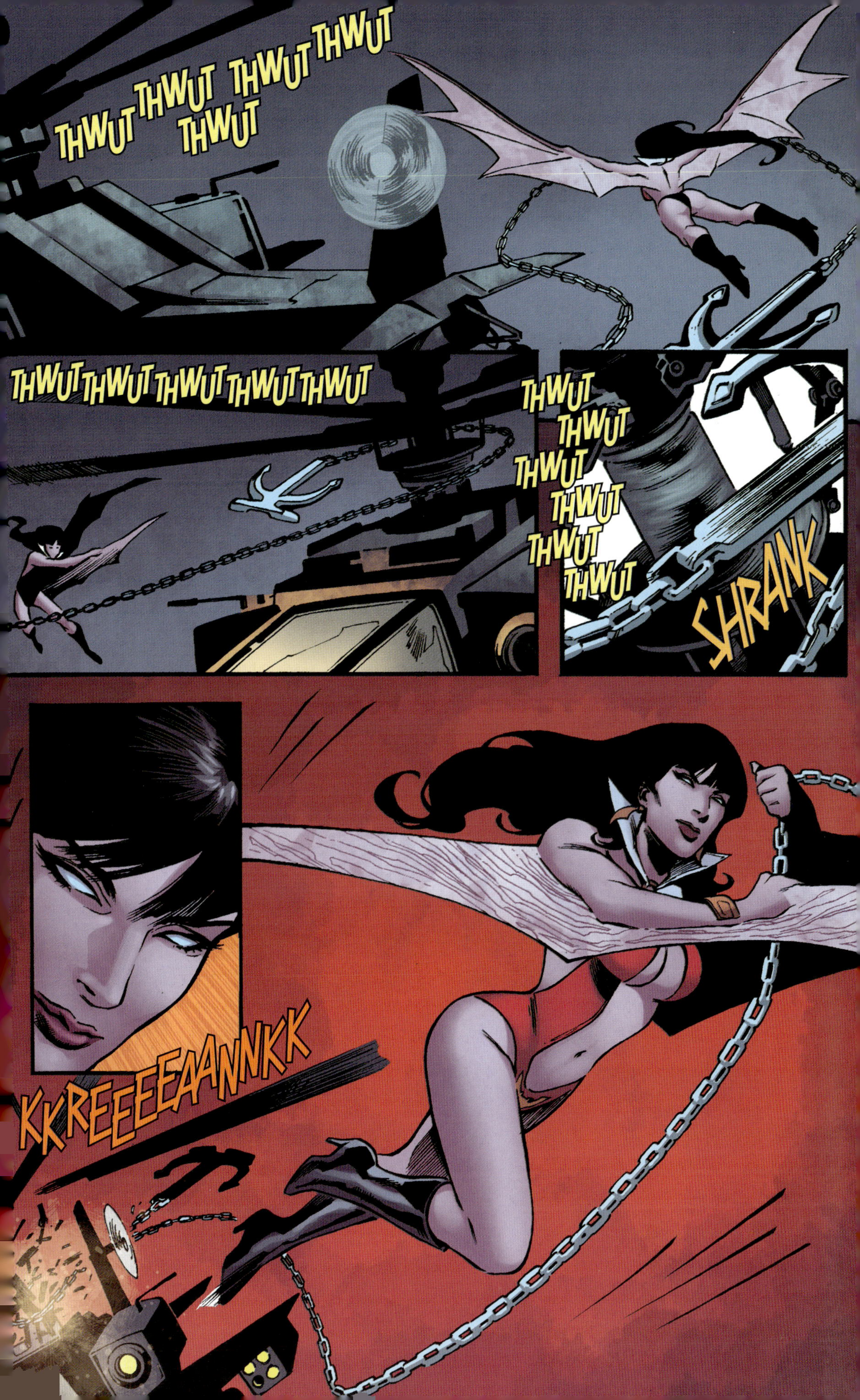
THWUT THWUT THWUT THWUT THWUT
THWUT THWUT THWUT THWUT THWUT
THWUT THWUT THWUT THWUT THWUT THWUT
SHRANK
KKREEEEAANNKK

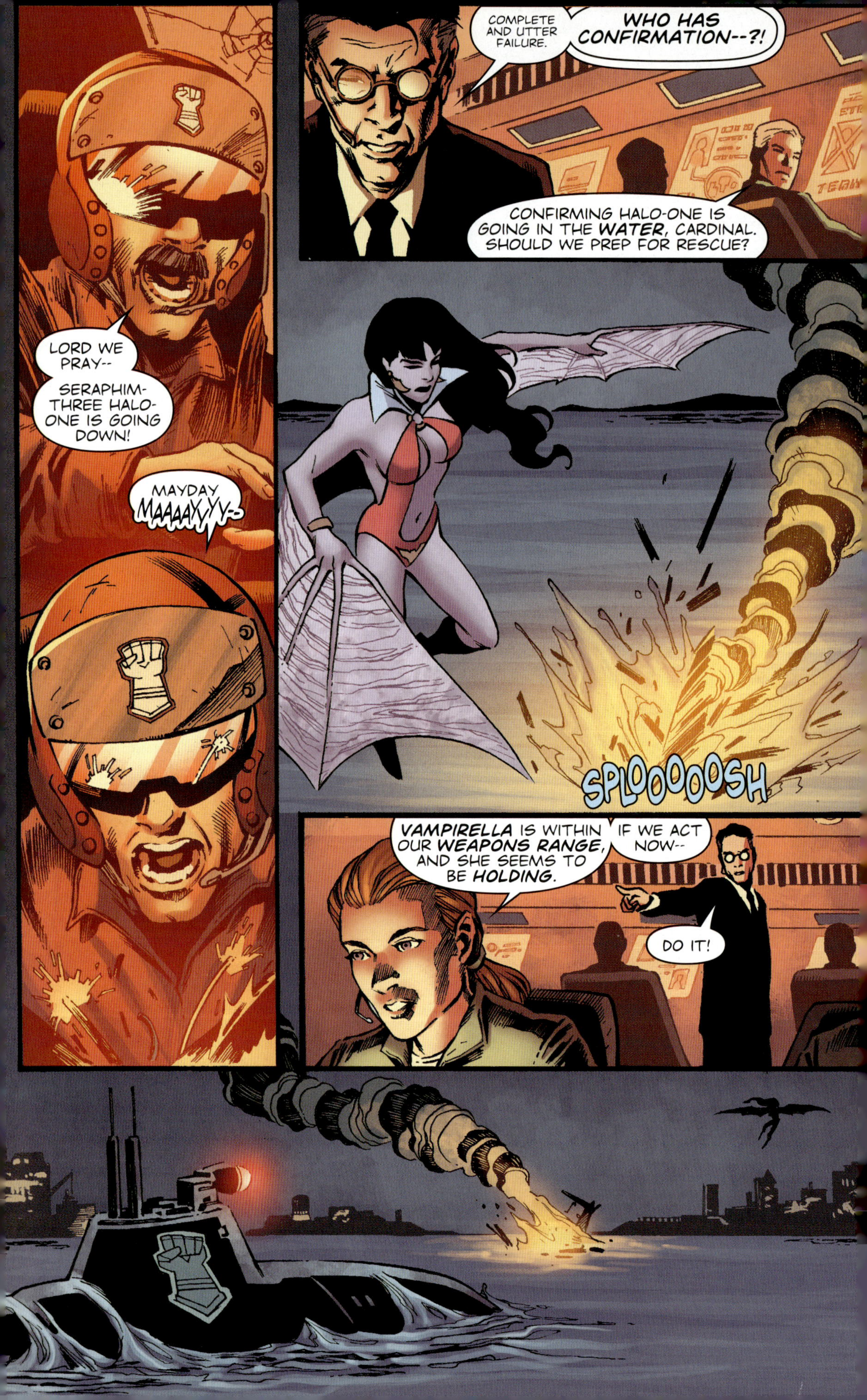

LORD WE PRAY--
SERAPHIM-THREE HALO-ONE IS GOING DOWN!
MAYDAY MAAAAYYYY-
COMPLETE AND UTTER FAILURE.
WHO HAS CONFIRMATION--?!
CONFIRMING HALO-ONE IS GOING IN THE WATER, CARDINAL. SHOULD WE PREP FOR RESCUE?
SPLOOOOOSH
VAMPIRELLA IS WITHIN OUR WEAPONS RANGE, AND SHE SEEMS TO BE HOLDING.
IF WE ACT NOW--
DO IT!

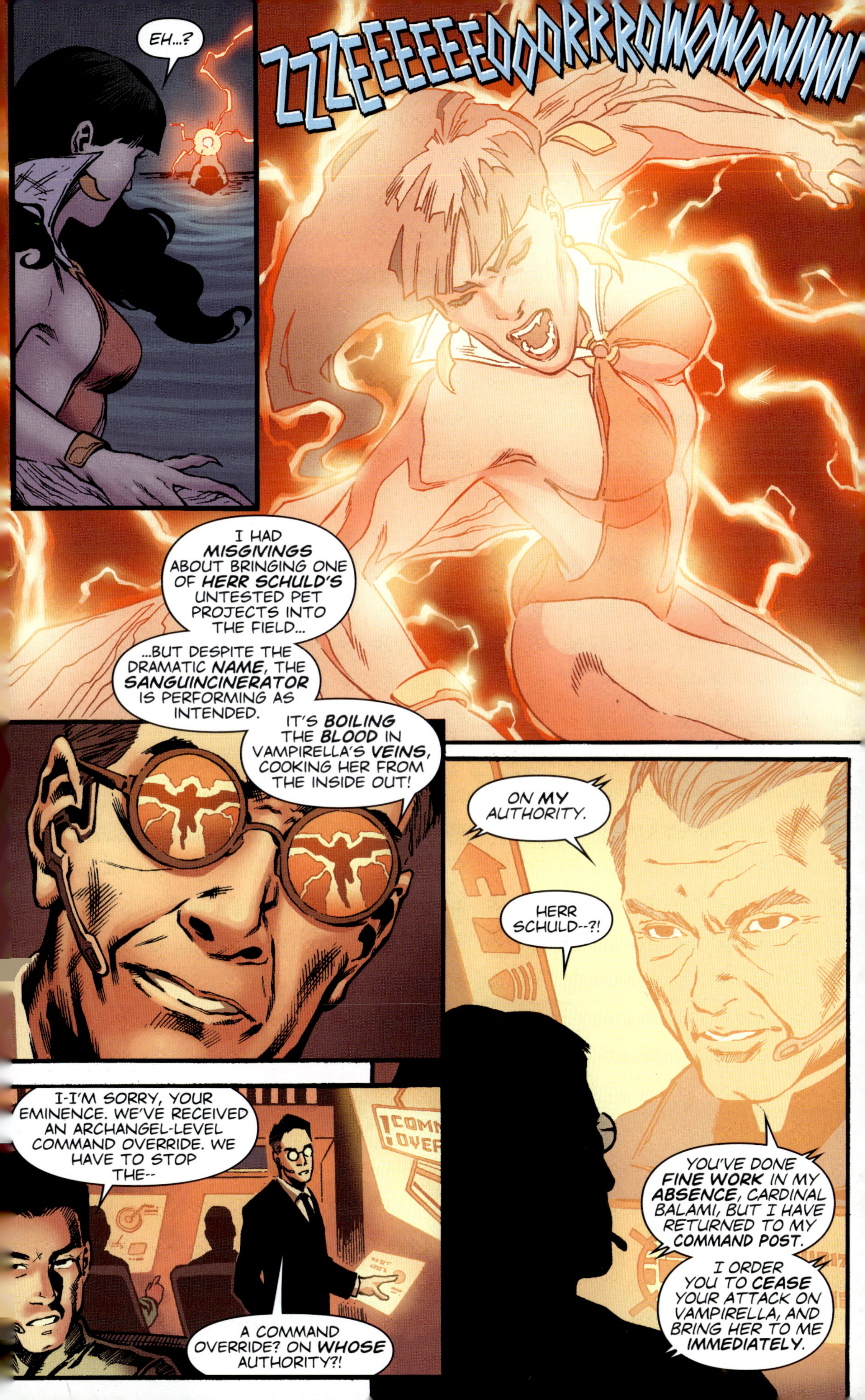
EH...?
ZZZEEEEEEEOOORRRROWOWOWNNN
I HAD MISGIVINGS ABOUT BRINGING ONE OF HERR SCHULD'S UNTESTED PET PROJECTS INTO THE FIELD...
...BUT DESPITE THE DRAMATIC NAME, THE SANGUINCINERATOR IS PERFORMING AS INTENDED.
IT'S BOILING THE BLOOD IN VAMPIRELLA'S VEINS, COOKING HER FROM THE INSIDE OUT!
I-I'M SORRY, YOUR EMINENCE. WE'VE RECEIVED AN ARCHANGEL-LEVEL COMMAND OVERRIDE. WE HAVE TO STOP THE--
A COMMAND OVERRIDE? ON WHOSE AUTHORITY?!
ON MY AUTHORITY.
HERR SCHULD--?!
YOU'VE DONE FINE WORK IN MY ABSENCE, CARDINAL BALAMI, BUT I HAVE RETURNED TO MY COMMAND POST.
I ORDER YOU TO CEASE YOUR ATTACK ON VAMPIRELLA, AND BRING HER TO ME IMMEDIATELY.

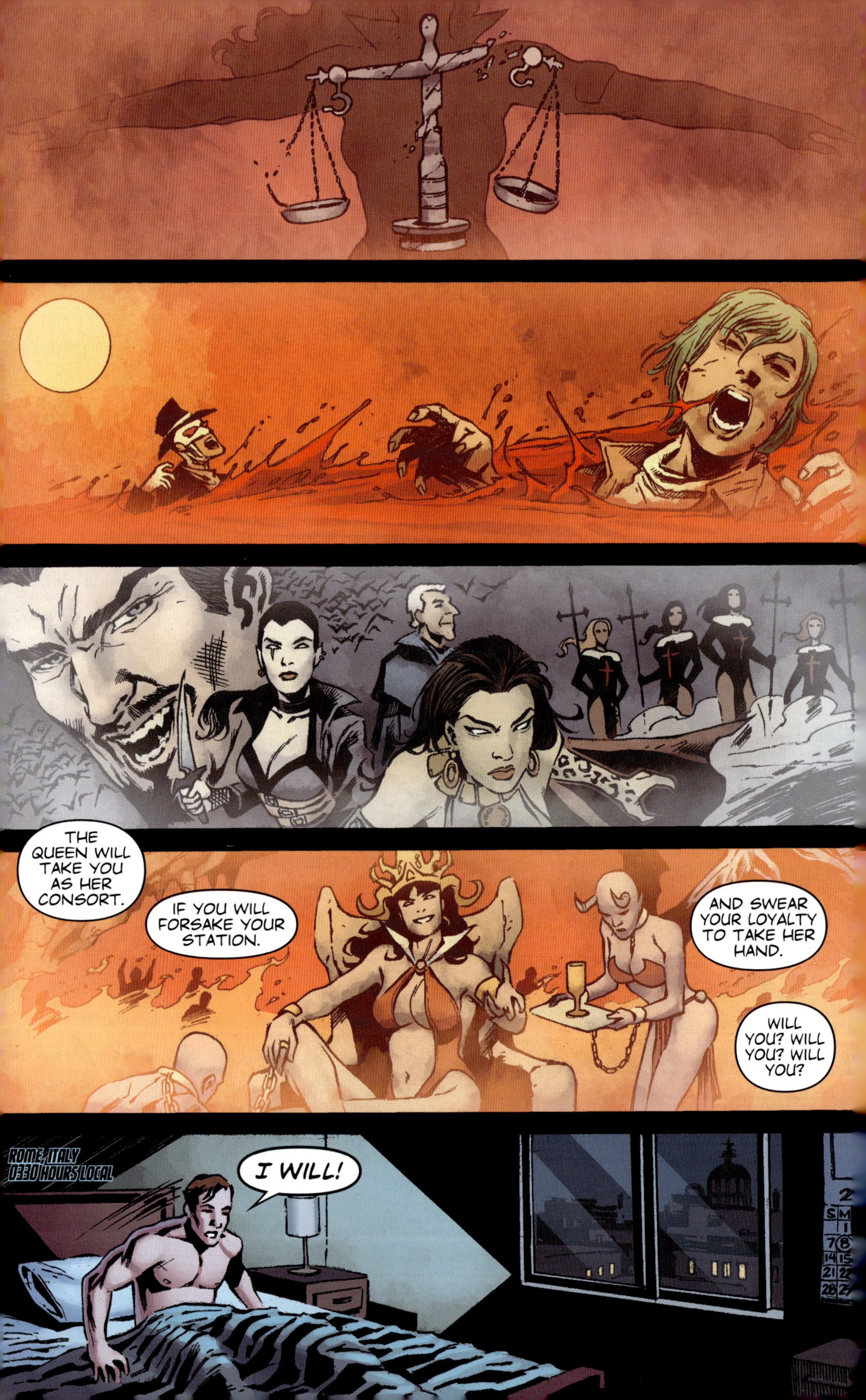
THE QUEEN WILL TAKE YOU AS HER CONSORT.
IF YOU WILL FORSAKE YOUR STATION.
AND SWEAR YOUR LOYALTY TO TAKE HER HAND.
WILL YOU? WILL YOU? WILL YOU?
ROME, ITALY 0330 HOURS LOCAL
I WILL!

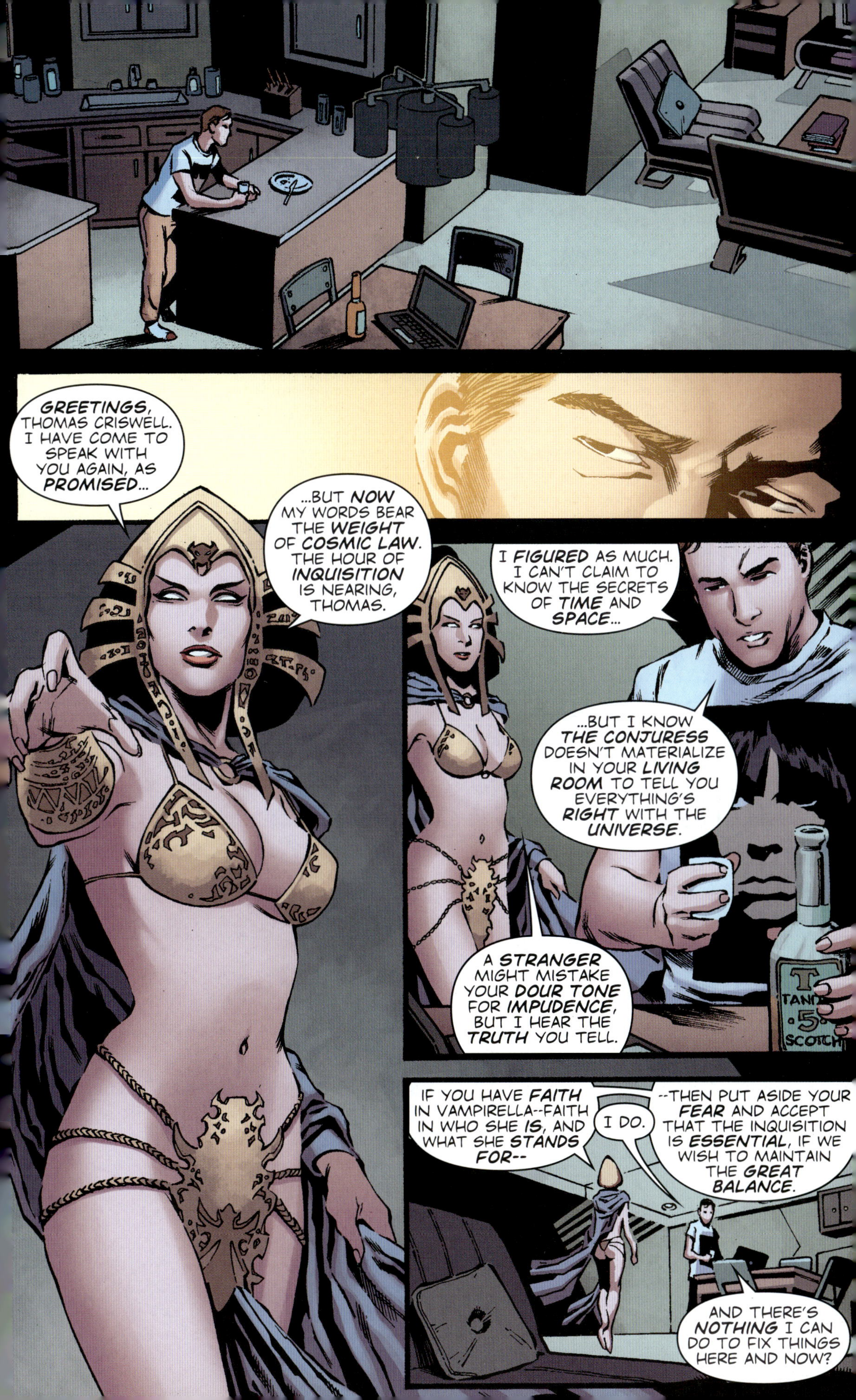
GREETINGS, THOMAS CRISWELL. I HAVE COME TO SPEAK WITH YOU AGAIN, AS PROMISED...
...BUT NOW MY WORDS BEAR THE WEIGHT OF COSMIC LAW. THE HOUR OF INQUISITION IS NEARING, THOMAS.
I FIGURED AS MUCH. I CAN'T CLAIM TO KNOW THE SECRETS OF TIME AND SPACE...
...BUT I KNOW THE CONJURESS DOESN'T MATERIALIZE IN YOUR LIVING ROOM TO TELL YOU EVERYTHING'S RIGHT WITH THE UNIVERSE.
A STRANGER MIGHT MISTAKE YOUR DOUR TONE FOR IMPUDENCE, BUT I HEAR THE TRUTH YOU TELL.
IF YOU HAVE FAITH IN VAMPIRELLA--FAITH IN WHO SHE IS, AND WHAT SHE STANDS FOR--
I DO.
--THEN PUT ASIDE YOUR FEAR AND ACCEPT THAT THE INQUISITION IS ESSENTIAL, IF WE WISH TO MAINTAIN THE GREAT BALANCE.
AND THERE'S NOTHING I CAN DO TO FIX THINGS HERE AND NOW?

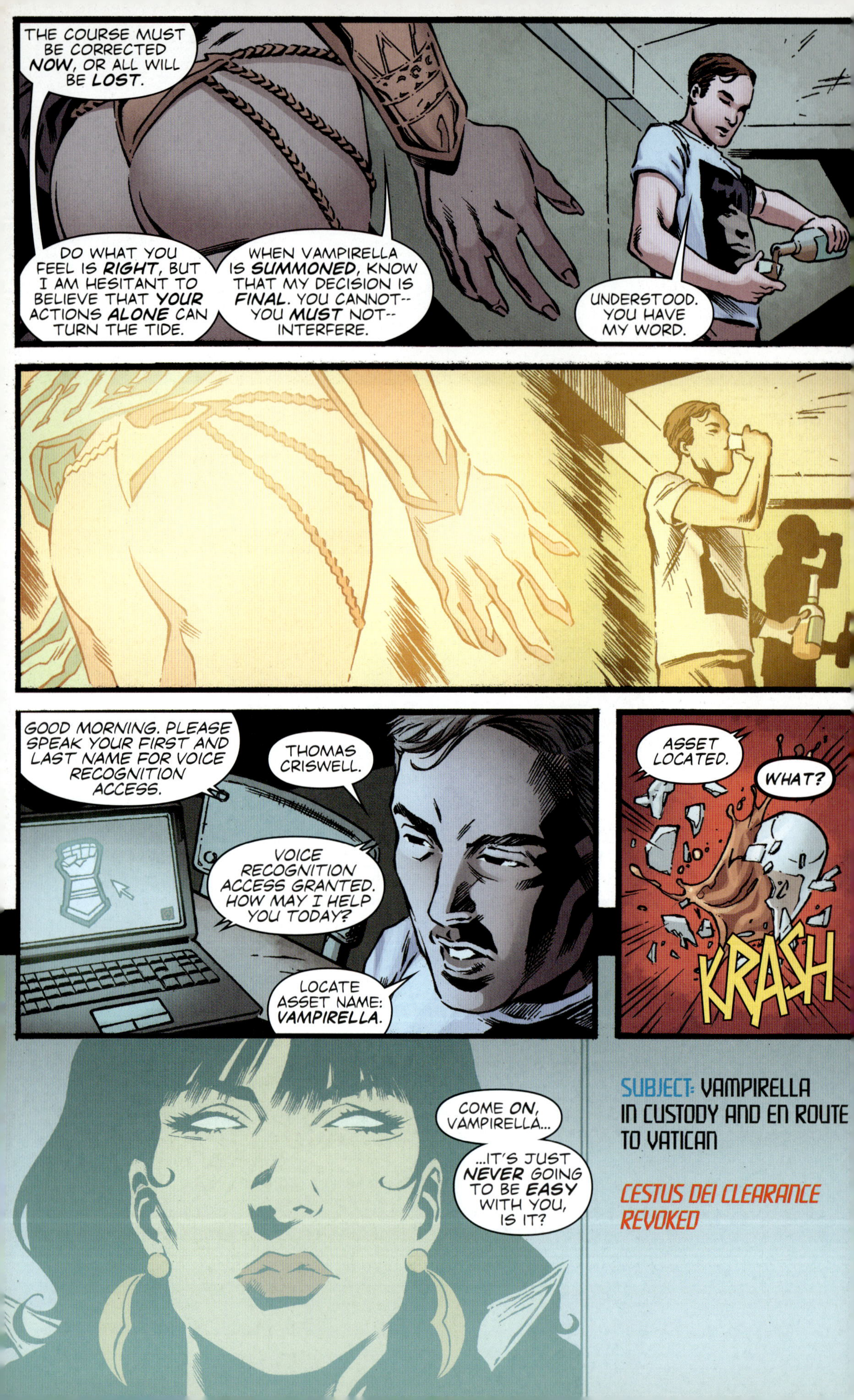
THE COURSE MUST BE CORRECTED NOW, OR ALL WILL BE LOST.
DO WHAT YOU FEEL IS RIGHT, BUT I AM HESITANT TO BELIEVE THAT YOUR ACTIONS ALONE CAN TURN THE TIDE.
WHEN VAMPIRELLA IS SUMMONED, KNOW THAT MY DECISION IS FINAL. YOU CANNOT-- YOU MUST NOT-- INTERFERE.
UNDERSTOOD. YOU HAVE MY WORD.
GOOD MORNING. PLEASE SPEAK YOUR FIRST AND LAST NAME FOR VOICE RECOGNITION ACCESS.
THOMAS CRISWELL.
VOICE RECOGNITION ACCESS GRANTED. HOW MAY I HELP YOU TODAY?
LOCATE ASSET NAME: VAMPIRELLA.
ASSET LOCATED.
WHAT?
KRASH
COME ON, VAMPIRELLA...
...IT'S JUST NEVER GOING TO BE EASY WITH YOU, IS IT?
SUBJECT: VAMPIRELLA IN CUSTODY AND EN ROUTE TO VATICAN
CESTUS DEI CLEARANCE REVOKED

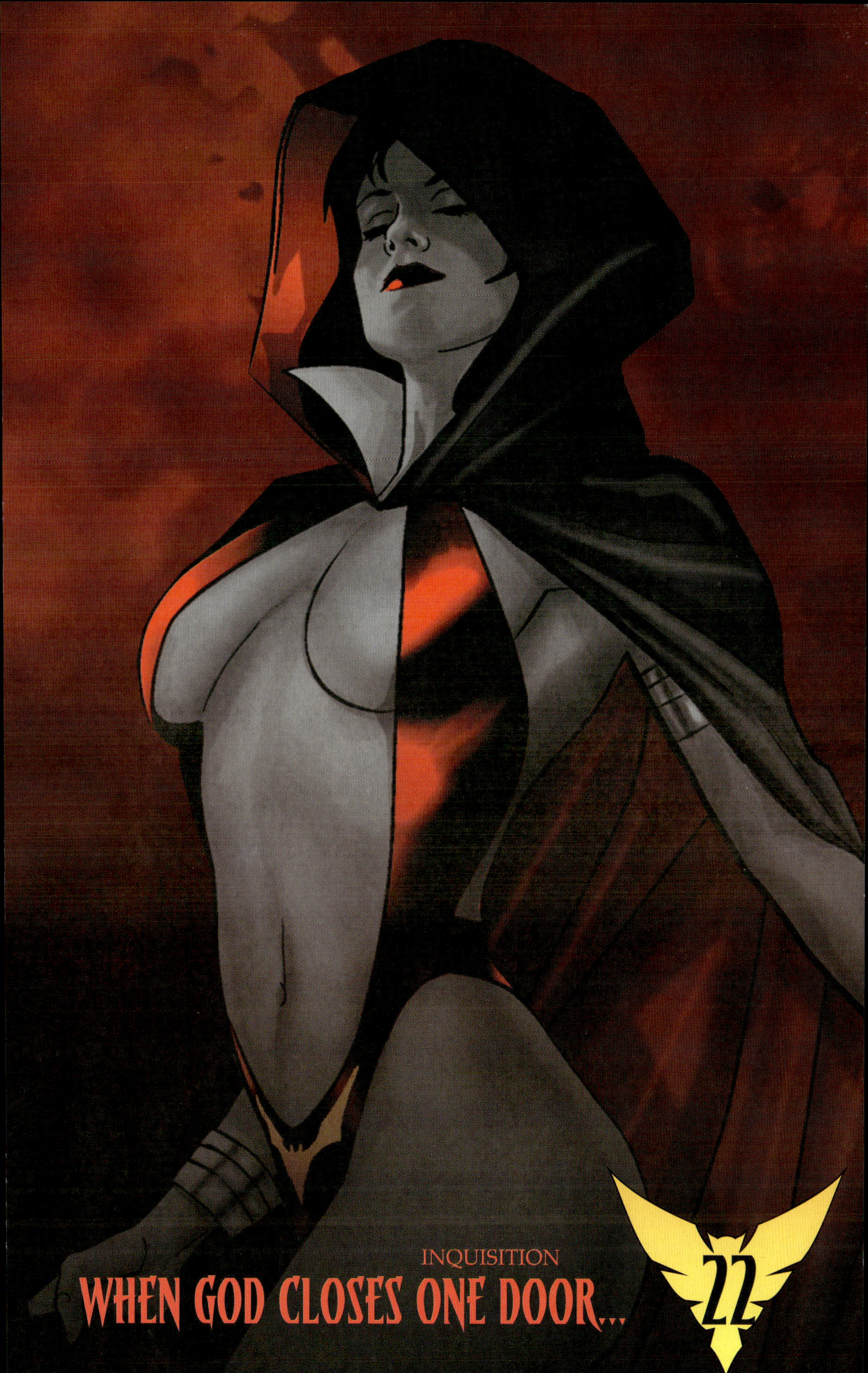
INQUISITION
WHEN GOD CLOSES ONE DOOR...
22

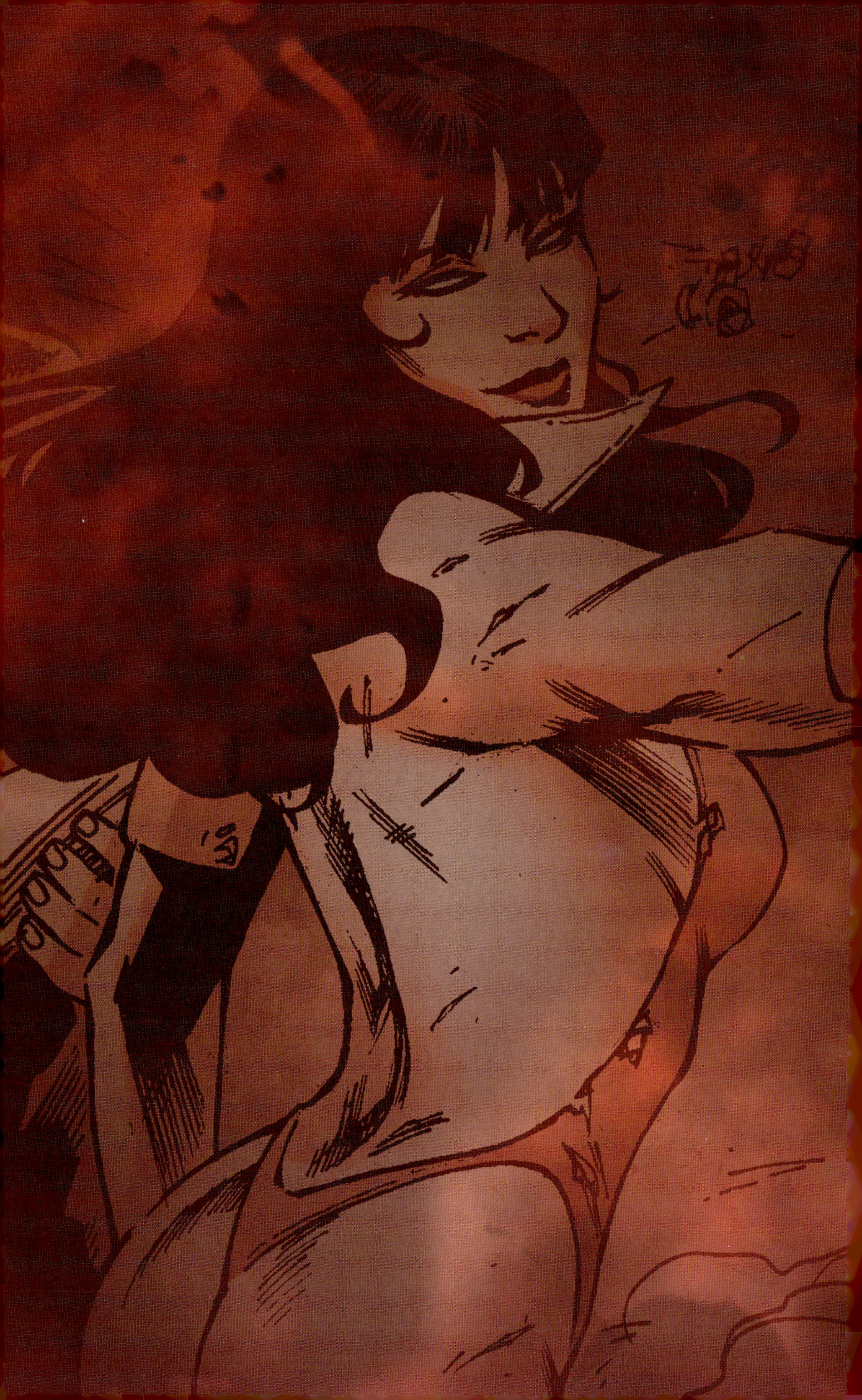

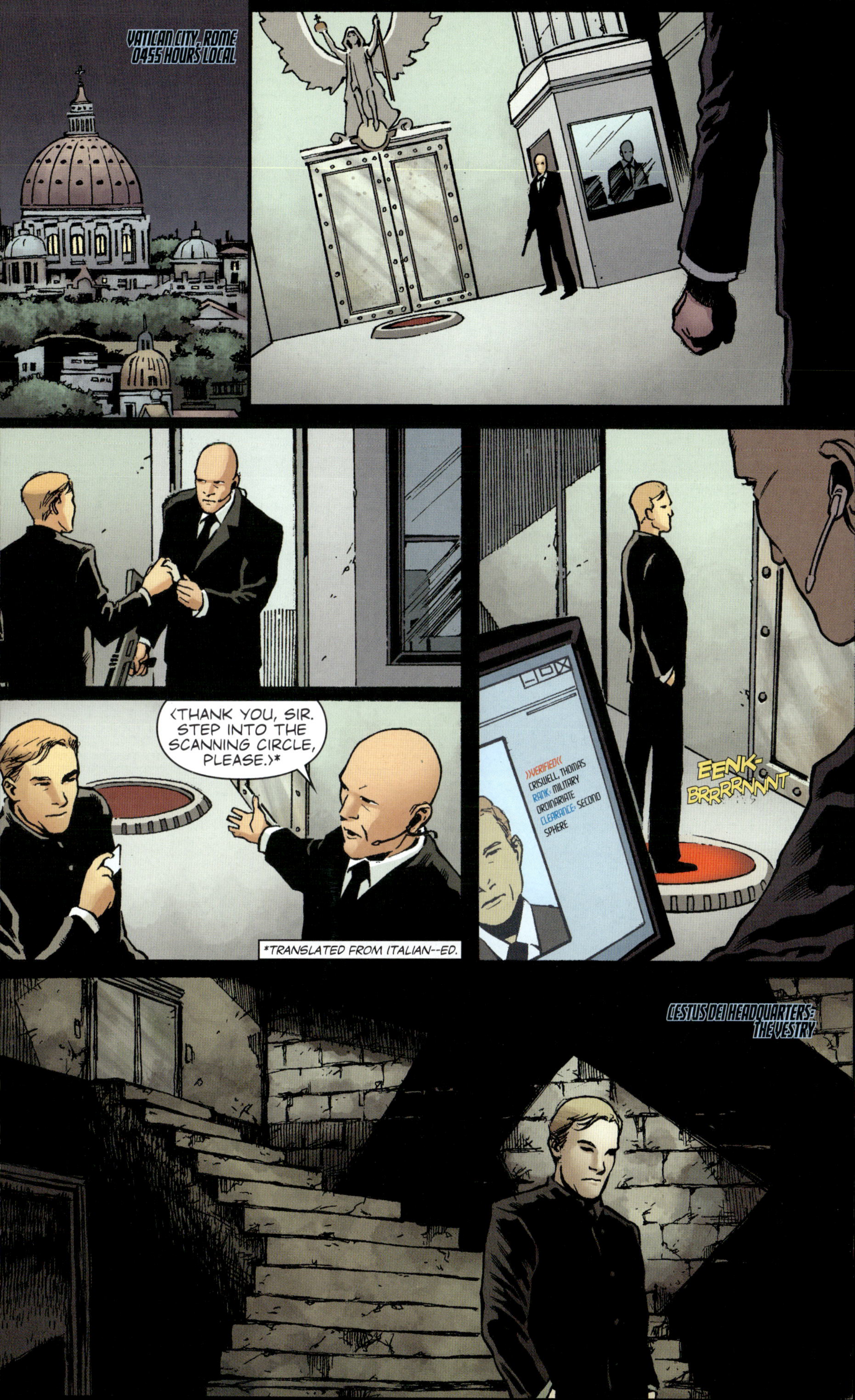
VATICAN CITY, ROME
0455 HOURS LOCAL
<THANK YOU, SIR. STEP INTO THE SCANNING CIRCLE, PLEASE.>*
*TRANSLATED FROM ITALIAN--ED.
»VERIFIED«
CRISWELL, THOMAS
RANK: MILITARY ORDINARIATE
CLEARANCE: SECOND SPHERE
EENK-BRRRRNNNT
CESTUS DEI HEADQUARTERS:
THE VESTRY

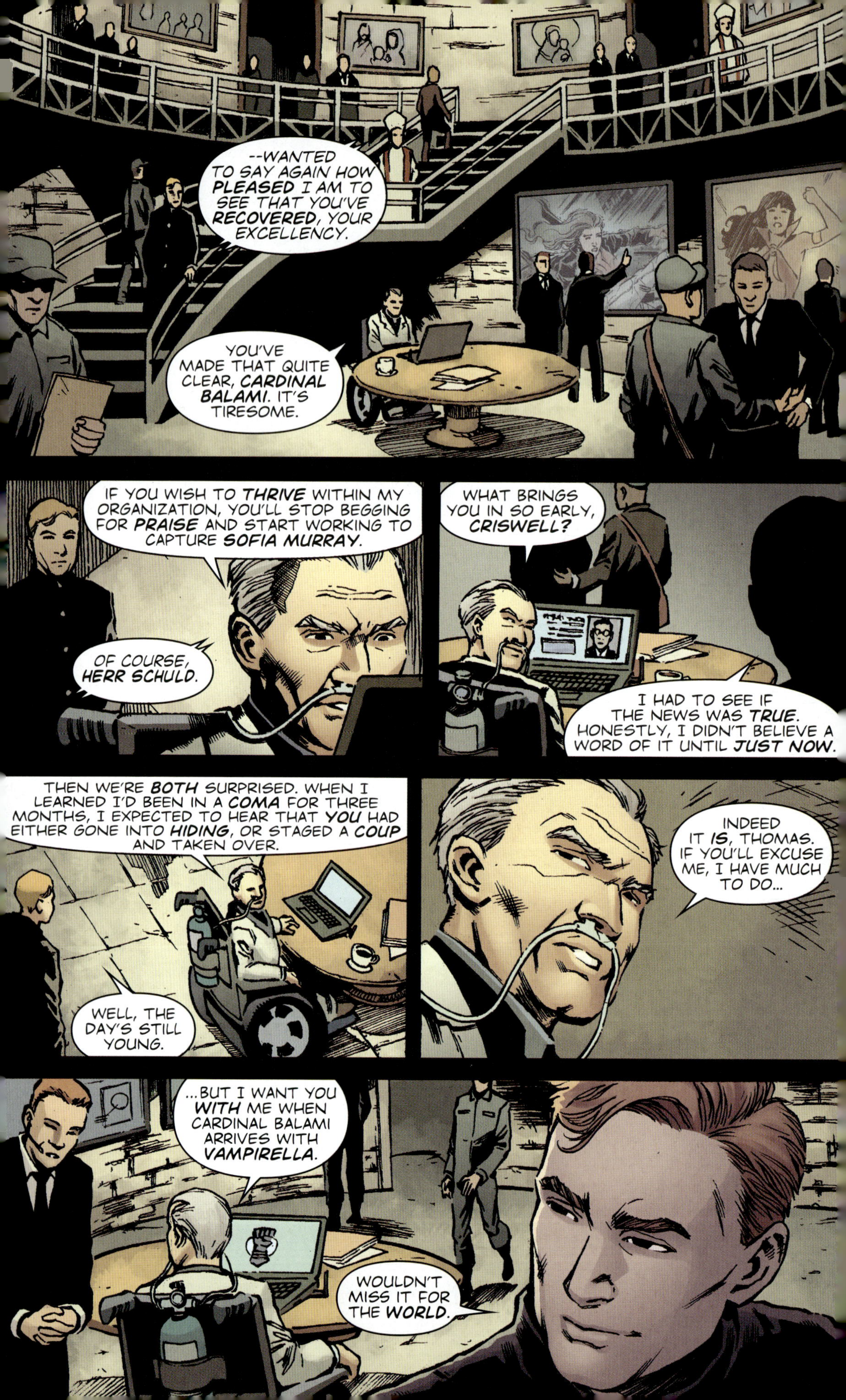
--WANTED TO SAY AGAIN HOW PLEASED I AM TO SEE THAT YOU'VE RECOVERED, YOUR EXCELLENCY.
YOU'VE MADE THAT QUITE CLEAR, CARDINAL BALAMI. IT'S TIRESOME.
IF YOU WISH TO THRIVE WITHIN MY ORGANIZATION, YOU'LL STOP BEGGING FOR PRAISE AND START WORKING TO CAPTURE SOFIA MURRAY.
OF COURSE, HERR SCHULD.
WHAT BRINGS YOU IN SO EARLY, CRISWELL?
I HAD TO SEE IF THE NEWS WAS TRUE. HONESTLY, I DIDN'T BELIEVE A WORD OF IT UNTIL JUST NOW.
THEN WE'RE BOTH SURPRISED. WHEN I LEARNED I'D BEEN IN A COMA FOR THREE MONTHS, I EXPECTED TO HEAR THAT YOU HAD EITHER GONE INTO HIDING, OR STAGED A COUP AND TAKEN OVER.
WELL, THE DAY'S STILL YOUNG.
INDEED IT IS, THOMAS. IF YOU'LL EXCUSE ME, I HAVE MUCH TO DO...
...BUT I WANT YOU WITH ME WHEN CARDINAL BALAMI ARRIVES WITH VAMPIRELLA.
WOULDN'T MISS IT FOR THE WORLD.

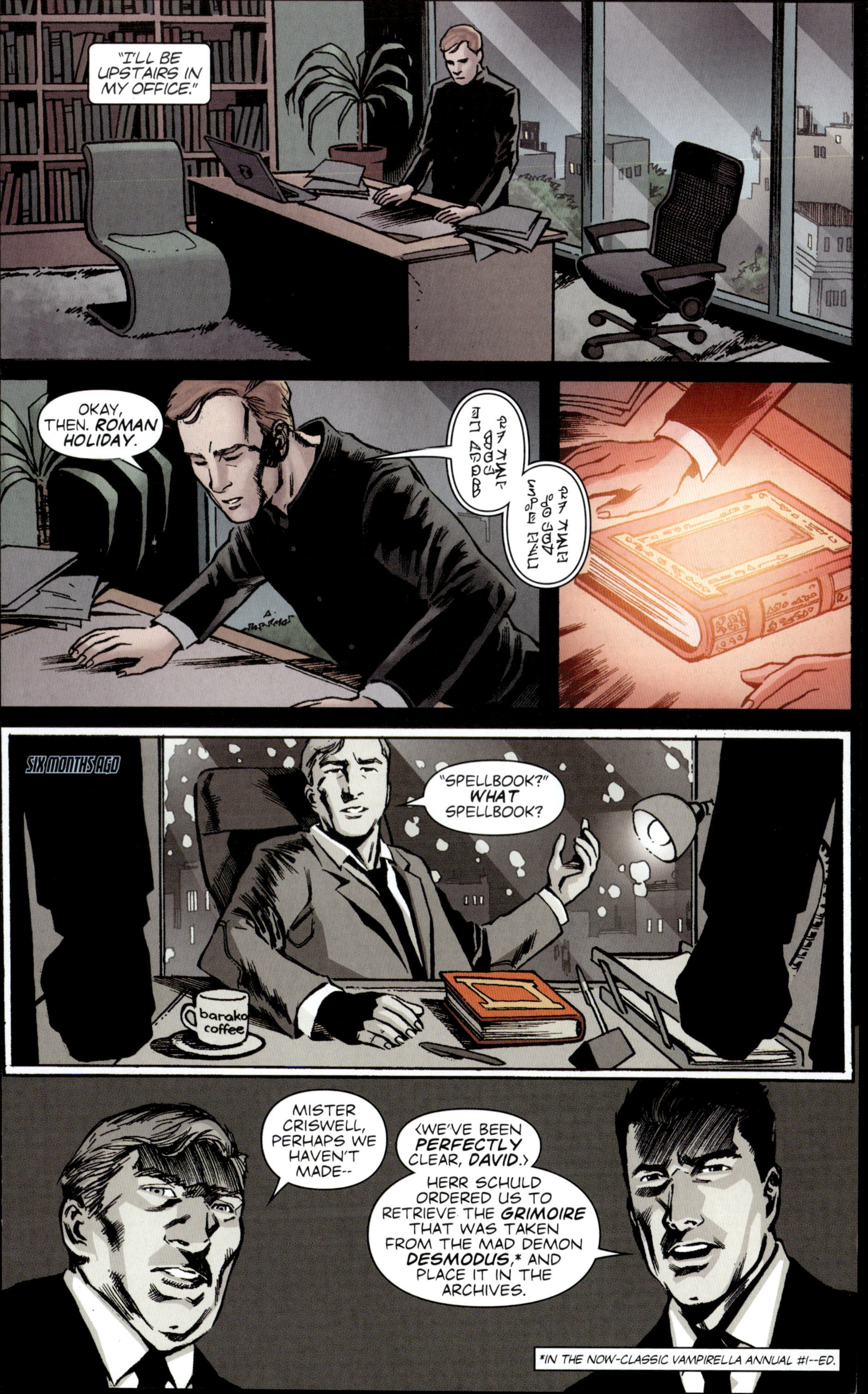
"I'LL BE UPSTAIRS IN MY OFFICE."
OKAY, THEN. ROMAN HOLIDAY.
SIX MONTHS AGO
"SPELLBOOK?" WHAT SPELLBOOK?
barako coffee
MISTER CRISWELL, PERHAPS WE HAVEN'T MADE--
‹WE'VE BEEN PERFECTLY CLEAR, DAVID.›
HERR SCHULD ORDERED US TO RETRIEVE THE GRIMOIRE THAT WAS TAKEN FROM THE MAD DEMON DESMODUS,* AND PLACE IT IN THE ARCHIVES.
*IN THE NOW-CLASSIC VAMPIRELLA ANNUAL #1--ED.

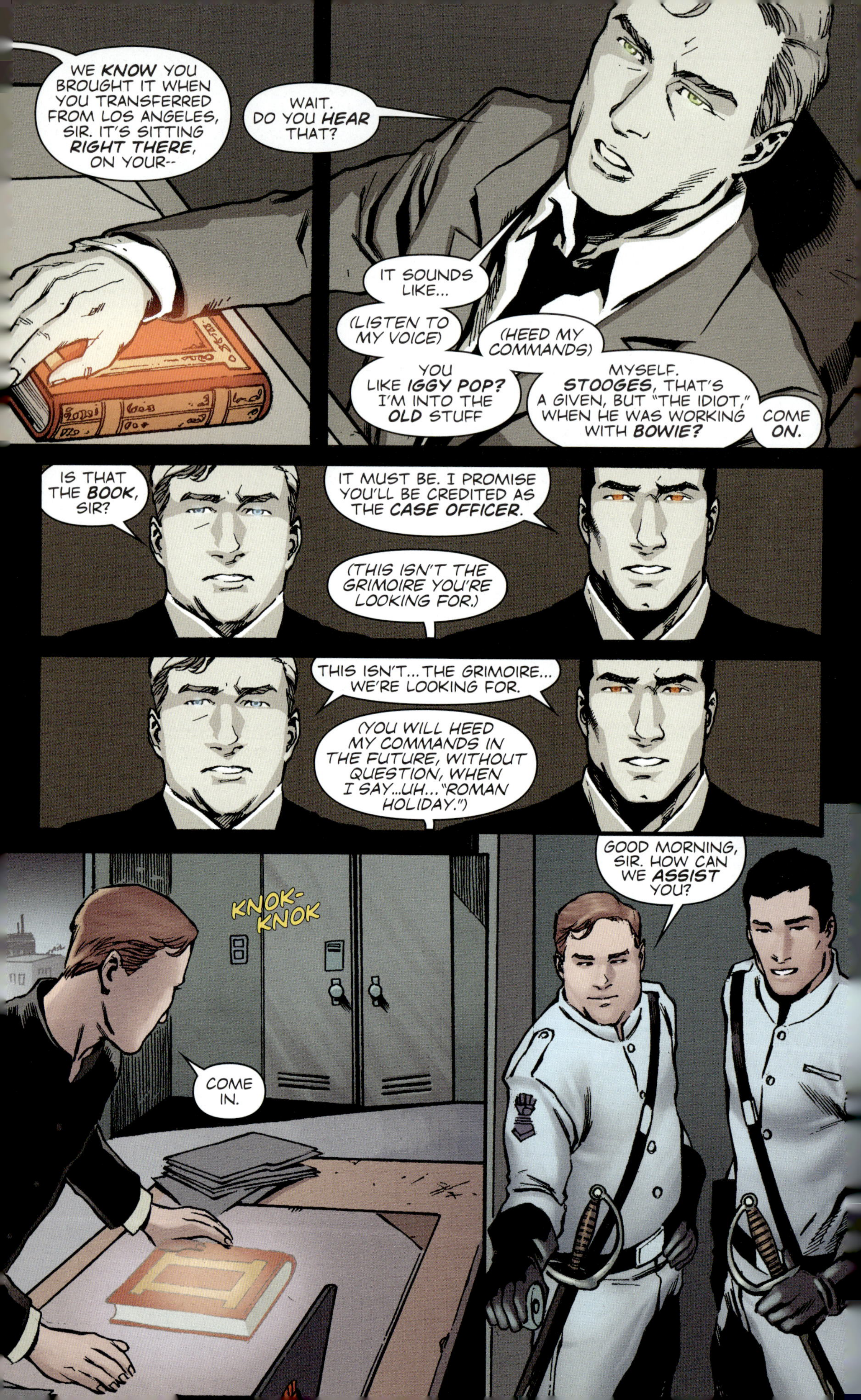
WE KNOW YOU BROUGHT IT WHEN YOU TRANSFERRED FROM LOS ANGELES, SIR. IT'S SITTING RIGHT THERE, ON YOUR--
WAIT. DO YOU HEAR THAT?
IT SOUNDS LIKE...
(LISTEN TO MY VOICE)
(HEED MY COMMANDS)
YOU LIKE IGGY POP? I'M INTO THE OLD STUFF
MYSELF. STOOGES, THAT'S A GIVEN, BUT "THE IDIOT," WHEN HE WAS WORKING WITH BOWIE?
COME ON.
IS THAT THE BOOK, SIR?
IT MUST BE. I PROMISE YOU'LL BE CREDITED AS THE CASE OFFICER.
(THIS ISN'T THE GRIMOIRE YOU'RE LOOKING FOR.)
THIS ISN'T...THE GRIMOIRE... WE'RE LOOKING FOR.
(YOU WILL HEED MY COMMANDS IN THE FUTURE, WITHOUT QUESTION, WHEN I SAY...UH... "ROMAN HOLIDAY.")
KNOK-KNOK
COME IN.
GOOD MORNING, SIR. HOW CAN WE ASSIST YOU?

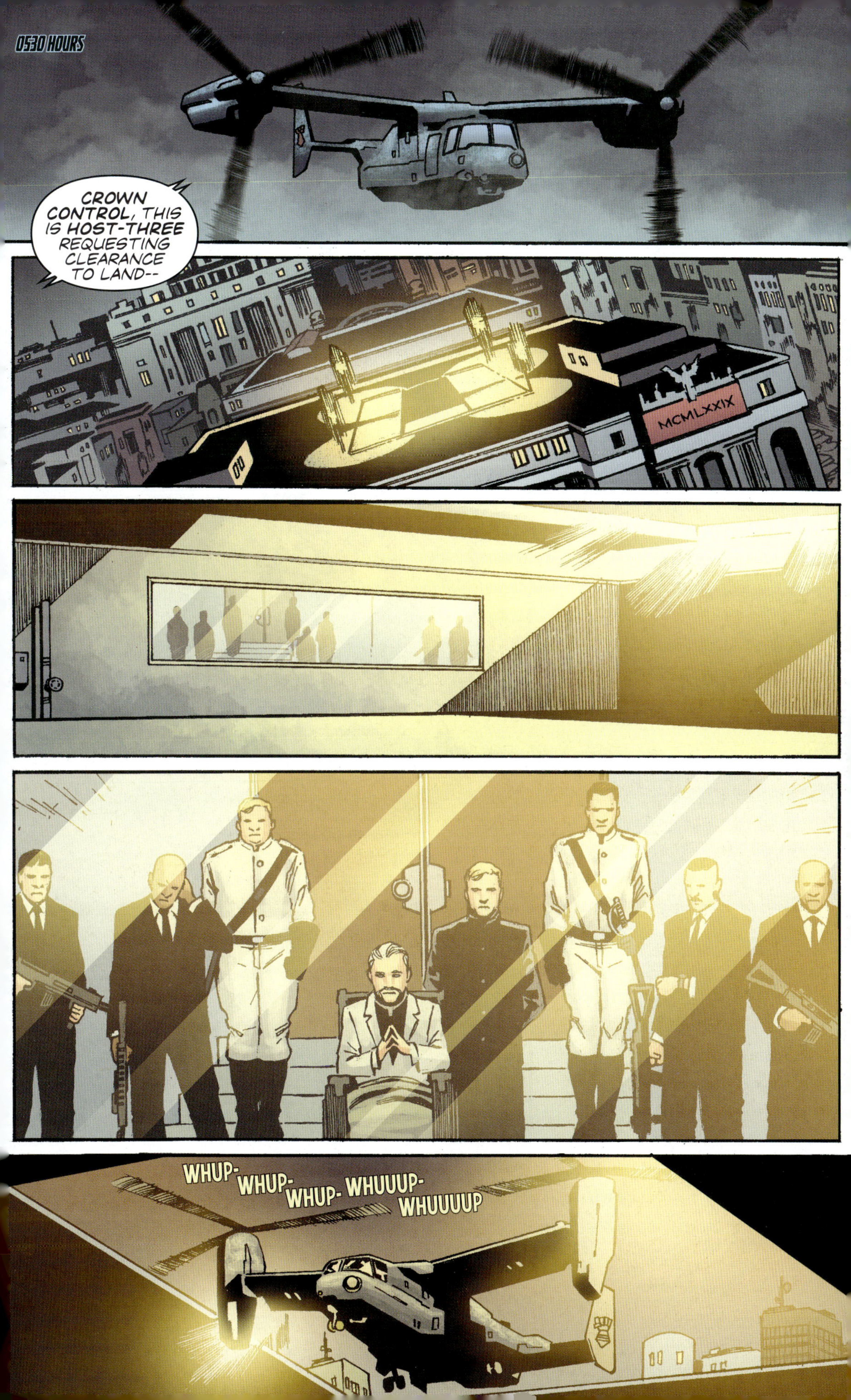
0530 HOURS
CROWN CONTROL, THIS IS HOST-THREE REQUESTING CLEARANCE TO LAND--
MCMLXXIX
WHUP- WHUP- WHUP- WHUUUP- WHUUUUP

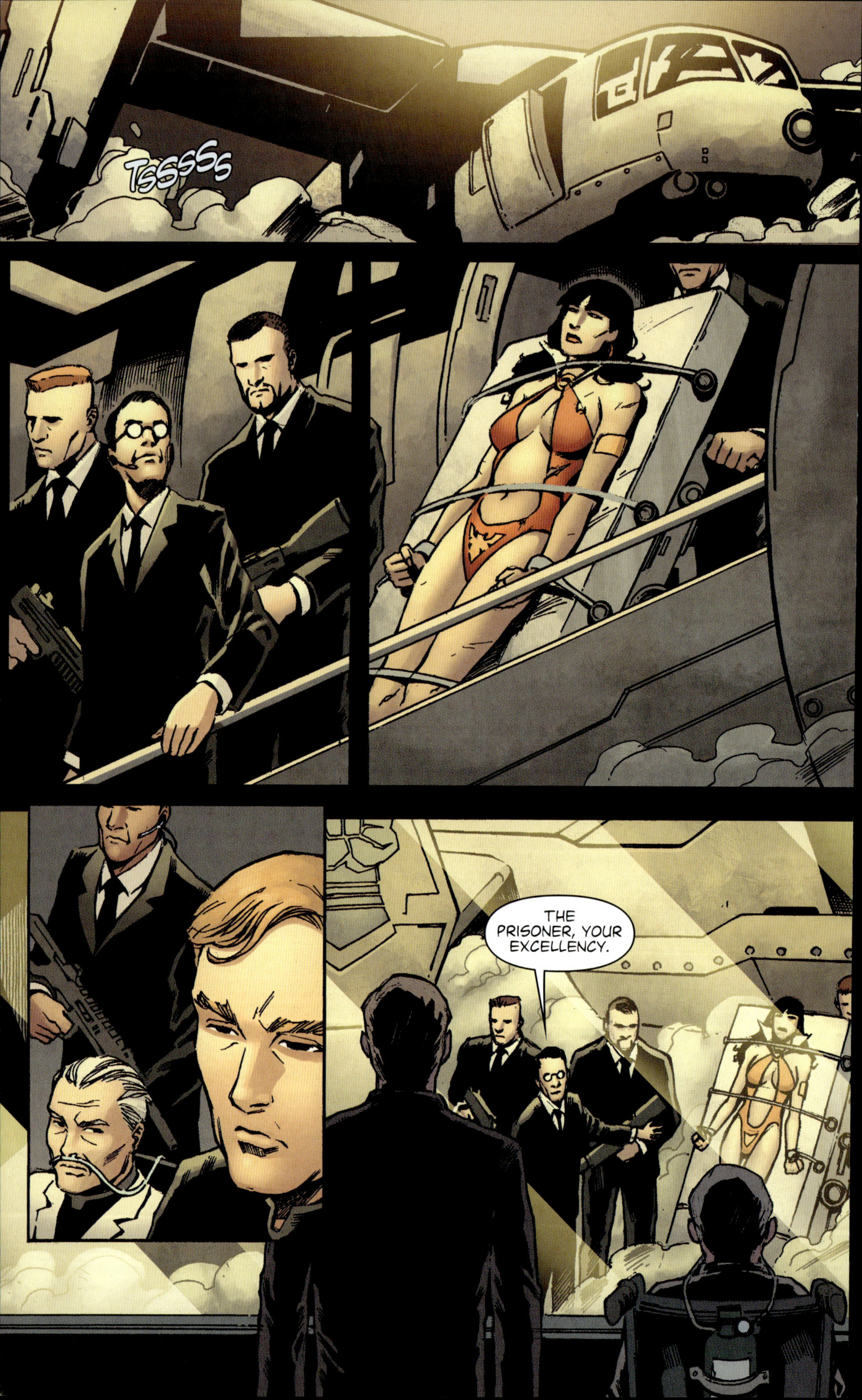
TSSSSS
THE PRISONER, YOUR EXCELLENCY.

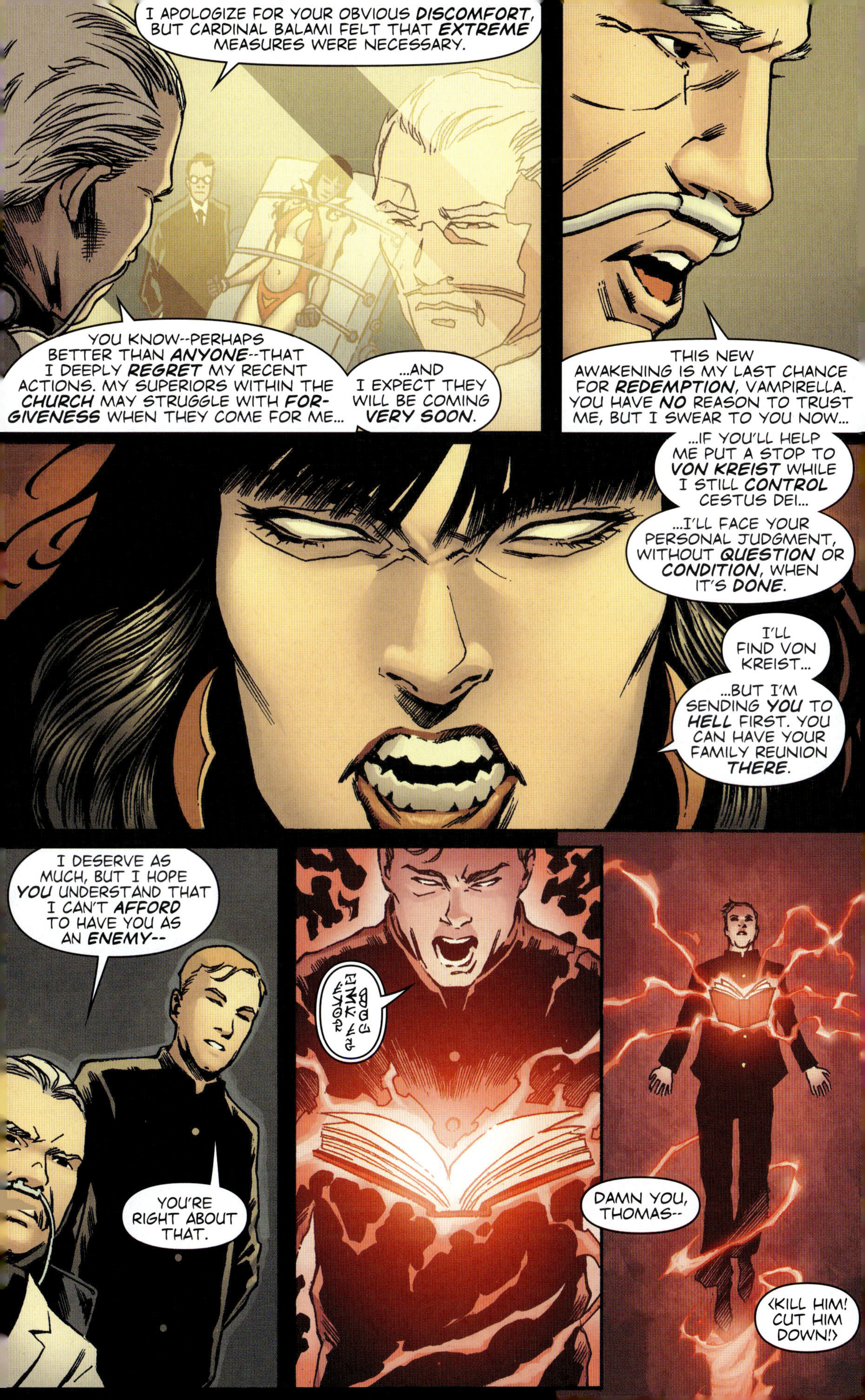
I APOLOGIZE FOR YOUR OBVIOUS DISCOMFORT, BUT CARDINAL BALAMI FELT THAT EXTREME MEASURES WERE NECESSARY.
YOU KNOW--PERHAPS BETTER THAN ANYONE--THAT I DEEPLY REGRET MY RECENT ACTIONS. MY SUPERIORS WITHIN THE CHURCH MAY STRUGGLE WITH FOR-GIVENESS WHEN THEY COME FOR ME...
...AND I EXPECT THEY WILL BE COMING VERY SOON.
THIS NEW AWAKENING IS MY LAST CHANCE FOR REDEMPTION, VAMPIRELLA. YOU HAVE NO REASON TO TRUST ME, BUT I SWEAR TO YOU NOW...
...IF YOU'LL HELP ME PUT A STOP TO VON KREIST WHILE I STILL CONTROL CESTUS DEI...
...I'LL FACE YOUR PERSONAL JUDGMENT, WITHOUT QUESTION OR CONDITION, WHEN IT'S DONE.
I'LL FIND VON KREIST...
...BUT I'M SENDING YOU TO HELL FIRST. YOU CAN HAVE YOUR FAMILY REUNION THERE.
I DESERVE AS MUCH, BUT I HOPE YOU UNDERSTAND THAT I CAN'T AFFORD TO HAVE YOU AS AN ENEMY--
YOU'RE RIGHT ABOUT THAT.
DAMN YOU, THOMAS--
‹KILL HIM! CUT HIM DOWN!›

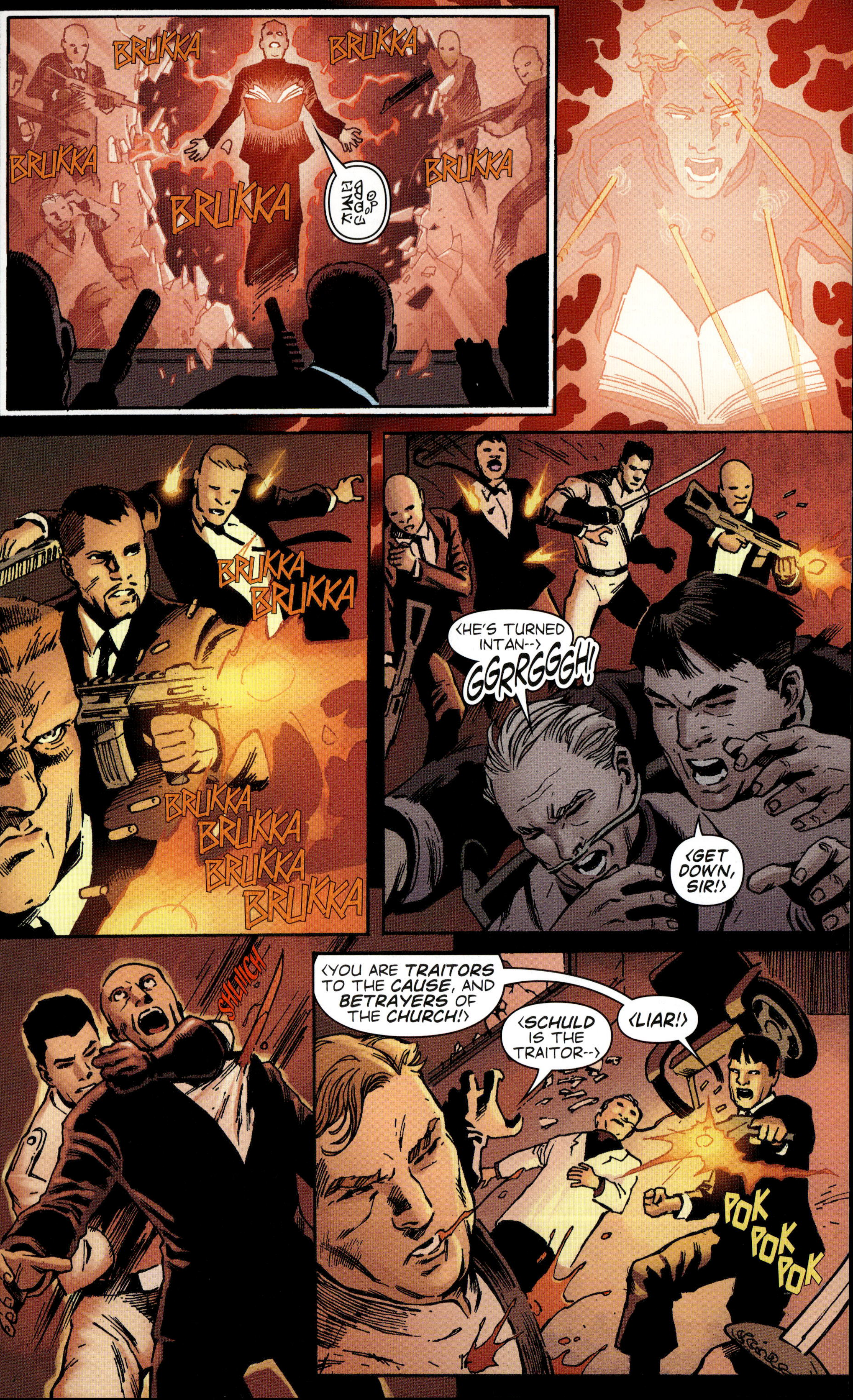
BRUKKA
BRUKKA
BRUKKA
BRUKKA
BRUKKA
BRUKKA
BRUKKA
BRUKKA
BRUKKA
BRUKKA
BRUKKA
‹HE'S TURNED INTAN--›
GGRRGGGH!
‹GET DOWN, SIR!›
‹YOU ARE TRAITORS TO THE CAUSE, AND BETRAYERS OF THE CHURCH!›
‹LIAR!›
‹SCHULD IS THE TRAITOR--›
POK
POK
POK

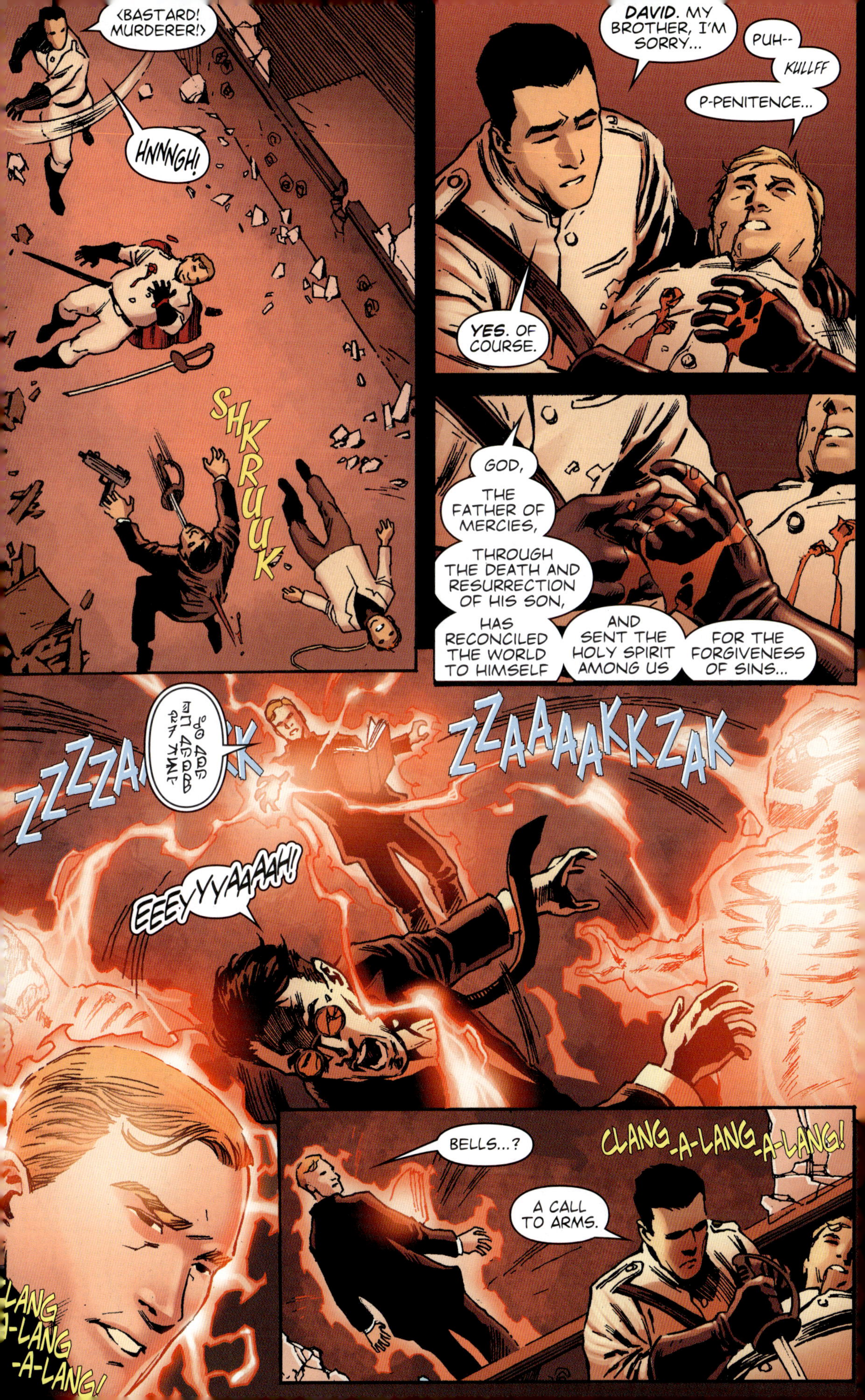
‹BASTARD! MURDERER!›
HNNNGH!
SHKRUUUK
DAVID. MY BROTHER, I'M SORRY...
PUH--
KULLFF
P-PENITENCE...
YES. OF COURSE.
GOD,
THE FATHER OF MERCIES,
THROUGH THE DEATH AND RESURRECTION OF HIS SON,
HAS RECONCILED THE WORLD TO HIMSELF
AND SENT THE HOLY SPIRIT AMONG US
FOR THE FORGIVENESS OF SINS...
ZZAAAAKKZAK
EEEYYYAAAAH!
BELLS...?
CLANG-A-LANG-A-LANG!
A CALL TO ARMS.
-A-LANG!

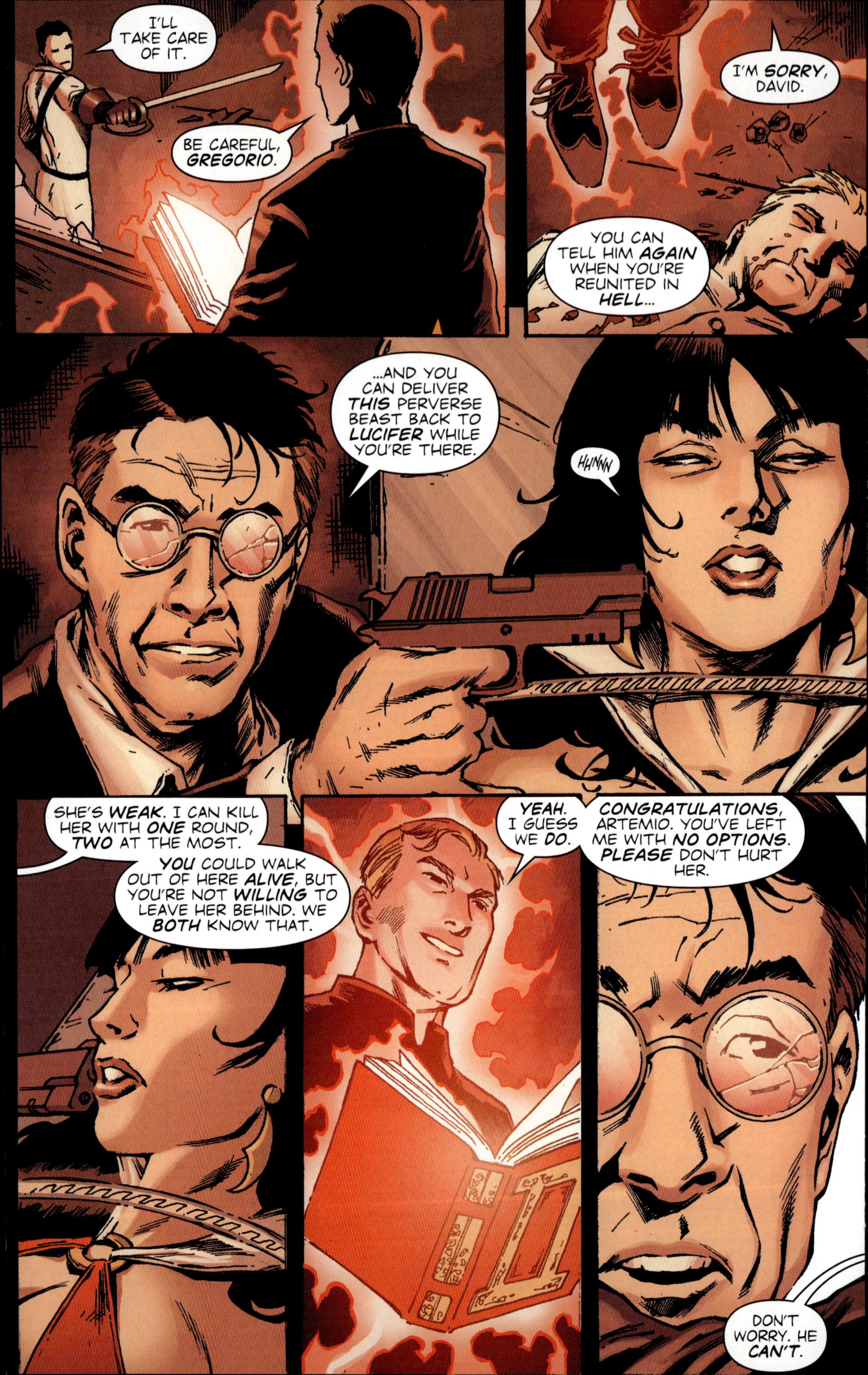
I'LL TAKE CARE OF IT.
BE CAREFUL, GREGORIO.
I'M SORRY, DAVID.
YOU CAN TELL HIM AGAIN WHEN YOU'RE REUNITED IN HELL...
...AND YOU CAN DELIVER THIS PERVERSE BEAST BACK TO LUCIFER WHILE YOU'RE THERE.
HHNNN
SHE'S WEAK. I CAN KILL HER WITH ONE ROUND, TWO AT THE MOST.
YOU COULD WALK OUT OF HERE ALIVE, BUT YOU'RE NOT WILLING TO LEAVE HER BEHIND. WE BOTH KNOW THAT.
YEAH. I GUESS WE DO.
CONGRATULATIONS, ARTEMIO. YOU'VE LEFT ME WITH NO OPTIONS. PLEASE DON'T HURT HER.
DON'T WORRY. HE CAN'T.

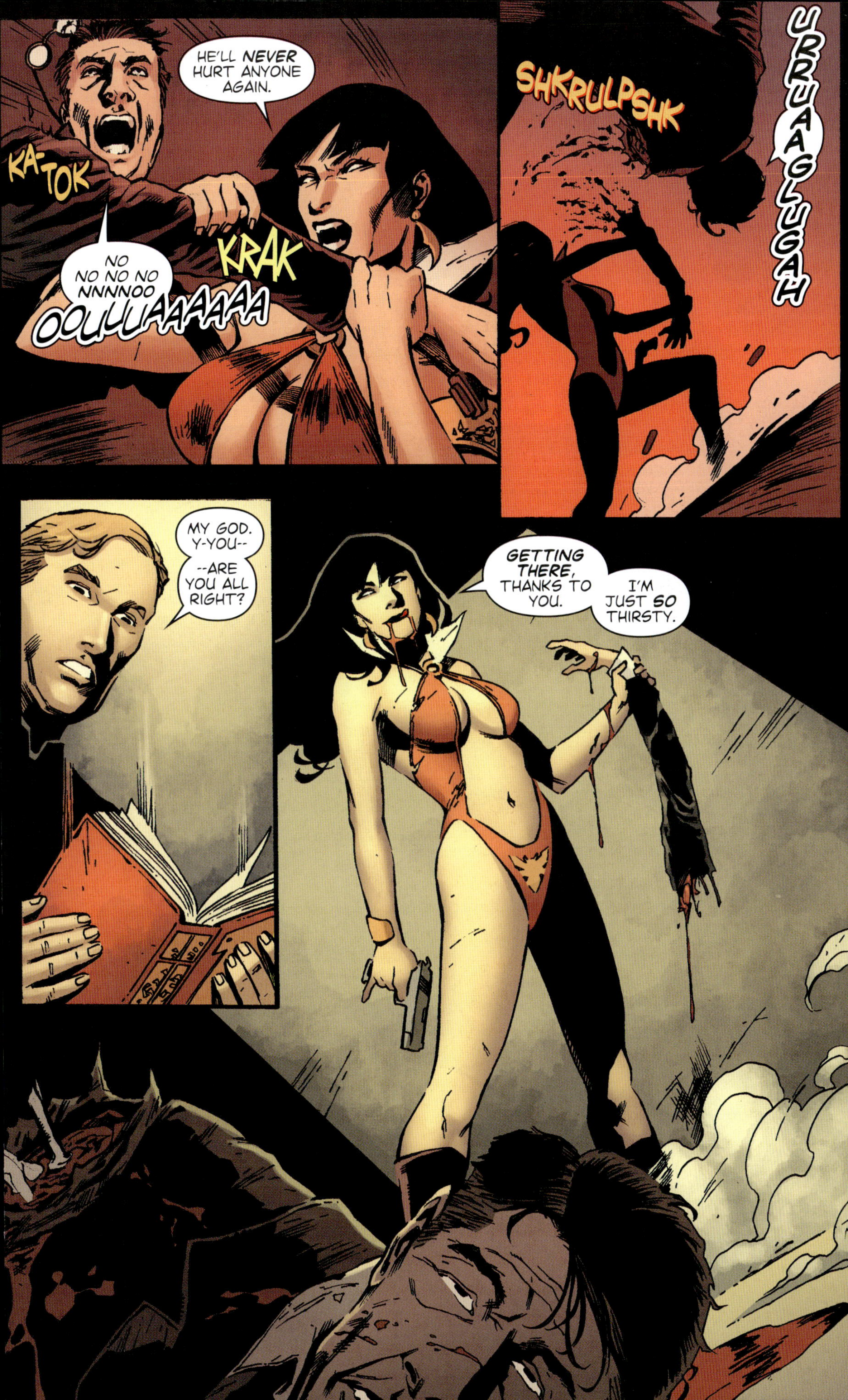
HE'LL NEVER HURT ANYONE AGAIN.
KA-TOK
NO NO NO NO NNNNOO
OOUUUAAAAAA
KRAK
SHKRULPSHK
URRUAAGLUGAH
MY GOD. Y-YOU--
--ARE YOU ALL RIGHT?
GETTING THERE, THANKS TO YOU.
I'M JUST SO THIRSTY.

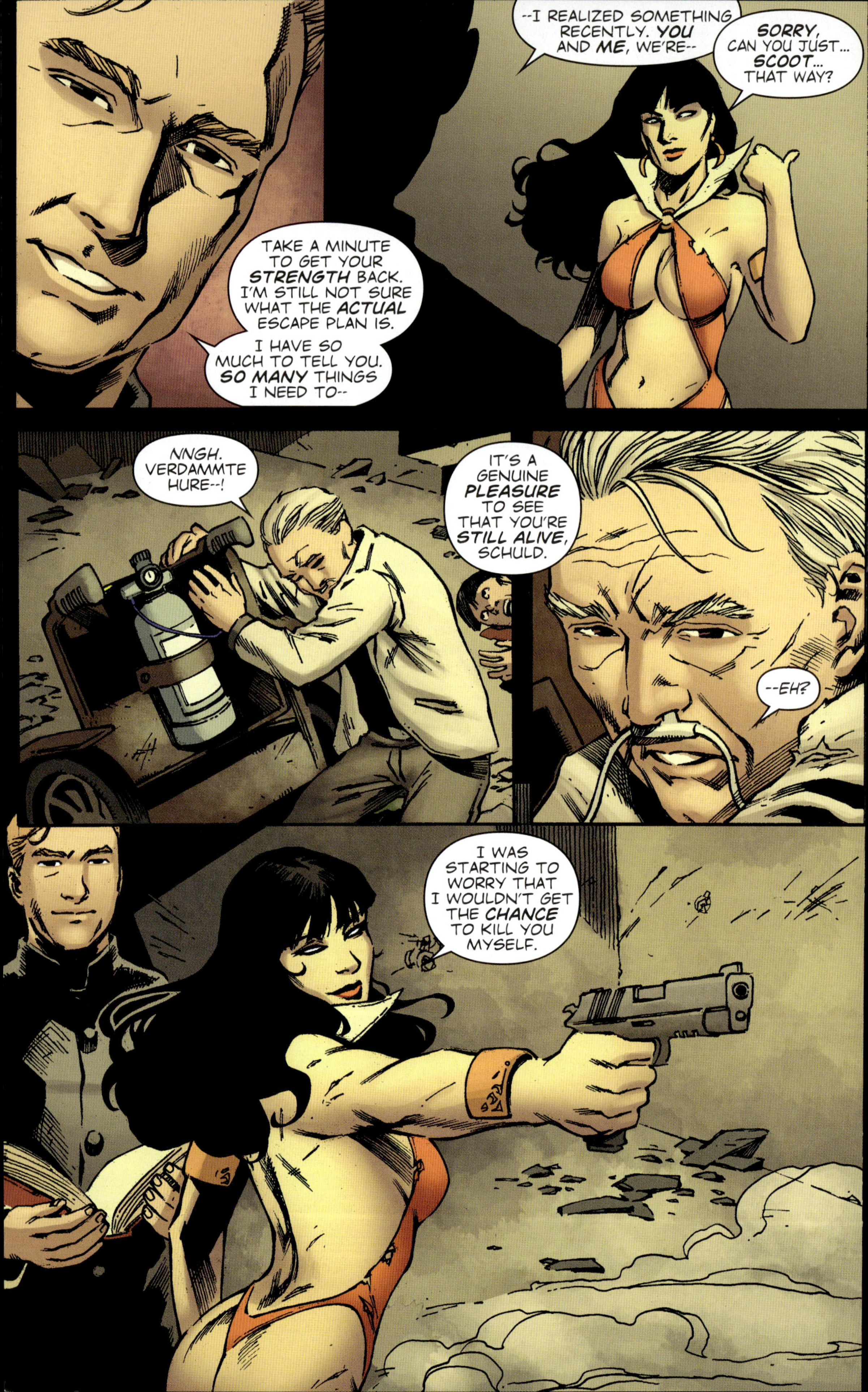

--I REALIZED SOMETHING RECENTLY. YOU AND ME, WE'RE--
SORRY, CAN YOU JUST... SCOOT... THAT WAY?
TAKE A MINUTE TO GET YOUR STRENGTH BACK. I'M STILL NOT SURE WHAT THE ACTUAL ESCAPE PLAN IS.
I HAVE SO MUCH TO TELL YOU. SO MANY THINGS I NEED TO--
NNGH. VERDAMMTE HURE--!
IT'S A GENUINE PLEASURE TO SEE THAT YOU'RE STILL ALIVE, SCHULD.
--EH?
I WAS STARTING TO WORRY THAT I WOULDN'T GET THE CHANCE TO KILL YOU MYSELF.

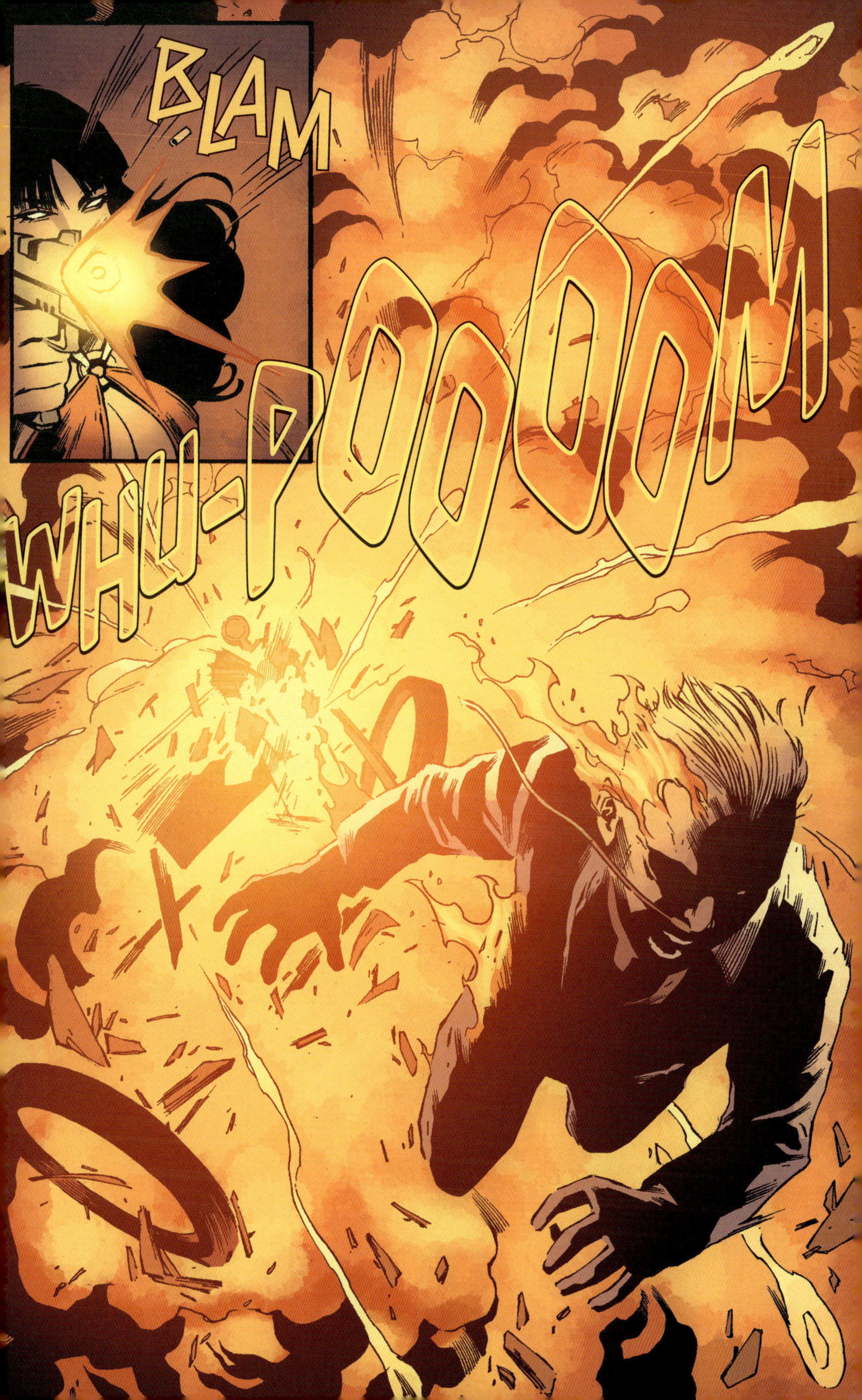
BLAM
WHU-POOOOOM

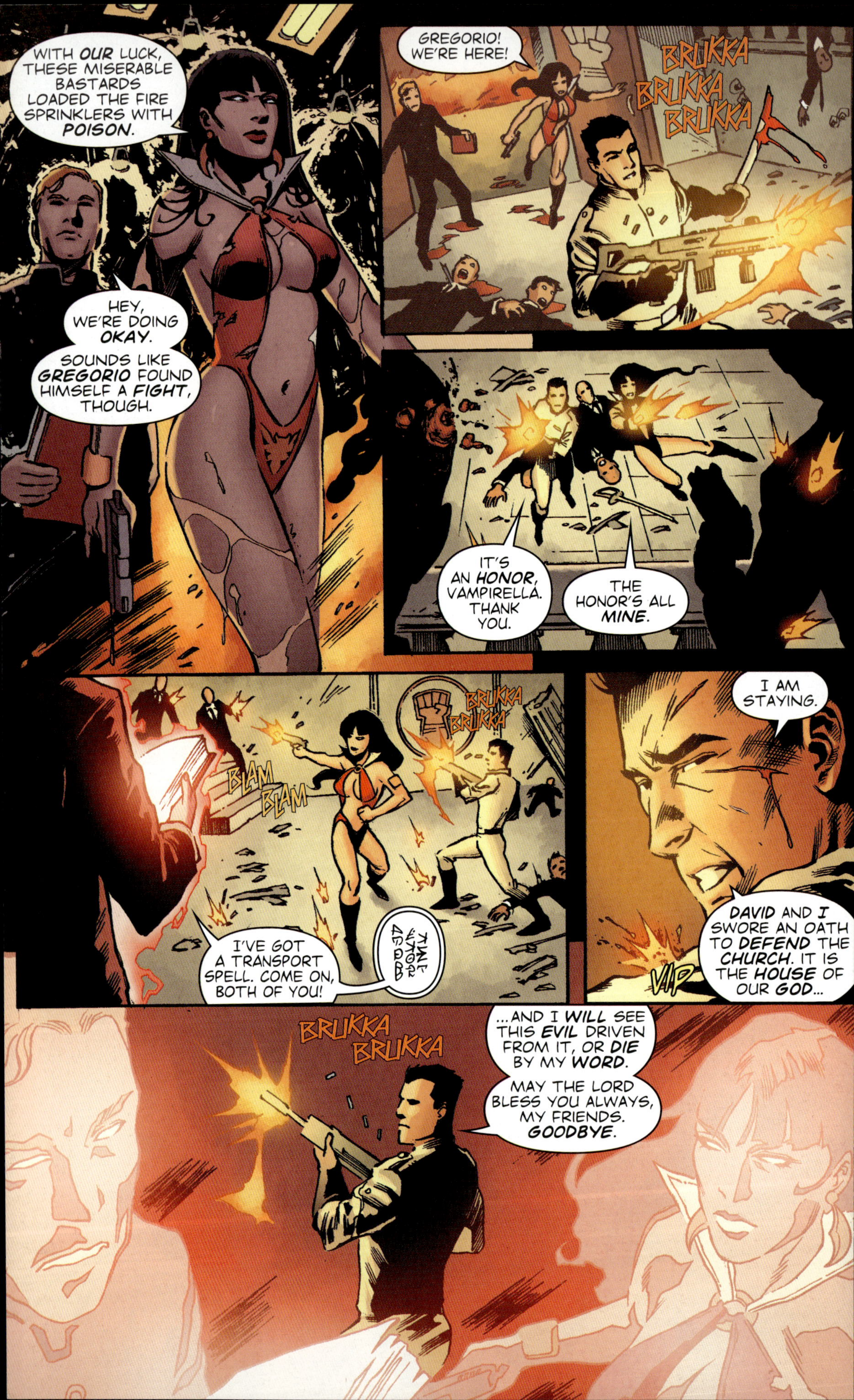
WITH OUR LUCK, THESE MISERABLE BASTARDS LOADED THE FIRE SPRINKLERS WITH POISON.
HEY, WE'RE DOING OKAY.
SOUNDS LIKE GREGORIO FOUND HIMSELF A FIGHT, THOUGH.
GREGORIO! WE'RE HERE!
BRUKKA BRUKKA BRUKKA
IT'S AN HONOR, VAMPIRELLA. THANK YOU.
THE HONOR'S ALL MINE.
BRUKKA BRUKKA
BLAM BLAM
I'VE GOT A TRANSPORT SPELL. COME ON, BOTH OF YOU!
I AM STAYING.
DAVID AND I SWORE AN OATH TO DEFEND THE CHURCH. IT IS THE HOUSE OF OUR GOD...
VIP
BRUKKA BRUKKA
...AND I WILL SEE THIS EVIL DRIVEN FROM IT, OR DIE BY MY WORD.
MAY THE LORD BLESS YOU ALWAYS, MY FRIENDS. GOODBYE.

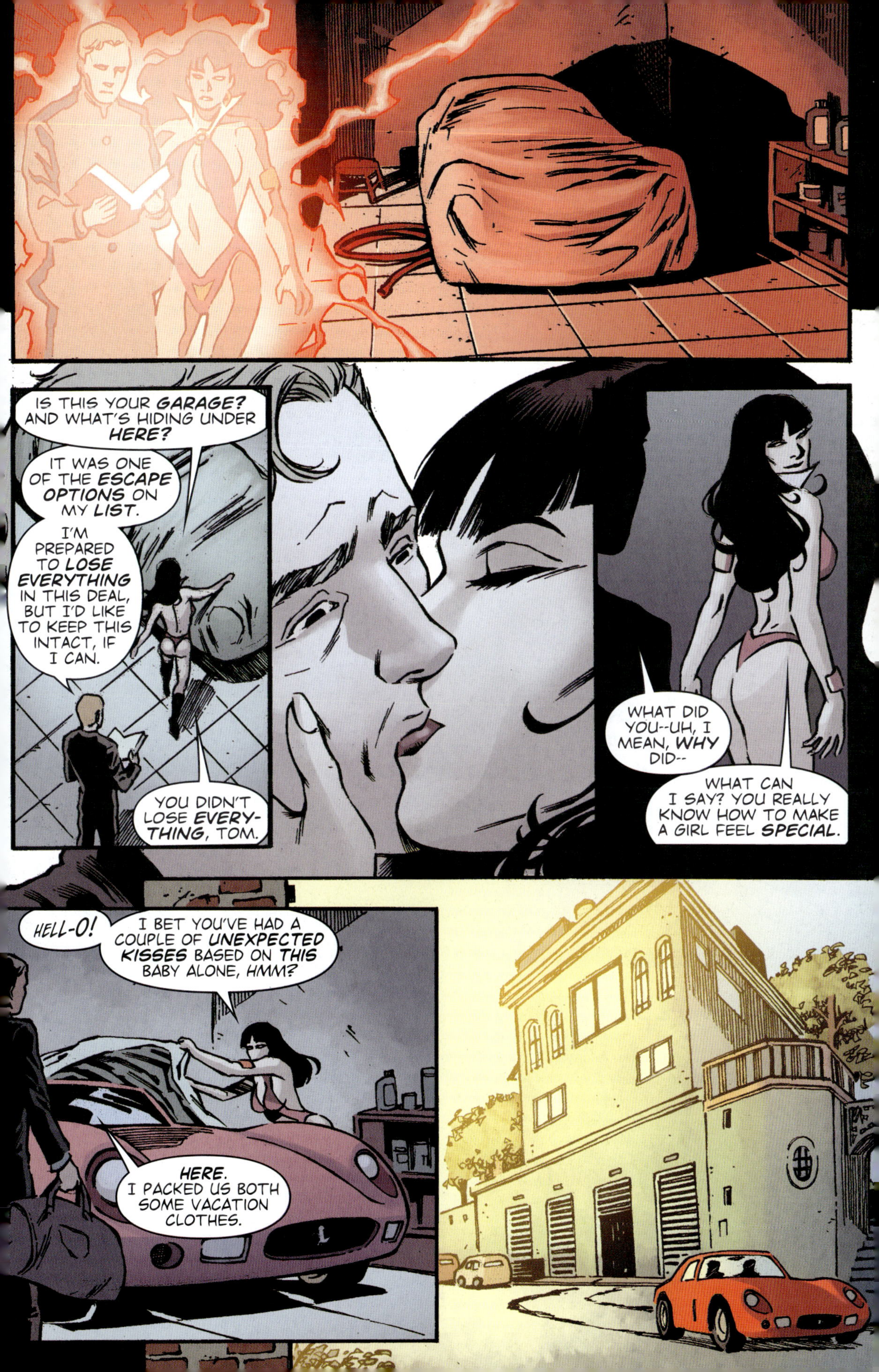
IS THIS YOUR GARAGE? AND WHAT'S HIDING UNDER HERE?
IT WAS ONE OF THE ESCAPE OPTIONS ON MY LIST.
I'M PREPARED TO LOSE EVERYTHING IN THIS DEAL, BUT I'D LIKE TO KEEP THIS INTACT, IF I CAN.
YOU DIDN'T LOSE EVERY-THING, TOM.
WHAT DID YOU--UH, I MEAN, WHY DID--
WHAT CAN I SAY? YOU REALLY KNOW HOW TO MAKE A GIRL FEEL SPECIAL.
HELL-O!
I BET YOU'VE HAD A COUPLE OF UNEXPECTED KISSES BASED ON THIS BABY ALONE, HMM?
HERE. I PACKED US BOTH SOME VACATION CLOTHES.

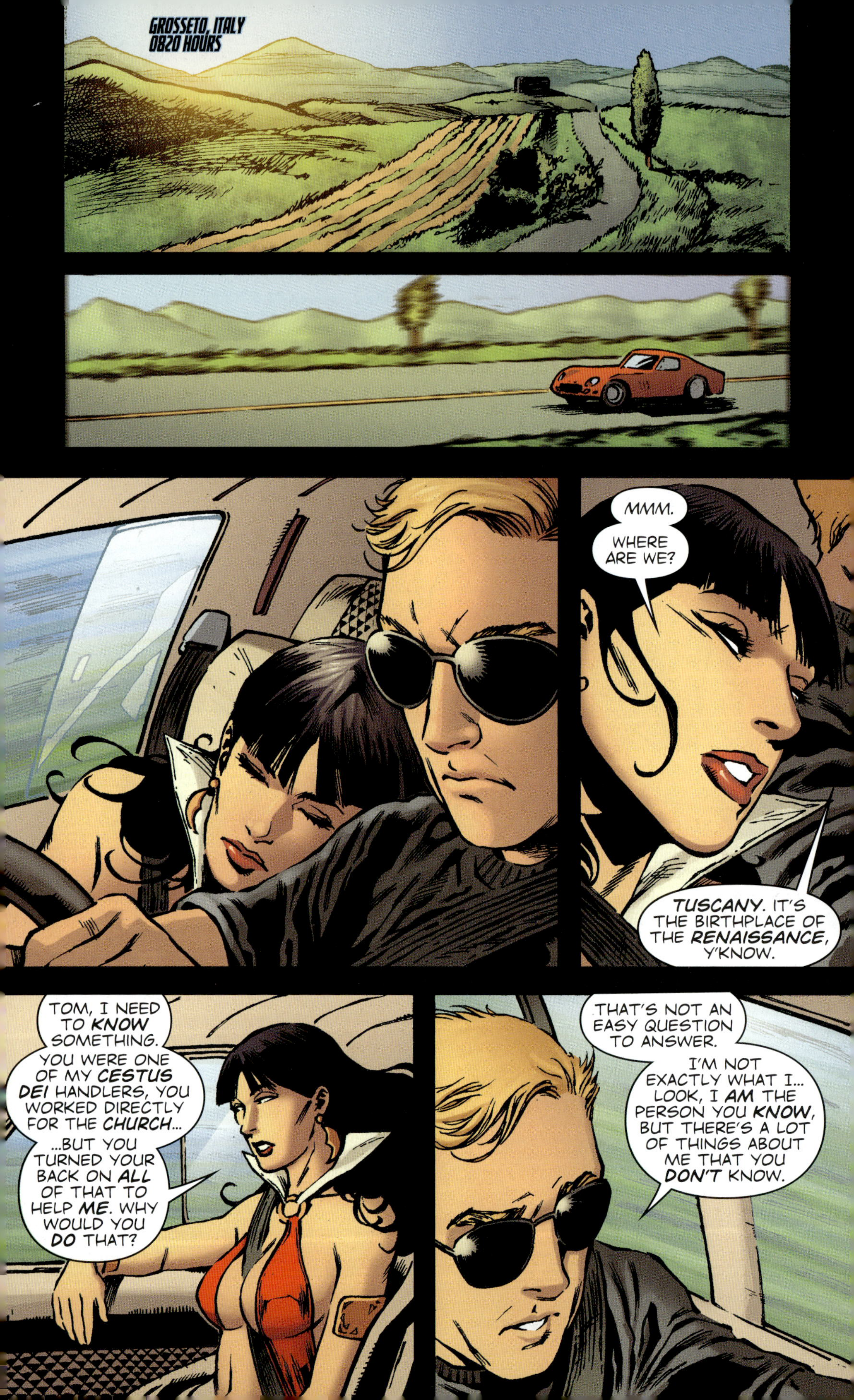
GROSSETO, ITALY
0820 HOURS
MMM.
WHERE ARE WE?
TUSCANY. IT'S THE BIRTHPLACE OF THE RENAISSANCE, Y'KNOW.
TOM, I NEED TO KNOW SOMETHING.
YOU WERE ONE OF MY CESTUS DEI HANDLERS, YOU WORKED DIRECTLY FOR THE CHURCH...
...BUT YOU TURNED YOUR BACK ON ALL OF THAT TO HELP ME. WHY WOULD YOU DO THAT?
THAT'S NOT AN EASY QUESTION TO ANSWER.
I'M NOT EXACTLY WHAT I... LOOK, I AM THE PERSON YOU KNOW, BUT THERE'S A LOT OF THINGS ABOUT ME THAT YOU DON'T KNOW.

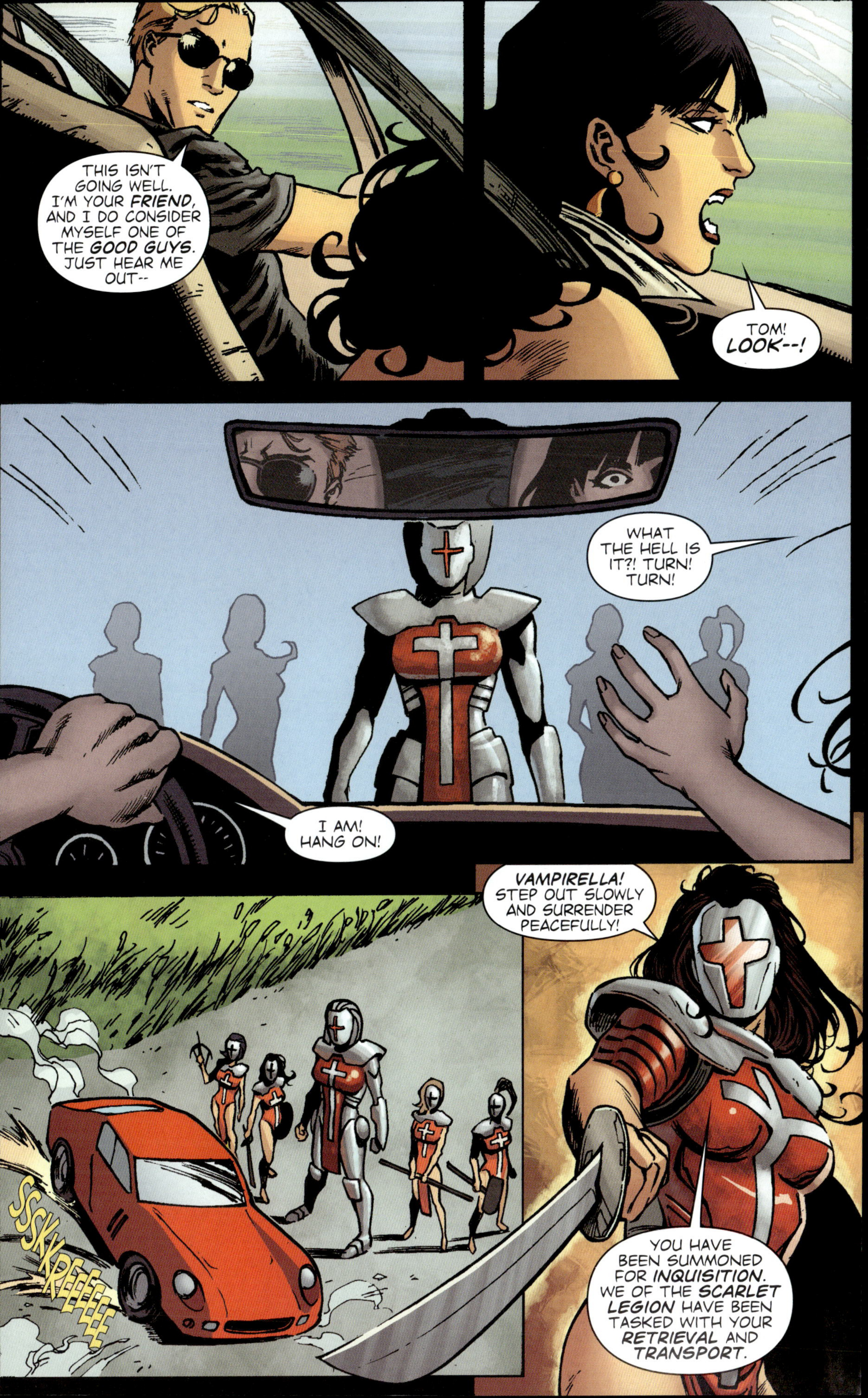
THIS ISN'T GOING WELL. I'M YOUR FRIEND, AND I DO CONSIDER MYSELF ONE OF THE GOOD GUYS. JUST HEAR ME OUT--
TOM! LOOK--!
WHAT THE HELL IS IT?! TURN! TURN!
I AM! HANG ON!
SSSKKREEEEEE
VAMPIRELLA! STEP OUT SLOWLY AND SURRENDER PEACEFULLY!
YOU HAVE BEEN SUMMONED FOR INQUISITION. WE OF THE SCARLET LEGION HAVE BEEN TASKED WITH YOUR RETRIEVAL AND TRANSPORT.

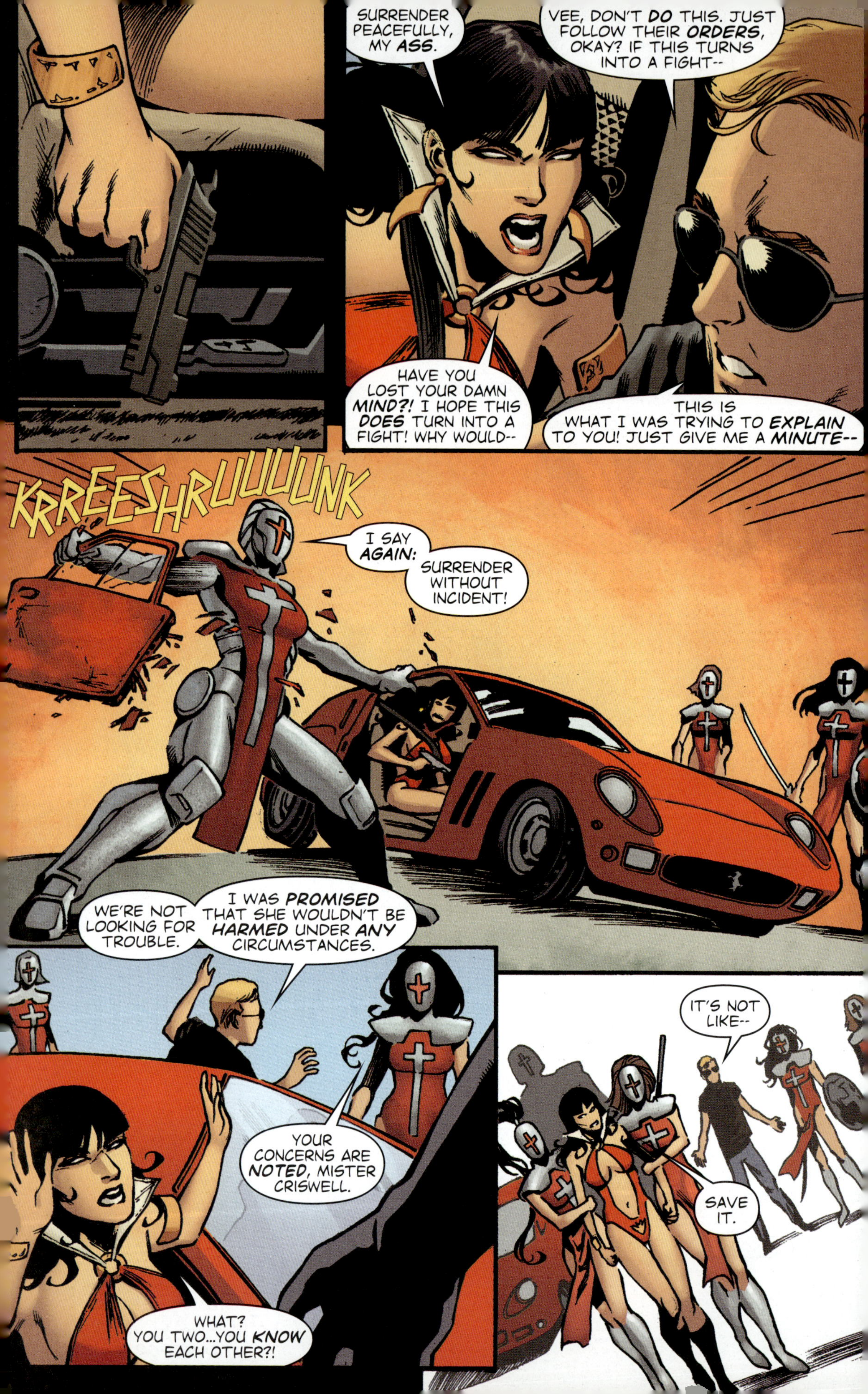
SURRENDER PEACEFULLY, MY ASS.
VEE, DON'T DO THIS. JUST FOLLOW THEIR ORDERS, OKAY? IF THIS TURNS INTO A FIGHT--
HAVE YOU LOST YOUR DAMN MIND?! I HOPE THIS DOES TURN INTO A FIGHT! WHY WOULD--
THIS IS WHAT I WAS TRYING TO EXPLAIN TO YOU! JUST GIVE ME A MINUTE--
KRREESHRUUUUNK
I SAY AGAIN:
SURRENDER WITHOUT INCIDENT!
WE'RE NOT LOOKING FOR TROUBLE.
I WAS PROMISED THAT SHE WOULDN'T BE HARMED UNDER ANY CIRCUMSTANCES.
YOUR CONCERNS ARE NOTED, MISTER CRISWELL.
WHAT? YOU TWO...YOU KNOW EACH OTHER?!
IT'S NOT LIKE--
SAVE IT.

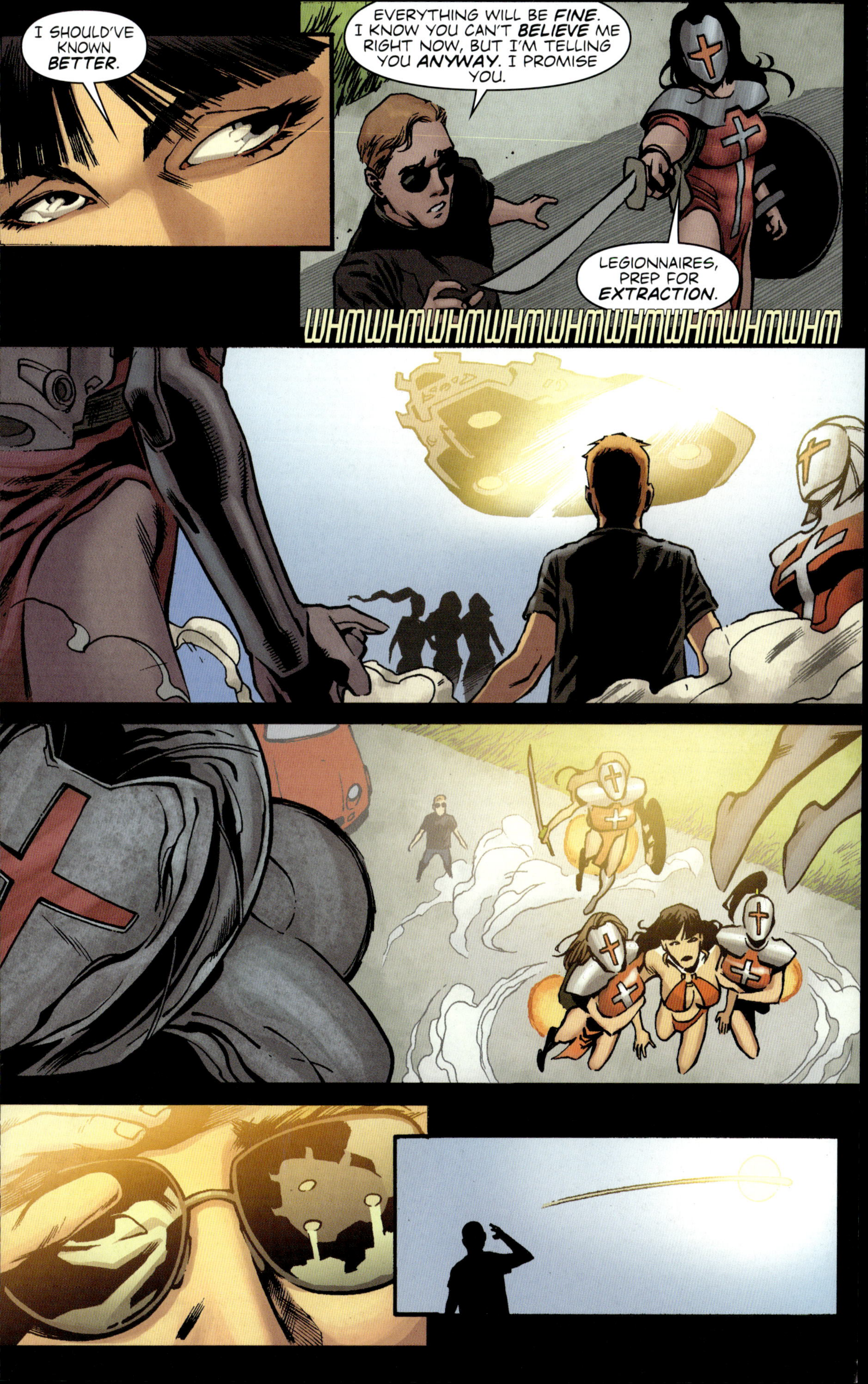
I SHOULD'VE KNOWN BETTER.
EVERYTHING WILL BE FINE. I KNOW YOU CAN'T BELIEVE ME RIGHT NOW, BUT I'M TELLING YOU ANYWAY. I PROMISE YOU.
LEGIONNAIRES, PREP FOR EXTRACTION.
WHMWHMWHMWHMWHMWHMWHMWHMWHMWHM

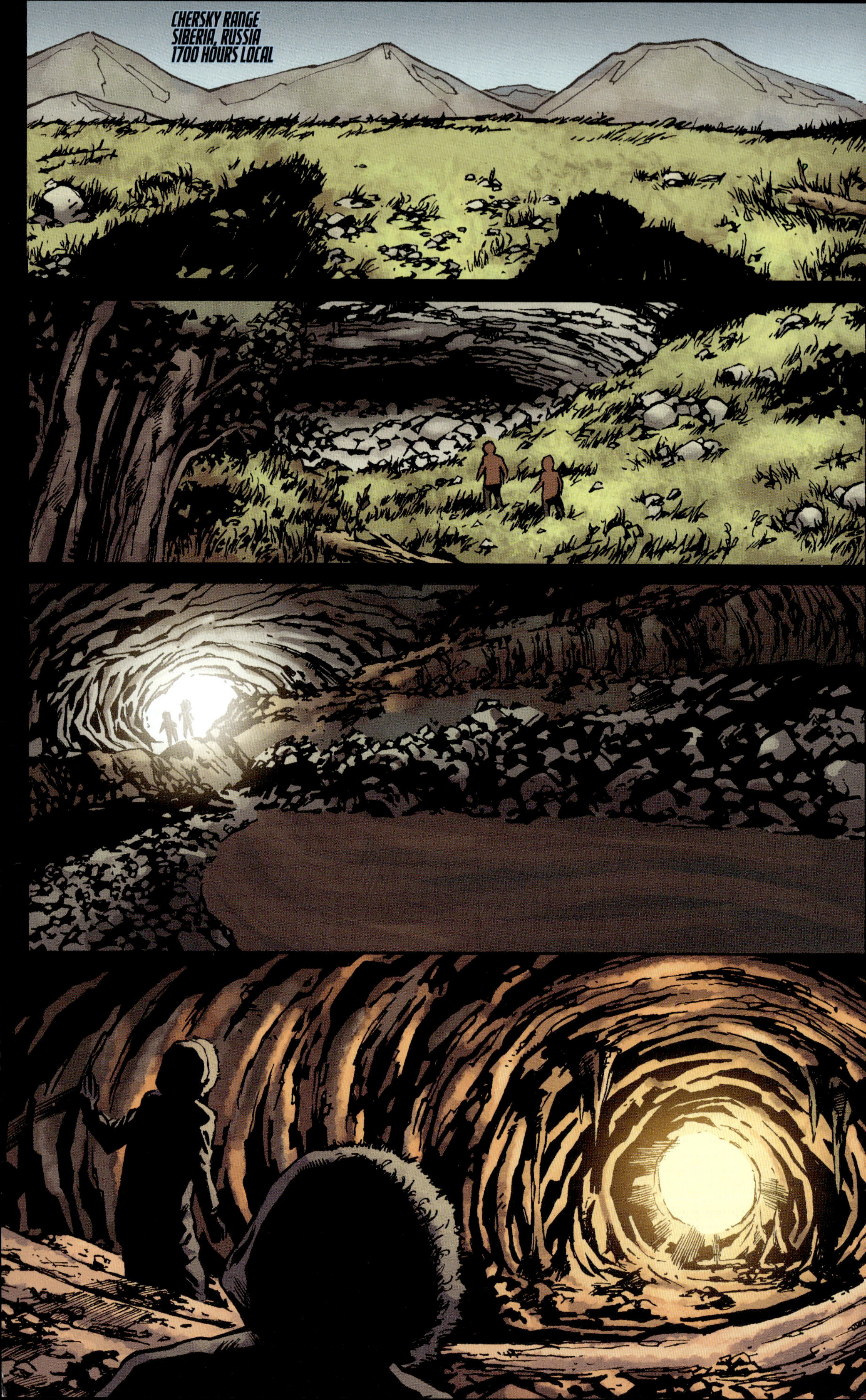
CHERSKY RANGE
SIBERIA, RUSSIA
1700 HOURS LOCAL

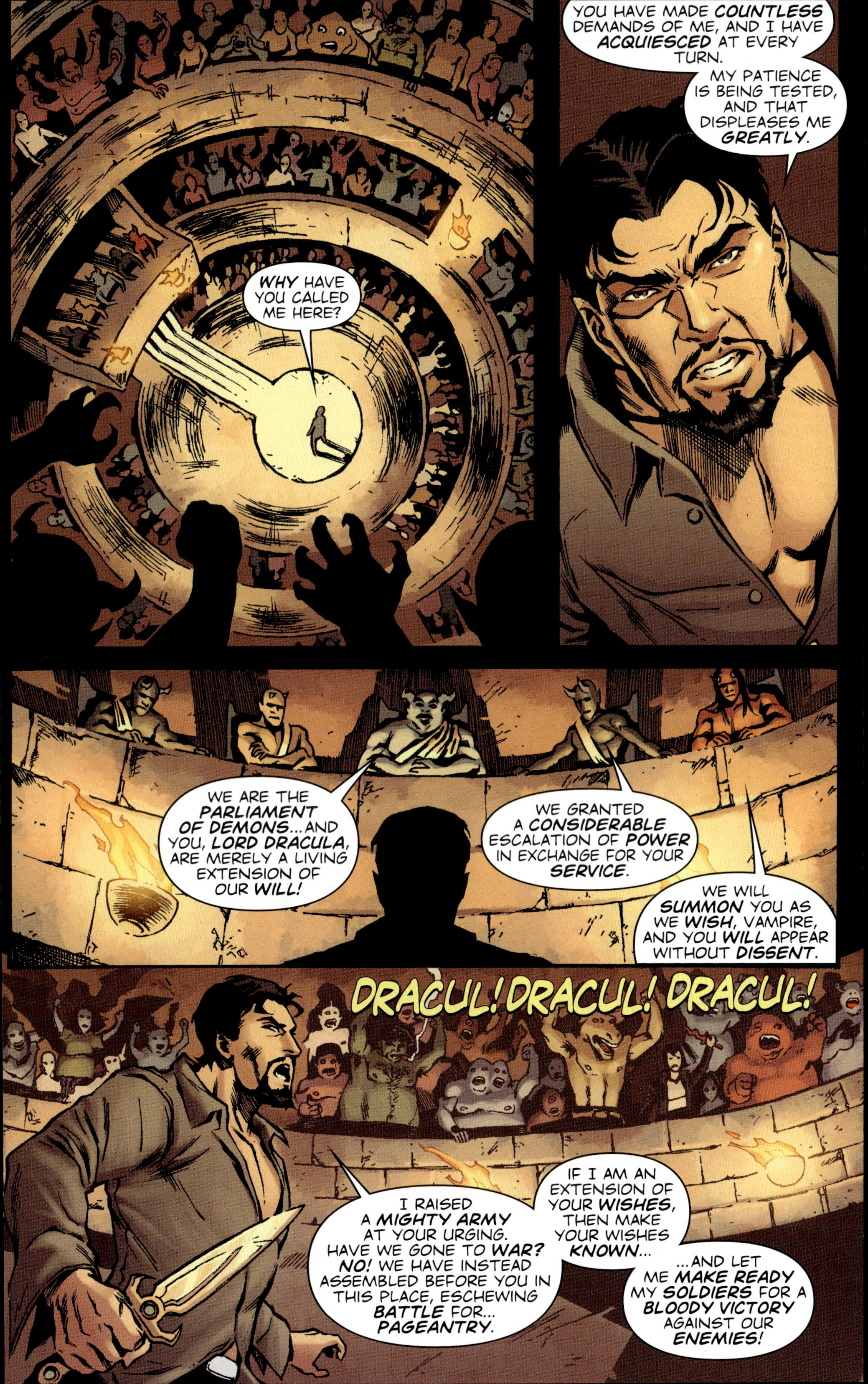
WHY HAVE YOU CALLED ME HERE?
YOU HAVE MADE COUNTLESS DEMANDS OF ME, AND I HAVE ACQUIESCED AT EVERY TURN.
MY PATIENCE IS BEING TESTED, AND THAT DISPLEASES ME GREATLY.
WE ARE THE PARLIAMENT OF DEMONS... AND YOU, LORD DRACULA, ARE MERELY A LIVING EXTENSION OF OUR WILL!
WE GRANTED A CONSIDERABLE ESCALATION OF POWER IN EXCHANGE FOR YOUR SERVICE.
WE WILL SUMMON YOU AS WE WISH, VAMPIRE, AND YOU WILL APPEAR WITHOUT DISSENT.
DRACUL! DRACUL! DRACUL!
I RAISED A MIGHTY ARMY AT YOUR URGING. HAVE WE GONE TO WAR? NO! WE HAVE INSTEAD ASSEMBLED BEFORE YOU IN THIS PLACE, ESCHEWING BATTLE FOR... PAGEANTRY.
IF I AM AN EXTENSION OF YOUR WISHES, THEN MAKE YOUR WISHES KNOWN...
...AND LET ME MAKE READY MY SOLDIERS FOR A BLOODY VICTORY AGAINST OUR ENEMIES!

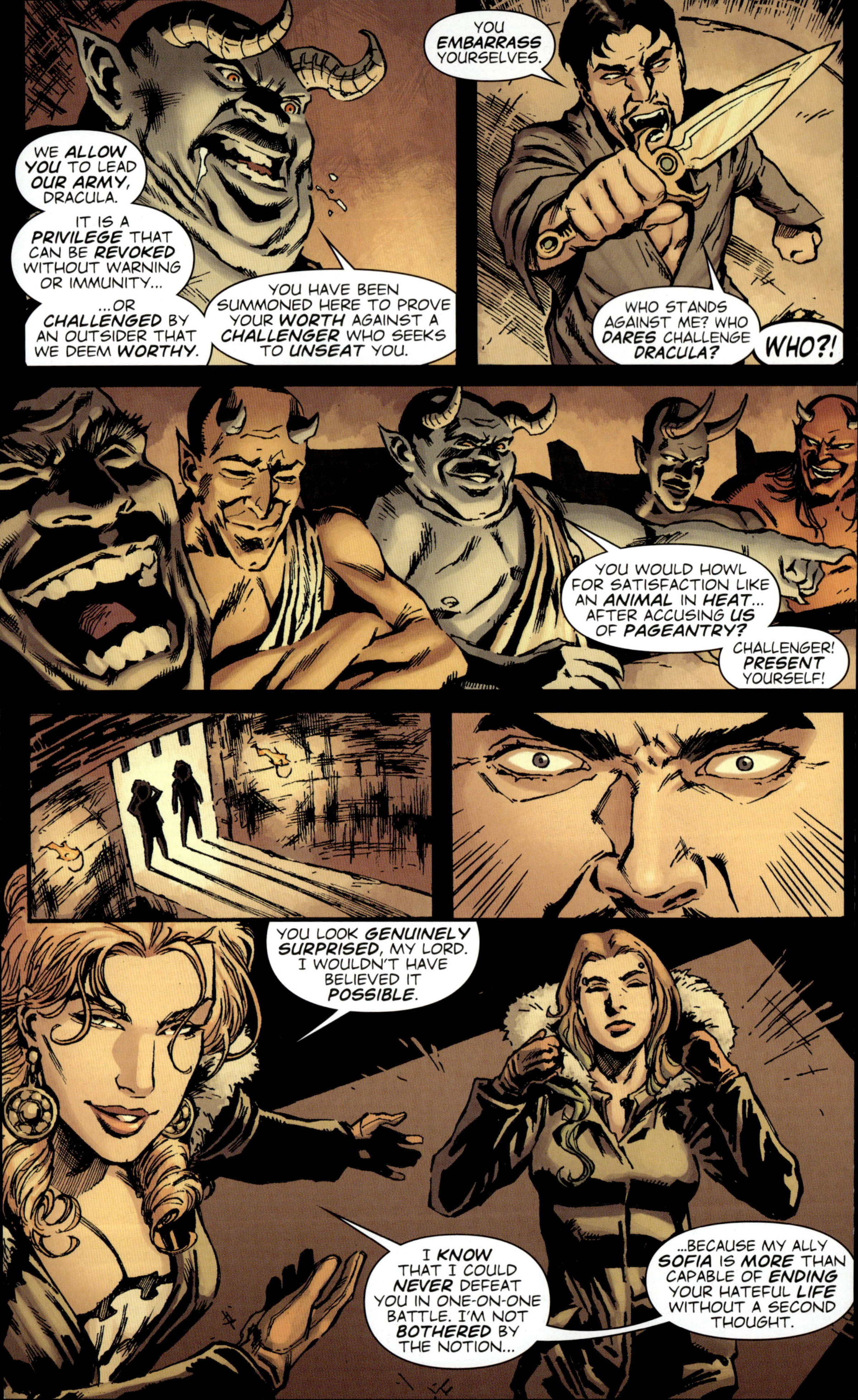
WE ALLOW YOU TO LEAD OUR ARMY, DRACULA.
IT IS A PRIVILEGE THAT CAN BE REVOKED WITHOUT WARNING OR IMMUNITY...
...OR CHALLENGED BY AN OUTSIDER THAT WE DEEM WORTHY.
YOU HAVE BEEN SUMMONED HERE TO PROVE YOUR WORTH AGAINST A CHALLENGER WHO SEEKS TO UNSEAT YOU.
YOU EMBARRASS YOURSELVES.
WHO STANDS AGAINST ME? WHO DARES CHALLENGE DRACULA?
WHO?!
YOU WOULD HOWL FOR SATISFACTION LIKE AN ANIMAL IN HEAT... AFTER ACCUSING US OF PAGEANTRY?
CHALLENGER! PRESENT YOURSELF!
YOU LOOK GENUINELY SURPRISED, MY LORD. I WOULDN'T HAVE BELIEVED IT POSSIBLE.
I KNOW THAT I COULD NEVER DEFEAT YOU IN ONE-ON-ONE BATTLE. I'M NOT BOTHERED BY THE NOTION...
...BECAUSE MY ALLY SOFIA IS MORE THAN CAPABLE OF ENDING YOUR HATEFUL LIFE WITHOUT A SECOND THOUGHT.

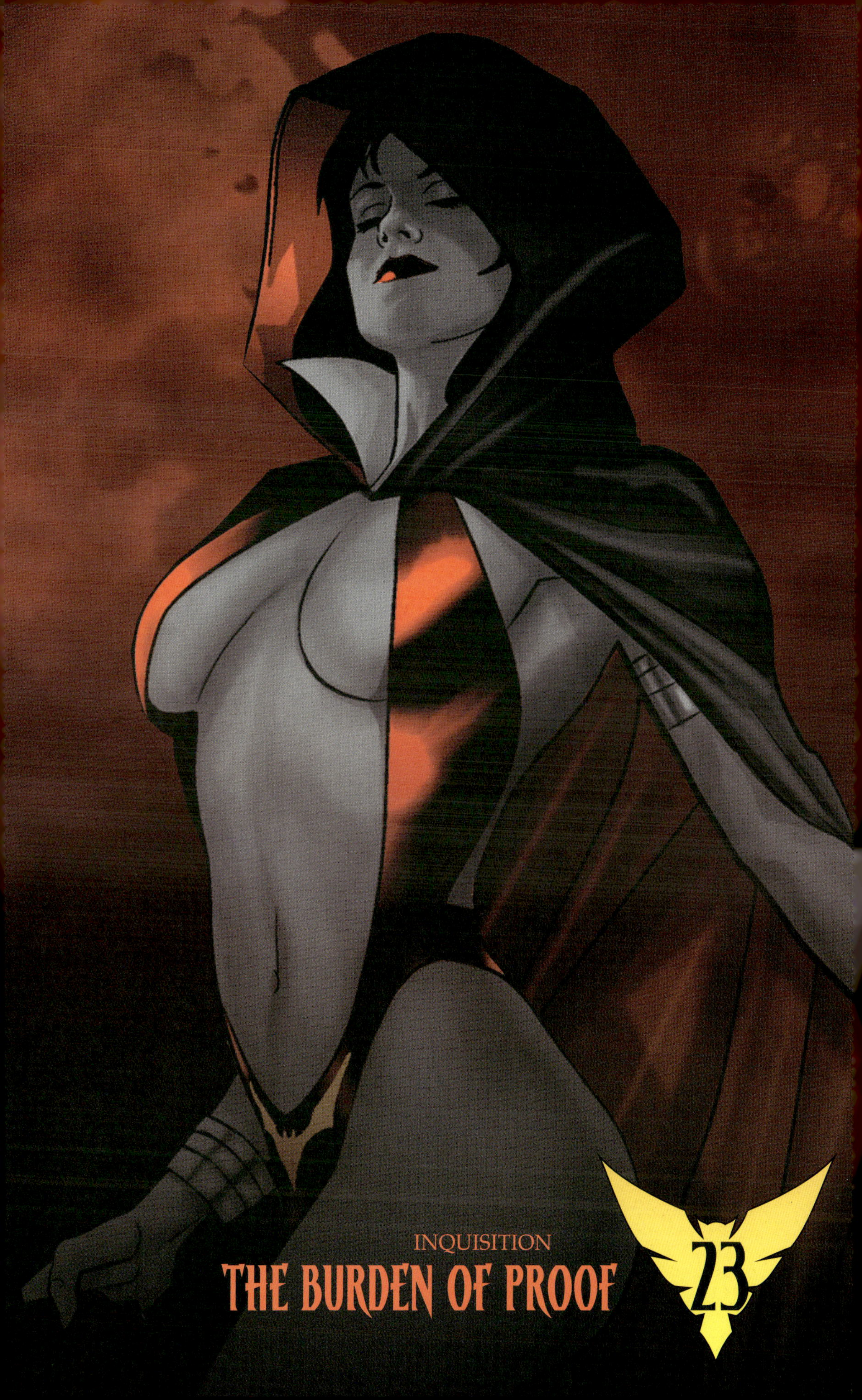
INQUISITION
THE BURDEN OF PROOF
23

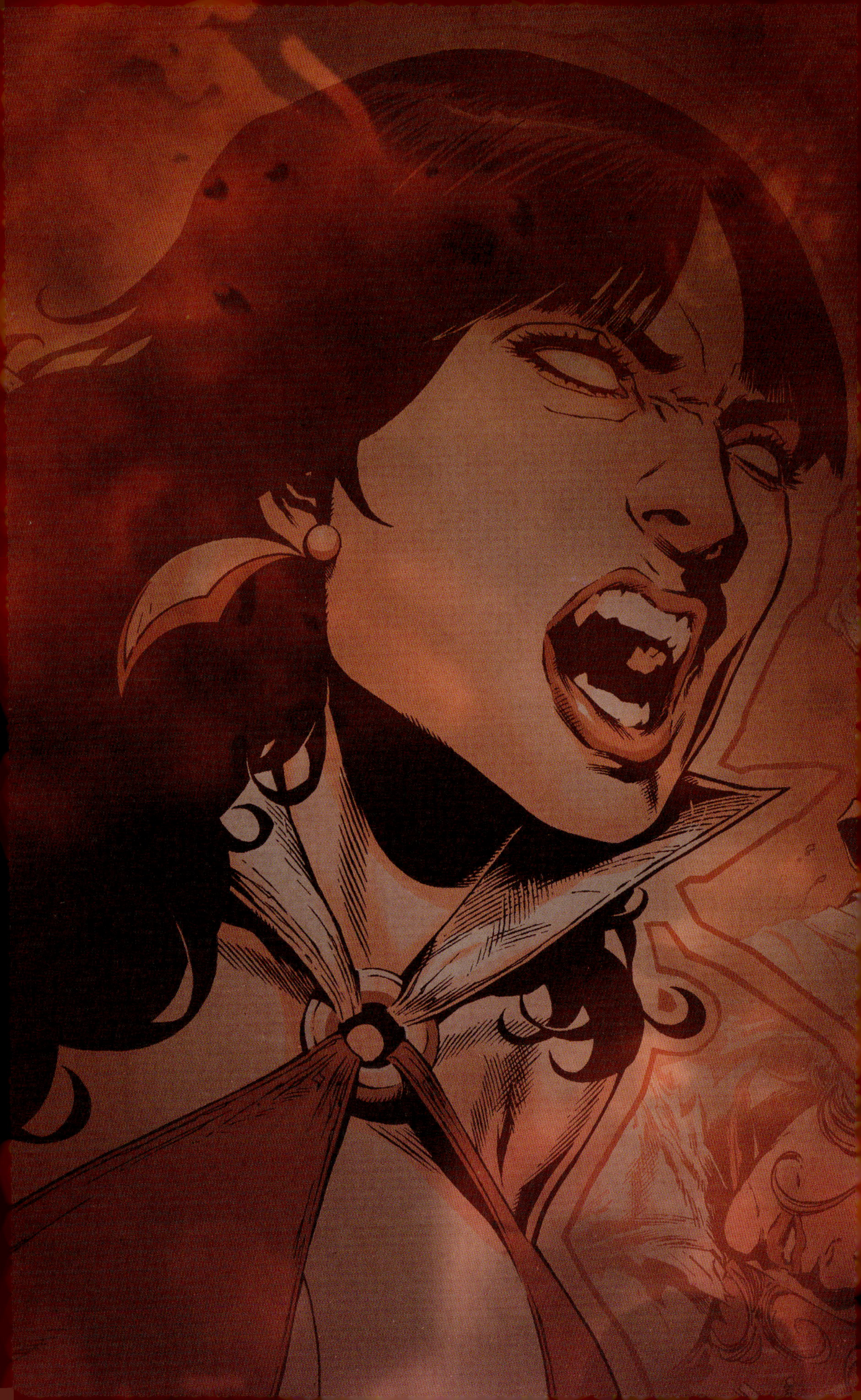

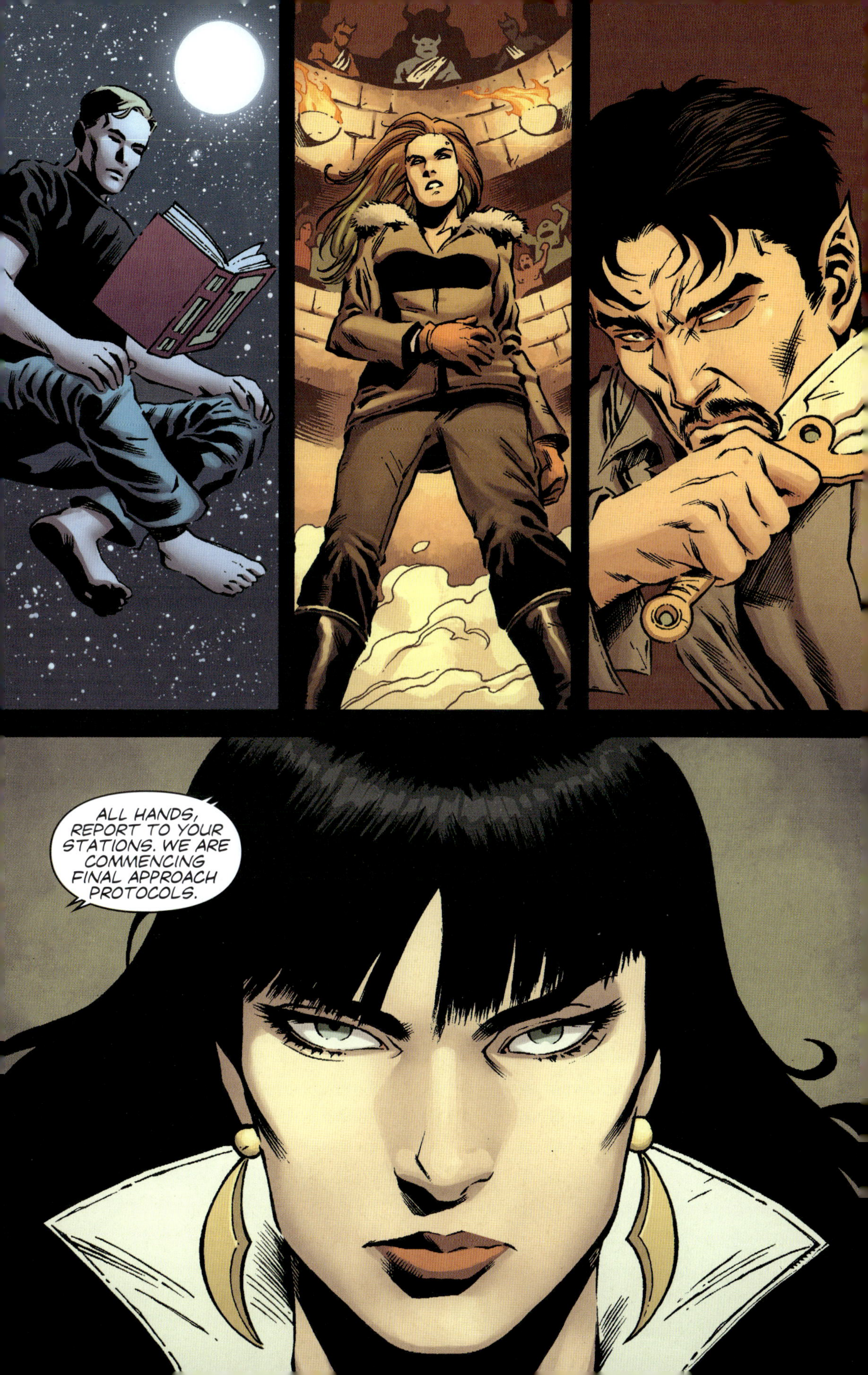
ALL HANDS, REPORT TO YOUR STATIONS. WE ARE COMMENCING FINAL APPROACH PROTOCOLS.

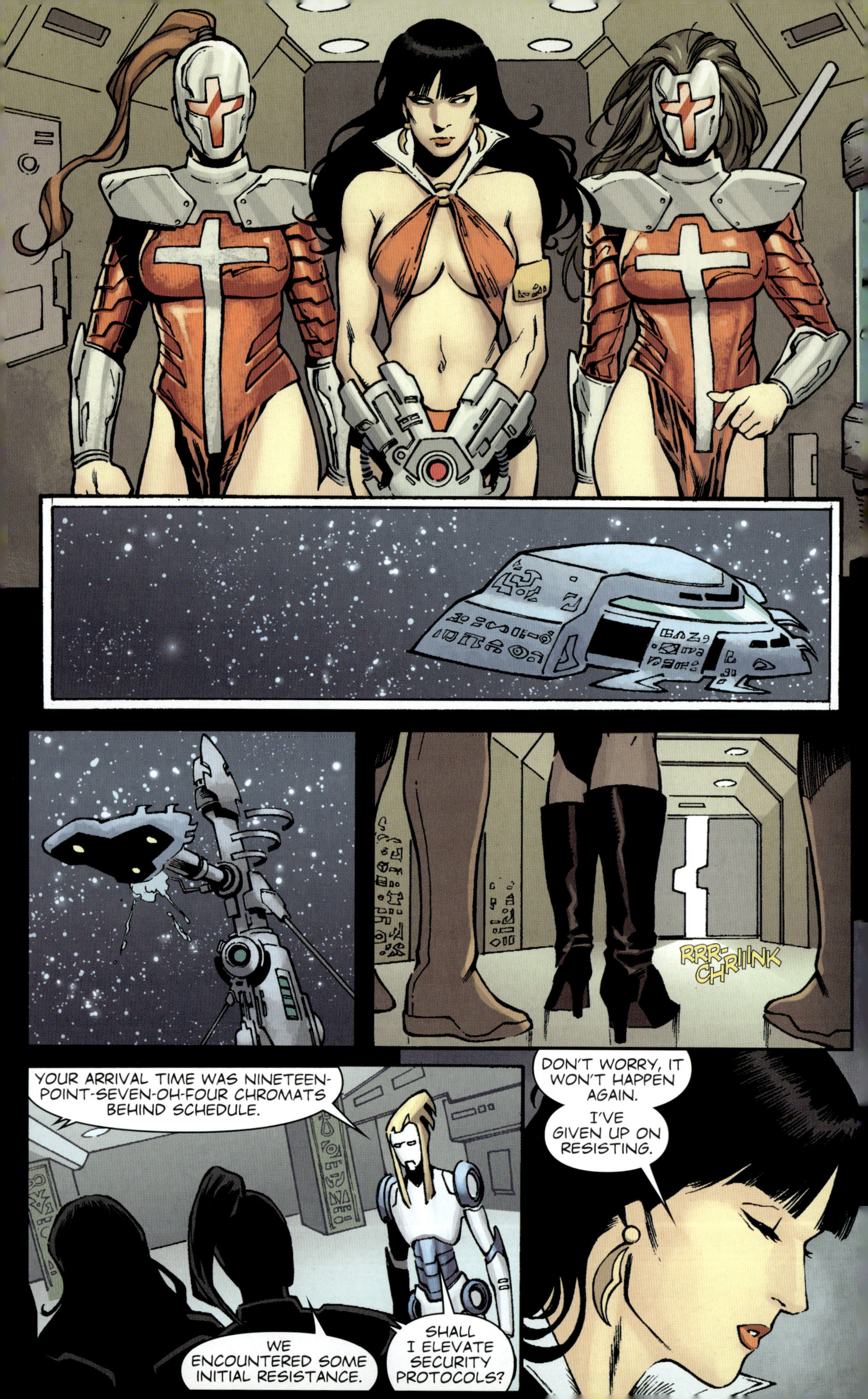
RRR-CHRIIINK
YOUR ARRIVAL TIME WAS NINETEEN-POINT-SEVEN-OH-FOUR CHROMATS BEHIND SCHEDULE.
WE ENCOUNTERED SOME INITIAL RESISTANCE.
SHALL I ELEVATE SECURITY PROTOCOLS?
DON'T WORRY, IT WON'T HAPPEN AGAIN.
I'VE GIVEN UP ON RESISTING.

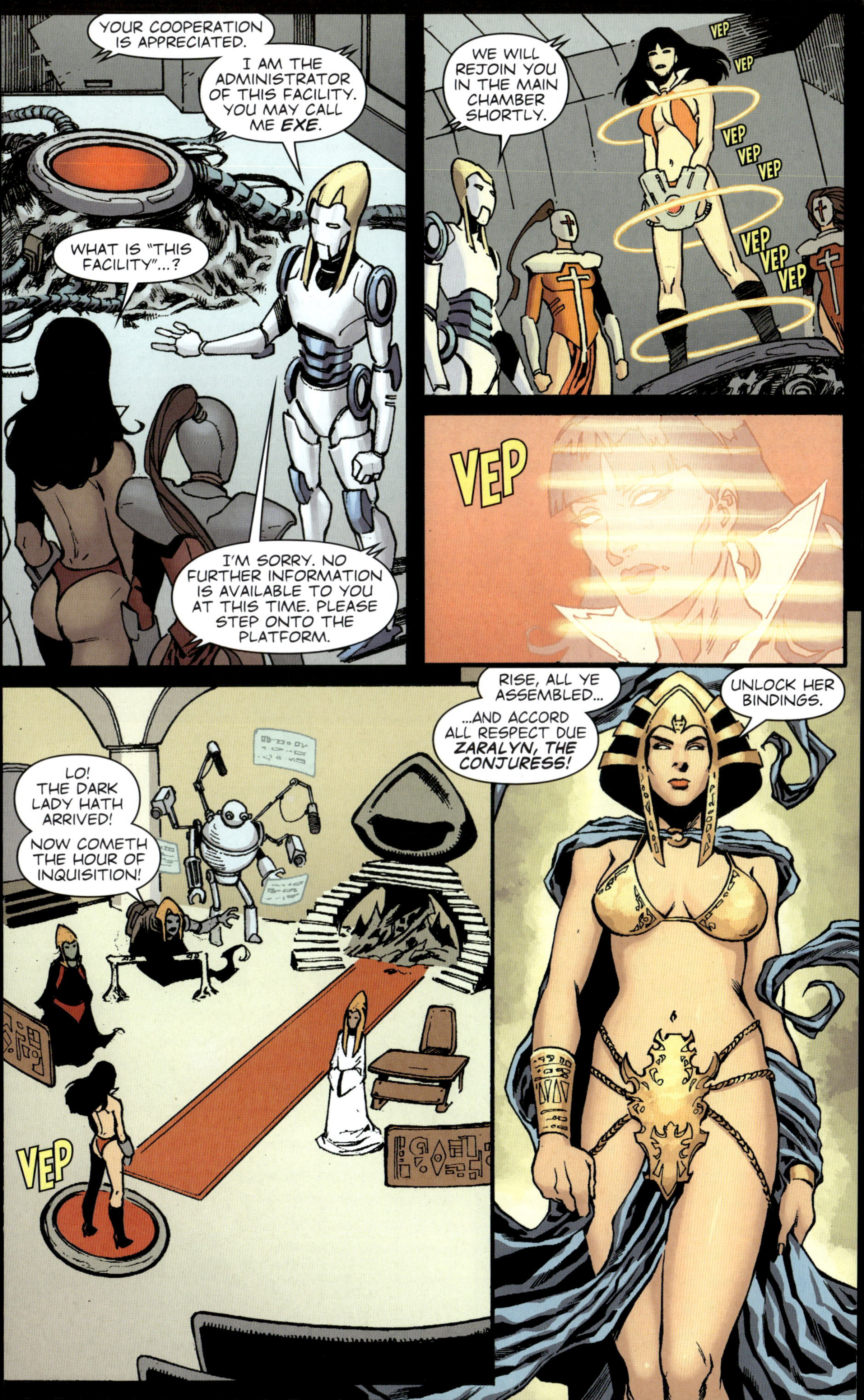
YOUR COOPERATION IS APPRECIATED.
I AM THE ADMINISTRATOR OF THIS FACILITY. YOU MAY CALL ME EXE.
WHAT IS "THIS FACILITY"...?
I'M SORRY. NO FURTHER INFORMATION IS AVAILABLE TO YOU AT THIS TIME. PLEASE STEP ONTO THE PLATFORM.
WE WILL REJOIN YOU IN THE MAIN CHAMBER SHORTLY.
VEP VEP
VEP VEP VEP
VEP VEP VEP
VEP
LO! THE DARK LADY HATH ARRIVED!
NOW COMETH THE HOUR OF INQUISITION!
VEP
RISE, ALL YE ASSEMBLED...
...AND ACCORD ALL RESPECT DUE ZARALYN, THE CONJURESS!
UNLOCK HER BINDINGS.

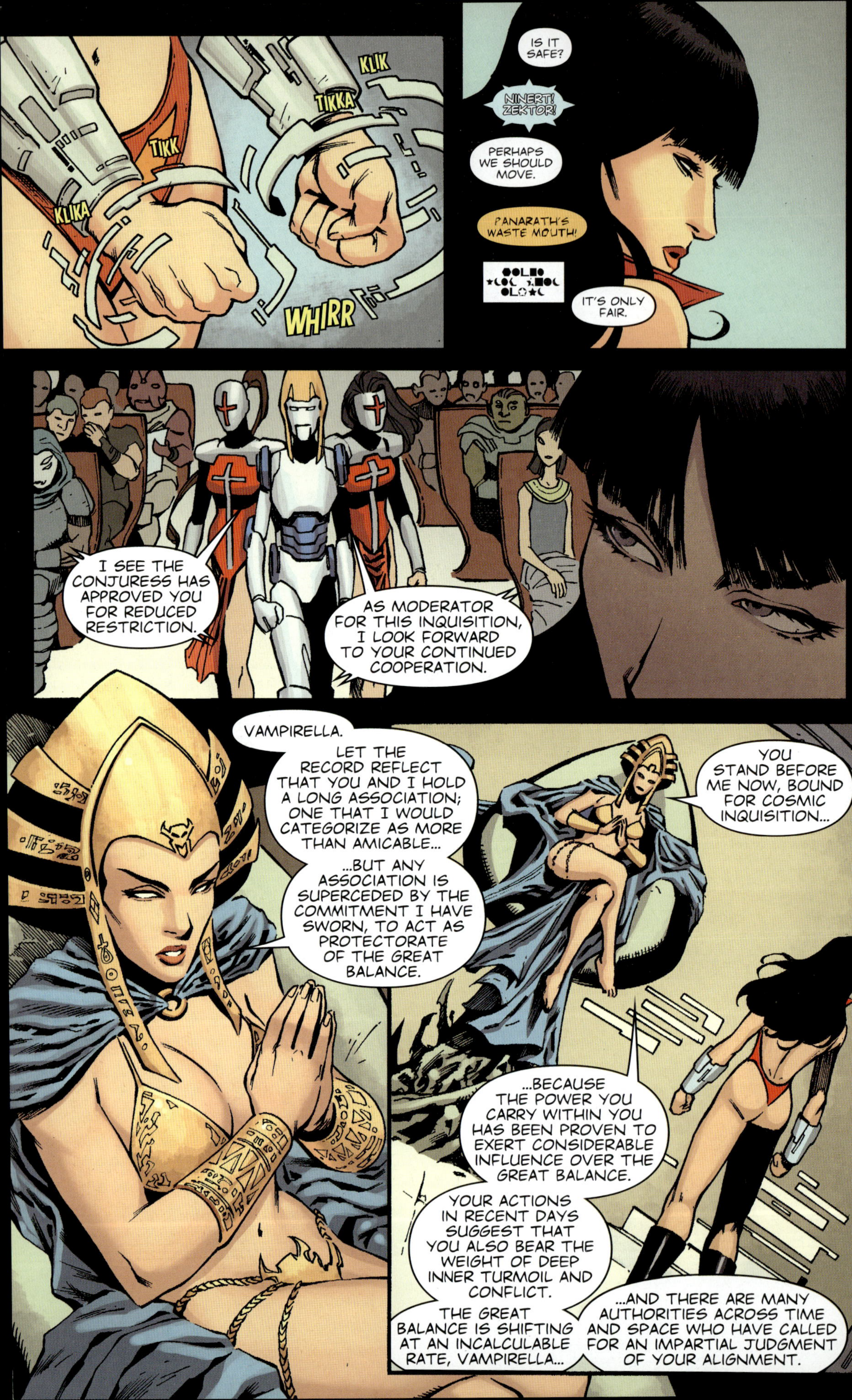
KLIK
TIKKA
TIKK
KLIKA
WHIRR
IS IT SAFE?
NINERT! ZEKTOR!
PERHAPS WE SHOULD MOVE.
PANARATH'S WASTE MOUTH!
IT'S ONLY FAIR.
I SEE THE CONJURESS HAS APPROVED YOU FOR REDUCED RESTRICTION.
AS MODERATOR FOR THIS INQUISITION, I LOOK FORWARD TO YOUR CONTINUED COOPERATION.
VAMPIRELLA.
LET THE RECORD REFLECT THAT YOU AND I HOLD A LONG ASSOCIATION; ONE THAT I WOULD CATEGORIZE AS MORE THAN AMICABLE...
...BUT ANY ASSOCIATION IS SUPERCEDED BY THE COMMITMENT I HAVE SWORN, TO ACT AS PROTECTORATE OF THE GREAT BALANCE.
YOU STAND BEFORE ME NOW, BOUND FOR COSMIC INQUISITION...
...BECAUSE THE POWER YOU CARRY WITHIN YOU HAS BEEN PROVEN TO EXERT CONSIDERABLE INFLUENCE OVER THE GREAT BALANCE.
YOUR ACTIONS IN RECENT DAYS SUGGEST THAT YOU ALSO BEAR THE WEIGHT OF DEEP INNER TURMOIL AND CONFLICT.
THE GREAT BALANCE IS SHIFTING AT AN INCALCULABLE RATE, VAMPIRELLA...
...AND THERE ARE MANY AUTHORITIES ACROSS TIME AND SPACE WHO HAVE CALLED FOR AN IMPARTIAL JUDGMENT OF YOUR ALIGNMENT.

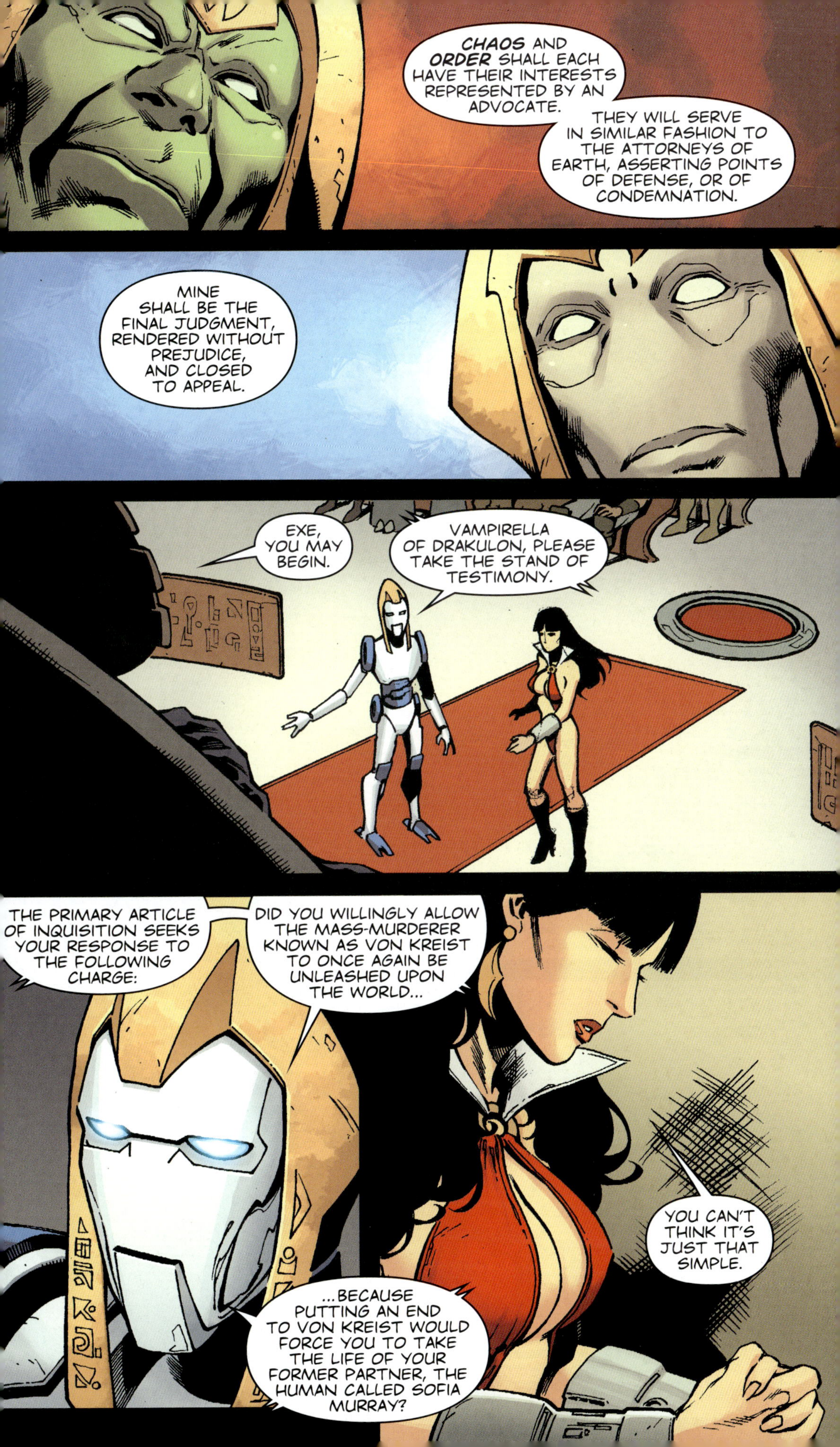
CHAOS AND ORDER SHALL EACH HAVE THEIR INTERESTS REPRESENTED BY AN ADVOCATE.
THEY WILL SERVE IN SIMILAR FASHION TO THE ATTORNEYS OF EARTH, ASSERTING POINTS OF DEFENSE, OR OF CONDEMNATION.
MINE SHALL BE THE FINAL JUDGMENT, RENDERED WITHOUT PREJUDICE, AND CLOSED TO APPEAL.
EXE, YOU MAY BEGIN.
VAMPIRELLA OF DRAKULON, PLEASE TAKE THE STAND OF TESTIMONY.
THE PRIMARY ARTICLE OF INQUISITION SEEKS YOUR RESPONSE TO THE FOLLOWING CHARGE:
DID YOU WILLINGLY ALLOW THE MASS-MURDERER KNOWN AS VON KREIST TO ONCE AGAIN BE UNLEASHED UPON THE WORLD...
...BECAUSE PUTTING AN END TO VON KREIST WOULD FORCE YOU TO TAKE THE LIFE OF YOUR FORMER PARTNER, THE HUMAN CALLED SOFIA MURRAY?
YOU CAN'T THINK IT'S JUST THAT SIMPLE.

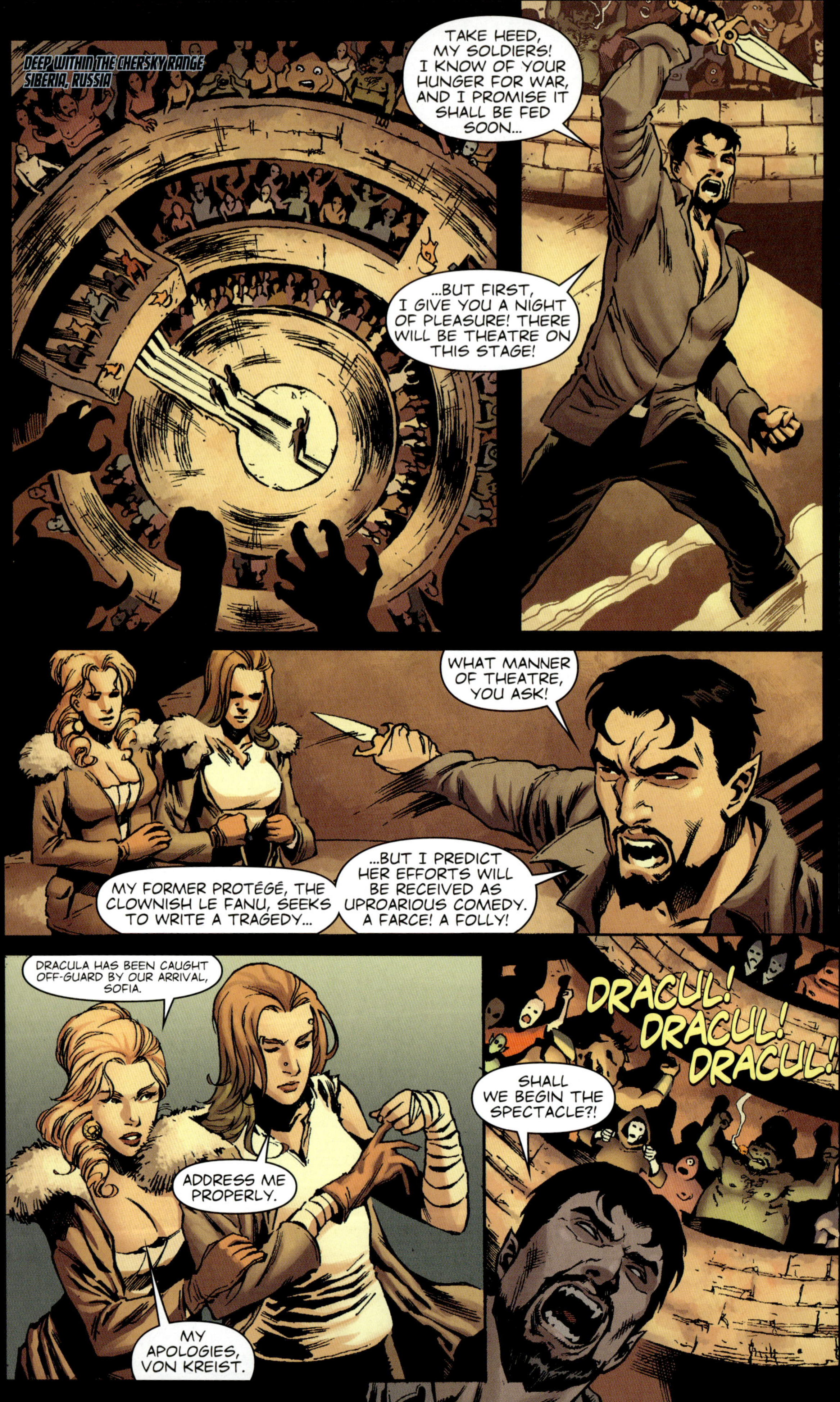
DEEP WITHIN THE CHERSKY RANGE SIBERIA, RUSSIA
TAKE HEED, MY SOLDIERS! I KNOW OF YOUR HUNGER FOR WAR, AND I PROMISE IT SHALL BE FED SOON...
...BUT FIRST, I GIVE YOU A NIGHT OF PLEASURE! THERE WILL BE THEATRE ON THIS STAGE!
WHAT MANNER OF THEATRE, YOU ASK!
MY FORMER PROTÉGÉ, THE CLOWNISH LE FANU, SEEKS TO WRITE A TRAGEDY...
...BUT I PREDICT HER EFFORTS WILL BE RECEIVED AS UPROARIOUS COMEDY. A FARCE! A FOLLY!
DRACULA HAS BEEN CAUGHT OFF-GUARD BY OUR ARRIVAL, SOFIA.
ADDRESS ME PROPERLY.
MY APOLOGIES, VON KREIST.
DRACUL! DRACUL! DRACUL!
SHALL WE BEGIN THE SPECTACLE?!

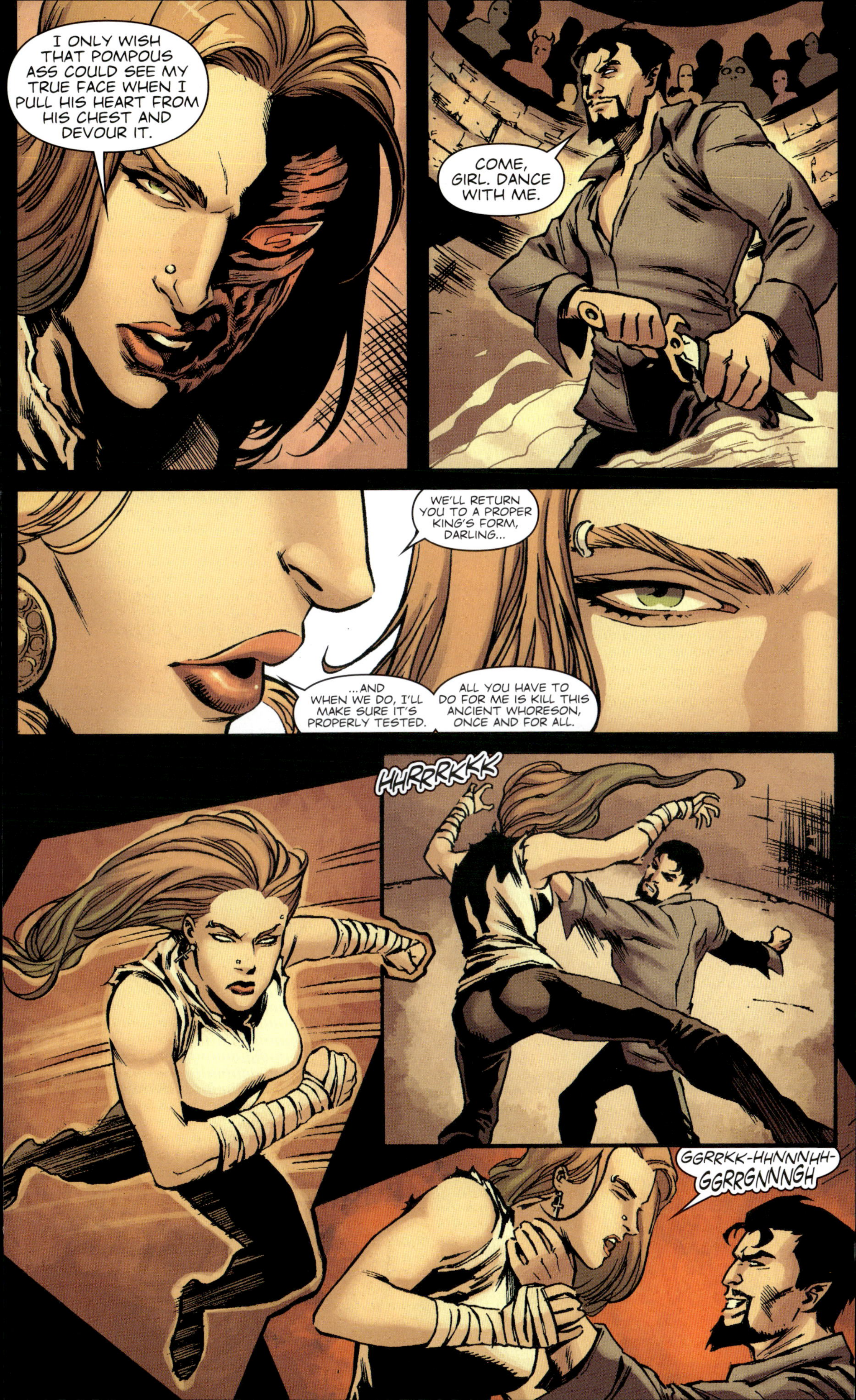
I ONLY WISH THAT POMPOUS ASS COULD SEE MY TRUE FACE WHEN I PULL HIS HEART FROM HIS CHEST AND DEVOUR IT.
COME, GIRL. DANCE WITH ME.
WE'LL RETURN YOU TO A PROPER KING'S FORM, DARLING...
...AND WHEN WE DO, I'LL MAKE SURE IT'S PROPERLY TESTED.
ALL YOU HAVE TO DO FOR ME IS KILL THIS ANCIENT WHORESON, ONCE AND FOR ALL.
HHRRRKKK
GGRRKK-HHNNNHH-GGRRGNNNGH

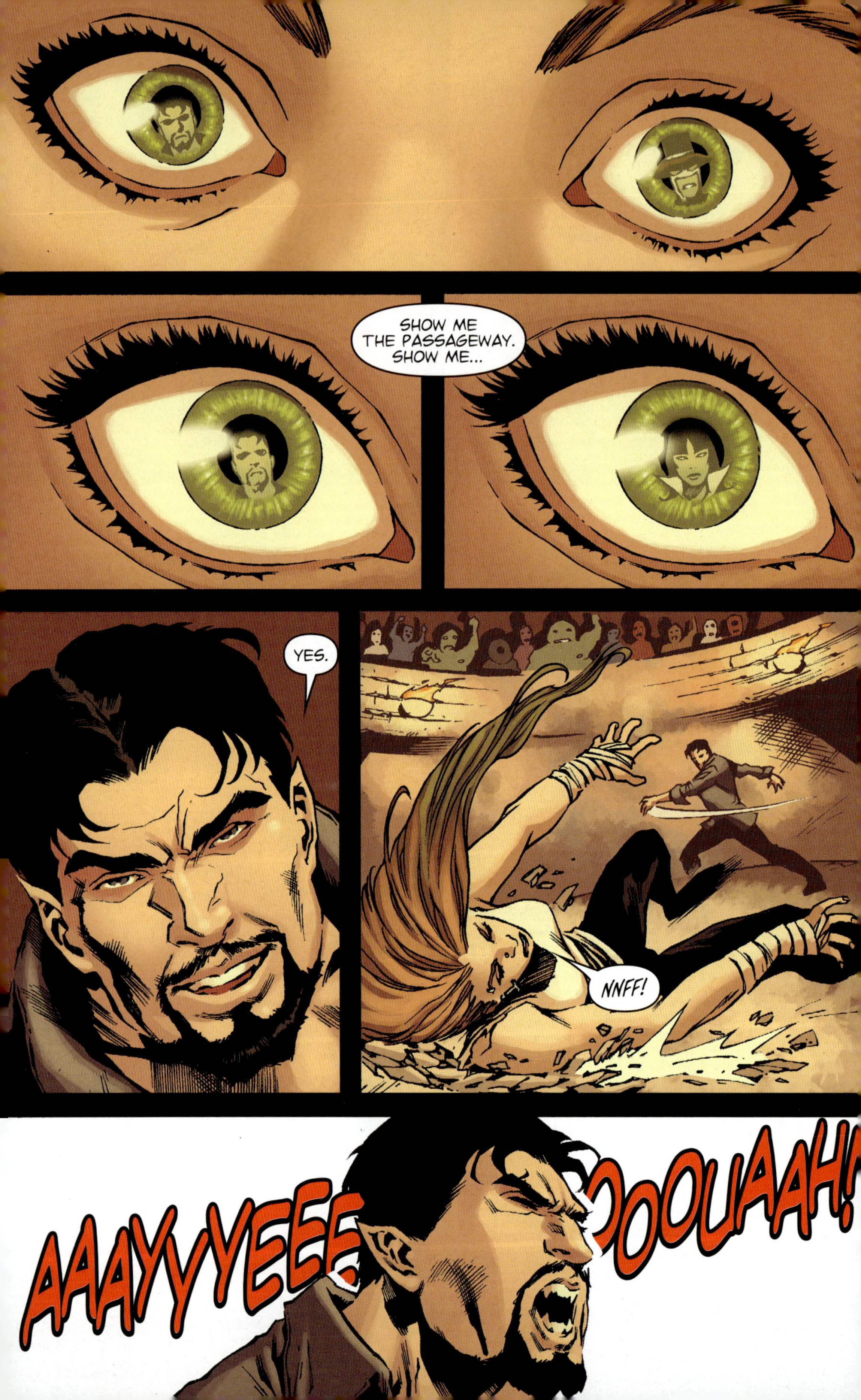
SHOW ME THE PASSAGEWAY. SHOW ME...
YES.
NNFF!
AAAYYYEEE
OOOUAAH!

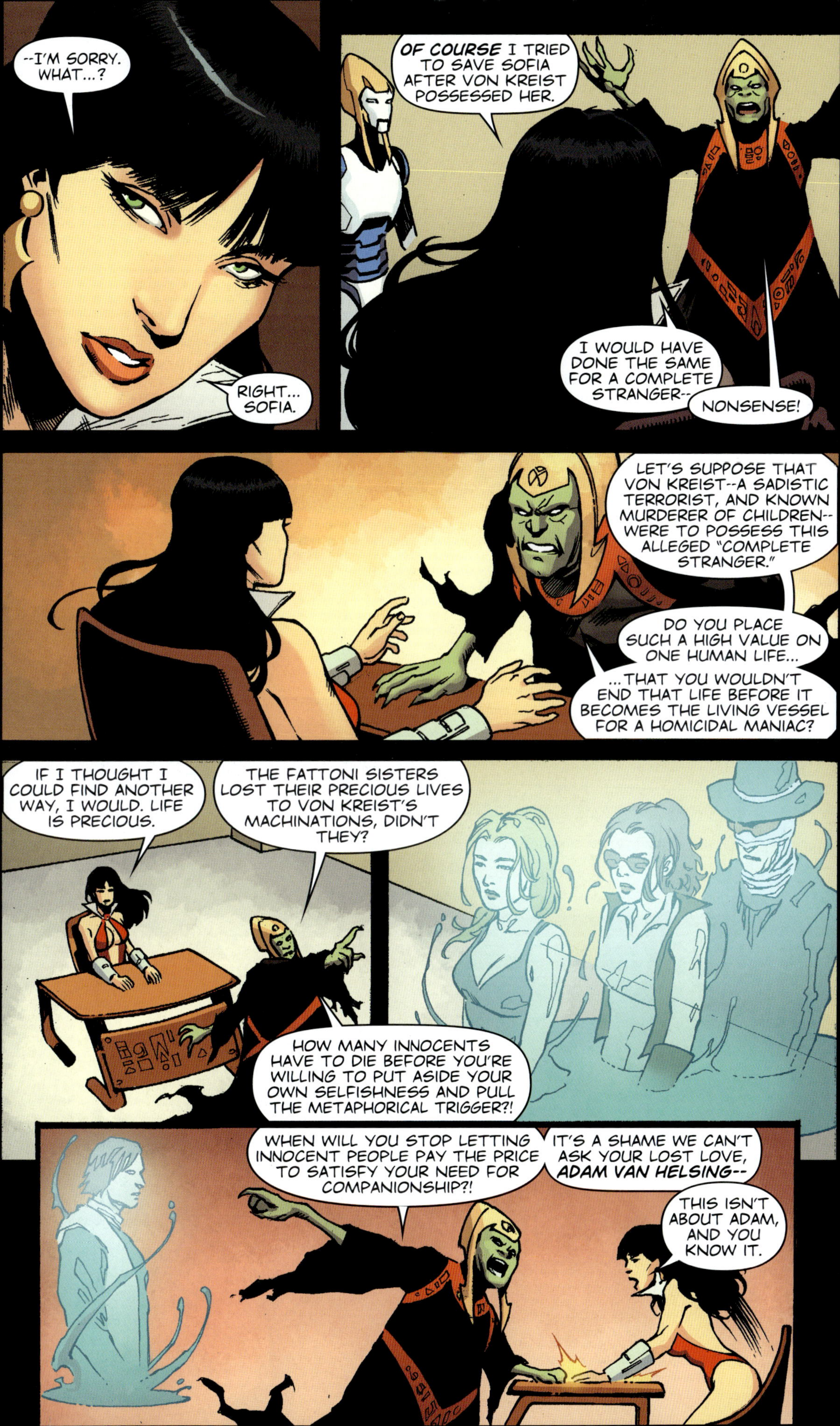
--I'M SORRY. WHAT...?
RIGHT... SOFIA.
OF COURSE I TRIED TO SAVE SOFIA AFTER VON KREIST POSSESSED HER.
I WOULD HAVE DONE THE SAME FOR A COMPLETE STRANGER--
NONSENSE!
LET'S SUPPOSE THAT VON KREIST--A SADISTIC TERRORIST, AND KNOWN MURDERER OF CHILDREN--WERE TO POSSESS THIS ALLEGED "COMPLETE STRANGER."
DO YOU PLACE SUCH A HIGH VALUE ON ONE HUMAN LIFE...
...THAT YOU WOULDN'T END THAT LIFE BEFORE IT BECOMES THE LIVING VESSEL FOR A HOMICIDAL MANIAC?
IF I THOUGHT I COULD FIND ANOTHER WAY, I WOULD. LIFE IS PRECIOUS.
THE FATTONI SISTERS LOST THEIR PRECIOUS LIVES TO VON KREIST'S MACHINATIONS, DIDN'T THEY?
HOW MANY INNOCENTS HAVE TO DIE BEFORE YOU'RE WILLING TO PUT ASIDE YOUR OWN SELFISHNESS AND PULL THE METAPHORICAL TRIGGER?!
WHEN WILL YOU STOP LETTING INNOCENT PEOPLE PAY THE PRICE TO SATISFY YOUR NEED FOR COMPANIONSHIP?!
IT'S A SHAME WE CAN'T ASK YOUR LOST LOVE, *ADAM VAN HELSING--*
THIS ISN'T ABOUT ADAM, AND YOU KNOW IT.

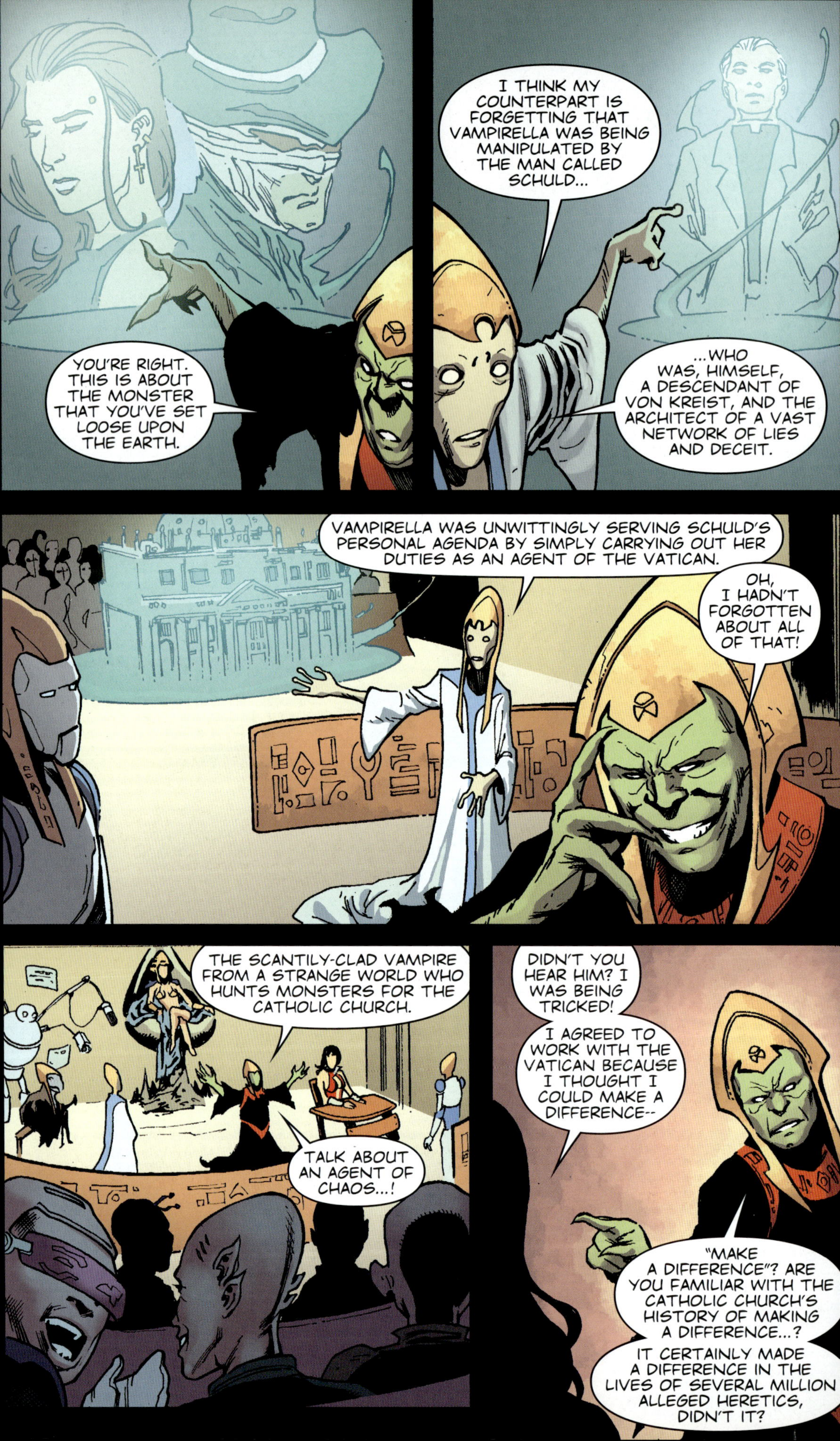
YOU'RE RIGHT. THIS IS ABOUT THE MONSTER THAT YOU'VE SET LOOSE UPON THE EARTH.
I THINK MY COUNTERPART IS FORGETTING THAT VAMPIRELLA WAS BEING MANIPULATED BY THE MAN CALLED SCHULD...
...WHO WAS, HIMSELF, A DESCENDANT OF VON KREIST, AND THE ARCHITECT OF A VAST NETWORK OF LIES AND DECEIT.
VAMPIRELLA WAS UNWITTINGLY SERVING SCHULD'S PERSONAL AGENDA BY SIMPLY CARRYING OUT HER DUTIES AS AN AGENT OF THE VATICAN.
OH, I HADN'T FORGOTTEN ABOUT ALL OF THAT!
THE SCANTILY-CLAD VAMPIRE FROM A STRANGE WORLD WHO HUNTS MONSTERS FOR THE CATHOLIC CHURCH.
TALK ABOUT AN AGENT OF CHAOS...!
DIDN'T YOU HEAR HIM? I WAS BEING TRICKED!
I AGREED TO WORK WITH THE VATICAN BECAUSE I THOUGHT I COULD MAKE A DIFFERENCE--
"MAKE A DIFFERENCE"? ARE YOU FAMILIAR WITH THE CATHOLIC CHURCH'S HISTORY OF MAKING A DIFFERENCE...?
IT CERTAINLY MADE A DIFFERENCE IN THE LIVES OF SEVERAL MILLION ALLEGED HERETICS, DIDN'T IT?

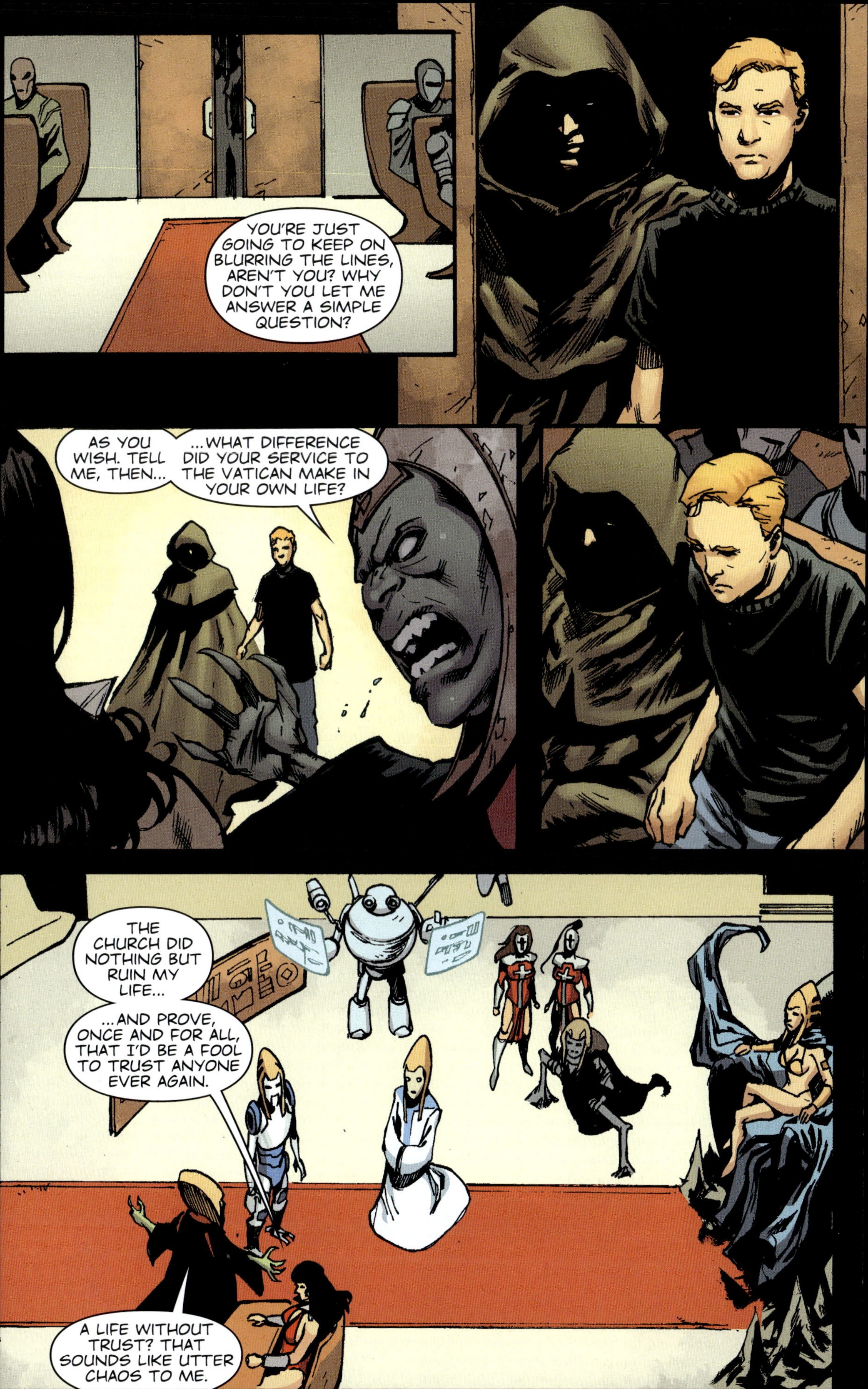
YOU'RE JUST GOING TO KEEP ON BLURRING THE LINES, AREN'T YOU? WHY DON'T YOU LET ME ANSWER A SIMPLE QUESTION?
AS YOU WISH. TELL ME, THEN...
...WHAT DIFFERENCE DID YOUR SERVICE TO THE VATICAN MAKE IN YOUR OWN LIFE?
THE CHURCH DID NOTHING BUT RUIN MY LIFE...
...AND PROVE, ONCE AND FOR ALL, THAT I'D BE A FOOL TO TRUST ANYONE EVER AGAIN.
A LIFE WITHOUT TRUST? THAT SOUNDS LIKE UTTER CHAOS TO ME.

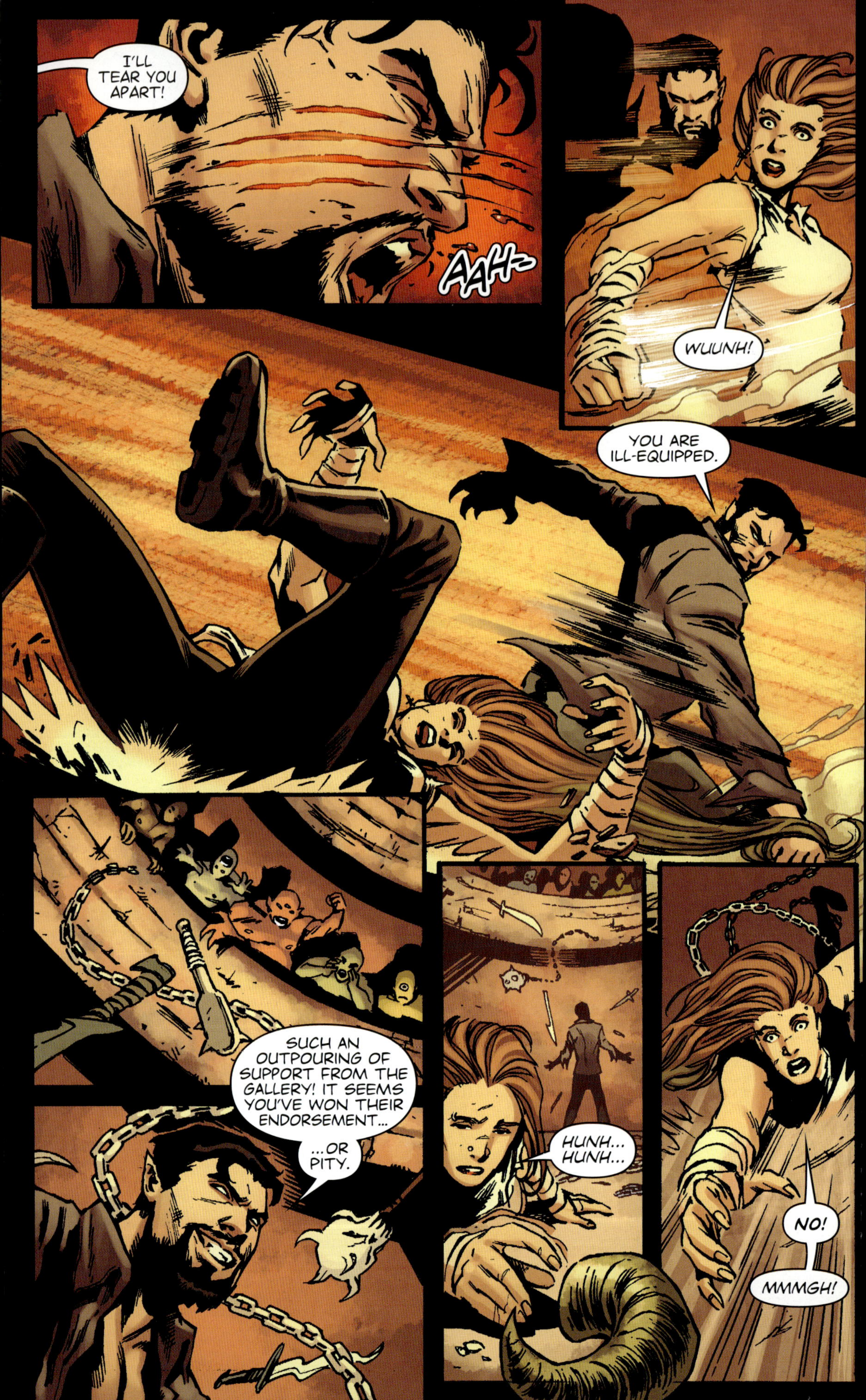
I'LL TEAR YOU APART!
AAH-
WUUNH!
YOU ARE ILL-EQUIPPED.
SUCH AN OUTPOURING OF SUPPORT FROM THE GALLERY! IT SEEMS YOU'VE WON THEIR ENDORSEMENT...
...OR PITY.
HUNH... HUNH...
NO!
MMMGH!

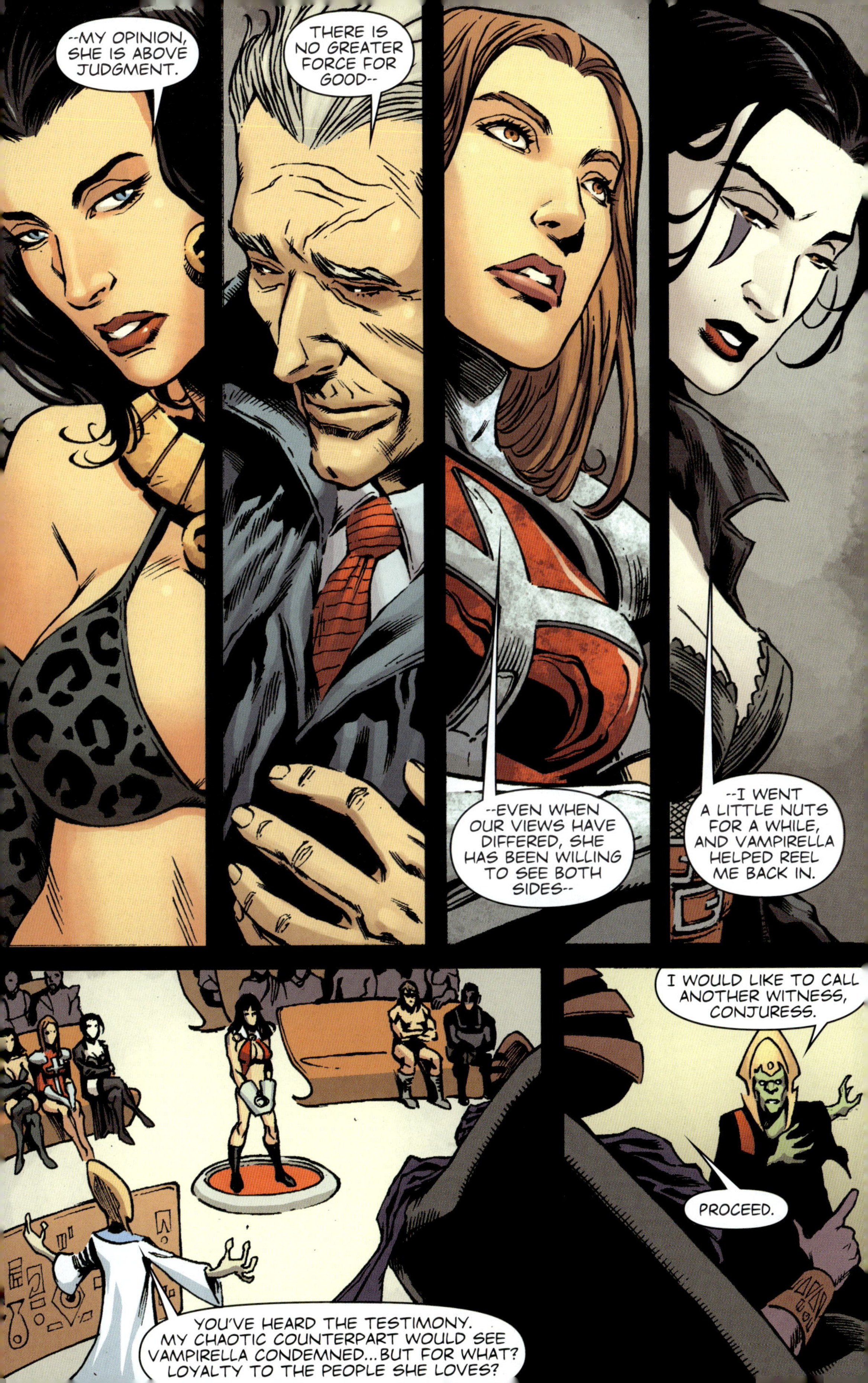
--MY OPINION, SHE IS ABOVE JUDGMENT.
THERE IS NO GREATER FORCE FOR GOOD--
--EVEN WHEN OUR VIEWS HAVE DIFFERED, SHE HAS BEEN WILLING TO SEE BOTH SIDES--
--I WENT A LITTLE NUTS FOR A WHILE, AND VAMPIRELLA HELPED REEL ME BACK IN.
YOU'VE HEARD THE TESTIMONY. MY CHAOTIC COUNTERPART WOULD SEE VAMPIRELLA CONDEMNED...BUT FOR WHAT? LOYALTY TO THE PEOPLE SHE LOVES?
I WOULD LIKE TO CALL ANOTHER WITNESS, CONJURESS.
PROCEED.

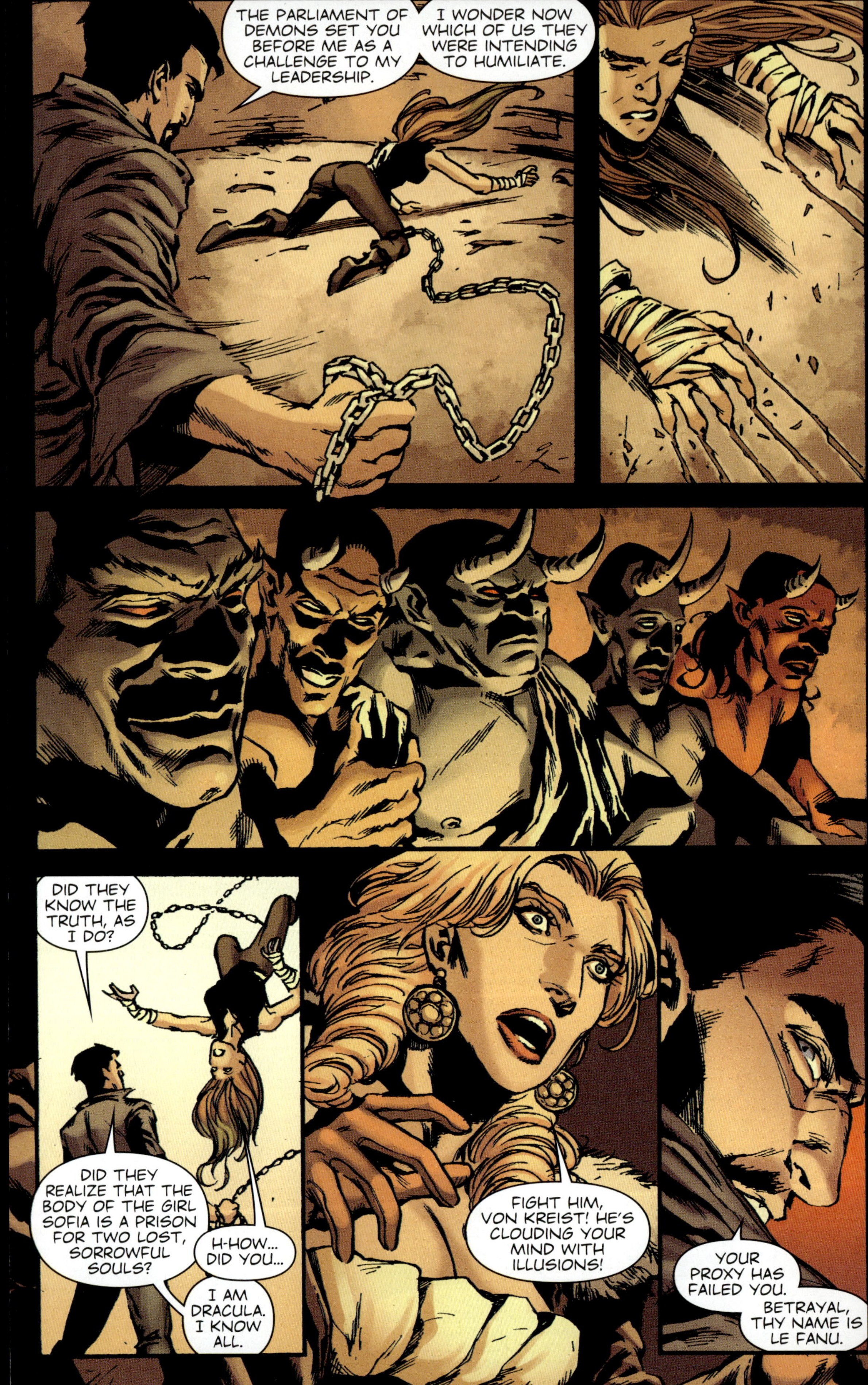
THE PARLIAMENT OF DEMONS SET YOU BEFORE ME AS A CHALLENGE TO MY LEADERSHIP.
I WONDER NOW WHICH OF US THEY WERE INTENDING TO HUMILIATE.
DID THEY KNOW THE TRUTH, AS I DO?
DID THEY REALIZE THAT THE BODY OF THE GIRL SOFIA IS A PRISON FOR TWO LOST, SORROWFUL SOULS?
H-HOW... DID YOU...
I AM DRACULA. I KNOW ALL.
FIGHT HIM, VON KREIST! HE'S CLOUDING YOUR MIND WITH ILLUSIONS!
YOUR PROXY HAS FAILED YOU.
BETRAYAL, THY NAME IS LE FANU.

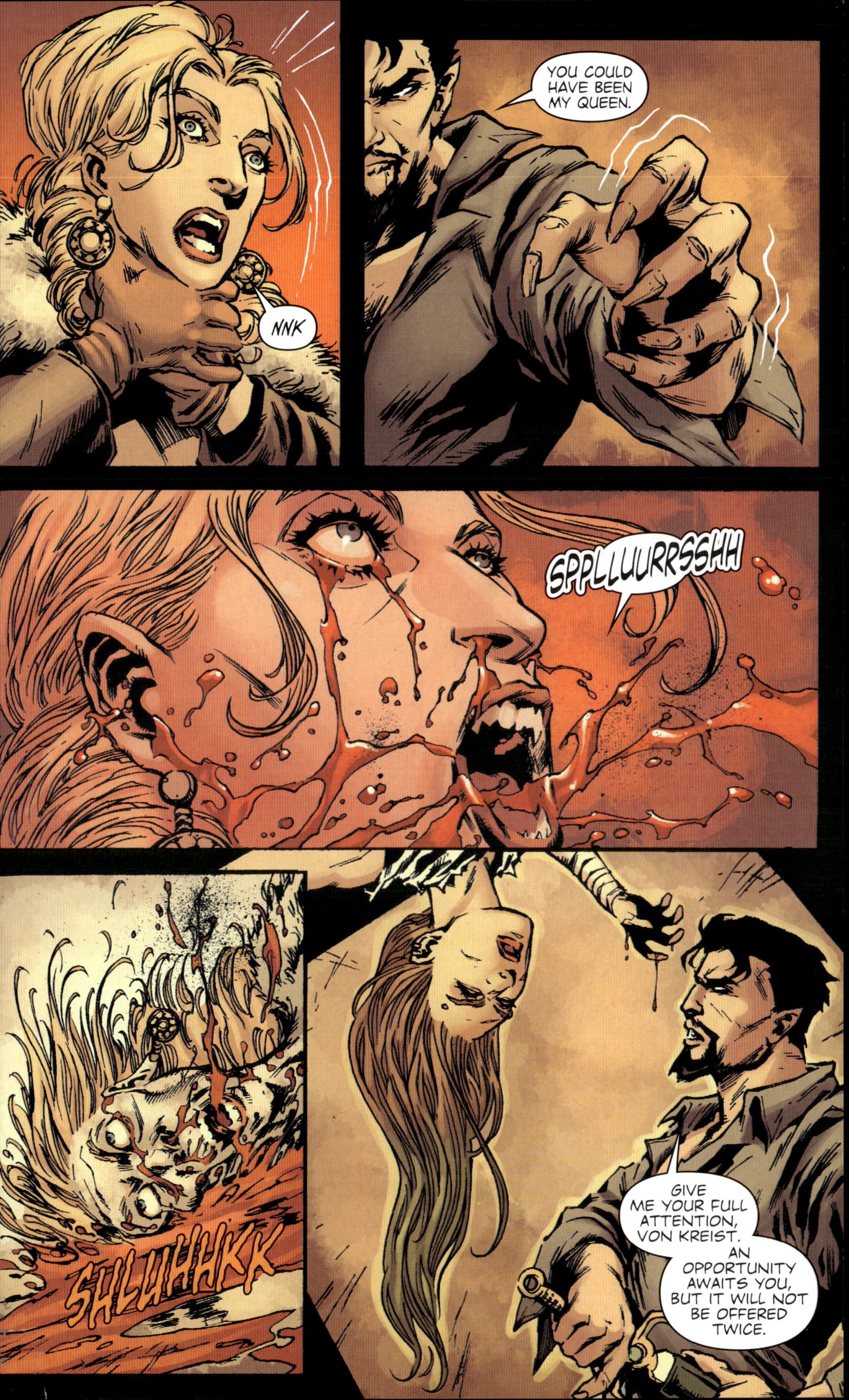
YOU COULD HAVE BEEN MY QUEEN.
NNK
SPPLLUURRSSHH
SHLUHHKK
GIVE ME YOUR FULL ATTENTION, VON KREIST.
AN OPPORTUNITY AWAITS YOU, BUT IT WILL NOT BE OFFERED TWICE.

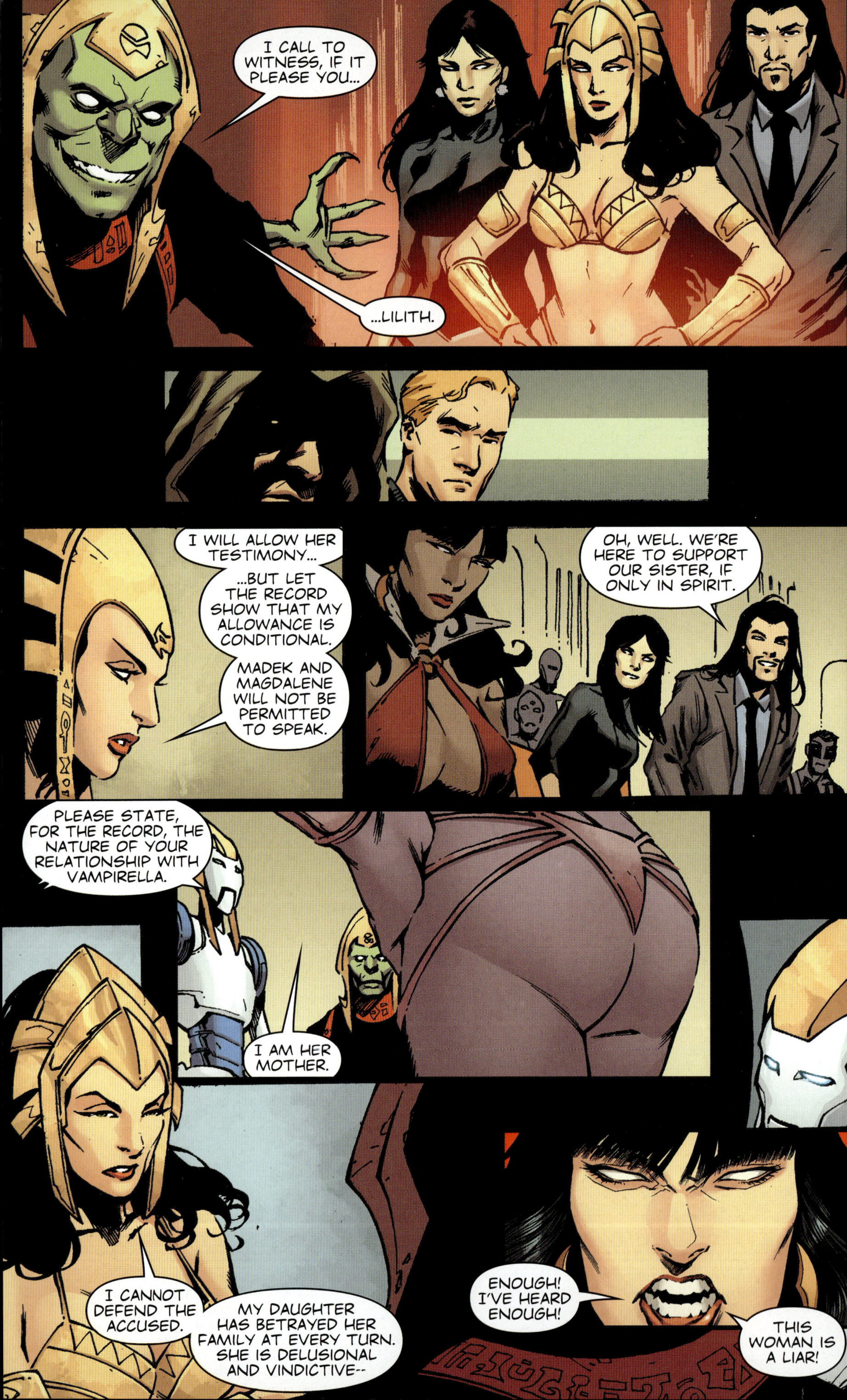

I CALL TO WITNESS, IF IT PLEASE YOU...
...LILITH.
I WILL ALLOW HER TESTIMONY...
...BUT LET THE RECORD SHOW THAT MY ALLOWANCE IS CONDITIONAL.
MADEK AND MAGDALENE WILL NOT BE PERMITTED TO SPEAK.
OH, WELL. WE'RE HERE TO SUPPORT OUR SISTER, IF ONLY IN SPIRIT.
PLEASE STATE, FOR THE RECORD, THE NATURE OF YOUR RELATIONSHIP WITH VAMPIRELLA.
I AM HER MOTHER.
I CANNOT DEFEND THE ACCUSED.
MY DAUGHTER HAS BETRAYED HER FAMILY AT EVERY TURN. SHE IS DELUSIONAL AND VINDICTIVE--
ENOUGH! I'VE HEARD ENOUGH!
THIS WOMAN IS A LIAR!

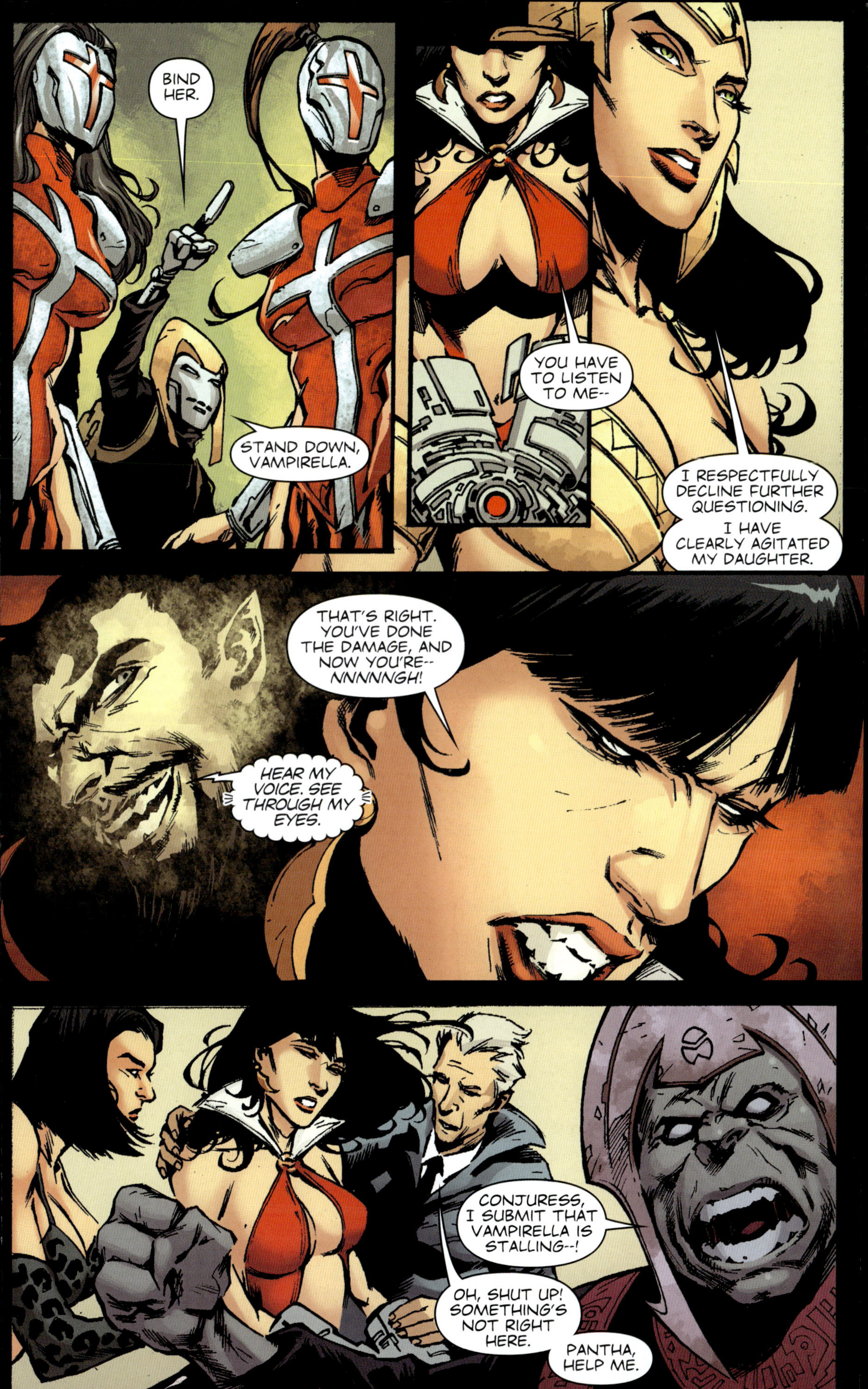
BIND HER.
STAND DOWN, VAMPIRELLA.
YOU HAVE TO LISTEN TO ME--
I RESPECTFULLY DECLINE FURTHER QUESTIONING.
I HAVE CLEARLY AGITATED MY DAUGHTER.
THAT'S RIGHT. YOU'VE DONE THE DAMAGE, AND NOW YOU'RE-- NNNNNGH!
HEAR MY VOICE. SEE THROUGH MY EYES.
CONJURESS, I SUBMIT THAT VAMPIRELLA IS STALLING--!
OH, SHUT UP! SOMETHING'S NOT RIGHT HERE.
PANTHA, HELP ME.

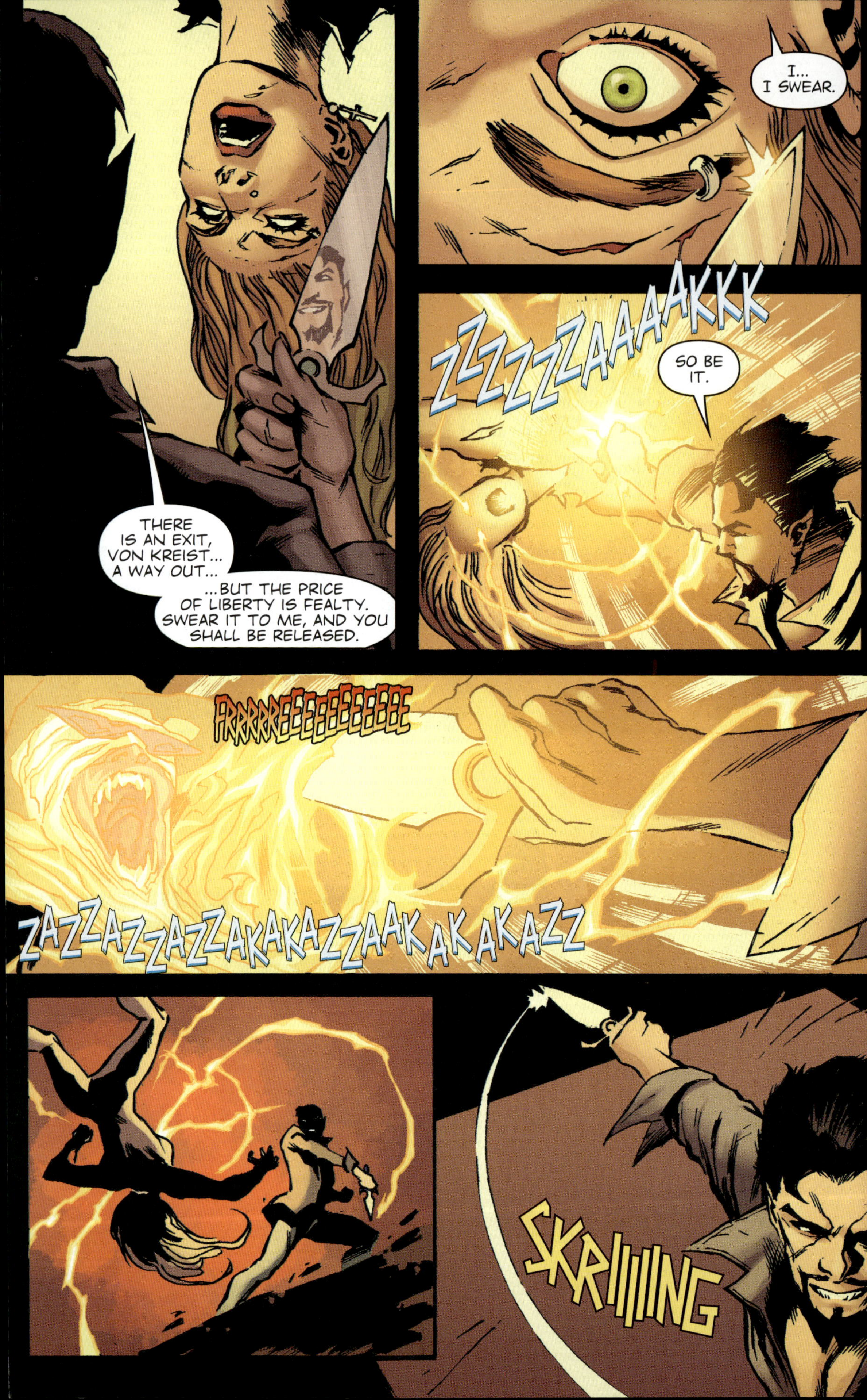

THERE IS AN EXIT, VON KREIST... A WAY OUT...
...BUT THE PRICE OF LIBERTY IS FEALTY. SWEAR IT TO ME, AND YOU SHALL BE RELEASED.
I... I SWEAR.
ZZZZZZAAAAAKKK
SO BE IT.
FRRRRREEEEEEEEEEE
ZAZZAZZAZZAKAKAZZAAKAKAKAZZ
SKRIIIIING

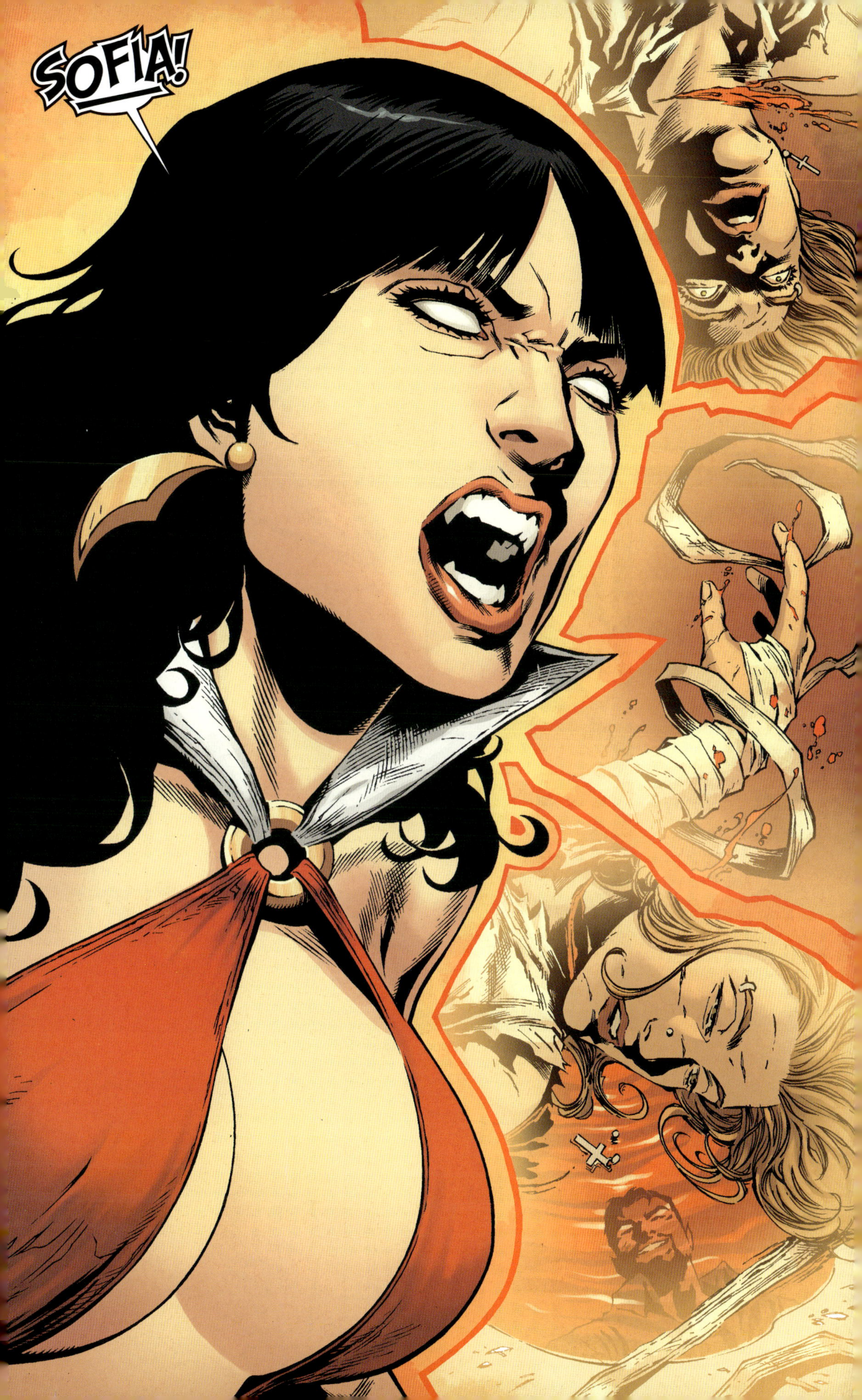
SOFIA!

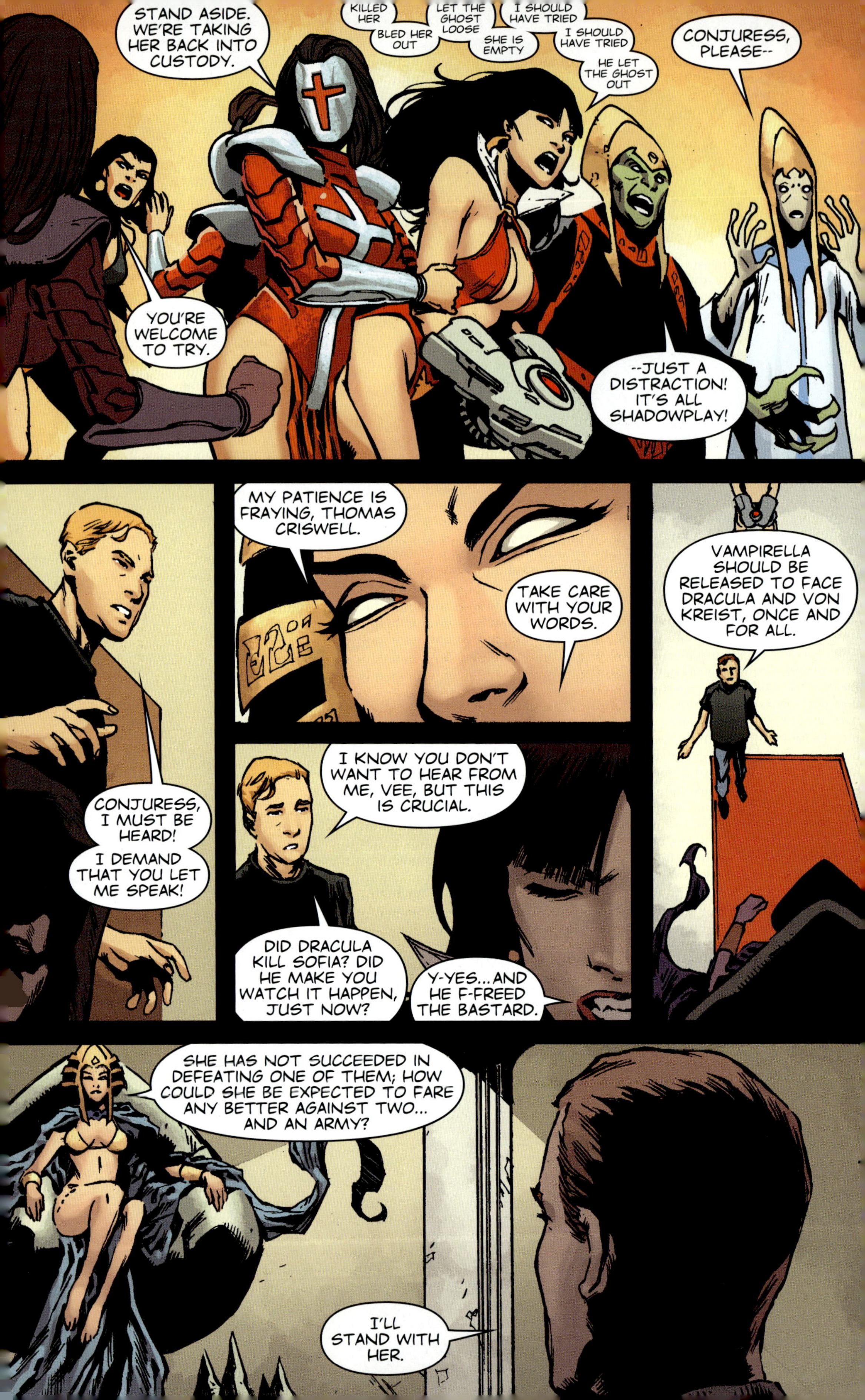
STAND ASIDE. WE'RE TAKING HER BACK INTO CUSTODY.
KILLED HER
BLED HER OUT
LET THE GHOST LOOSE
SHE IS EMPTY
I SHOULD HAVE TRIED
I SHOULD HAVE TRIED
HE LET THE GHOST OUT
CONJURESS, PLEASE--
YOU'RE WELCOME TO TRY.
--JUST A DISTRACTION! IT'S ALL SHADOWPLAY!
MY PATIENCE IS FRAYING, THOMAS CRISWELL.
TAKE CARE WITH YOUR WORDS.
VAMPIRELLA SHOULD BE RELEASED TO FACE DRACULA AND VON KREIST, ONCE AND FOR ALL.
CONJURESS, I MUST BE HEARD!
I DEMAND THAT YOU LET ME SPEAK!
I KNOW YOU DON'T WANT TO HEAR FROM ME, VEE, BUT THIS IS CRUCIAL.
DID DRACULA KILL SOFIA? DID HE MAKE YOU WATCH IT HAPPEN, JUST NOW?
Y-YES...AND HE F-FREED THE BASTARD.
SHE HAS NOT SUCCEEDED IN DEFEATING ONE OF THEM; HOW COULD SHE BE EXPECTED TO FARE ANY BETTER AGAINST TWO... AND AN ARMY?
I'LL STAND WITH HER.

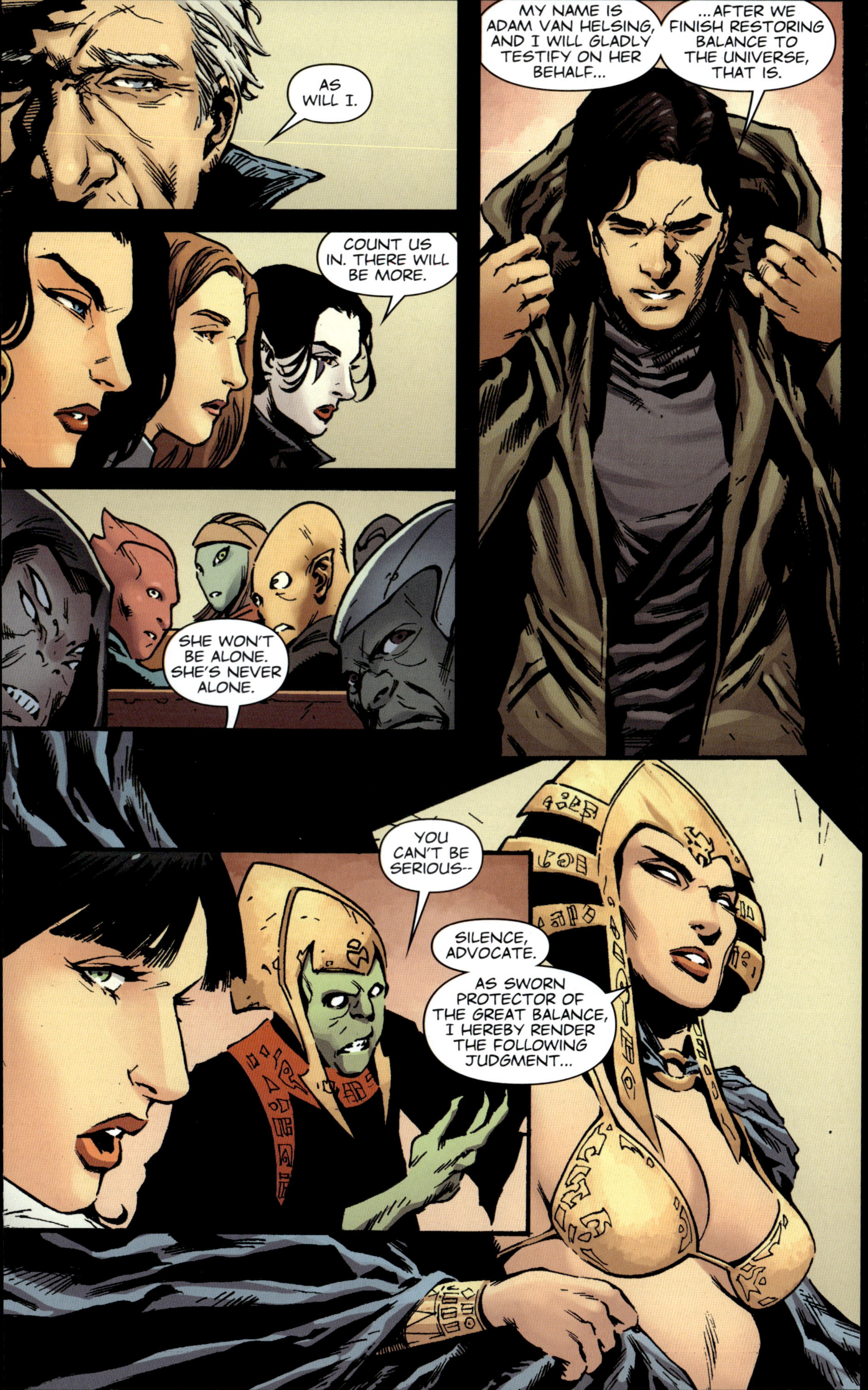
AS WILL I.
COUNT US IN. THERE WILL BE MORE.
SHE WON'T BE ALONE. SHE'S NEVER ALONE.
MY NAME IS ADAM VAN HELSING, AND I WILL GLADLY TESTIFY ON HER BEHALF...
...AFTER WE FINISH RESTORING BALANCE TO THE UNIVERSE, THAT IS.
YOU CAN'T BE SERIOUS--
SILENCE, ADVOCATE.
AS SWORN PROTECTOR OF THE GREAT BALANCE, I HEREBY RENDER THE FOLLOWING JUDGMENT...

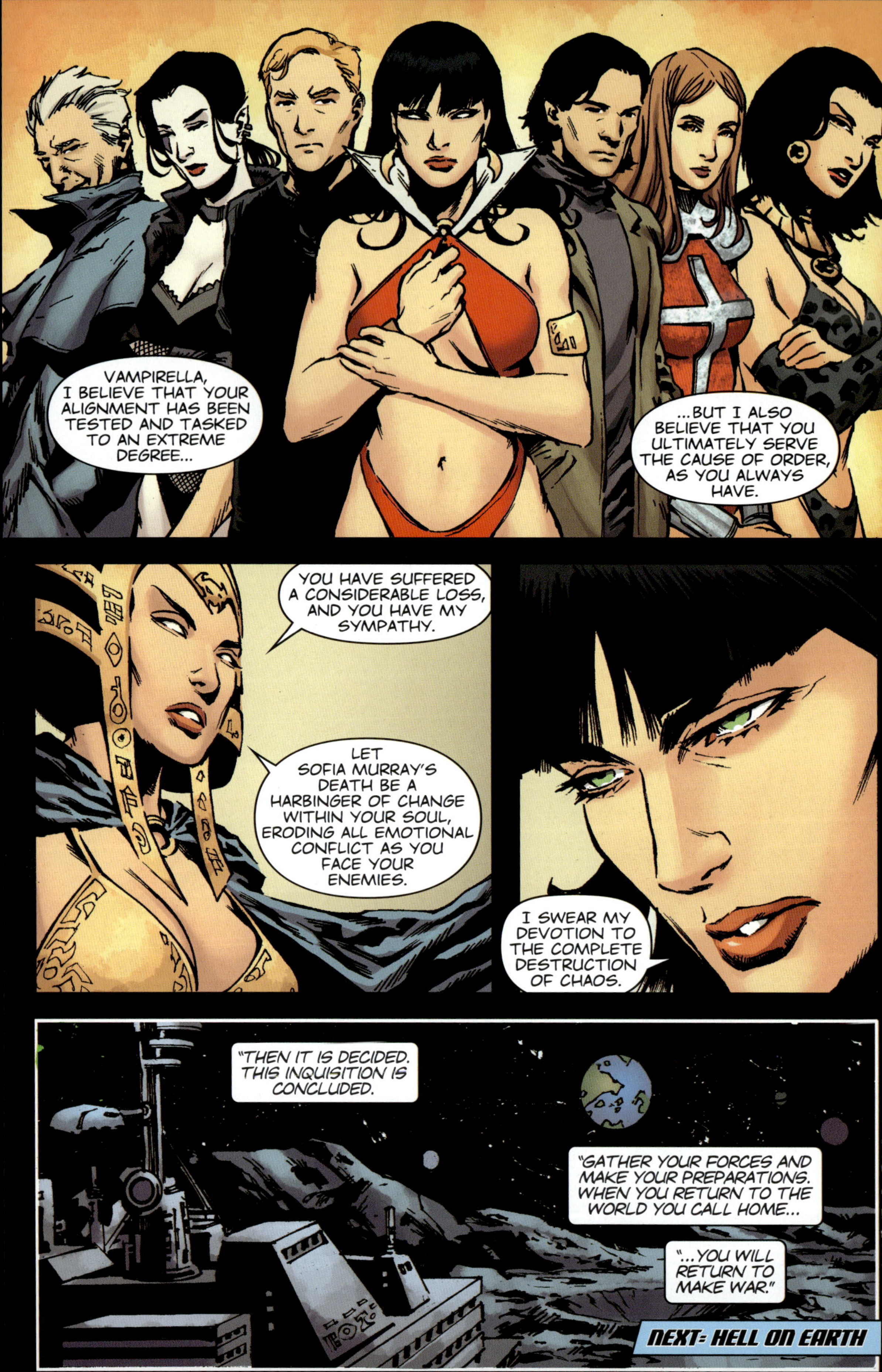
VAMPIRELLA, I BELIEVE THAT YOUR ALIGNMENT HAS BEEN TESTED AND TASKED TO AN EXTREME DEGREE...
...BUT I ALSO BELIEVE THAT YOU ULTIMATELY SERVE THE CAUSE OF ORDER, AS YOU ALWAYS HAVE.
YOU HAVE SUFFERED A CONSIDERABLE LOSS, AND YOU HAVE MY SYMPATHY.
LET SOFIA MURRAY'S DEATH BE A HARBINGER OF CHANGE WITHIN YOUR SOUL, ERODING ALL EMOTIONAL CONFLICT AS YOU FACE YOUR ENEMIES.
I SWEAR MY DEVOTION TO THE COMPLETE DESTRUCTION OF CHAOS.
"THEN IT IS DECIDED. THIS INQUISITION IS CONCLUDED.
"GATHER YOUR FORCES AND MAKE YOUR PREPARATIONS. WHEN YOU RETURN TO THE WORLD YOU CALL HOME...
"...YOU WILL RETURN TO MAKE WAR."
NEXT: HELL ON EARTH

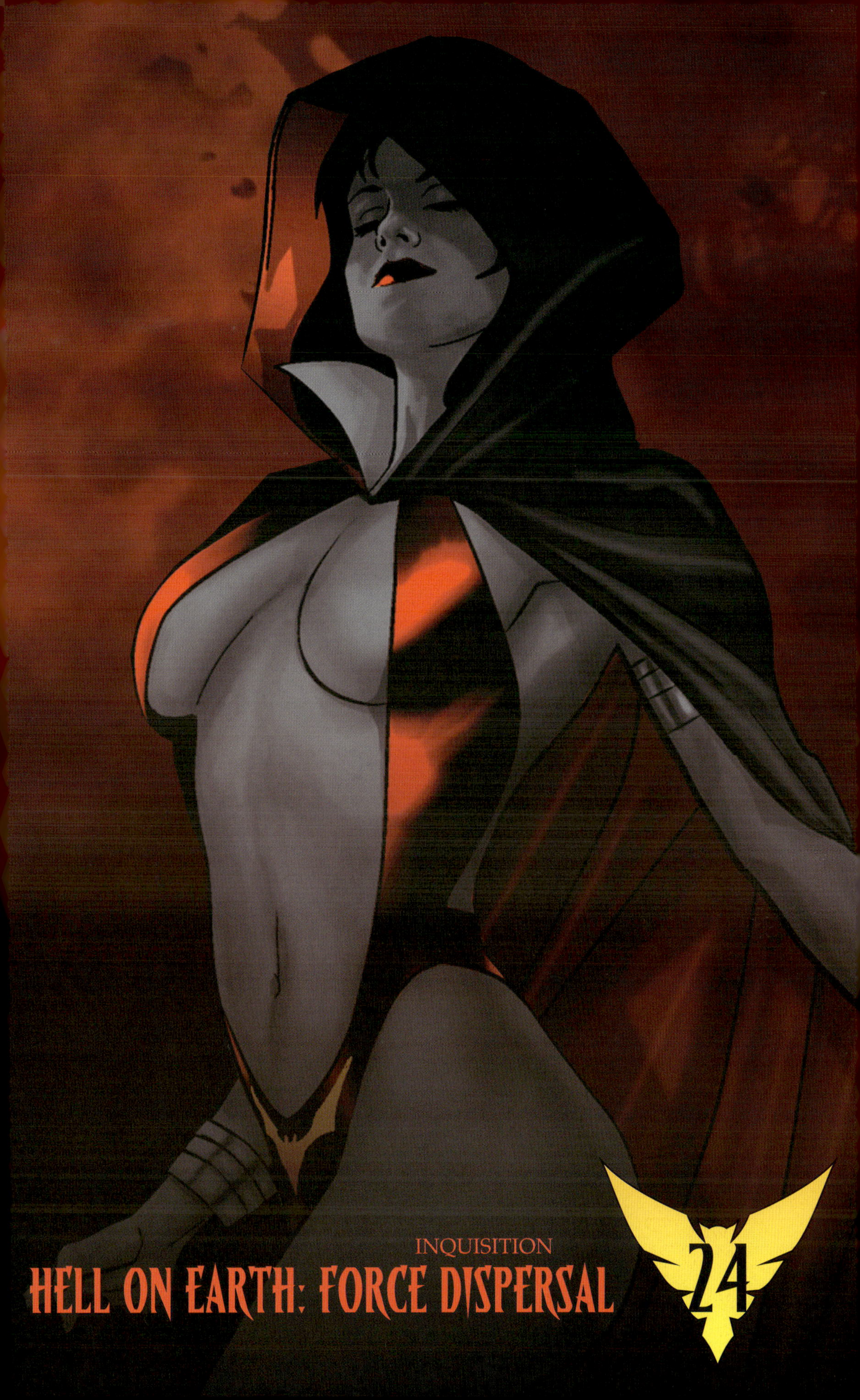
INQUISITION
HELL ON EARTH: FORCE DISPERSAL
24

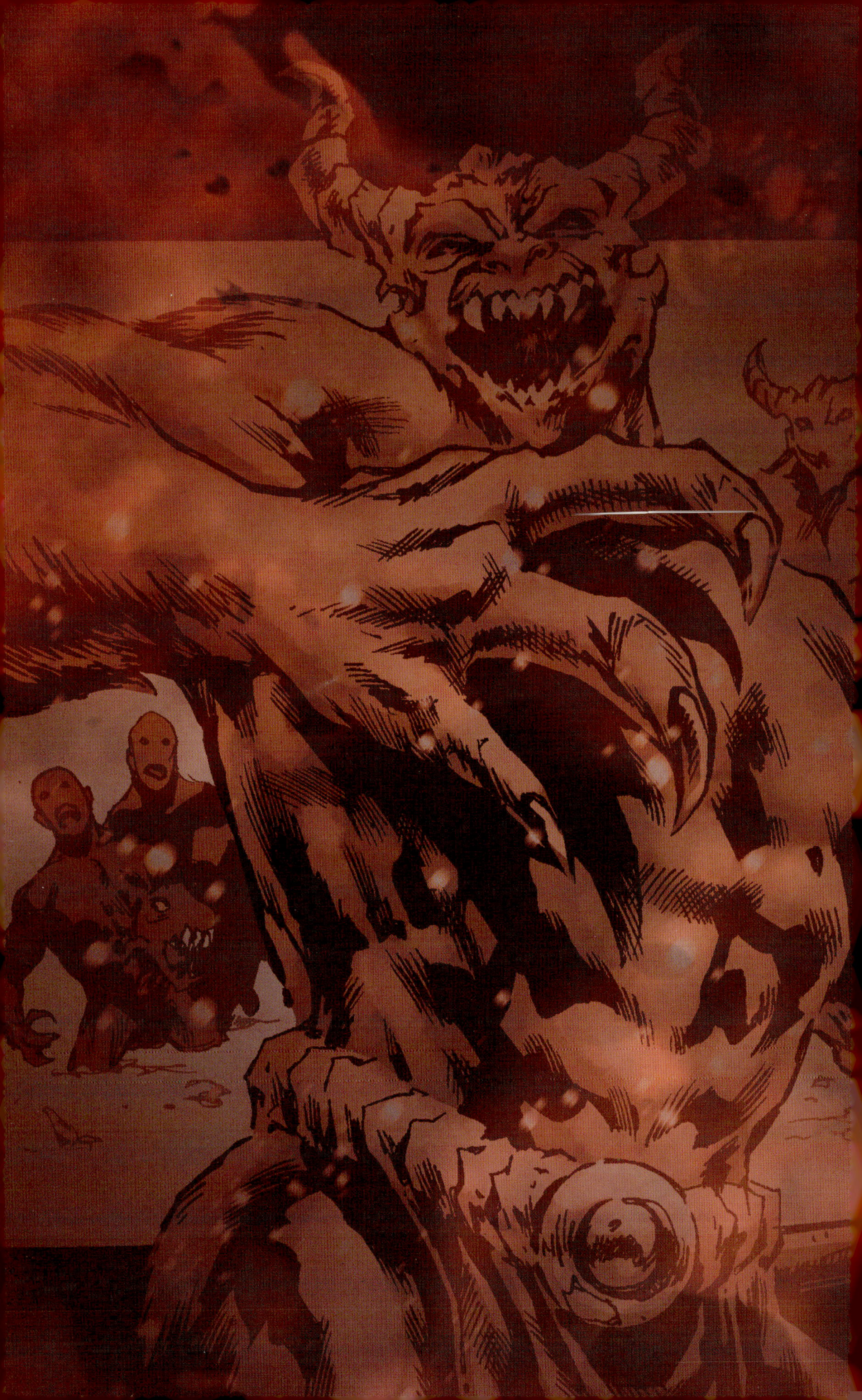

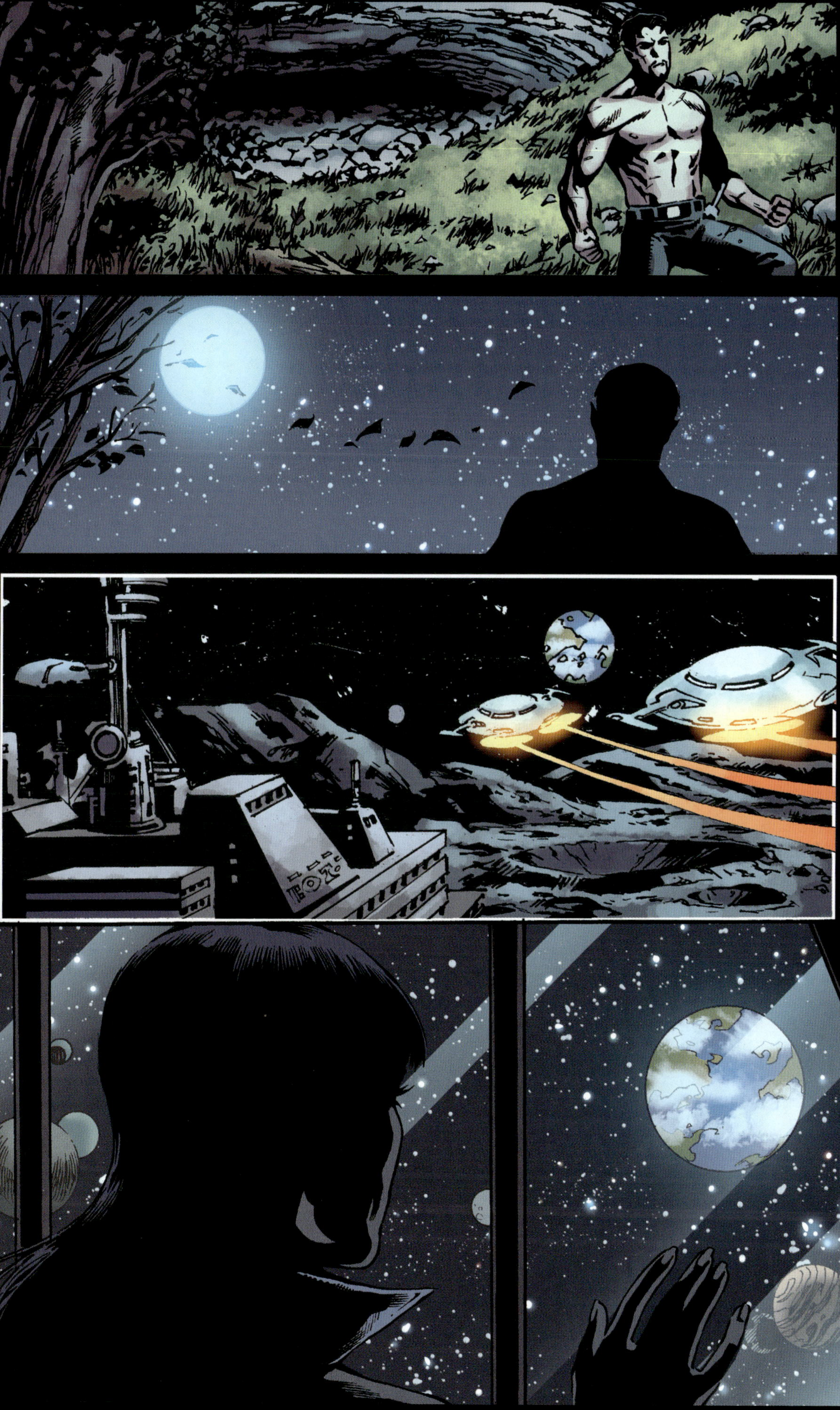

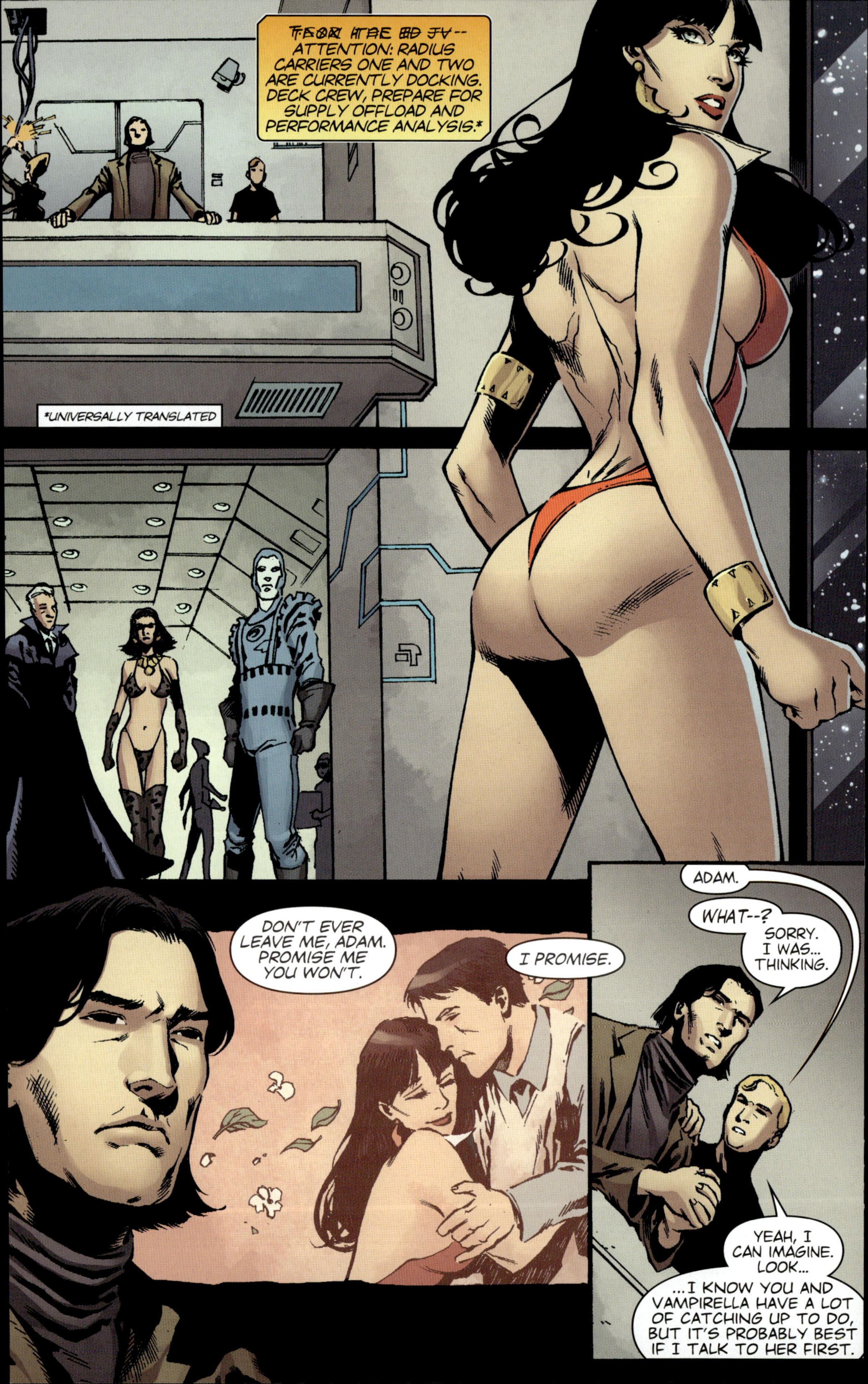
ATTENTION: RADIUS CARRIERS ONE AND TWO ARE CURRENTLY DOCKING. DECK CREW, PREPARE FOR SUPPLY OFFLOAD AND PERFORMANCE ANALYSIS.*
*UNIVERSALLY TRANSLATED
DON'T EVER LEAVE ME, ADAM. PROMISE ME YOU WON'T.
I PROMISE.
ADAM.
WHAT--?
SORRY. I WAS... THINKING.
YEAH, I CAN IMAGINE. LOOK...
...I KNOW YOU AND VAMPIRELLA HAVE A LOT OF CATCHING UP TO DO, BUT IT'S PROBABLY BEST IF I TALK TO HER FIRST.

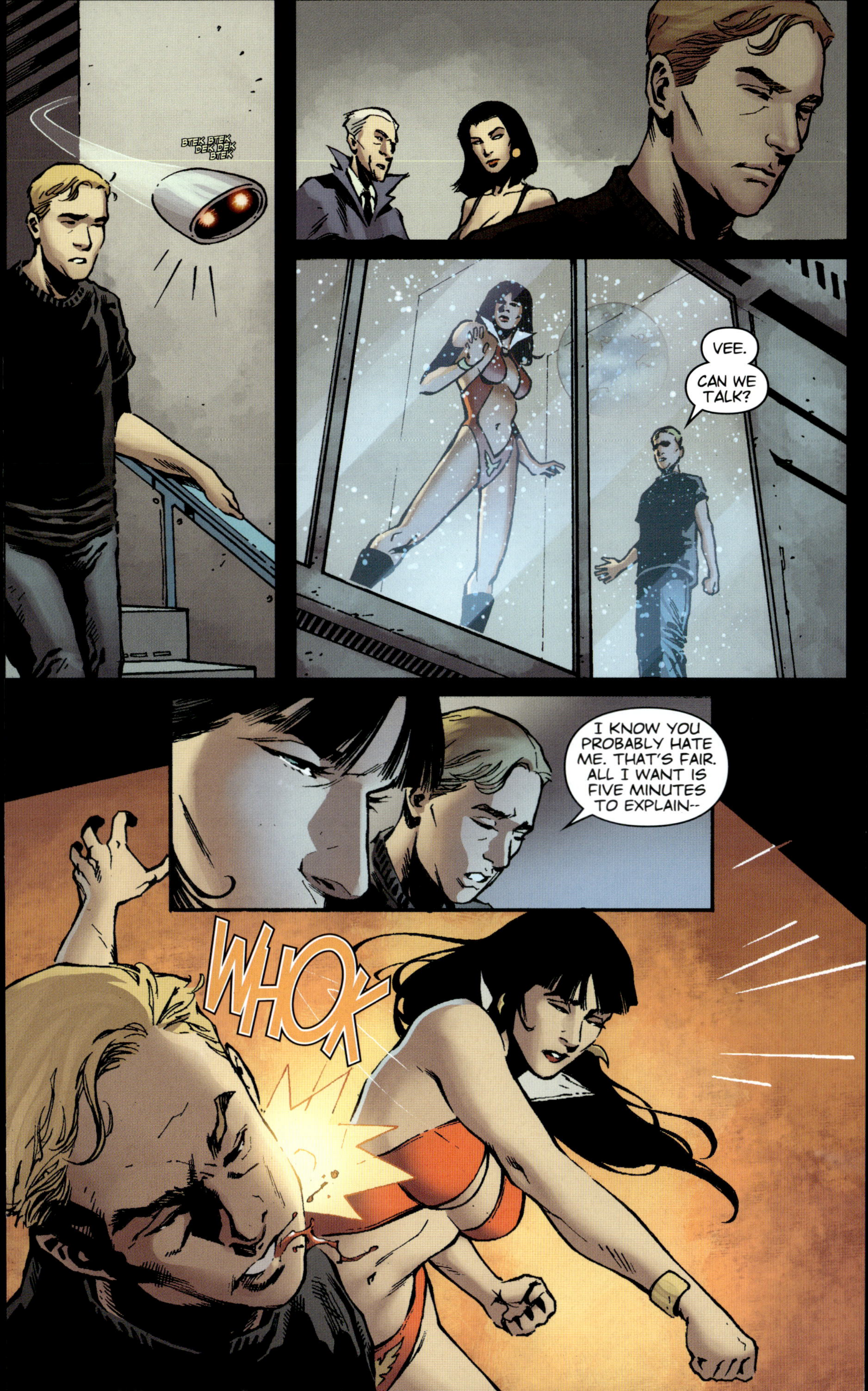
BTEK BTEK DEK DEK BTEK
VEE.
CAN WE TALK?
I KNOW YOU PROBABLY HATE ME. THAT'S FAIR. ALL I WANT IS FIVE MINUTES TO EXPLAIN--
WHOK

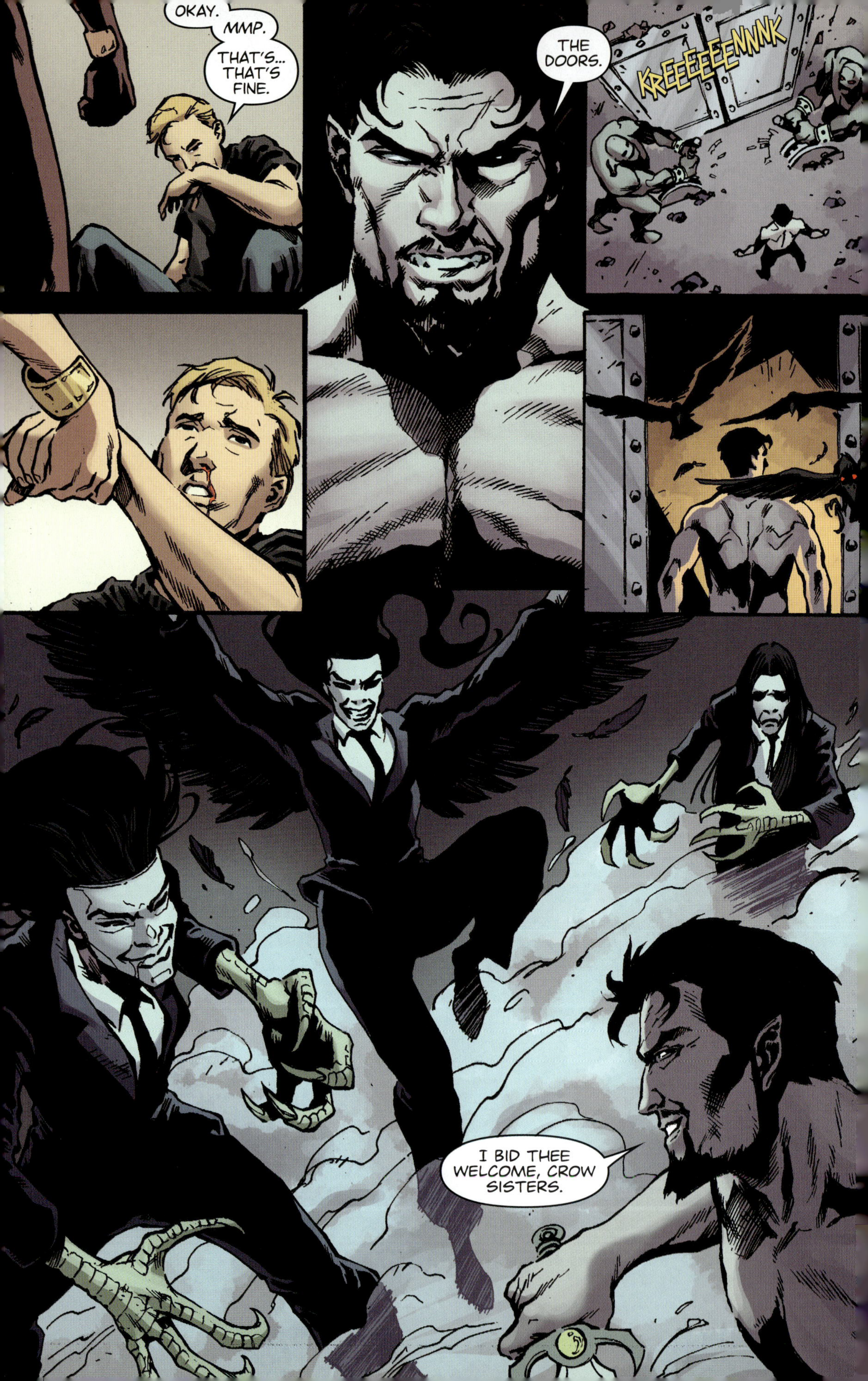
OKAY.
MMP.
THAT'S... THAT'S FINE.
THE DOORS.
KREEEEEEENNNK
I BID THEE WELCOME, CROW SISTERS.

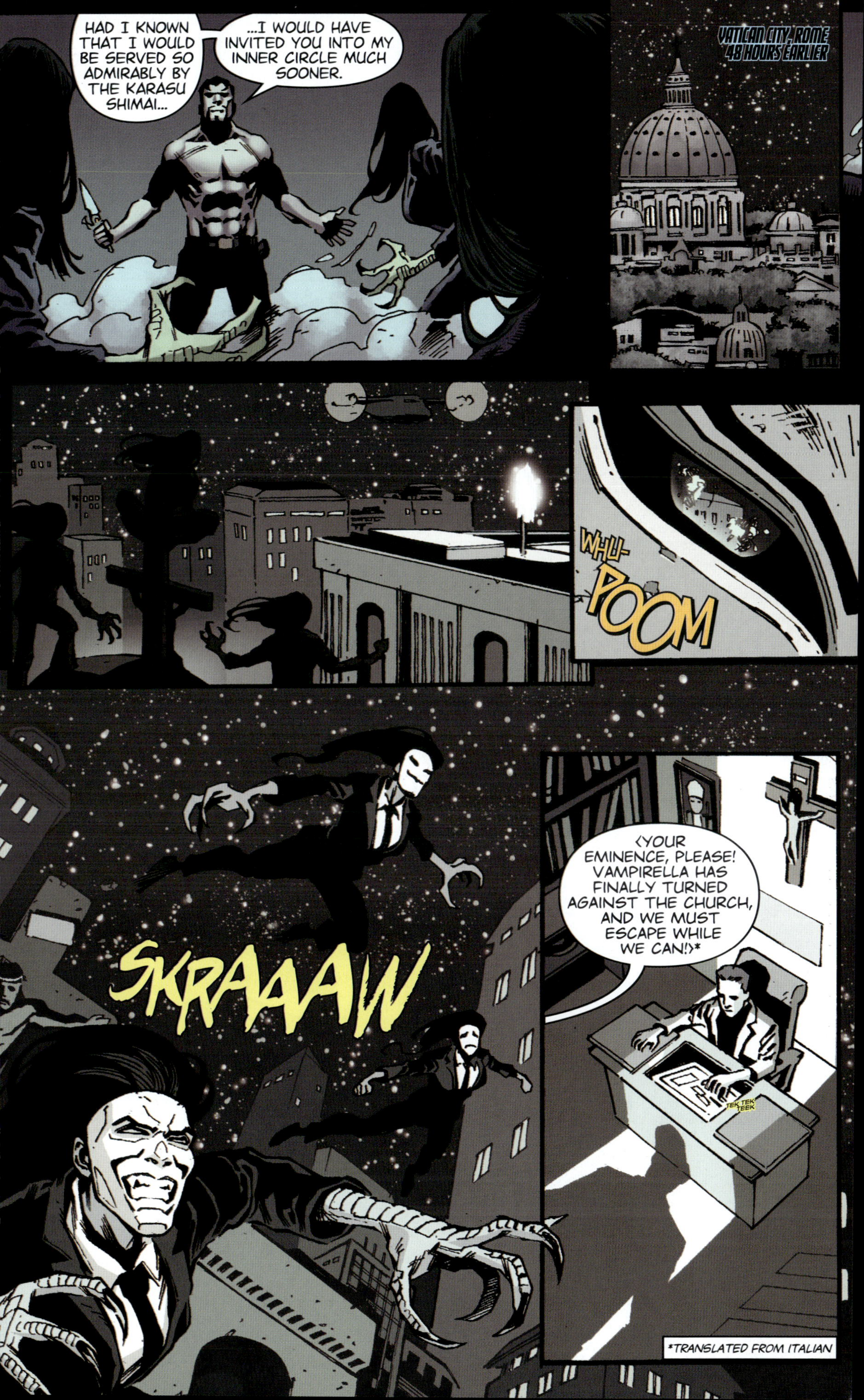
HAD I KNOWN THAT I WOULD BE SERVED SO ADMIRABLY BY THE KARASU SHIMAI...
...I WOULD HAVE INVITED YOU INTO MY INNER CIRCLE MUCH SOONER.
VATICAN CITY, ROME
48 HOURS EARLIER
WHU-POOM
SKRAAAAW
<YOUR EMINENCE, PLEASE! VAMPIRELLA HAS FINALLY TURNED AGAINST THE CHURCH, AND WE MUST ESCAPE WHILE WE CAN!>*
TEK TEK TEEK
*TRANSLATED FROM ITALIAN

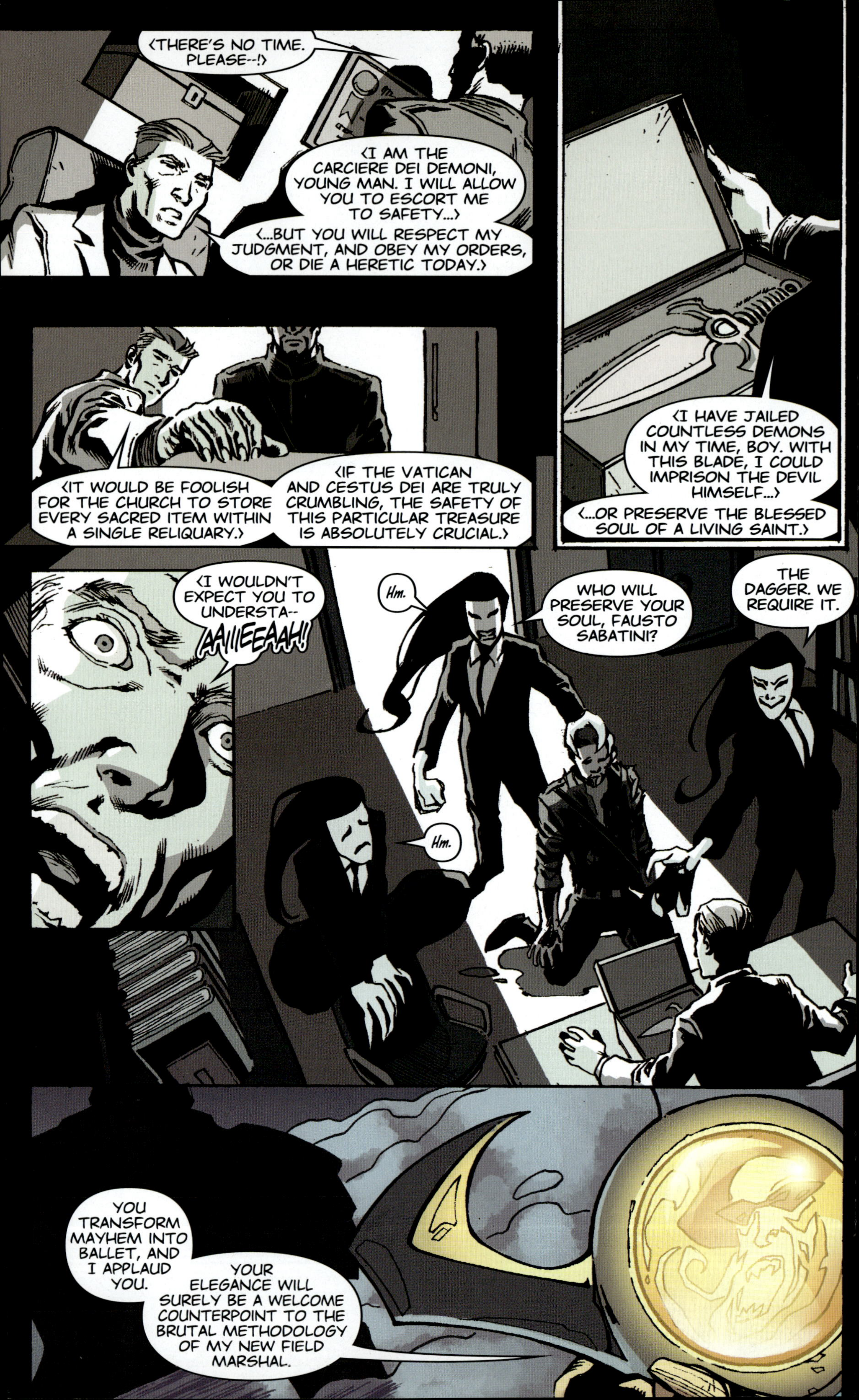
‹THERE'S NO TIME. PLEASE--!›
‹I AM THE CARCIERE DEI DEMONI, YOUNG MAN. I WILL ALLOW YOU TO ESCORT ME TO SAFETY...›
‹...BUT YOU WILL RESPECT MY JUDGMENT, AND OBEY MY ORDERS, OR DIE A HERETIC TODAY.›
‹IT WOULD BE FOOLISH FOR THE CHURCH TO STORE EVERY SACRED ITEM WITHIN A SINGLE RELIQUARY.›
‹IF THE VATICAN AND CESTUS DEI ARE TRULY CRUMBLING, THE SAFETY OF THIS PARTICULAR TREASURE IS ABSOLUTELY CRUCIAL.›
‹I HAVE JAILED COUNTLESS DEMONS IN MY TIME, BOY. WITH THIS BLADE, I COULD IMPRISON THE DEVIL HIMSELF...›
‹...OR PRESERVE THE BLESSED SOUL OF A LIVING SAINT.›
‹I WOULDN'T EXPECT YOU TO UNDERSTA--
AAIIEEAAH!
Hm.
WHO WILL PRESERVE YOUR SOUL, FAUSTO SABATINI?
THE DAGGER. WE REQUIRE IT.
Hm.
YOU TRANSFORM MAYHEM INTO BALLET, AND I APPLAUD YOU.
YOUR ELEGANCE WILL SURELY BE A WELCOME COUNTERPOINT TO THE BRUTAL METHODOLOGY OF MY NEW FIELD MARSHAL.

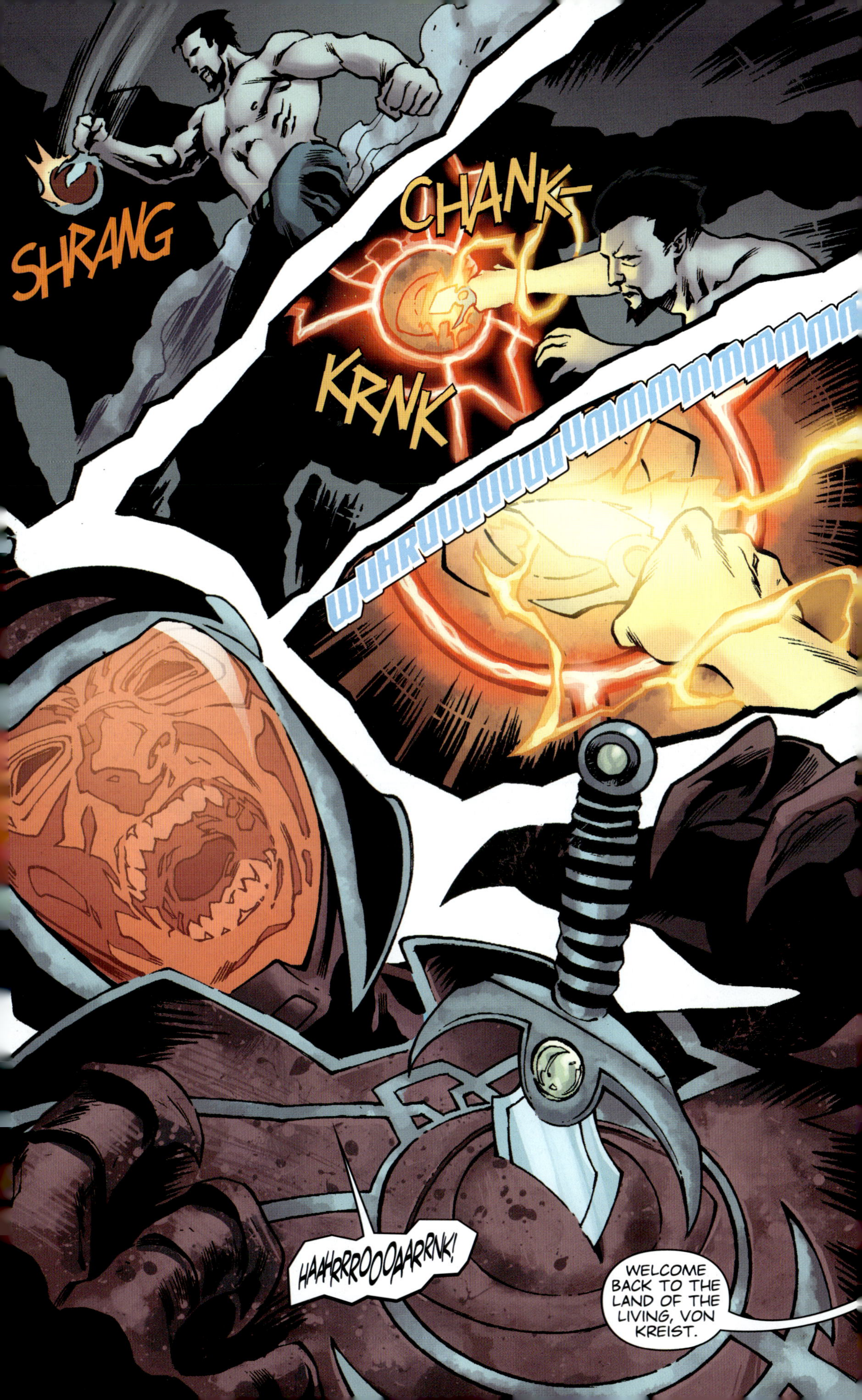
SHRANG
CHANK-
KRNK
WUHRUUUUUUUUUMMMMMMMMMMMMMMMM
HAAHRRROOOOAARRNK!
WELCOME BACK TO THE LAND OF THE LIVING, VON KREIST.

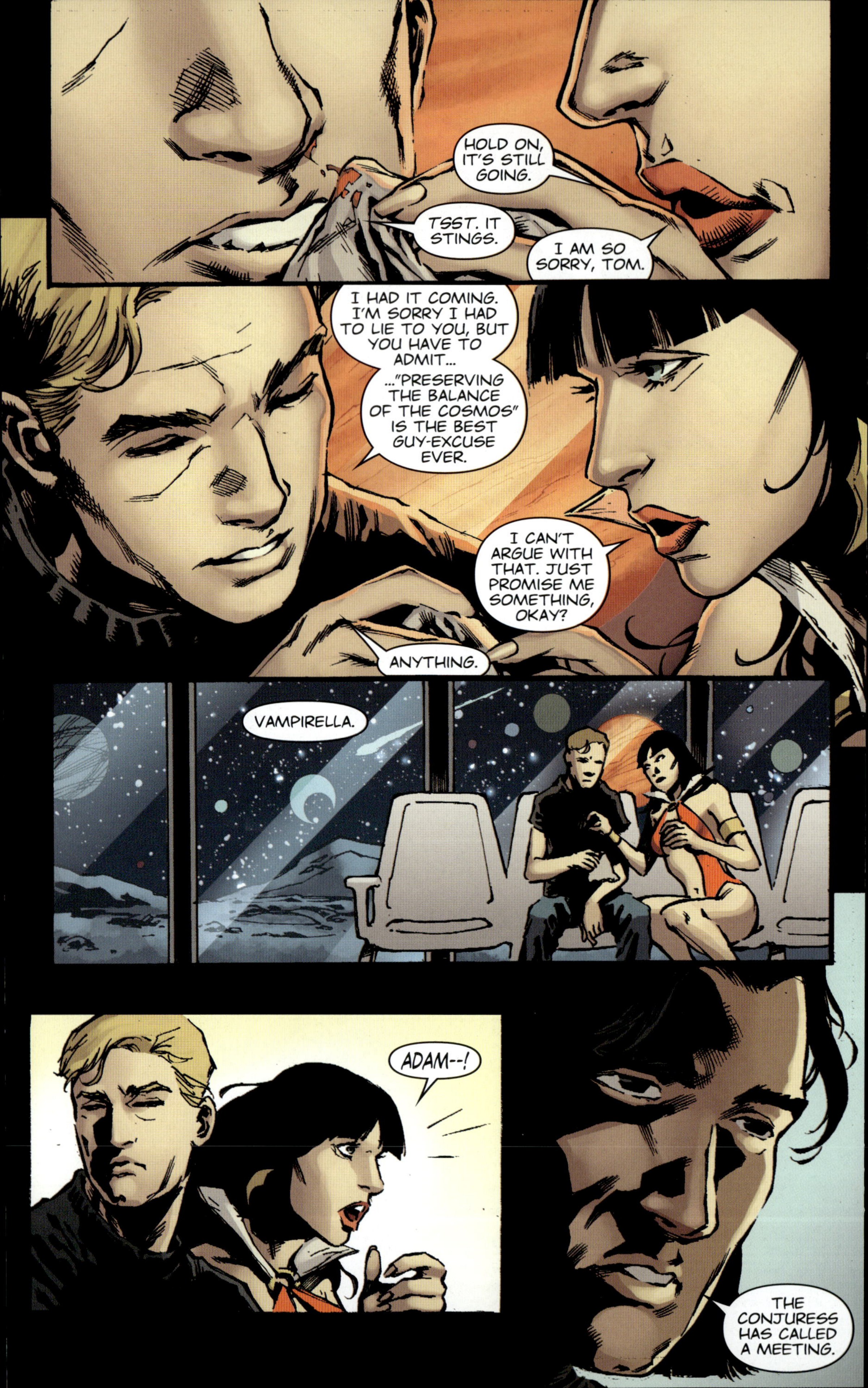
HOLD ON, IT'S STILL GOING.
TSST. IT STINGS.
I AM SO SORRY, TOM.
I HAD IT COMING. I'M SORRY I HAD TO LIE TO YOU, BUT YOU HAVE TO ADMIT...
..."PRESERVING THE BALANCE OF THE COSMOS" IS THE BEST GUY-EXCUSE EVER.
I CAN'T ARGUE WITH THAT. JUST PROMISE ME SOMETHING, OKAY?
ANYTHING.
VAMPIRELLA.
ADAM--!
THE CONJURESS HAS CALLED A MEETING.

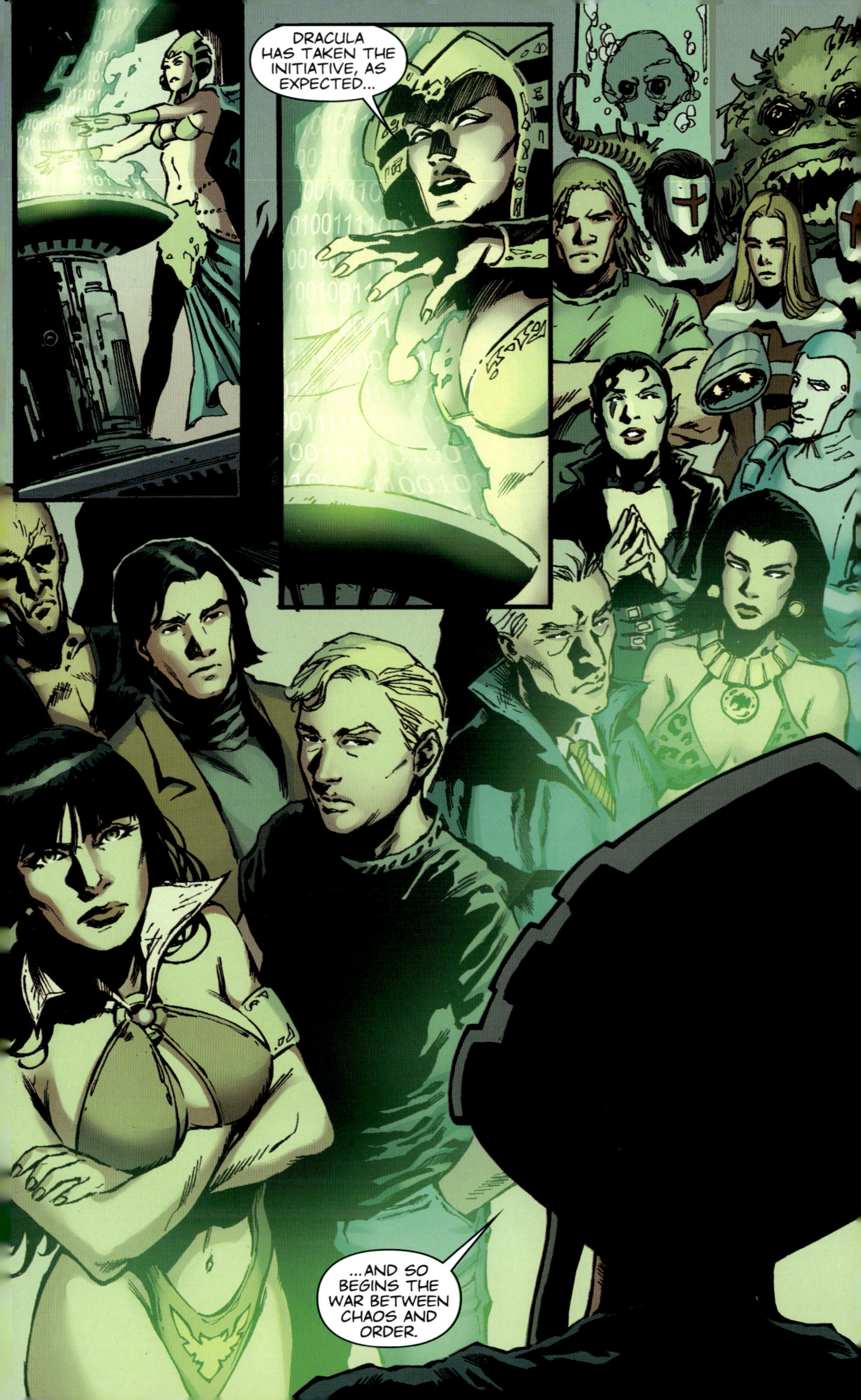
DRACULA HAS TAKEN THE INITIATIVE, AS EXPECTED...
...AND SO BEGINS THE WAR BETWEEN CHAOS AND ORDER.

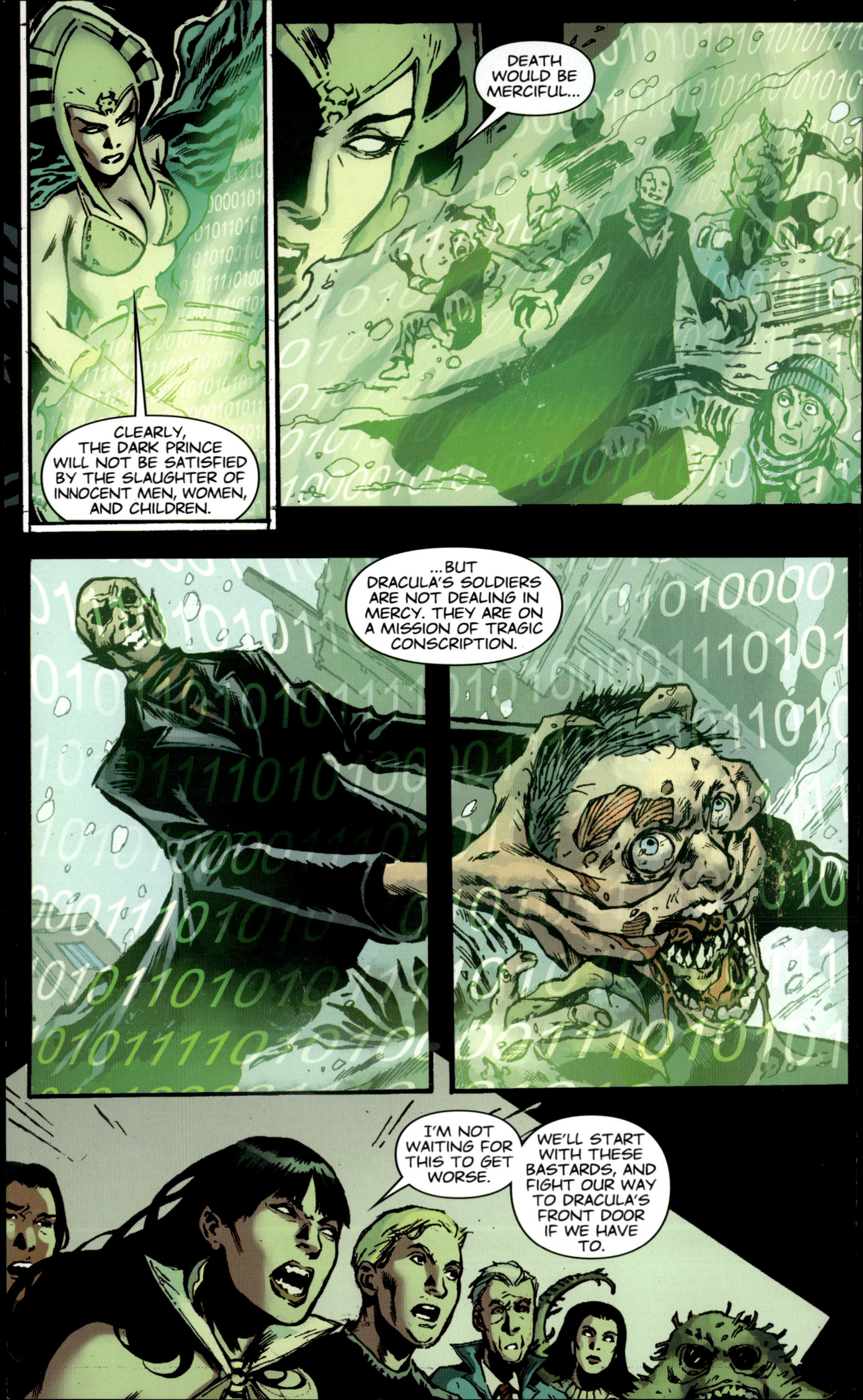
CLEARLY, THE DARK PRINCE WILL NOT BE SATISFIED BY THE SLAUGHTER OF INNOCENT MEN, WOMEN, AND CHILDREN.
DEATH WOULD BE MERCIFUL...
...BUT DRACULA'S SOLDIERS ARE NOT DEALING IN MERCY. THEY ARE ON A MISSION OF TRAGIC CONSCRIPTION.
I'M NOT WAITING FOR THIS TO GET WORSE.
WE'LL START WITH THESE BASTARDS, AND FIGHT OUR WAY TO DRACULA'S FRONT DOOR IF WE HAVE TO.

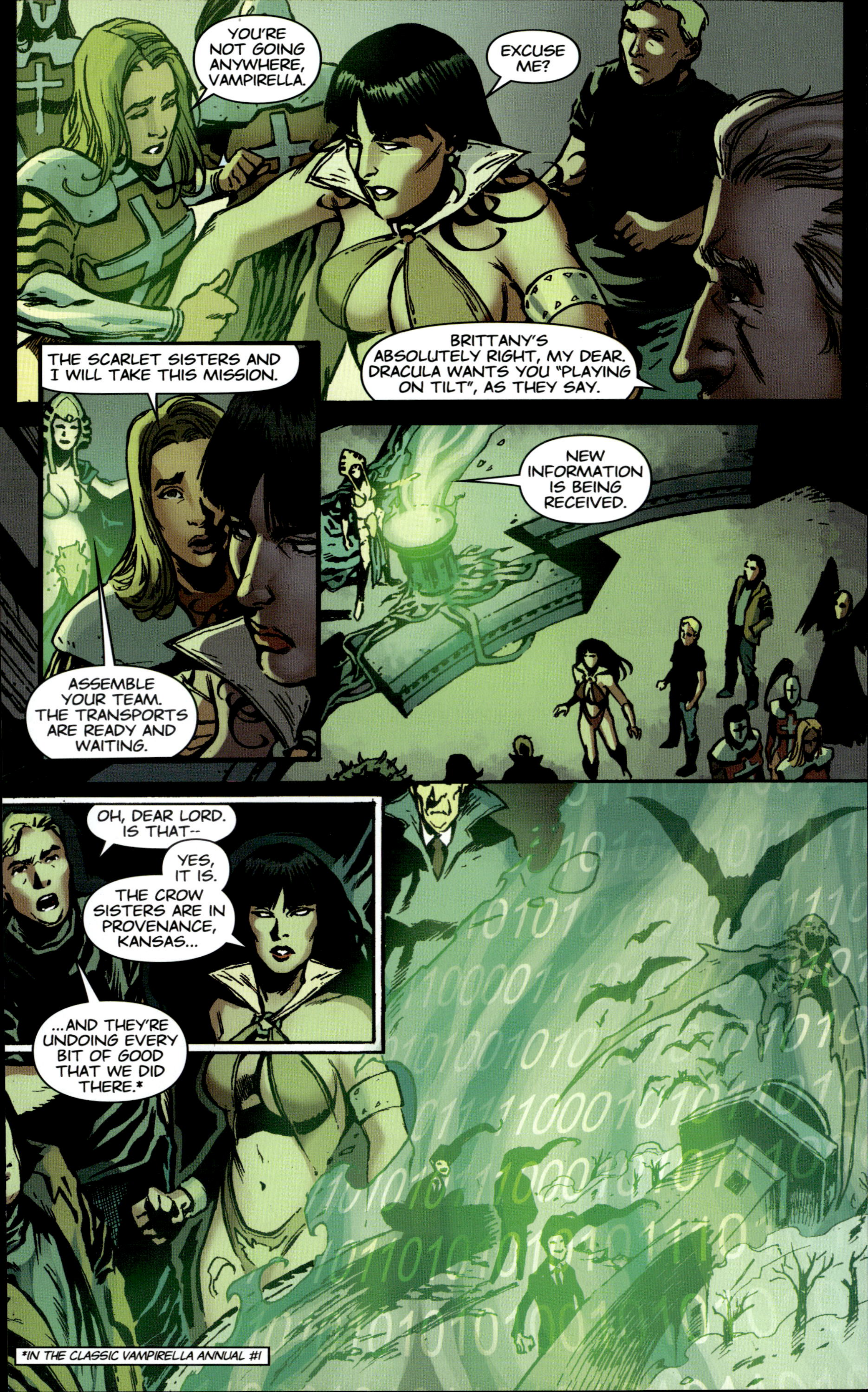
YOU'RE NOT GOING ANYWHERE, VAMPIRELLA.
EXCUSE ME?
BRITTANY'S ABSOLUTELY RIGHT, MY DEAR. DRACULA WANTS YOU "PLAYING ON TILT", AS THEY SAY.
THE SCARLET SISTERS AND I WILL TAKE THIS MISSION.
ASSEMBLE YOUR TEAM. THE TRANSPORTS ARE READY AND WAITING.
NEW INFORMATION IS BEING RECEIVED.
OH, DEAR LORD. IS THAT--
YES, IT IS.
THE CROW SISTERS ARE IN PROVENANCE, KANSAS...
...AND THEY'RE UNDOING EVERY BIT OF GOOD THAT WE DID THERE.*
*IN THE CLASSIC VAMPIRELLA ANNUAL #1

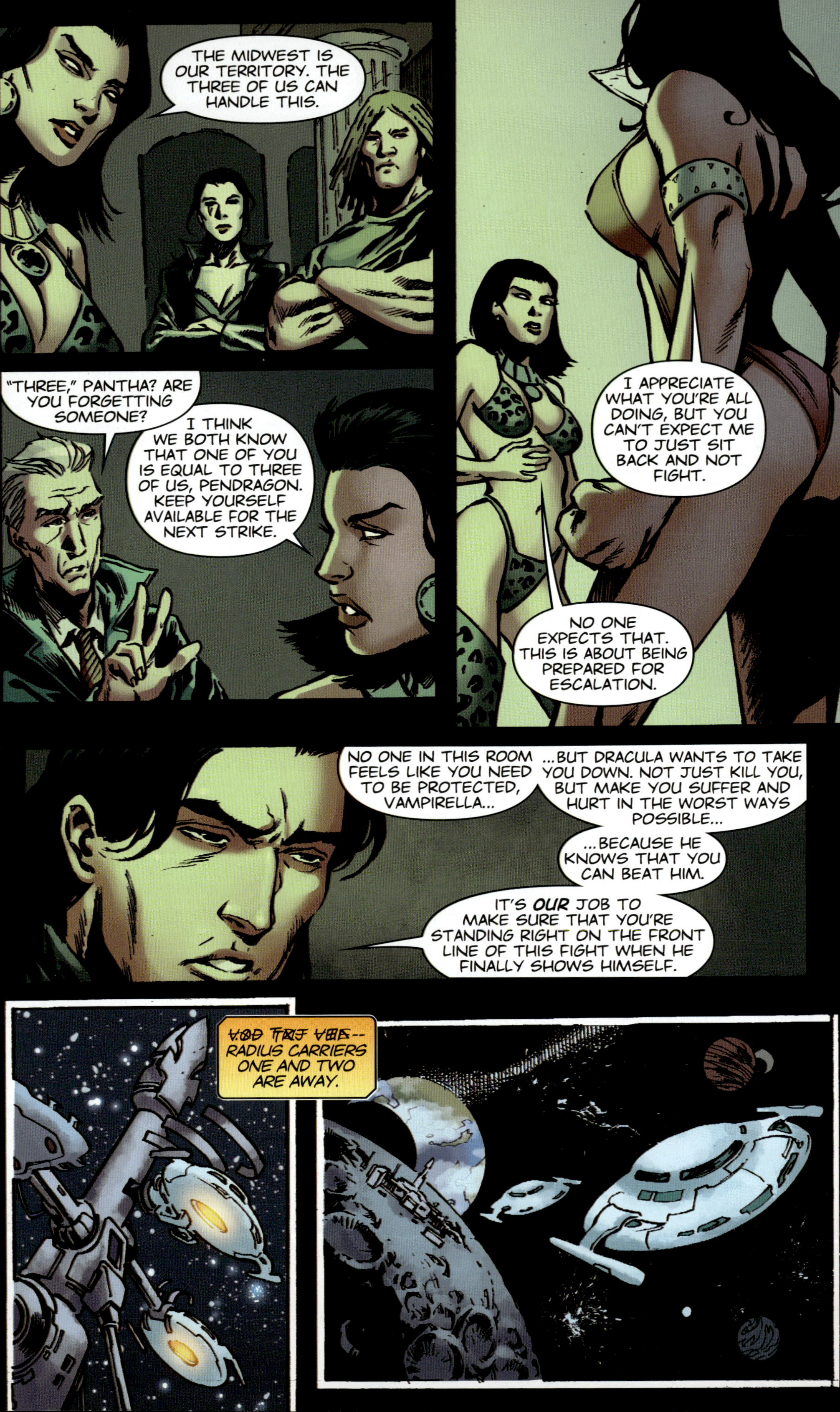
THE MIDWEST IS OUR TERRITORY. THE THREE OF US CAN HANDLE THIS.
"THREE," PANTHA? ARE YOU FORGETTING SOMEONE?
I THINK WE BOTH KNOW THAT ONE OF YOU IS EQUAL TO THREE OF US, PENDRAGON. KEEP YOURSELF AVAILABLE FOR THE NEXT STRIKE.
I APPRECIATE WHAT YOU'RE ALL DOING, BUT YOU CAN'T EXPECT ME TO JUST SIT BACK AND NOT FIGHT.
NO ONE EXPECTS THAT. THIS IS ABOUT BEING PREPARED FOR ESCALATION.
NO ONE IN THIS ROOM FEELS LIKE YOU NEED TO BE PROTECTED, VAMPIRELLA...
...BUT DRACULA WANTS TO TAKE YOU DOWN. NOT JUST KILL YOU, BUT MAKE YOU SUFFER AND HURT IN THE WORST WAYS POSSIBLE...
...BECAUSE HE KNOWS THAT YOU CAN BEAT HIM.
IT'S ***OUR*** JOB TO MAKE SURE THAT YOU'RE STANDING RIGHT ON THE FRONT LINE OF THIS FIGHT WHEN HE FINALLY SHOWS HIMSELF.
RADIUS CARRIERS ONE AND TWO ARE AWAY.

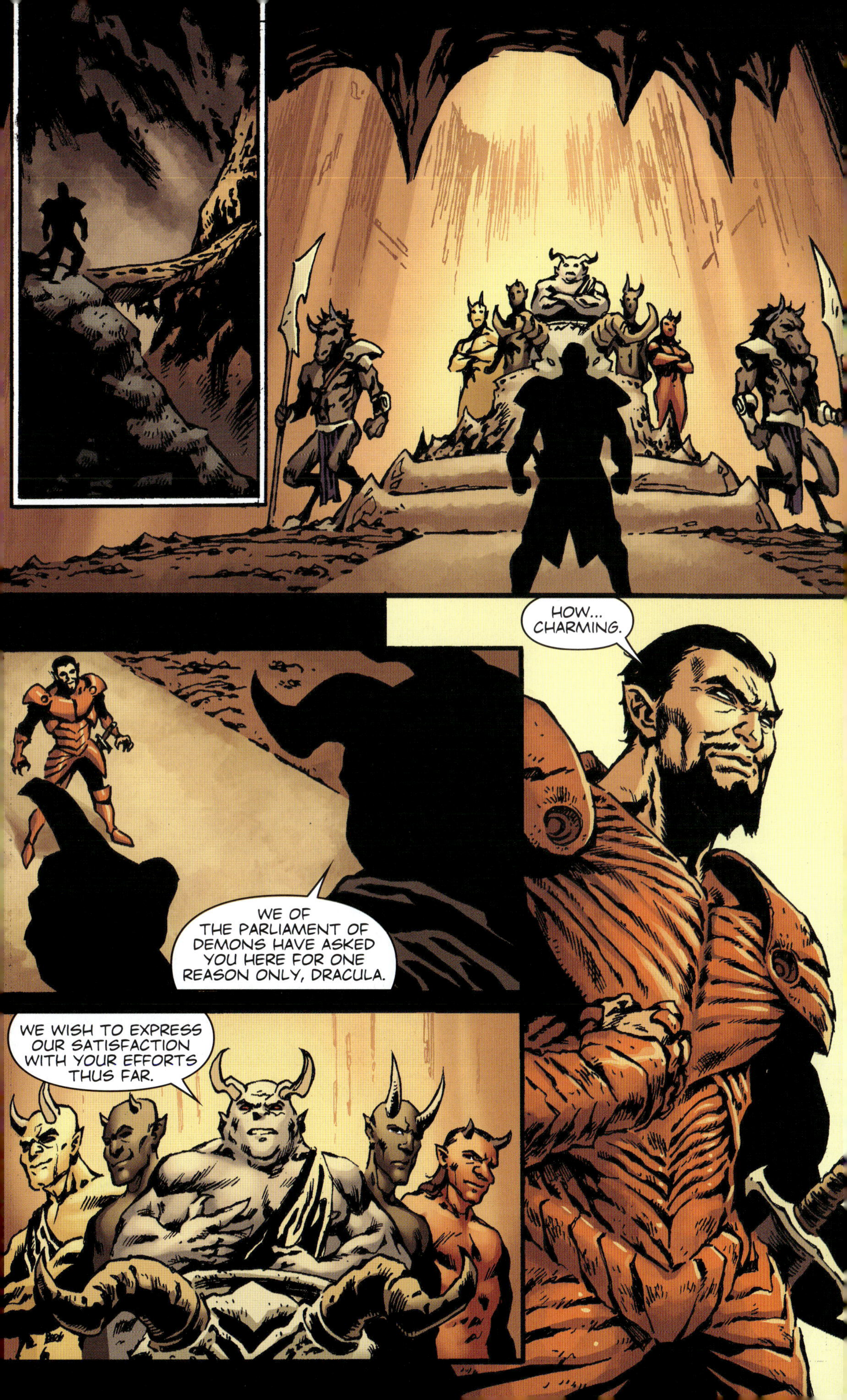

HOW... CHARMING.
WE OF THE PARLIAMENT OF DEMONS HAVE ASKED YOU HERE FOR ONE REASON ONLY, DRACULA.
WE WISH TO EXPRESS OUR SATISFACTION WITH YOUR EFFORTS THUS FAR.

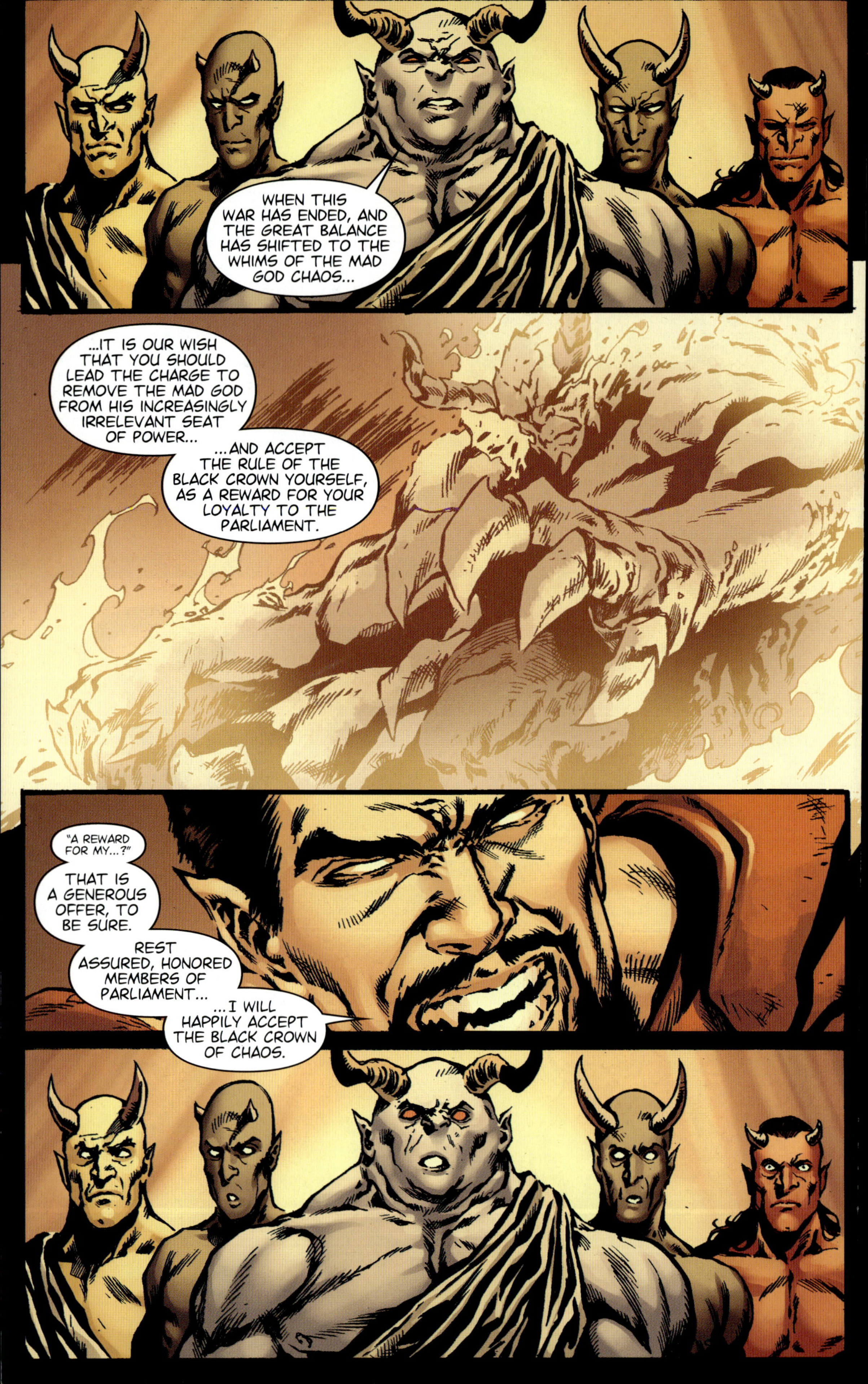
WHEN THIS WAR HAS ENDED, AND THE GREAT BALANCE HAS SHIFTED TO THE WHIMS OF THE MAD GOD CHAOS...
...IT IS OUR WISH THAT YOU SHOULD LEAD THE CHARGE TO REMOVE THE MAD GOD FROM HIS INCREASINGLY IRRELEVANT SEAT OF POWER...
...AND ACCEPT THE RULE OF THE BLACK CROWN YOURSELF, AS A REWARD FOR YOUR LOYALTY TO THE PARLIAMENT.
"A REWARD FOR MY...?"
THAT IS A GENEROUS OFFER, TO BE SURE.
REST ASSURED, HONORED MEMBERS OF PARLIAMENT...
...I WILL HAPPILY ACCEPT THE BLACK CROWN OF CHAOS.

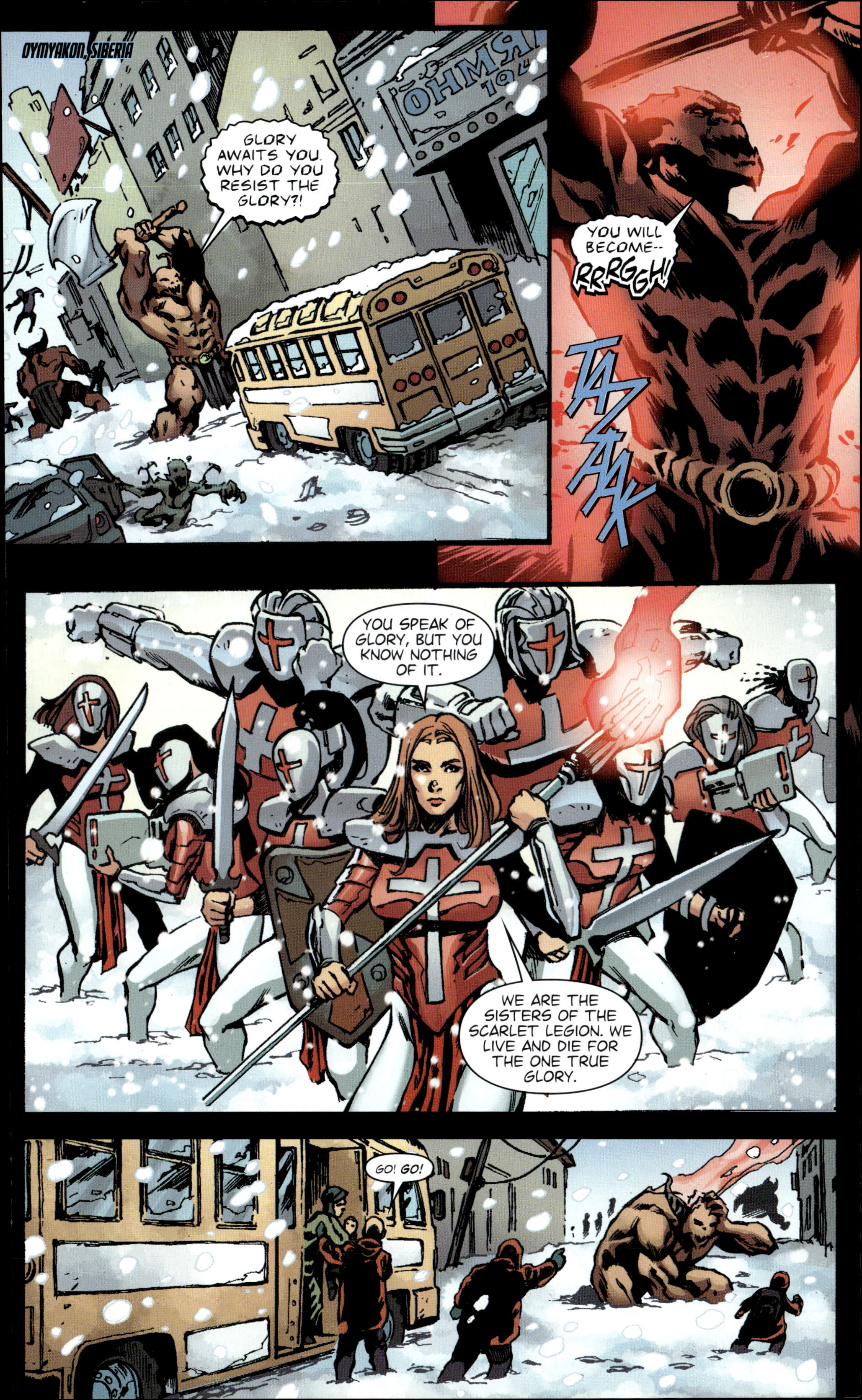
OYMYAKON, SIBERIA
GLORY AWAITS YOU. WHY DO YOU RESIST THE GLORY?!
YOU WILL BECOME-- RRRGGH!
TAZAAK
YOU SPEAK OF GLORY, BUT YOU KNOW NOTHING OF IT.
WE ARE THE SISTERS OF THE SCARLET LEGION. WE LIVE AND DIE FOR THE ONE TRUE GLORY.
GO! GO!

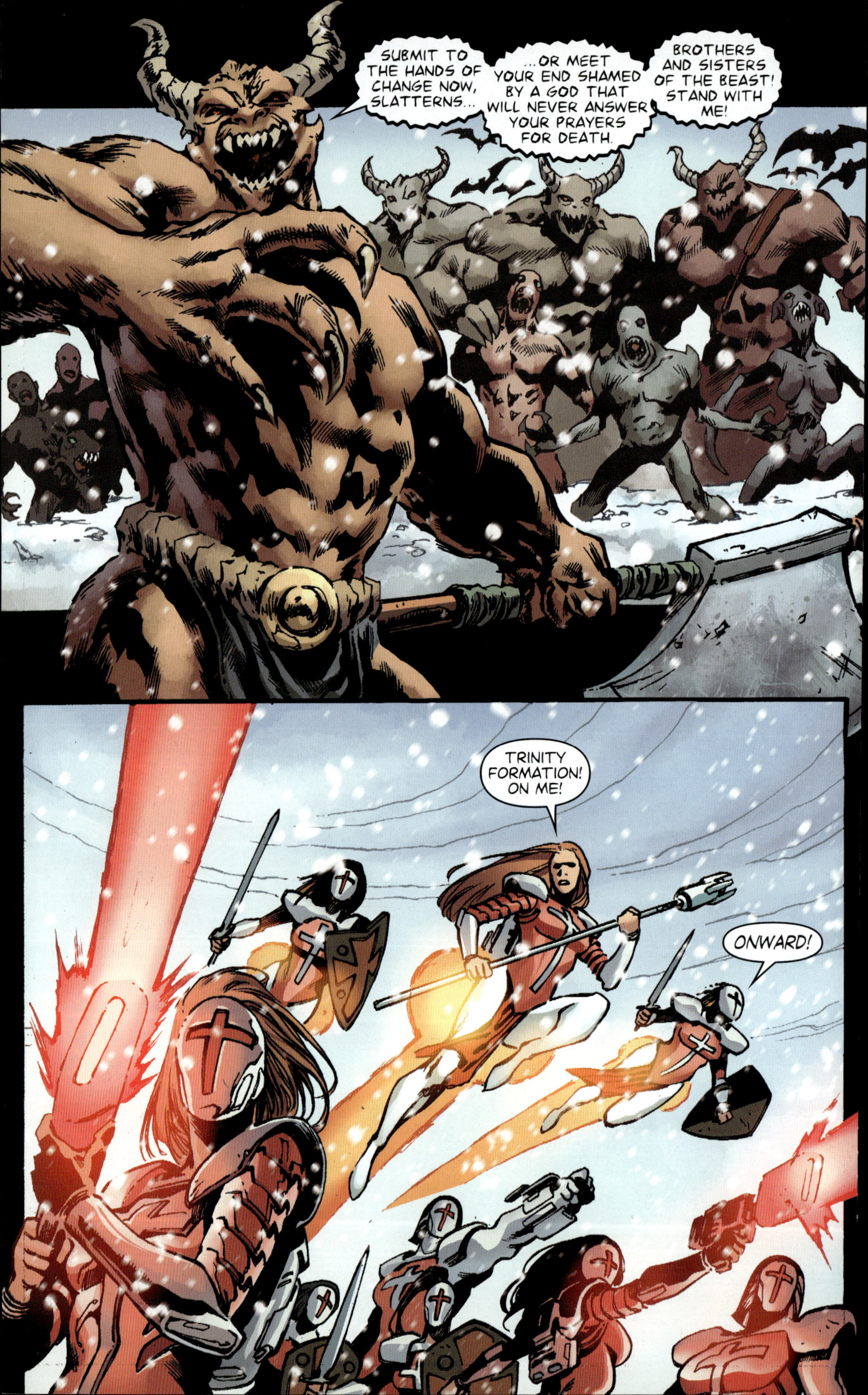
SUBMIT TO THE HANDS OF CHANGE NOW, SLATTERNS...
...OR MEET YOUR END SHAMED BY A GOD THAT WILL NEVER ANSWER YOUR PRAYERS FOR DEATH.
BROTHERS AND SISTERS OF THE BEAST! STAND WITH ME!
TRINITY FORMATION! ON ME!
ONWARD!

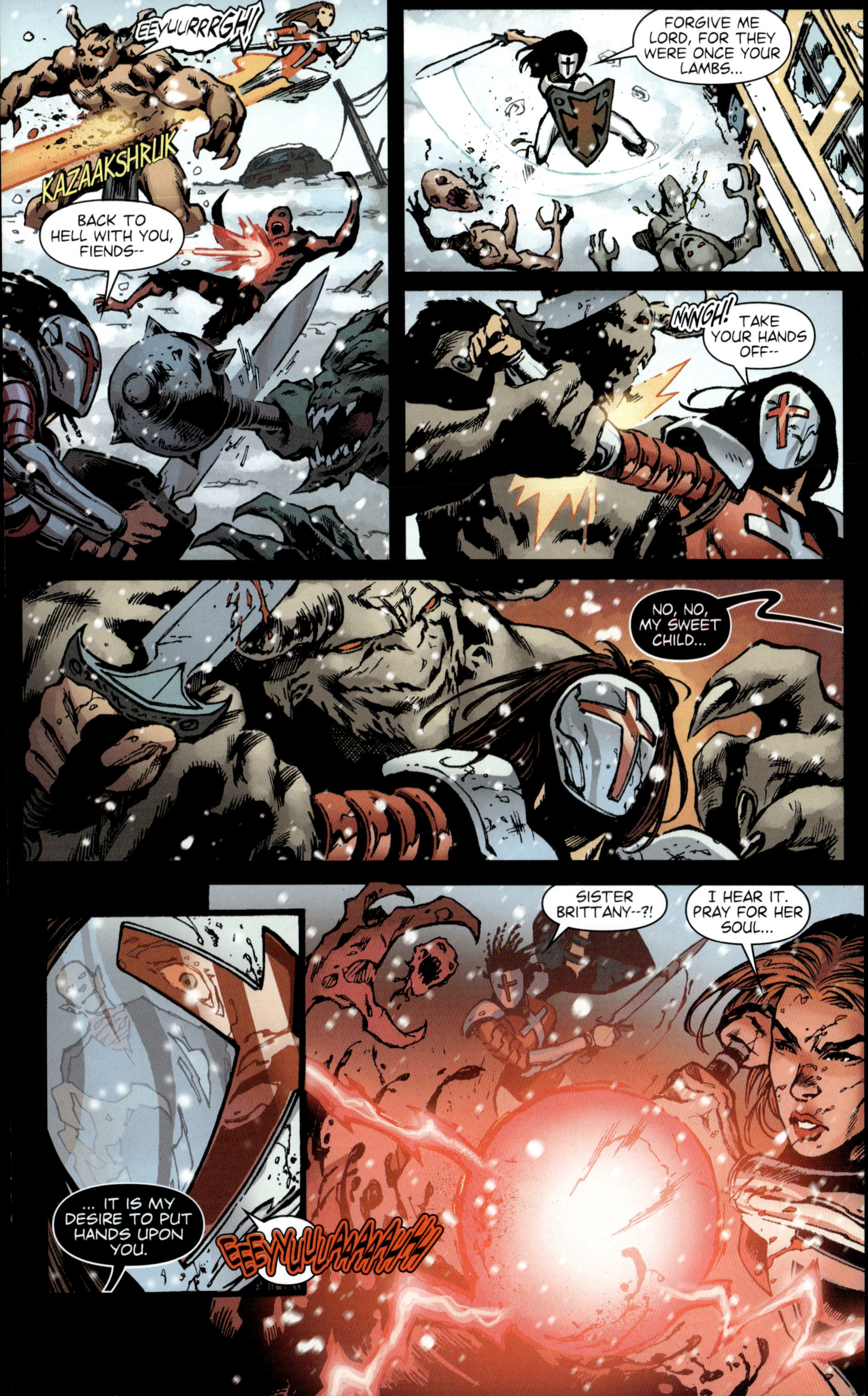
EEYUURRRGH!
KAZAAKSHRUK
BACK TO HELL WITH YOU, FIENDS--
FORGIVE ME LORD, FOR THEY WERE ONCE YOUR LAMBS...
NNNGH!
TAKE YOUR HANDS OFF--
NO, NO, MY SWEET CHILD...
... IT IS MY DESIRE TO PUT HANDS UPON YOU.
EEEYYUUUAAAHHH!!
SISTER BRITTANY--?!
I HEAR IT. PRAY FOR HER SOUL...

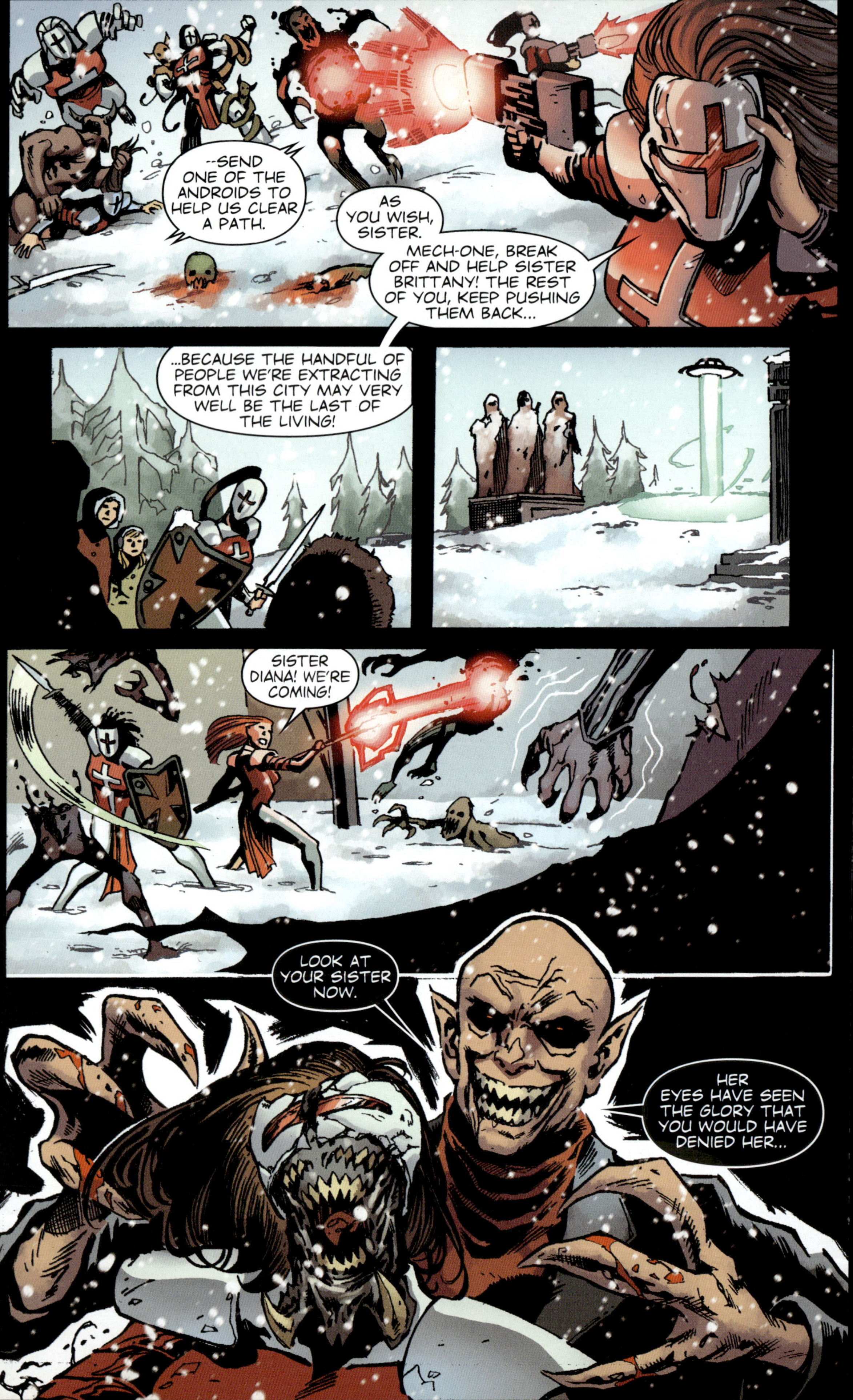
--SEND ONE OF THE ANDROIDS TO HELP US CLEAR A PATH.
AS YOU WISH, SISTER.
MECH-ONE, BREAK OFF AND HELP SISTER BRITTANY! THE REST OF YOU, KEEP PUSHING THEM BACK...
...BECAUSE THE HANDFUL OF PEOPLE WE'RE EXTRACTING FROM THIS CITY MAY VERY WELL BE THE LAST OF THE LIVING!
SISTER DIANA! WE'RE COMING!
LOOK AT YOUR SISTER NOW.
HER EYES HAVE SEEN THE GLORY THAT YOU WOULD HAVE DENIED HER...

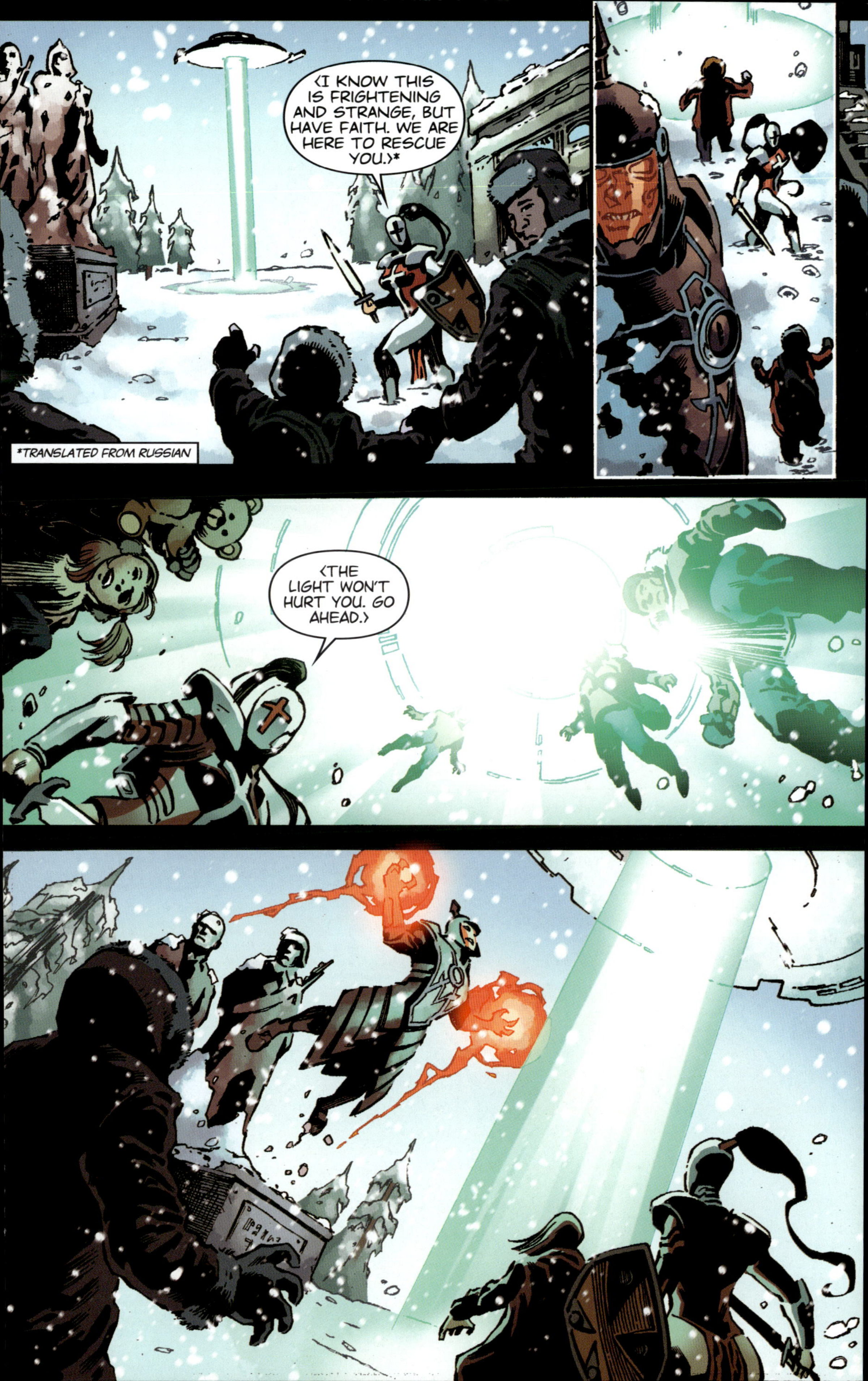

<I KNOW THIS IS FRIGHTENING AND STRANGE, BUT HAVE FAITH. WE ARE HERE TO RESCUE YOU.>*
*TRANSLATED FROM RUSSIAN
<THE LIGHT WON'T HURT YOU. GO AHEAD.>

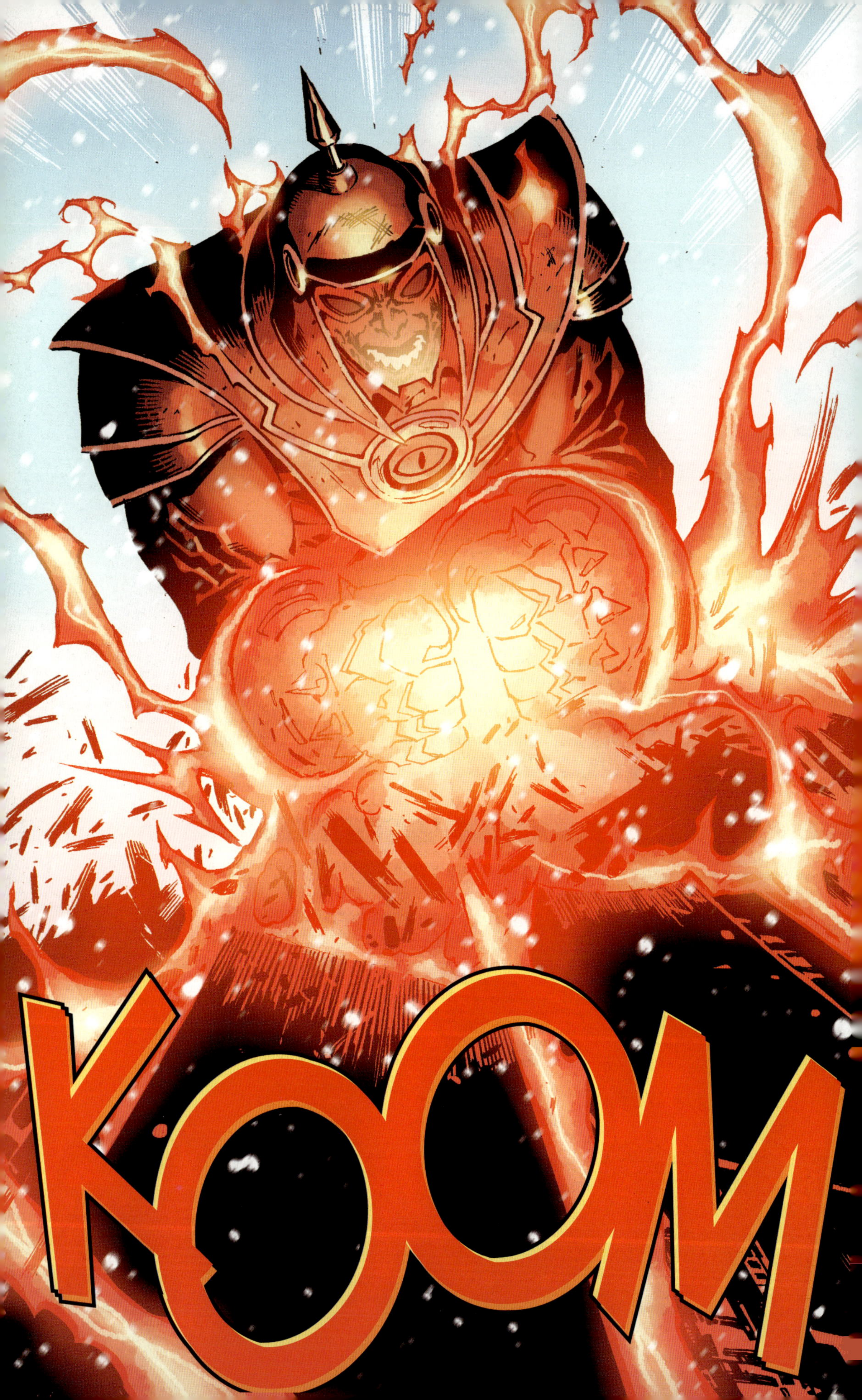
KOOM

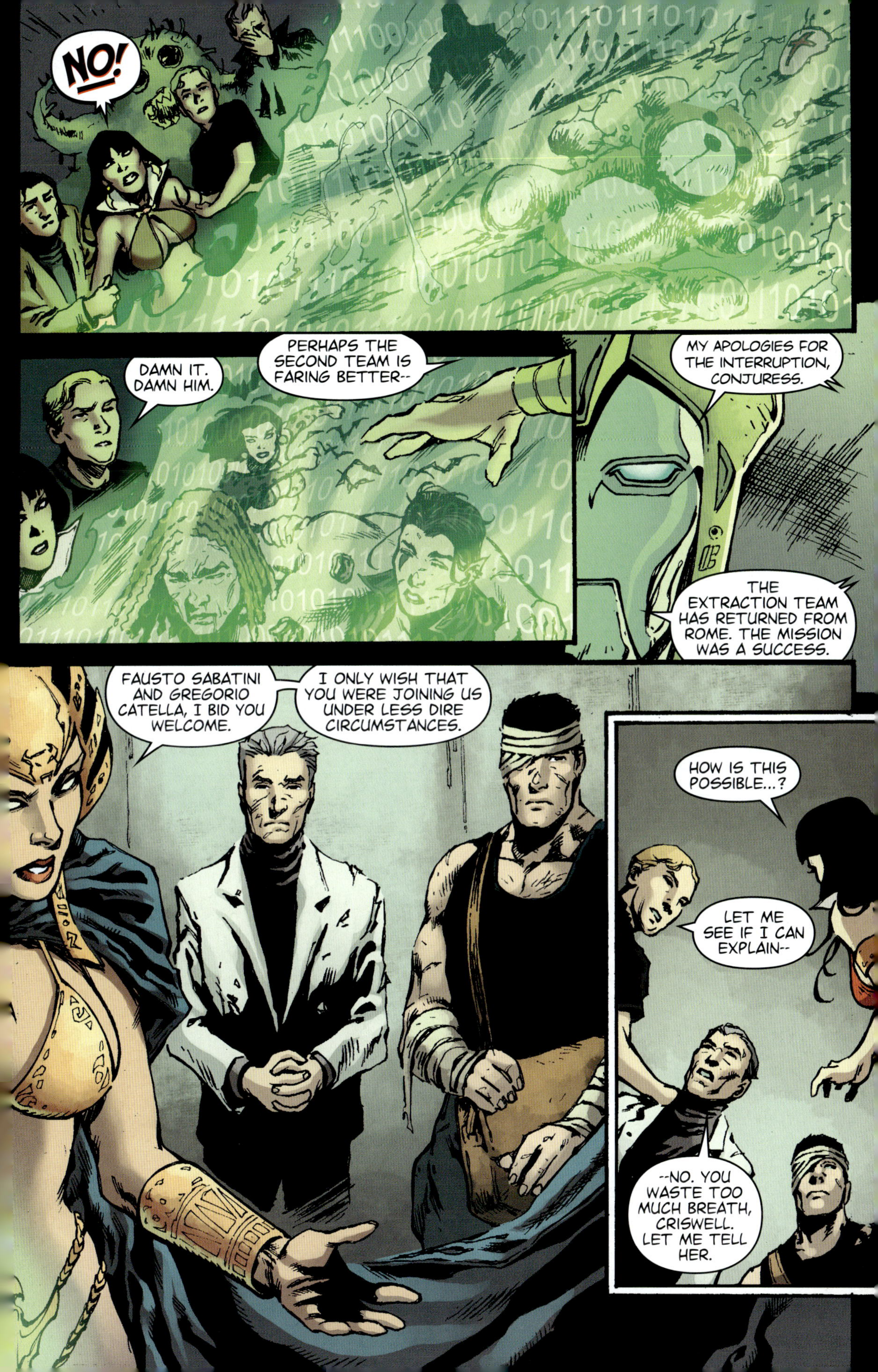
NO!
DAMN IT. DAMN HIM.
PERHAPS THE SECOND TEAM IS FARING BETTER--
MY APOLOGIES FOR THE INTERRUPTION, CONJURESS.
THE EXTRACTION TEAM HAS RETURNED FROM ROME. THE MISSION WAS A SUCCESS.
FAUSTO SABATINI AND GREGORIO CATELLA, I BID YOU WELCOME.
I ONLY WISH THAT YOU WERE JOINING US UNDER LESS DIRE CIRCUMSTANCES.
HOW IS THIS POSSIBLE...?
LET ME SEE IF I CAN EXPLAIN--
--NO. YOU WASTE TOO MUCH BREATH, CRISWELL. LET ME TELL HER.

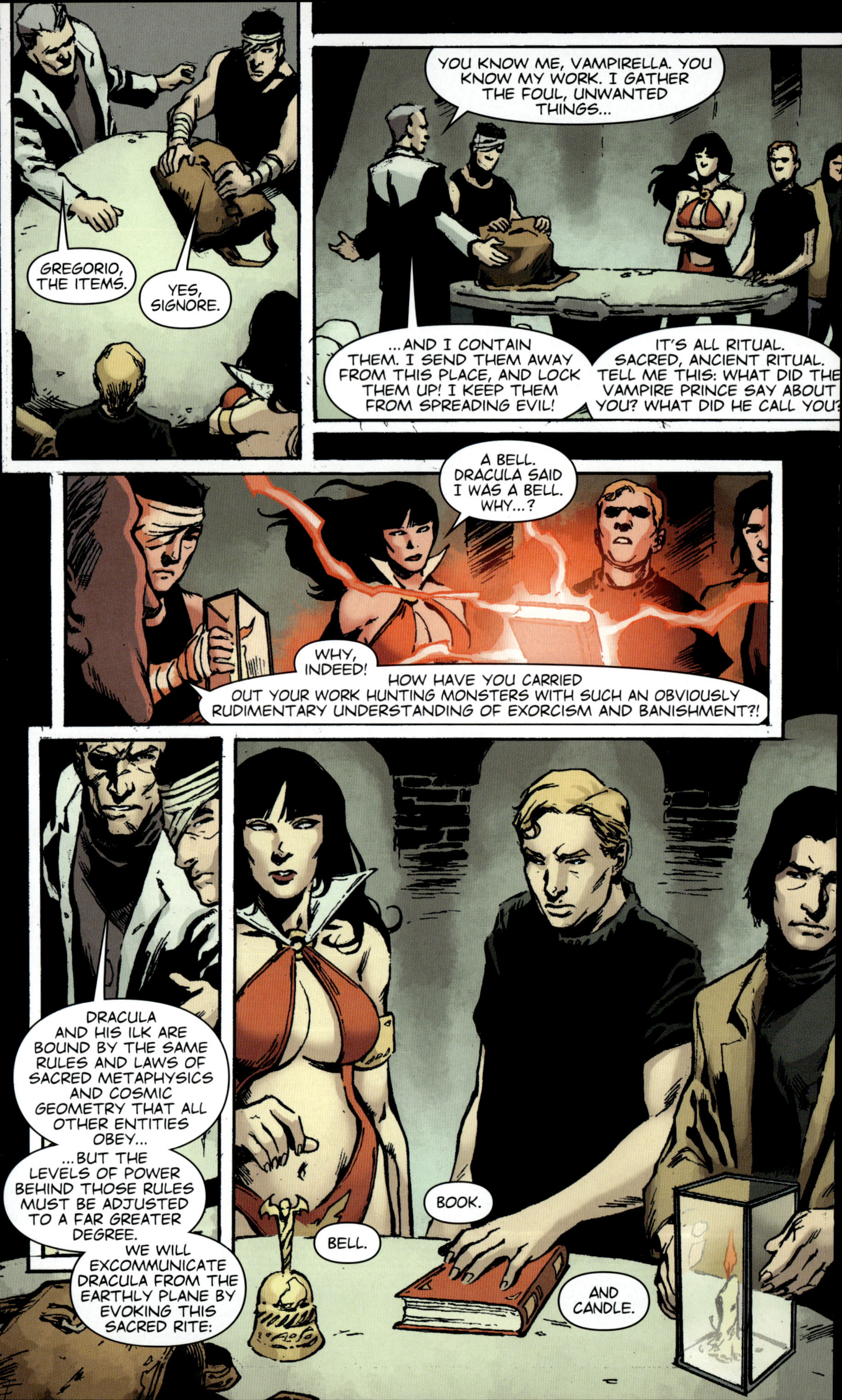
GREGORIO, THE ITEMS.
YES, SIGNORE.
YOU KNOW ME, VAMPIRELLA. YOU KNOW MY WORK. I GATHER THE FOUL, UNWANTED THINGS...
...AND I CONTAIN THEM. I SEND THEM AWAY FROM THIS PLACE, AND LOCK THEM UP! I KEEP THEM FROM SPREADING EVIL!
IT'S ALL RITUAL. SACRED, ANCIENT RITUAL. TELL ME THIS: WHAT DID THE VAMPIRE PRINCE SAY ABOUT YOU? WHAT DID HE CALL YOU?
A BELL. DRACULA SAID I WAS A BELL. WHY...?
WHY, INDEED!
HOW HAVE YOU CARRIED OUT YOUR WORK HUNTING MONSTERS WITH SUCH AN OBVIOUSLY RUDIMENTARY UNDERSTANDING OF EXORCISM AND BANISHMENT?!
DRACULA AND HIS ILK ARE BOUND BY THE SAME RULES AND LAWS OF SACRED METAPHYSICS AND COSMIC GEOMETRY THAT ALL OTHER ENTITIES OBEY...
...BUT THE LEVELS OF POWER BEHIND THOSE RULES MUST BE ADJUSTED TO A FAR GREATER DEGREE.
WE WILL EXCOMMUNICATE DRACULA FROM THE EARTHLY PLANE BY EVOKING THIS SACRED RITE:
BELL.
BOOK.
AND CANDLE.

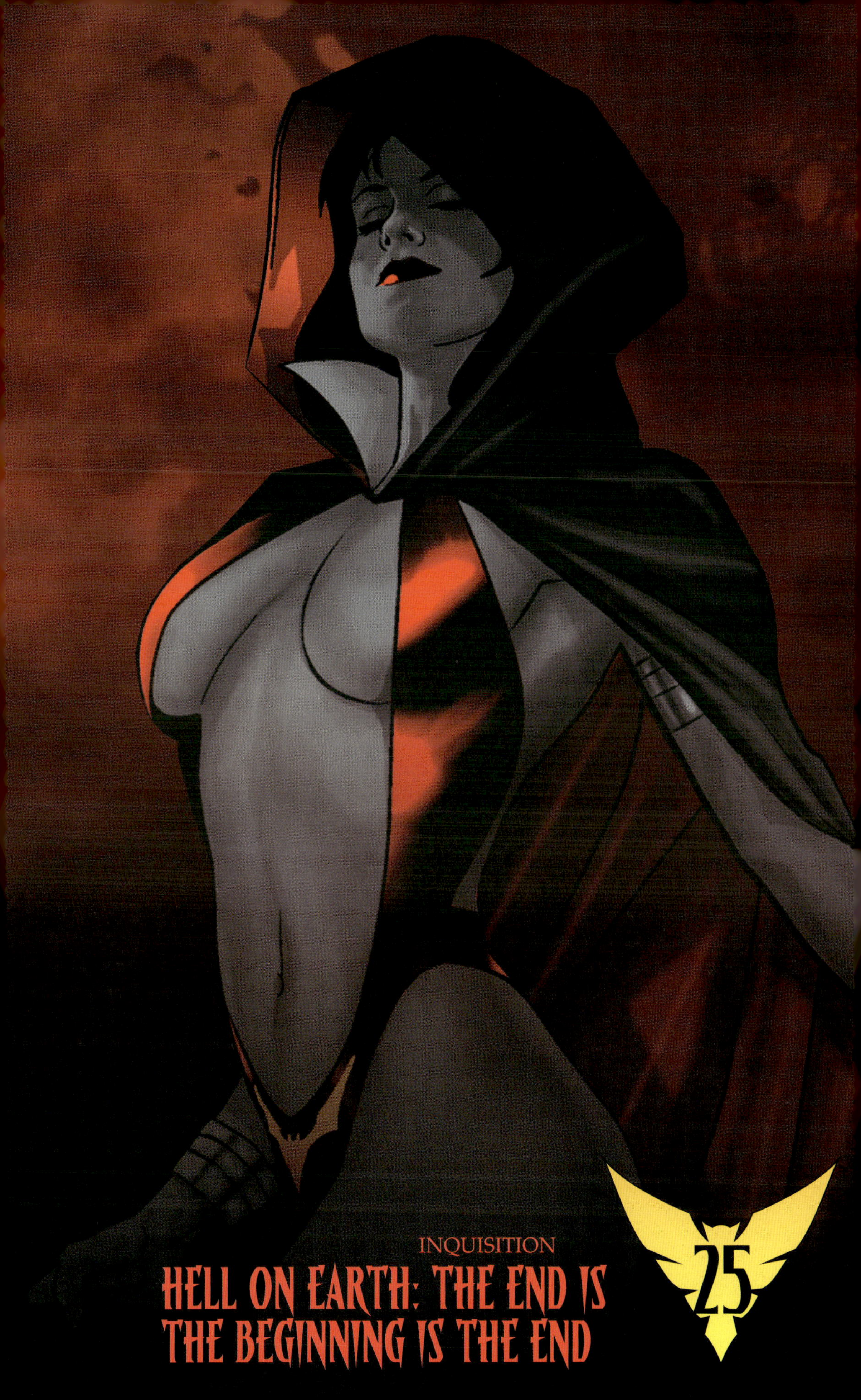
INQUISITION
HELL ON EARTH: THE END IS
THE BEGINNING IS THE END
25

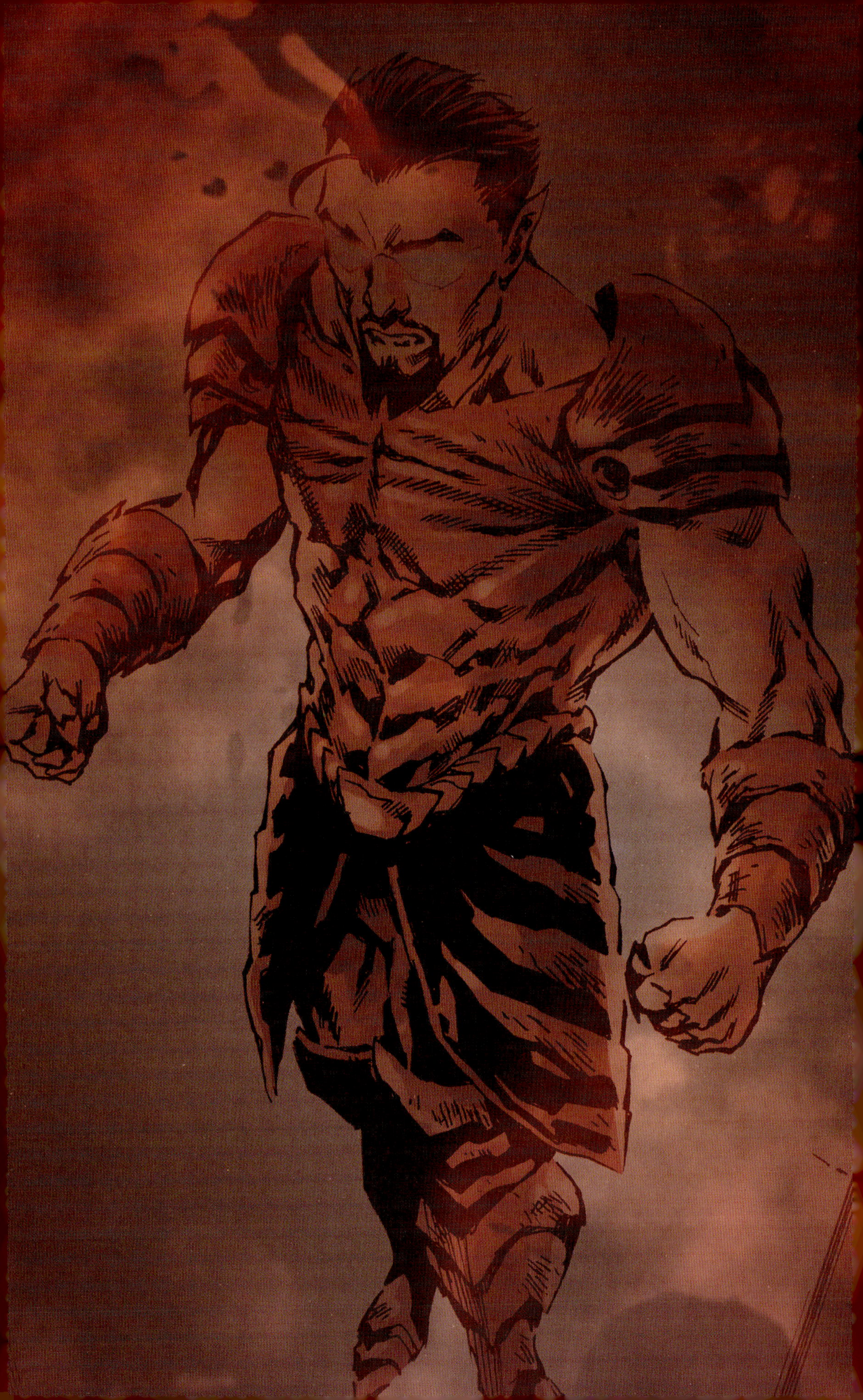

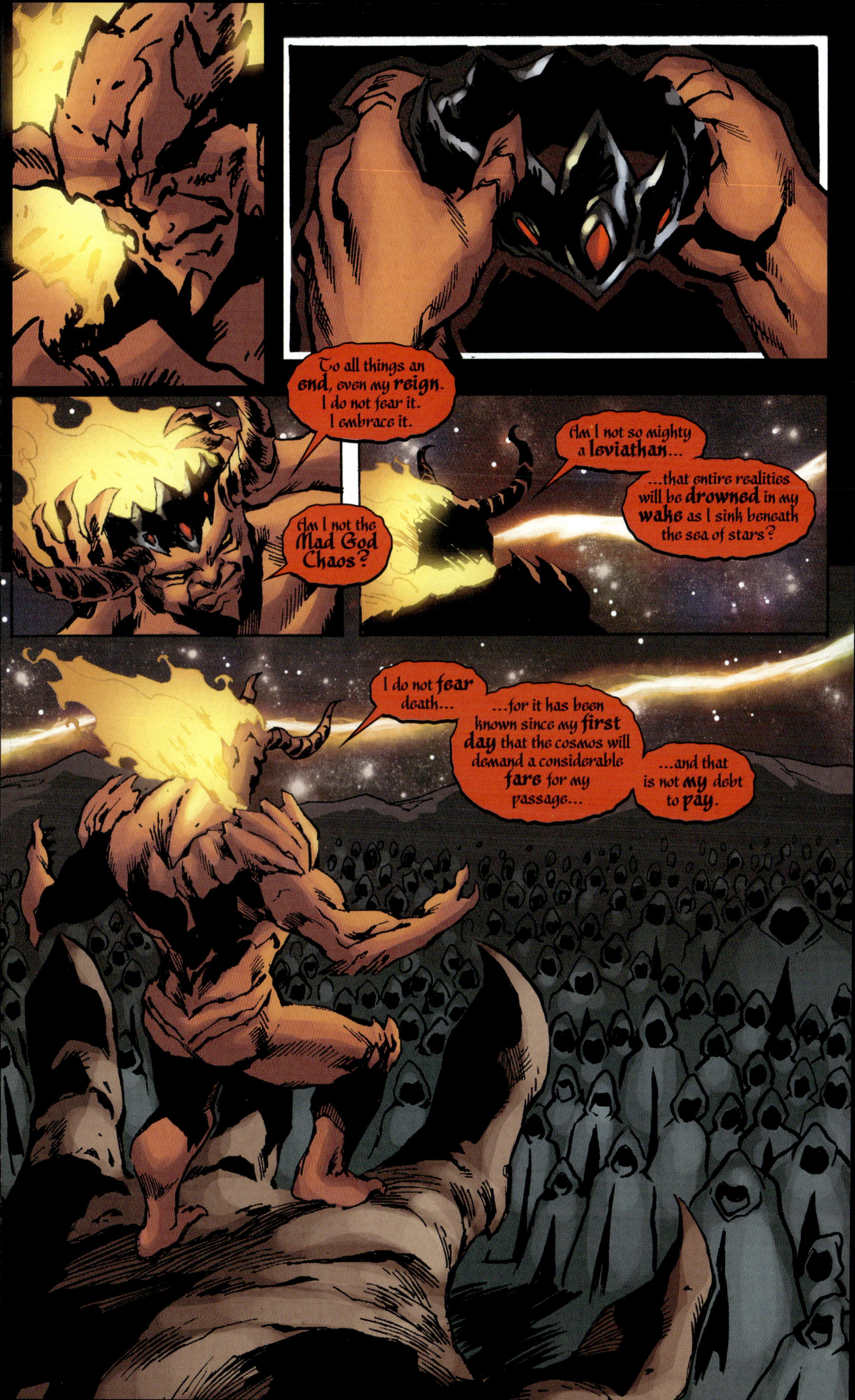
To all things an end, even my reign. I do not fear it. I embrace it.
Am I not the Mad God Chaos?
Am I not so mighty a leviathan...
...that entire realities will be drowned in my wake as I sink beneath the sea of stars?
I do not fear death...
...for it has been known since my first day that the cosmos will demand a considerable fare for my passage...
...and that is not my debt to pay.

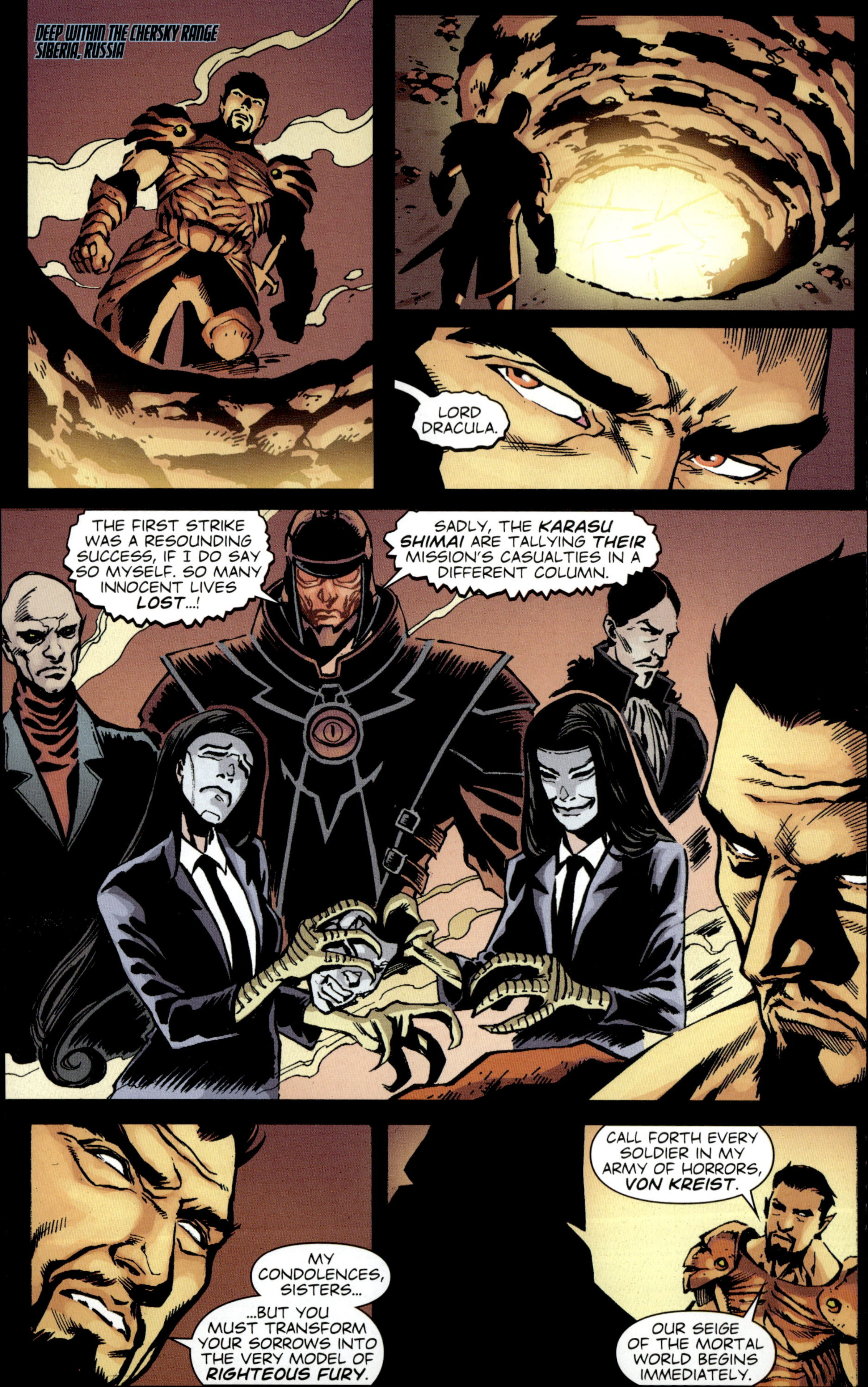
DEEP WITHIN THE CHERSKY RANGE
SIBERIA, RUSSIA
LORD DRACULA.
THE FIRST STRIKE WAS A RESOUNDING SUCCESS, IF I DO SAY SO MYSELF. SO MANY INNOCENT LIVES LOST...!
SADLY, THE KARASU SHIMAI ARE TALLYING THEIR MISSION'S CASUALTIES IN A DIFFERENT COLUMN.
MY CONDOLENCES, SISTERS...
...BUT YOU MUST TRANSFORM YOUR SORROWS INTO THE VERY MODEL OF RIGHTEOUS FURY.
CALL FORTH EVERY SOLDIER IN MY ARMY OF HORRORS, VON KREIST.
OUR SEIGE OF THE MORTAL WORLD BEGINS IMMEDIATELY.

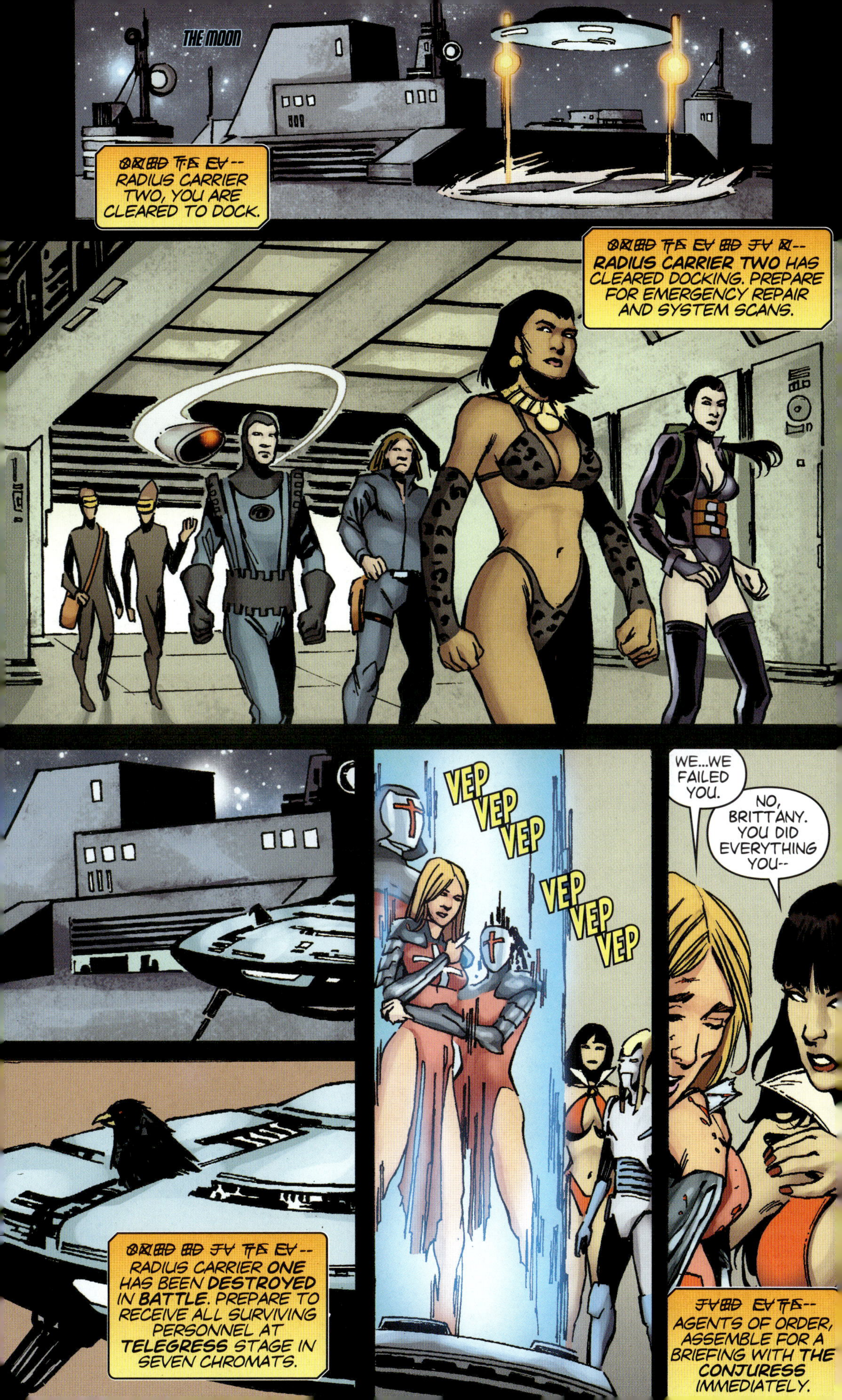
THE MOON
RADIUS CARRIER TWO, YOU ARE CLEARED TO DOCK.
RADIUS CARRIER TWO HAS CLEARED DOCKING. PREPARE FOR EMERGENCY REPAIR AND SYSTEM SCANS.
RADIUS CARRIER ONE HAS BEEN DESTROYED IN BATTLE. PREPARE TO RECEIVE ALL SURVIVING PERSONNEL AT TELEGRESS STAGE IN SEVEN CHROMATS.
VEP VEP VEP
VEP VEP VEP
WE...WE FAILED YOU.
NO, BRITTANY. YOU DID EVERYTHING YOU--
AGENTS OF ORDER, ASSEMBLE FOR A BRIEFING WITH THE CONJURESS IMMEDIATELY.

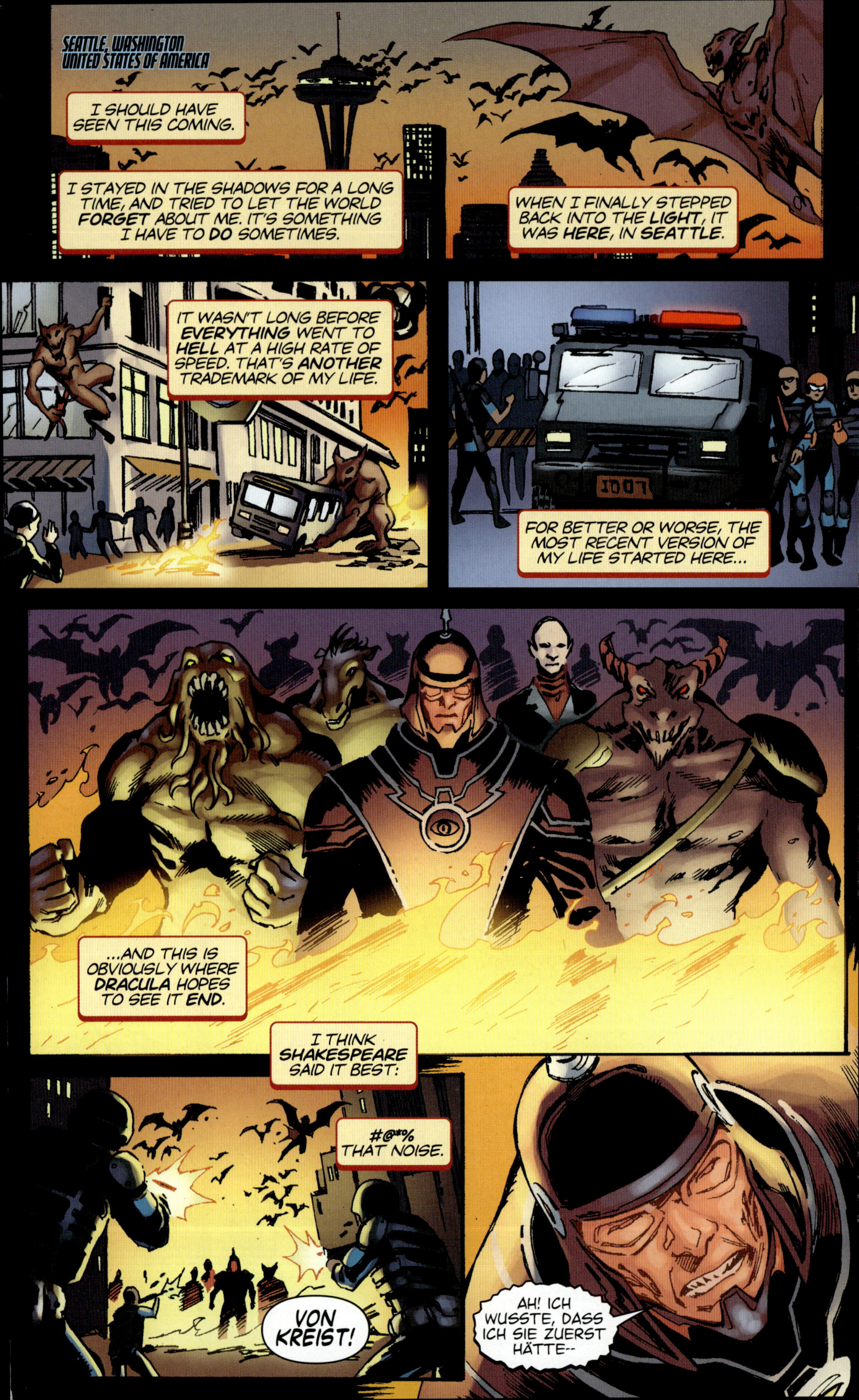
SEATTLE, WASHINGTON
UNITED STATES OF AMERICA
I SHOULD HAVE SEEN THIS COMING.
I STAYED IN THE SHADOWS FOR A LONG TIME, AND TRIED TO LET THE WORLD FORGET ABOUT ME. IT'S SOMETHING I HAVE TO DO SOMETIMES.
WHEN I FINALLY STEPPED BACK INTO THE LIGHT, IT WAS HERE, IN SEATTLE.
IT WASN'T LONG BEFORE EVERYTHING WENT TO HELL AT A HIGH RATE OF SPEED. THAT'S ANOTHER TRADEMARK OF MY LIFE.
FOR BETTER OR WORSE, THE MOST RECENT VERSION OF MY LIFE STARTED HERE...
...AND THIS IS OBVIOUSLY WHERE DRACULA HOPES TO SEE IT END.
I THINK SHAKESPEARE SAID IT BEST:
#@*% THAT NOISE.
VON KREIST!
AH! ICH WUSSTE, DASS ICH SIE ZUERST HÄTTE--

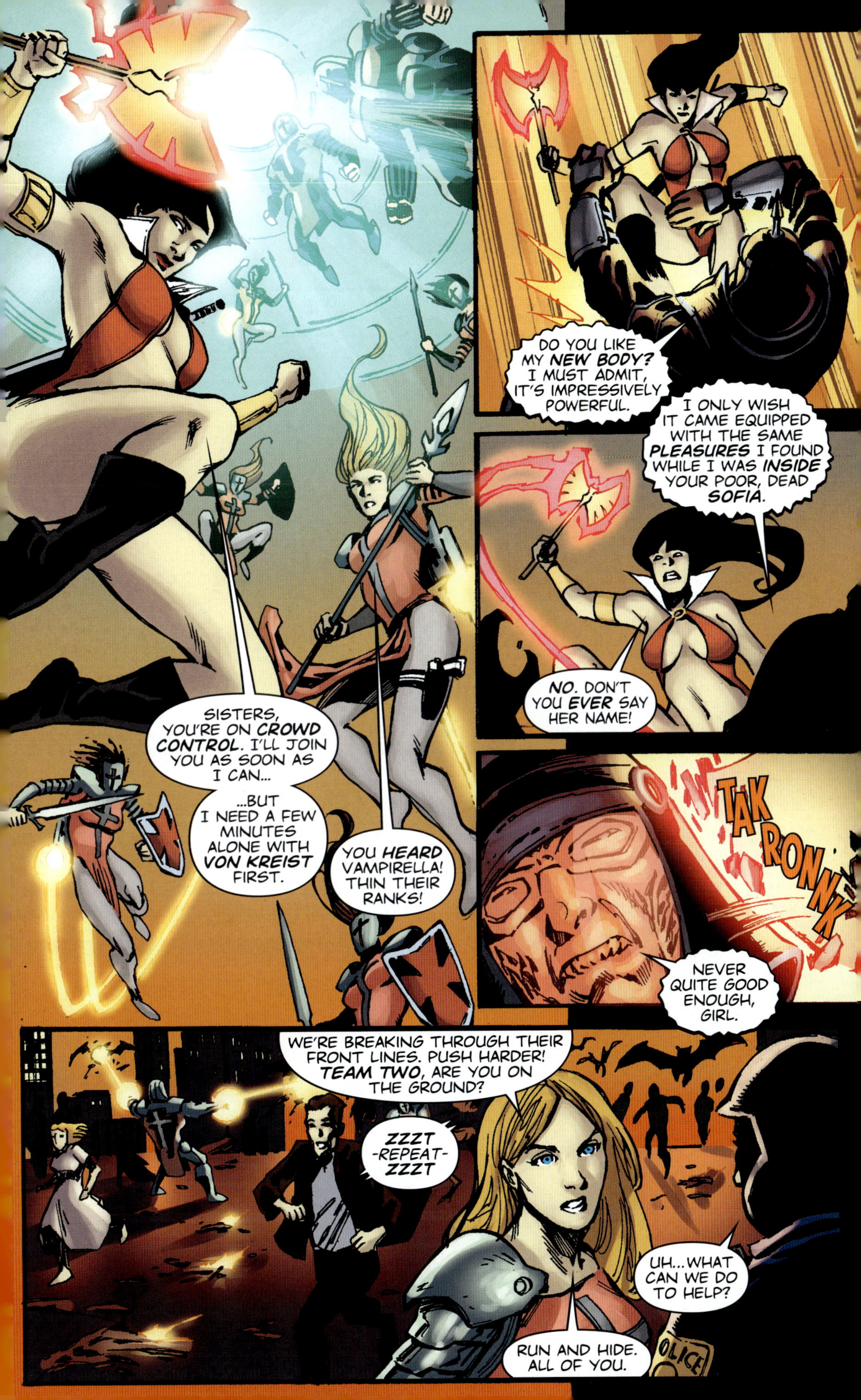
SISTERS, YOU'RE ON CROWD CONTROL. I'LL JOIN YOU AS SOON AS I CAN...
...BUT I NEED A FEW MINUTES ALONE WITH VON KREIST FIRST.
YOU HEARD VAMPIRELLA! THIN THEIR RANKS!
DO YOU LIKE MY NEW BODY? I MUST ADMIT, IT'S IMPRESSIVELY POWERFUL.
I ONLY WISH IT CAME EQUIPPED WITH THE SAME PLEASURES I FOUND WHILE I WAS INSIDE YOUR POOR, DEAD SOFIA.
NO. DON'T YOU EVER SAY HER NAME!
TAK RONNK
NEVER QUITE GOOD ENOUGH, GIRL.
WE'RE BREAKING THROUGH THEIR FRONT LINES. PUSH HARDER! TEAM TWO, ARE YOU ON THE GROUND?
ZZZT -REPEAT- ZZZT
UH...WHAT CAN WE DO TO HELP?
RUN AND HIDE. ALL OF YOU.

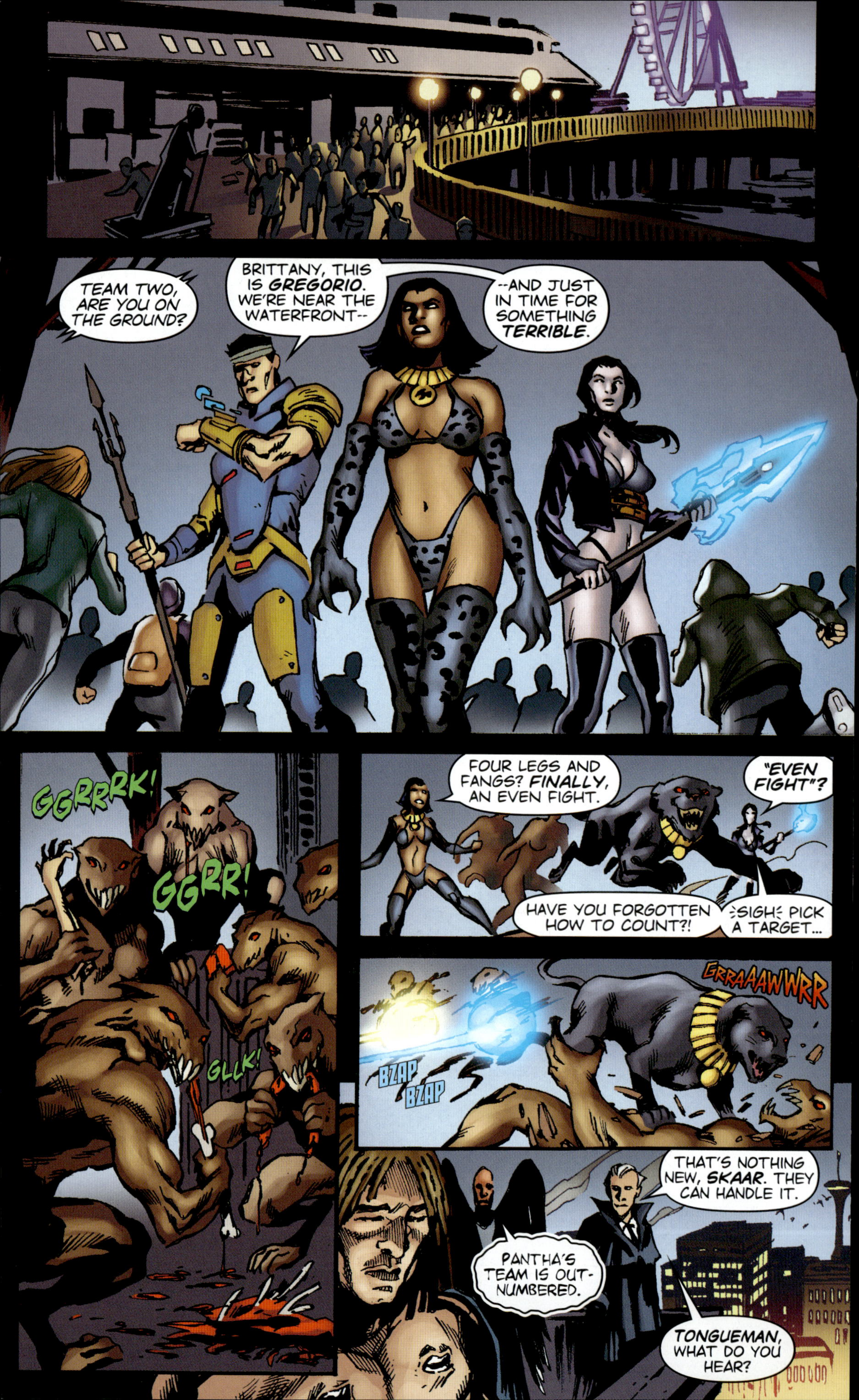
TEAM TWO, ARE YOU ON THE GROUND?
BRITTANY, THIS IS GREGORIO. WE'RE NEAR THE WATERFRONT--
--AND JUST IN TIME FOR SOMETHING TERRIBLE.
GGRRRK!
GGRR!
GLLK!
FOUR LEGS AND FANGS? FINALLY, AN EVEN FIGHT.
"EVEN FIGHT"?
HAVE YOU FORGOTTEN HOW TO COUNT?!
SIGH PICK A TARGET...
GRRAAAWWRR
BZAP
BZAP
THAT'S NOTHING NEW, SKAAR. THEY CAN HANDLE IT.
PANTHA'S TEAM IS OUT-NUMBERED.
TONGUEMAN, WHAT DO YOU HEAR?

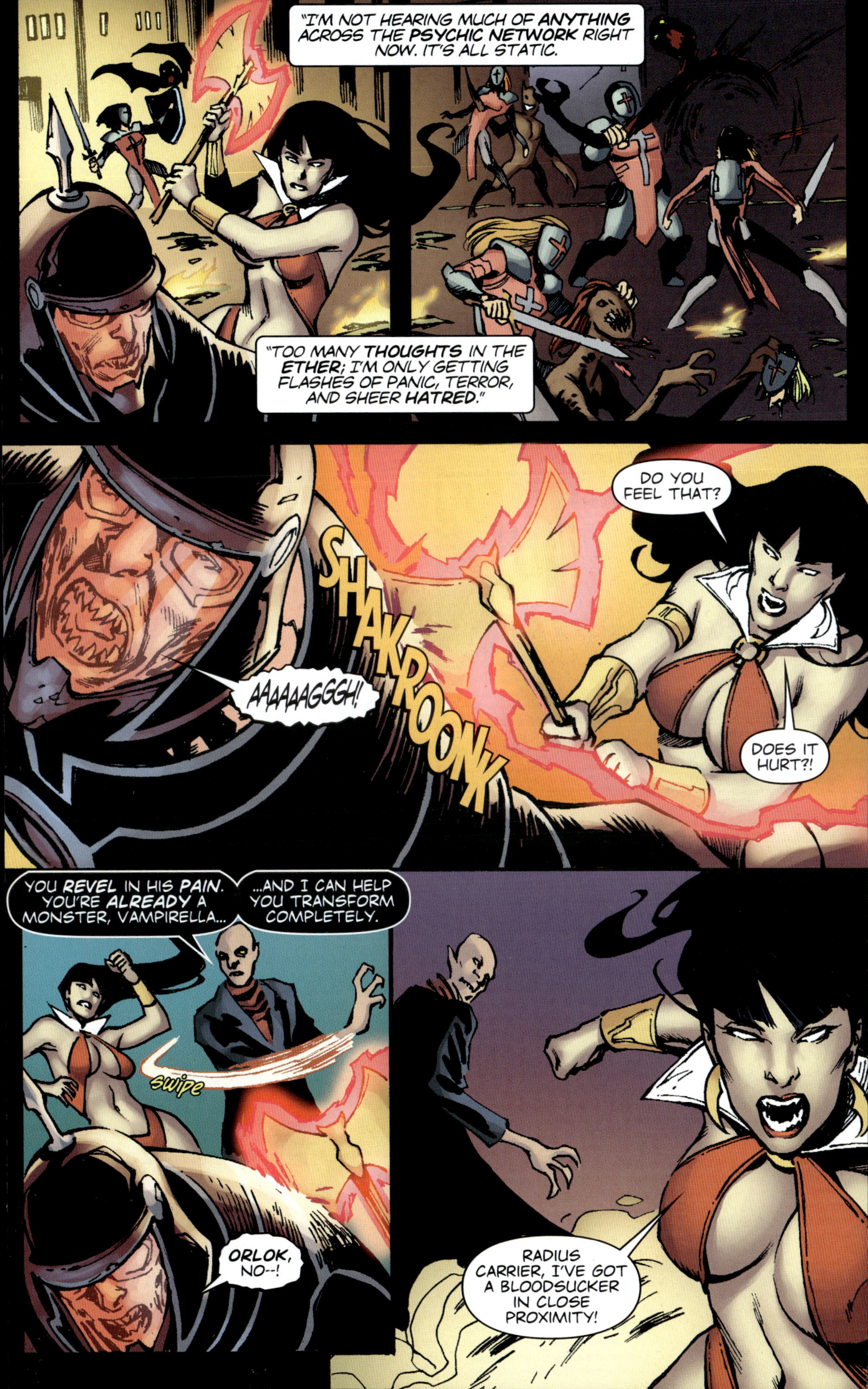
"I'M NOT HEARING MUCH OF ANYTHING ACROSS THE PSYCHIC NETWORK RIGHT NOW. IT'S ALL STATIC.
"TOO MANY THOUGHTS IN THE ETHER; I'M ONLY GETTING FLASHES OF PANIC, TERROR, AND SHEER HATRED."
DO YOU FEEL THAT?
SHAKROONK
AAAAAAGGGH!
DOES IT HURT?!
YOU REVEL IN HIS PAIN. YOU'RE ALREADY A MONSTER, VAMPIRELLA...
...AND I CAN HELP YOU TRANSFORM COMPLETELY.
swipe
ORLOK, NO--!
RADIUS CARRIER, I'VE GOT A BLOODSUCKER IN CLOSE PROXIMITY!

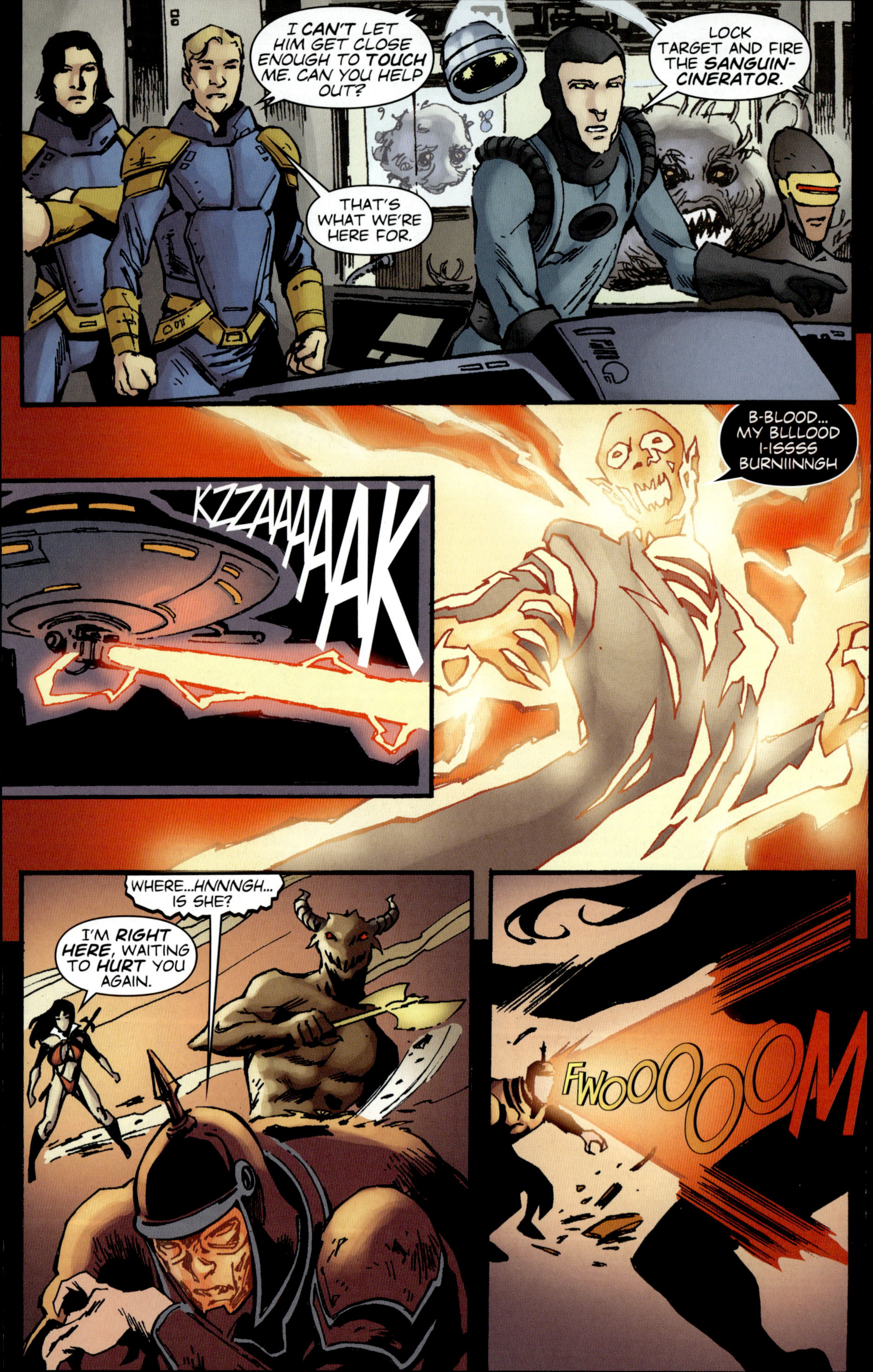

I **CAN'T** LET HIM GET CLOSE ENOUGH TO **TOUCH** ME. CAN YOU HELP OUT?
THAT'S WHAT WE'RE HERE FOR.
LOCK TARGET AND FIRE THE **SANGUIN-CINERATOR**.
KZZAAAAAAK
B-BLOOD... MY BLLLOOD I-ISSSS BURNIINNGH
WHERE...HNNNGH... IS SHE?
I'M **RIGHT HERE**, WAITING TO **HURT** YOU AGAIN.
FWOOOOOOM

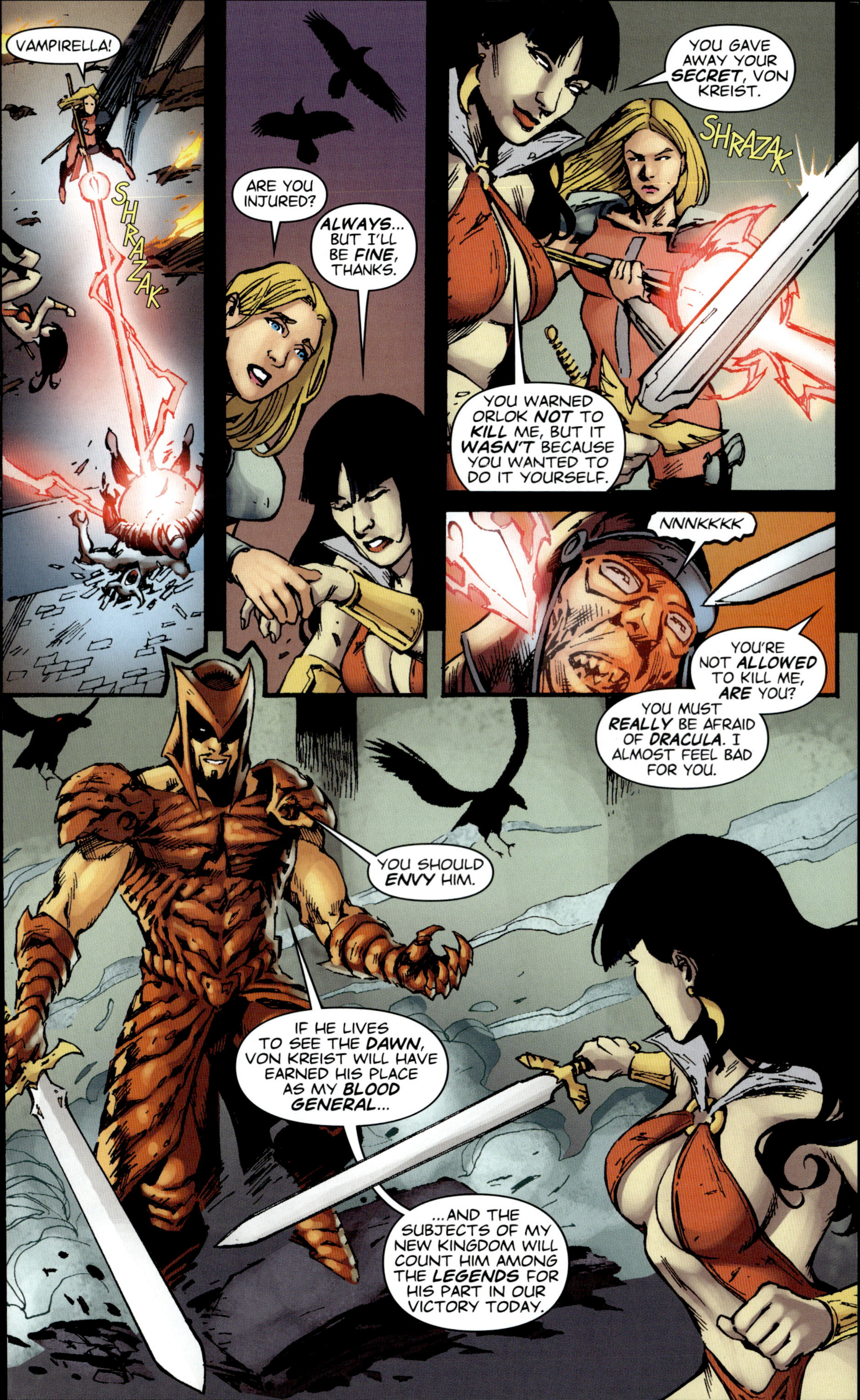
VAMPIRELLA!
SHRAZAK
ARE YOU INJURED?
ALWAYS... BUT I'LL BE FINE, THANKS.
YOU GAVE AWAY YOUR SECRET, VON KREIST.
SHRAZAK
YOU WARNED ORLOK NOT TO KILL ME, BUT IT WASN'T BECAUSE YOU WANTED TO DO IT YOURSELF.
NNNKKKK
YOU'RE NOT ALLOWED TO KILL ME, ARE YOU?
YOU MUST REALLY BE AFRAID OF DRACULA. I ALMOST FEEL BAD FOR YOU.
YOU SHOULD ENVY HIM.
IF HE LIVES TO SEE THE DAWN, VON KREIST WILL HAVE EARNED HIS PLACE AS MY BLOOD GENERAL...
...AND THE SUBJECTS OF MY NEW KINGDOM WILL COUNT HIM AMONG THE LEGENDS FOR HIS PART IN OUR VICTORY TODAY.

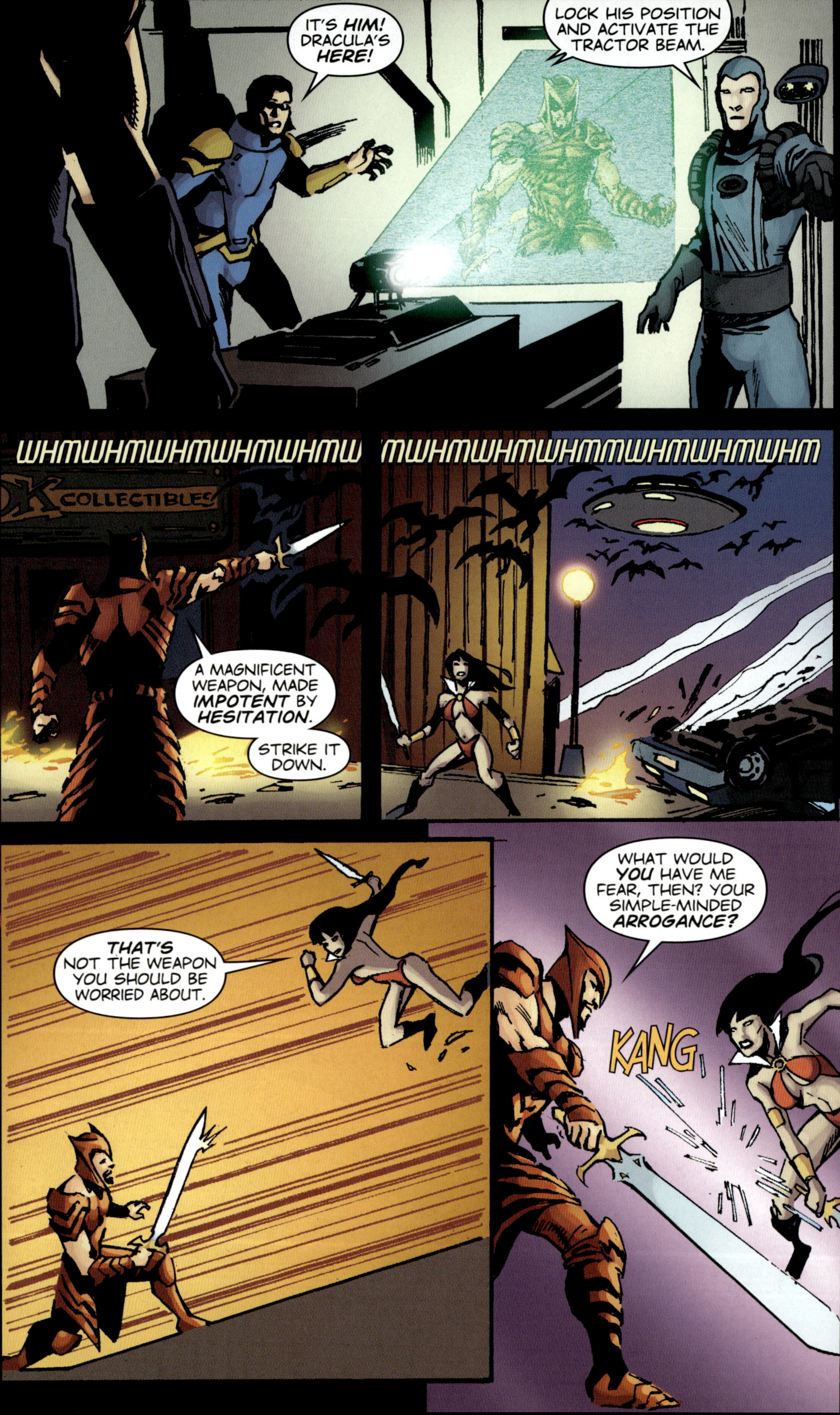
IT'S HIM! DRACULA'S HERE!
LOCK HIS POSITION AND ACTIVATE THE TRACTOR BEAM.
WHMWHMWHMWHMWHMWHMWHMWHMWHMWHMWHMWHM
COLLECTIBLES
A MAGNIFICENT WEAPON, MADE IMPOTENT BY HESITATION.
STRIKE IT DOWN.
THAT'S NOT THE WEAPON YOU SHOULD BE WORRIED ABOUT.
WHAT WOULD YOU HAVE ME FEAR, THEN? YOUR SIMPLE-MINDED ARROGANCE?
KANG

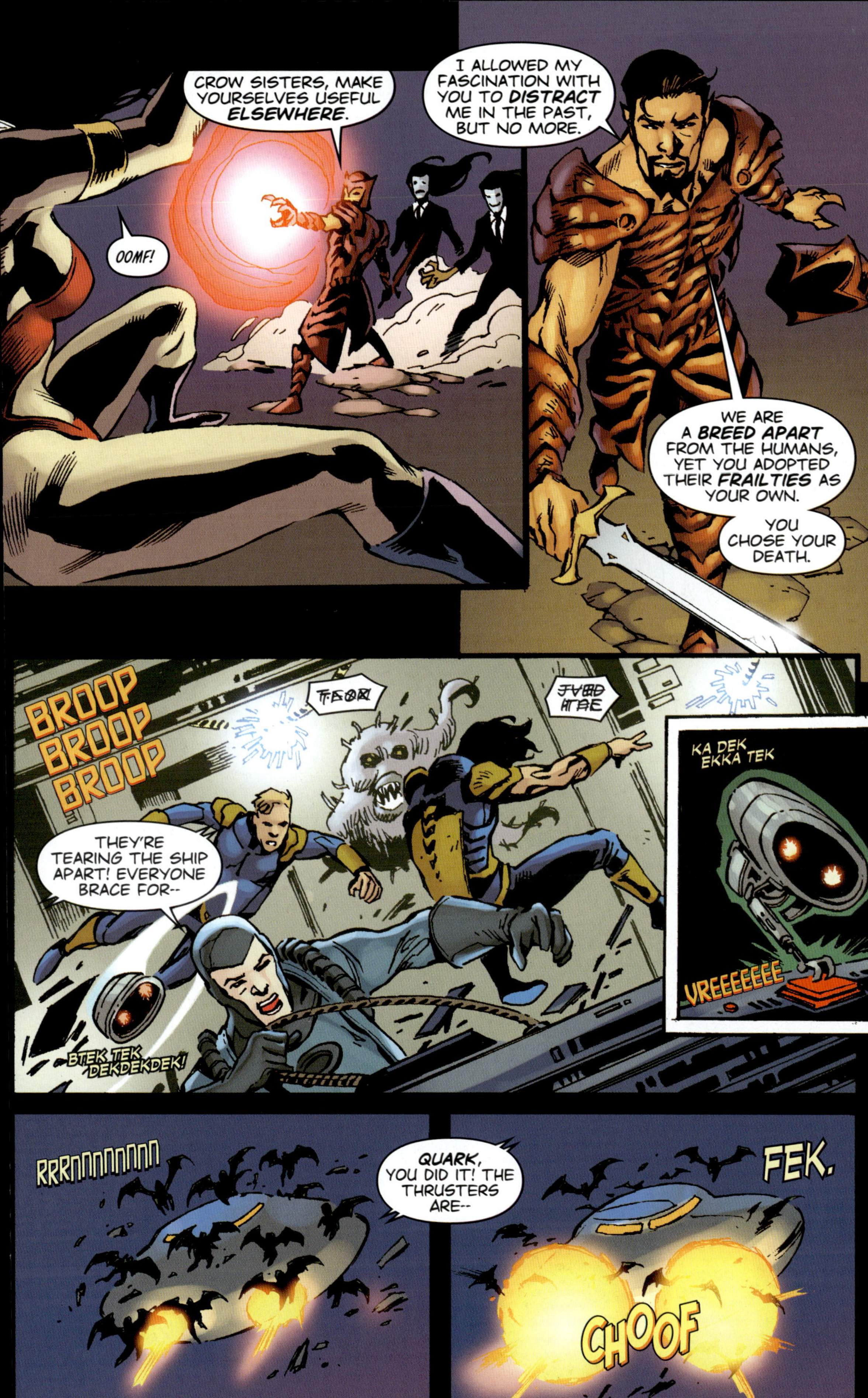
CROW SISTERS, MAKE YOURSELVES USEFUL ELSEWHERE.
OOMF!
I ALLOWED MY FASCINATION WITH YOU TO DISTRACT ME IN THE PAST, BUT NO MORE.
WE ARE A BREED APART FROM THE HUMANS, YET YOU ADOPTED THEIR FRAILTIES AS YOUR OWN.
YOU CHOSE YOUR DEATH.
BROOP BROOP BROOP
THEY'RE TEARING THE SHIP APART! EVERYONE BRACE FOR--
BTEK TEK DEKDEKDEK!
KA DEK EKKA TEK
VREEEEEEE
RRRnnnnnnnn
QUARK, YOU DID IT! THE THRUSTERS ARE--
FEK.
CHOOF

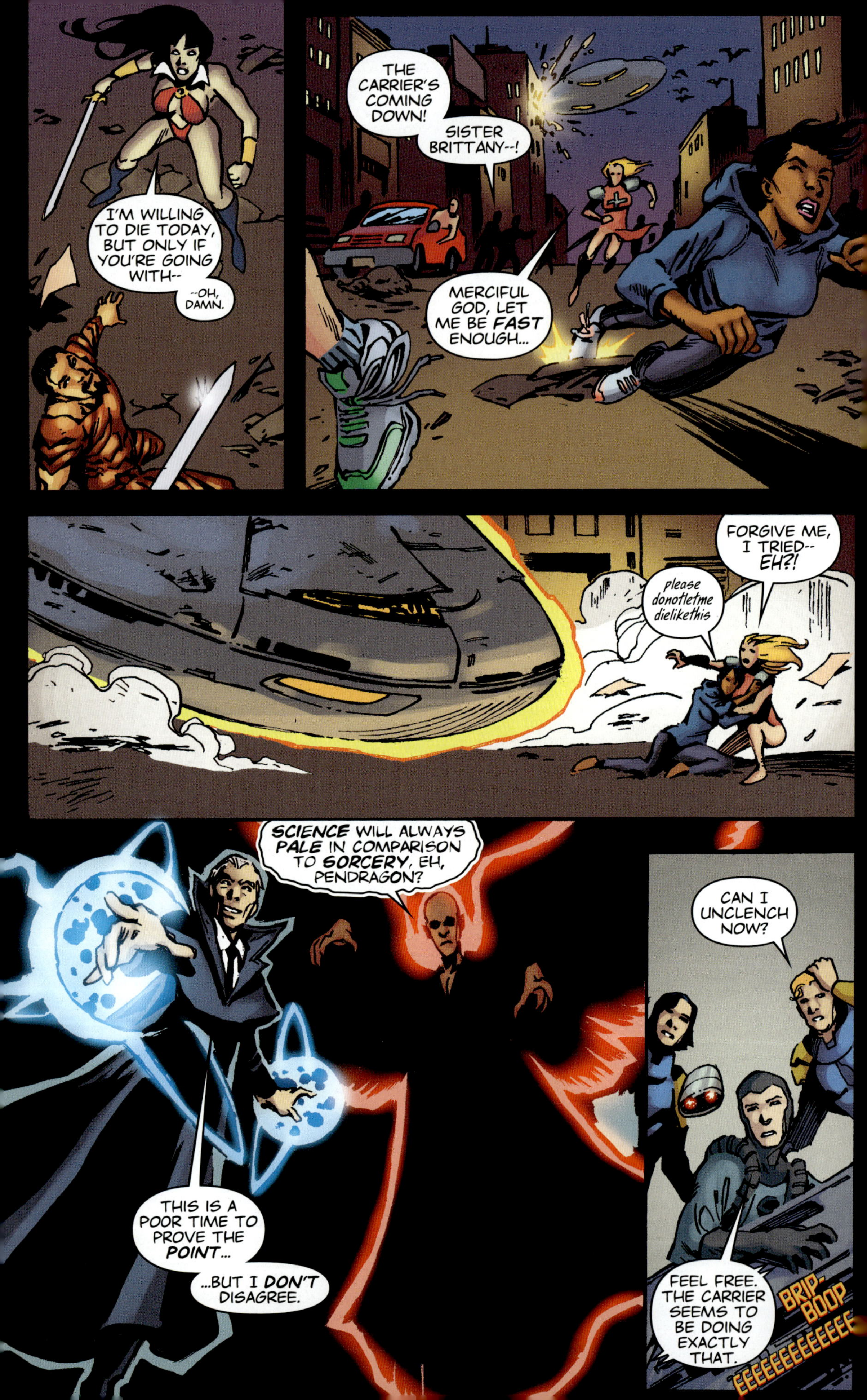
I'M WILLING TO DIE TODAY, BUT ONLY IF YOU'RE GOING WITH--
--OH, DAMN.
THE CARRIER'S COMING DOWN!
SISTER BRITTANY--!
MERCIFUL GOD, LET ME BE **FAST** ENOUGH...
FORGIVE ME, I TRIED-- **EH?!**
please donotletme dielikethis
SCIENCE WILL ALWAYS **PALE** IN COMPARISON TO **SORCERY**, EH, PENDRAGON?
THIS IS A POOR TIME TO PROVE THE **POINT**...
...BUT I **DON'T** DISAGREE.
CAN I UNCLENCH NOW?
FEEL FREE. THE CARRIER SEEMS TO BE DOING EXACTLY THAT.
BRIP-BOOP
EEEEEEEEEEEE

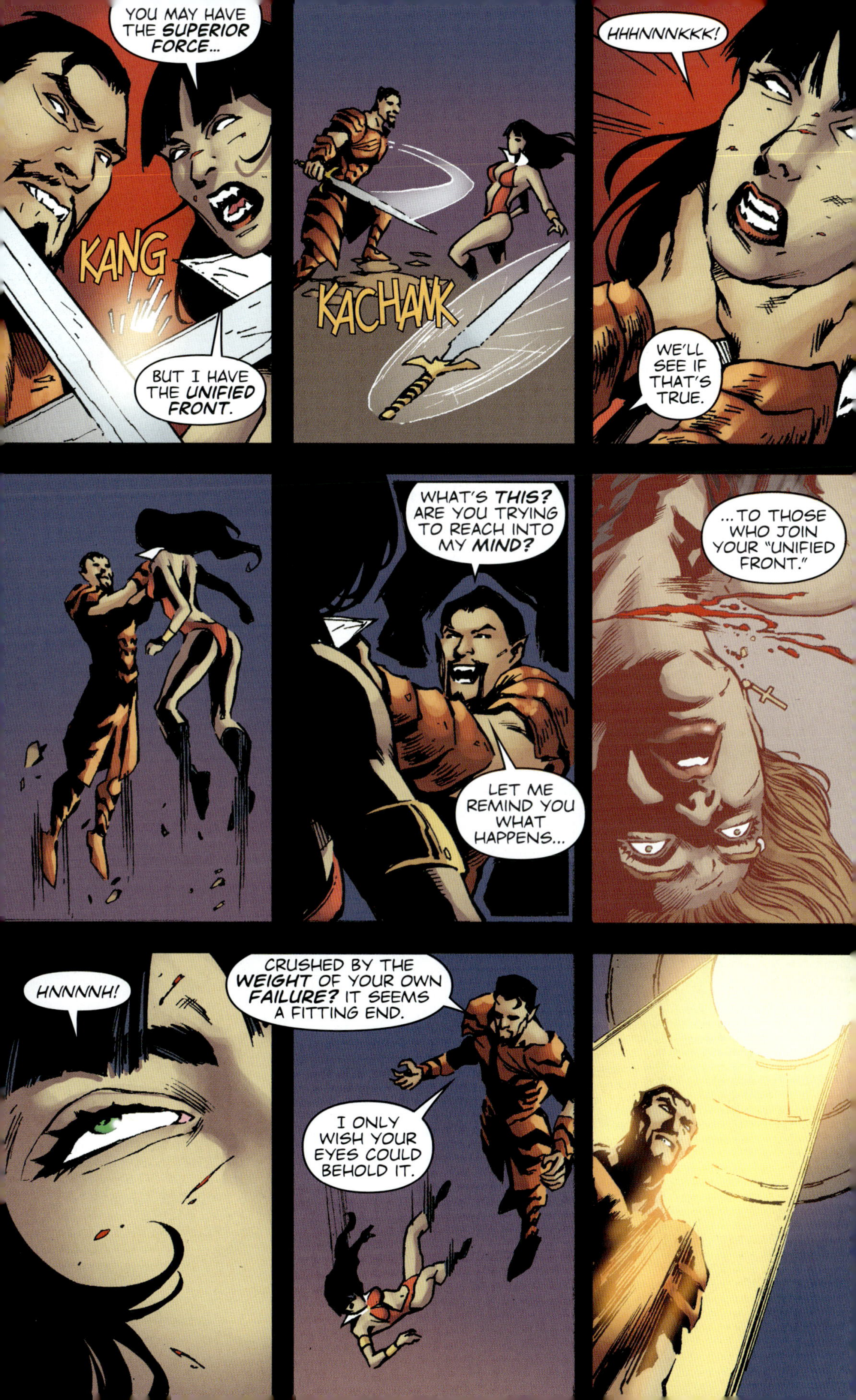
YOU MAY HAVE THE SUPERIOR FORCE...
KANG
BUT I HAVE THE UNIFIED FRONT.
KACHANK
HHHNNNKKK!
WE'LL SEE IF THAT'S TRUE.
WHAT'S THIS? ARE YOU TRYING TO REACH INTO MY MIND?
LET ME REMIND YOU WHAT HAPPENS...
...TO THOSE WHO JOIN YOUR "UNIFIED FRONT."
HNNNNH!
CRUSHED BY THE WEIGHT OF YOUR OWN FAILURE? IT SEEMS A FITTING END.
I ONLY WISH YOUR EYES COULD BEHOLD IT.

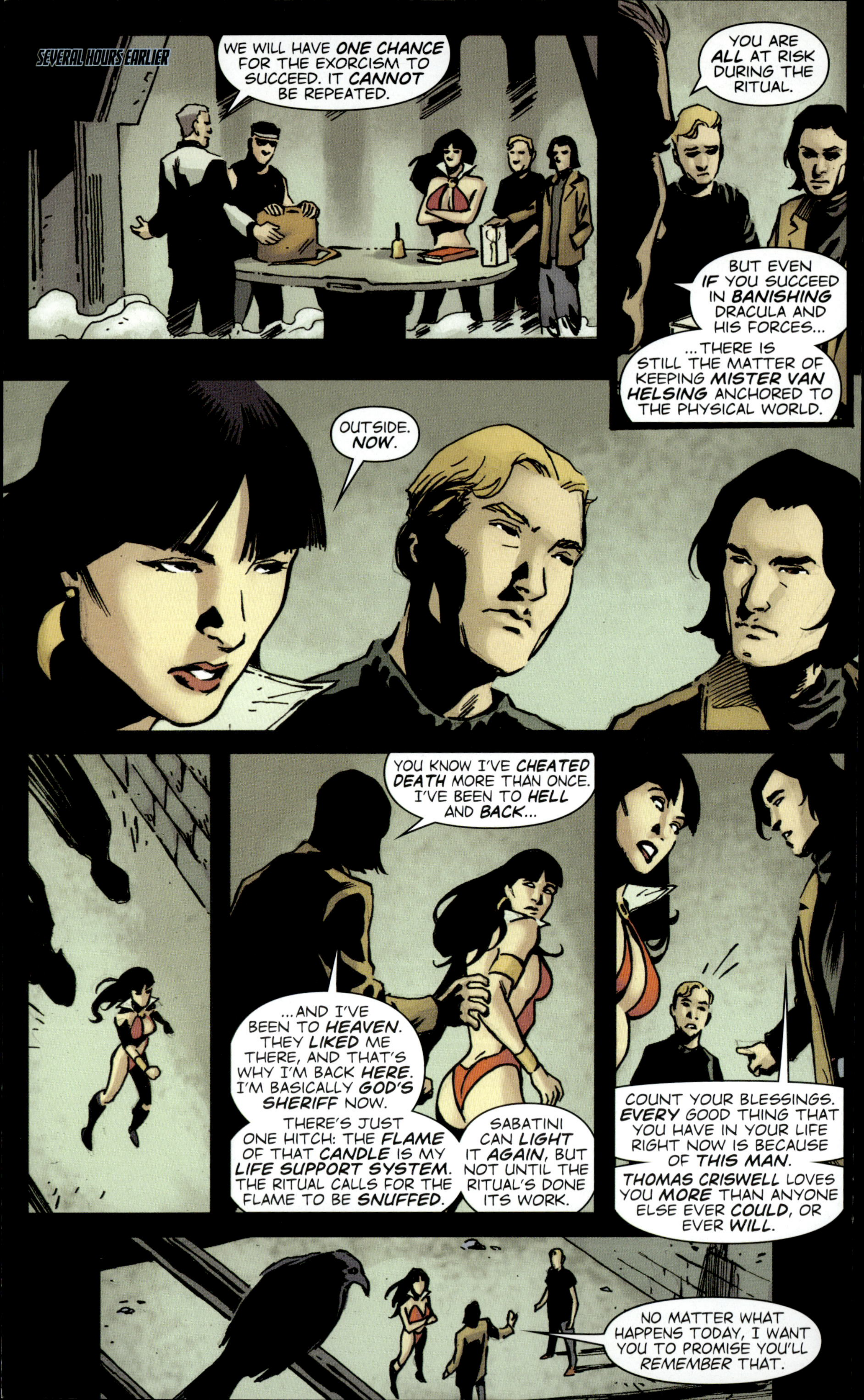
SEVERAL HOURS EARLIER
WE WILL HAVE ONE CHANCE FOR THE EXORCISM TO SUCCEED. IT CANNOT BE REPEATED.
YOU ARE ALL AT RISK DURING THE RITUAL.
BUT EVEN IF YOU SUCCEED IN BANISHING DRACULA AND HIS FORCES...
...THERE IS STILL THE MATTER OF KEEPING MISTER VAN HELSING ANCHORED TO THE PHYSICAL WORLD.
OUTSIDE. NOW.
YOU KNOW I'VE CHEATED DEATH MORE THAN ONCE. I'VE BEEN TO HELL AND BACK...
...AND I'VE BEEN TO HEAVEN. THEY LIKED ME THERE, AND THAT'S WHY I'M BACK HERE. I'M BASICALLY GOD'S SHERIFF NOW.
THERE'S JUST ONE HITCH: THE FLAME OF THAT CANDLE IS MY LIFE SUPPORT SYSTEM. THE RITUAL CALLS FOR THE FLAME TO BE SNUFFED.
SABATINI CAN LIGHT IT AGAIN, BUT NOT UNTIL THE RITUAL'S DONE ITS WORK.
COUNT YOUR BLESSINGS. EVERY GOOD THING THAT YOU HAVE IN YOUR LIFE RIGHT NOW IS BECAUSE OF THIS MAN.
THOMAS CRISWELL LOVES YOU MORE THAN ANYONE ELSE EVER COULD, OR EVER WILL.
NO MATTER WHAT HAPPENS TODAY, I WANT YOU TO PROMISE YOU'LL REMEMBER THAT.

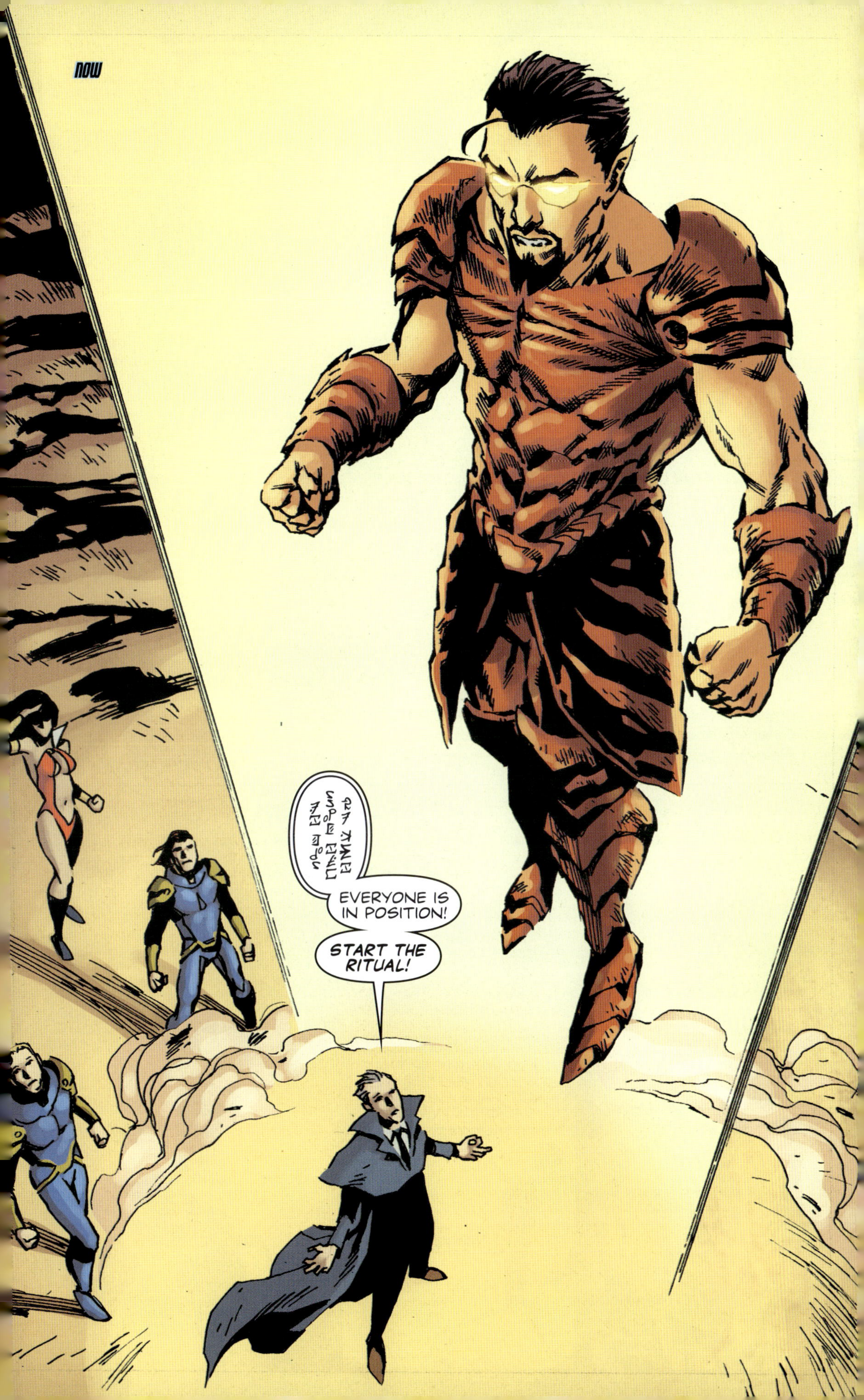
NOW
EVERYONE IS IN POSITION!
START THE RITUAL!

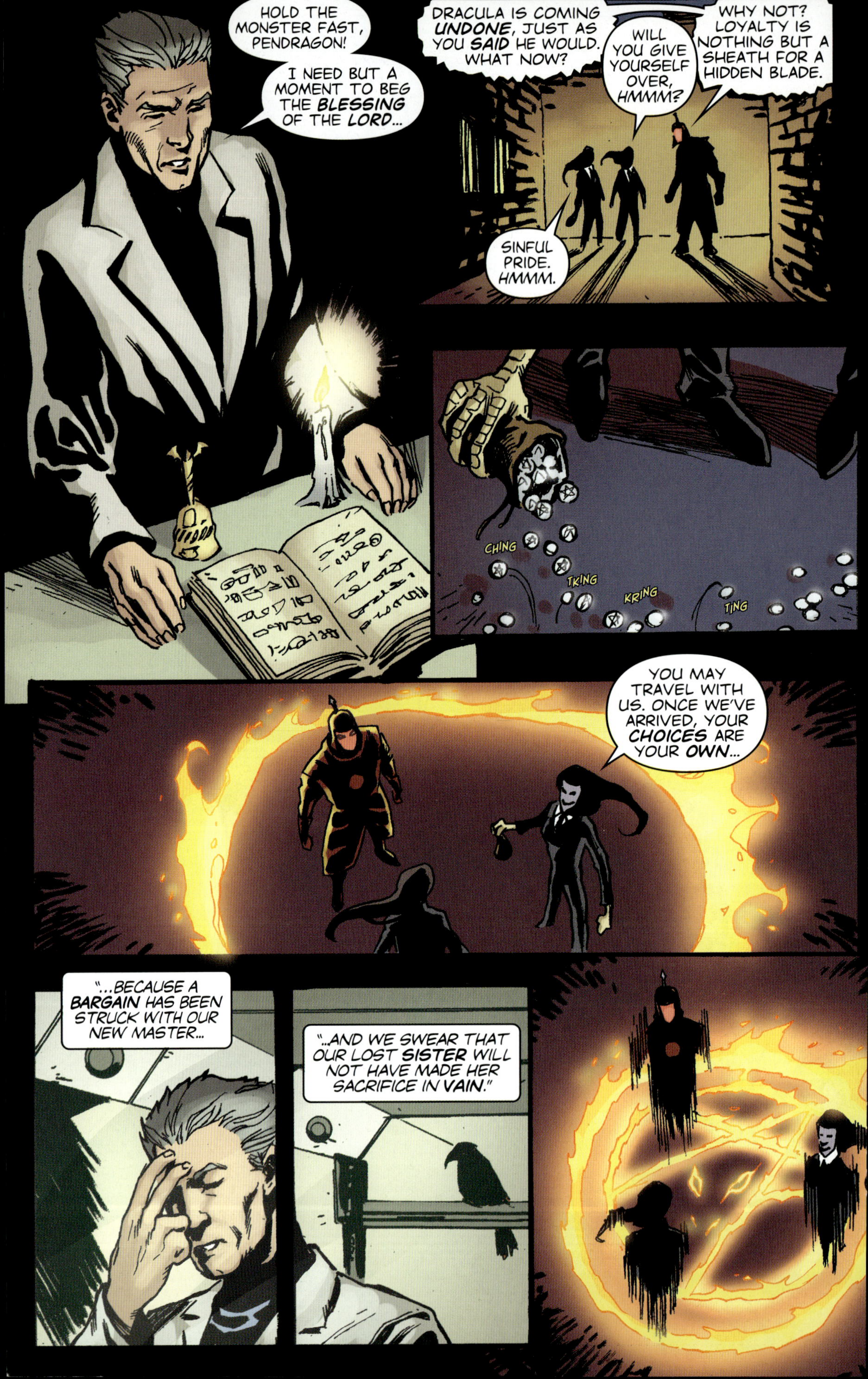
HOLD THE MONSTER FAST, PENDRAGON!
I NEED BUT A MOMENT TO BEG THE BLESSING OF THE LORD...
DRACULA IS COMING UNDONE, JUST AS YOU SAID HE WOULD. WHAT NOW?
WILL YOU GIVE YOURSELF OVER, HMMM?
WHY NOT? LOYALTY IS NOTHING BUT A SHEATH FOR A HIDDEN BLADE.
SINFUL PRIDE. HMMM.
CHING
TKING
KRING
TING
YOU MAY TRAVEL WITH US. ONCE WE'VE ARRIVED, YOUR CHOICES ARE YOUR OWN...
"...BECAUSE A BARGAIN HAS BEEN STRUCK WITH OUR NEW MASTER...
"...AND WE SWEAR THAT OUR LOST SISTER WILL NOT HAVE MADE HER SACRIFICE IN VAIN."

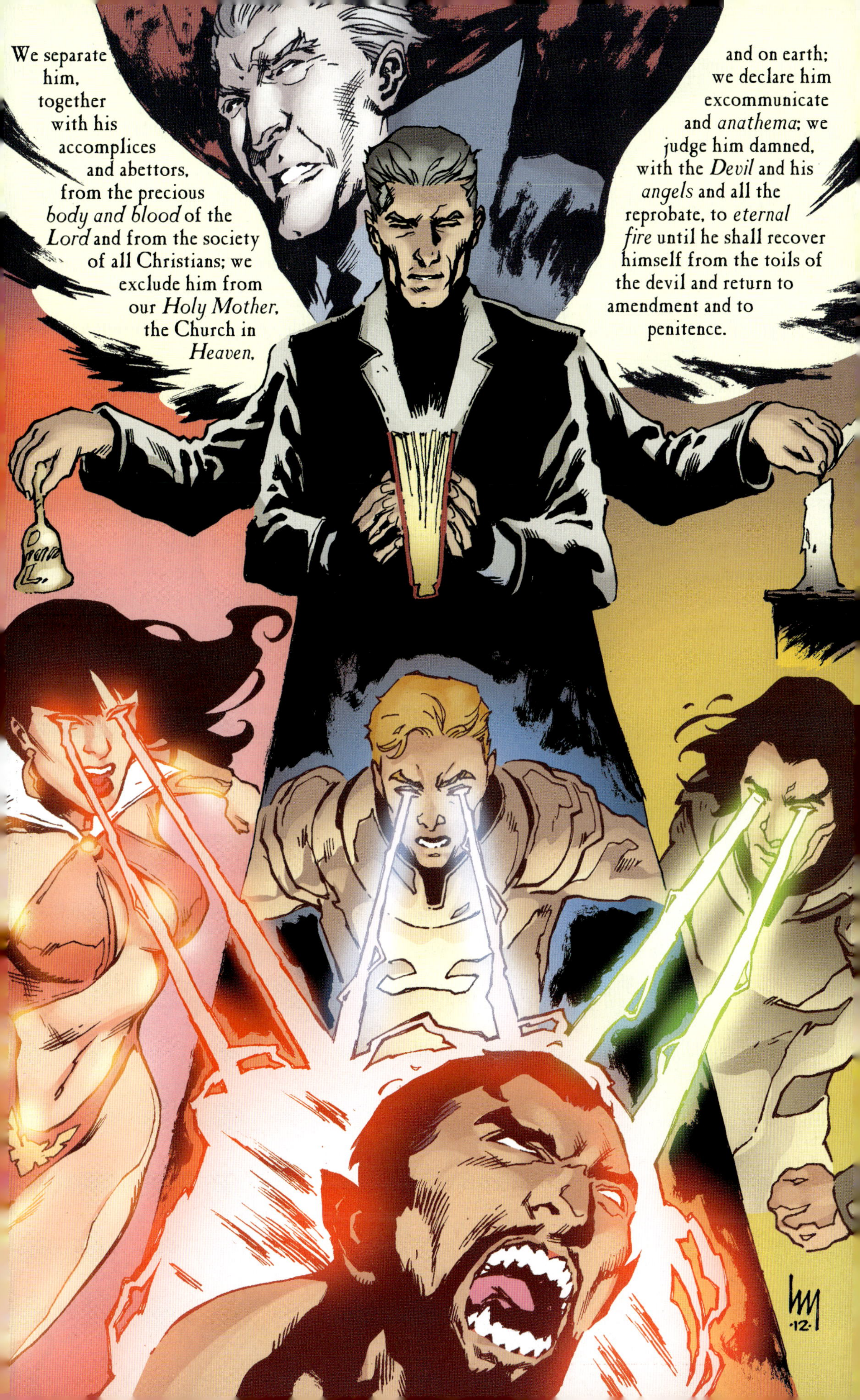

We separate him, together with his accomplices and abettors, from the precious *body and blood* of the *Lord* and from the society of all Christians; we exclude him from our *Holy Mother*, the Church in *Heaven*,
and on earth; we declare him excommunicate and *anathema*; we judge him damned, with the *Devil* and his *angels* and all the reprobate, to *eternal fire* until he shall recover himself from the toils of the devil and return to amendment and to penitence.

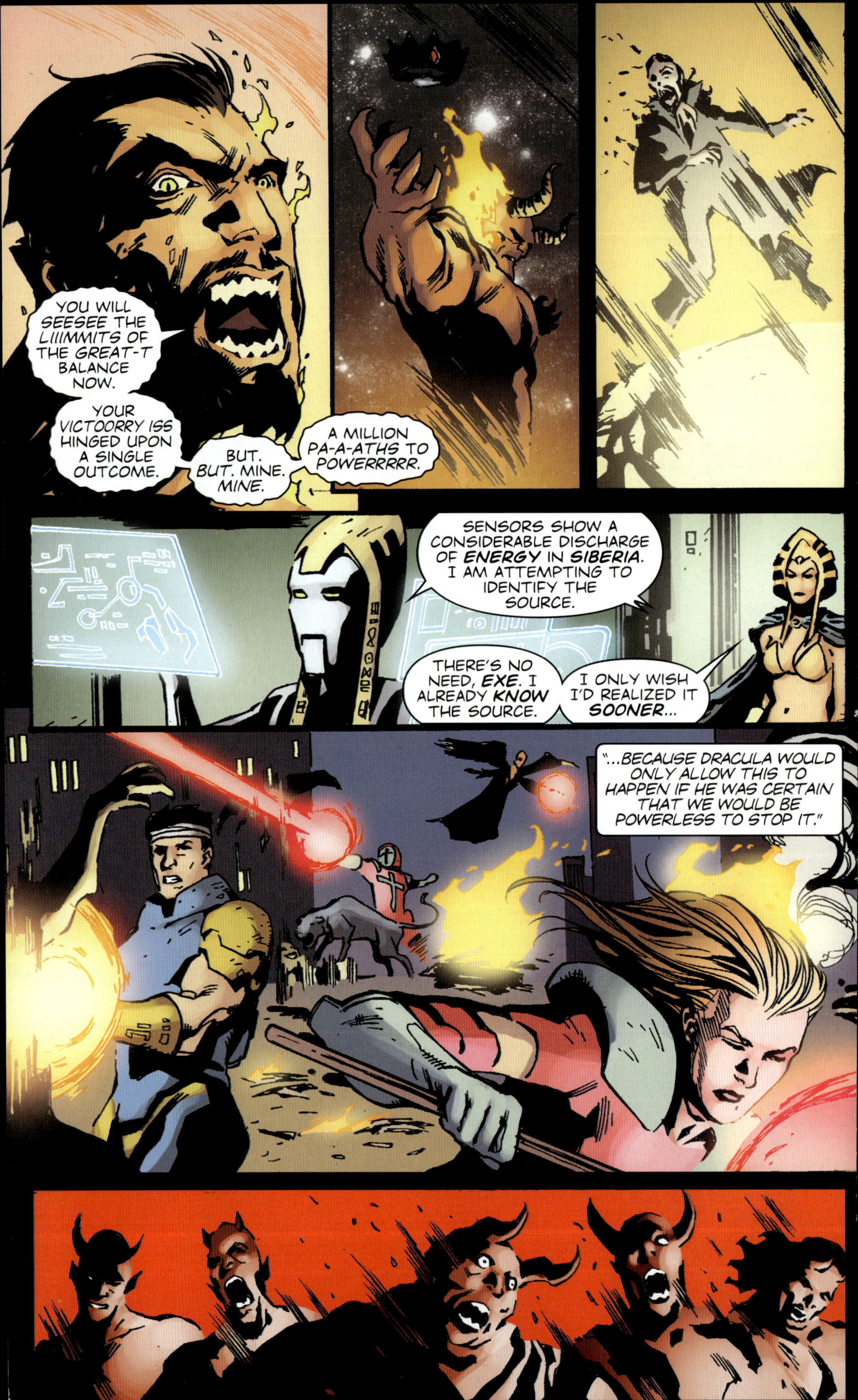
YOU WILL SEESEE THE LIIIMMITS OF THE GREAT-T BALANCE NOW.
YOUR VICTOORRY ISS HINGED UPON A SINGLE OUTCOME.
BUT. BUT. MINE. MINE.
A MILLION PA-A-ATHS TO POWERRRRR.
SENSORS SHOW A CONSIDERABLE DISCHARGE OF ENERGY IN SIBERIA. I AM ATTEMPTING TO IDENTIFY THE SOURCE.
THERE'S NO NEED, EXE. I ALREADY KNOW THE SOURCE.
I ONLY WISH I'D REALIZED IT SOONER...
"...BECAUSE DRACULA WOULD ONLY ALLOW THIS TO HAPPEN IF HE WAS CERTAIN THAT WE WOULD BE POWERLESS TO STOP IT."

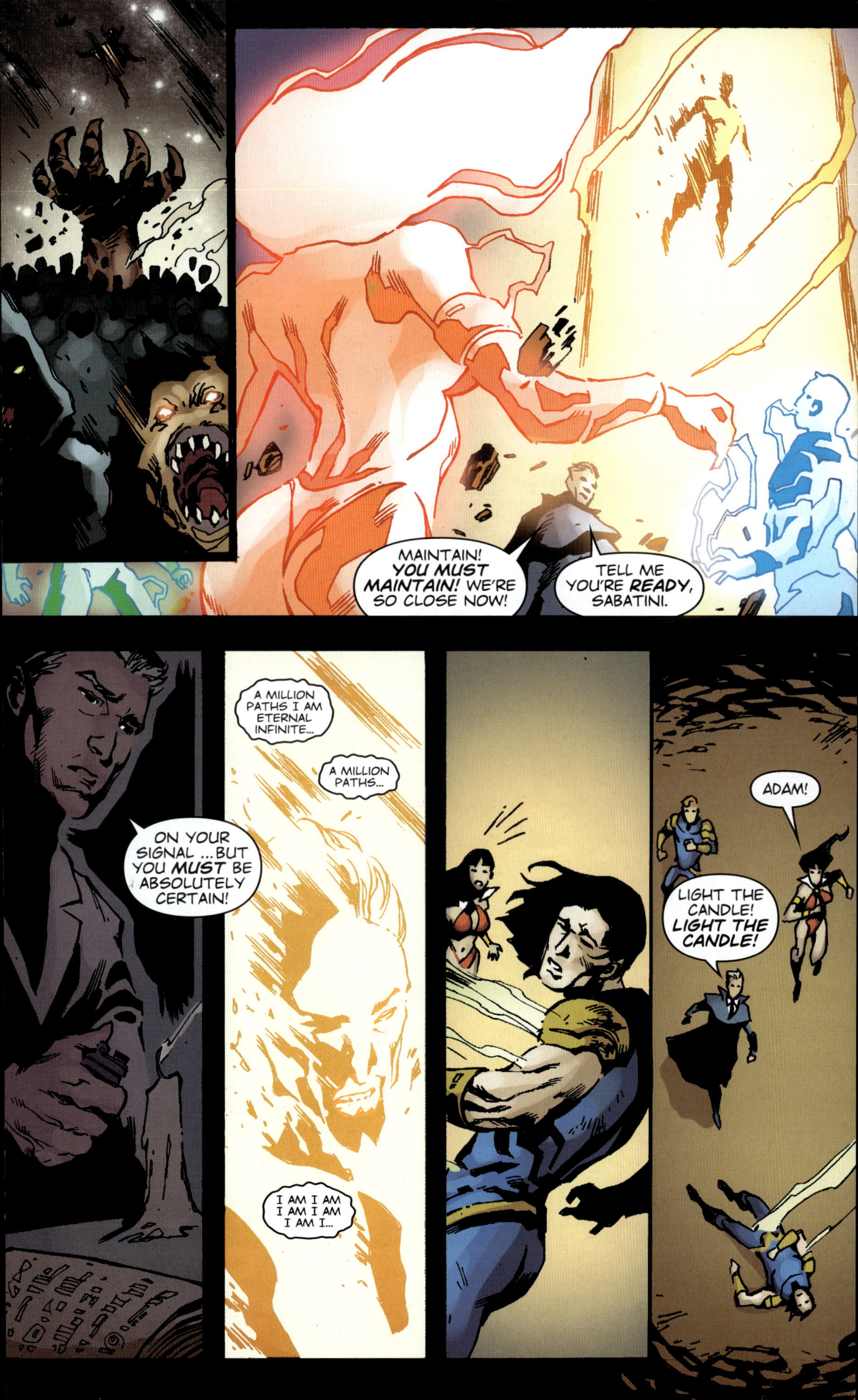
MAINTAIN! YOU MUST MAINTAIN! WE'RE SO CLOSE NOW!
TELL ME YOU'RE READY, SABATINI.
ON YOUR SIGNAL ...BUT YOU MUST BE ABSOLUTELY CERTAIN!
A MILLION PATHS I AM ETERNAL INFINITE...
A MILLION PATHS...
I AM I AM I AM I AM I AM I...
ADAM!
LIGHT THE CANDLE! LIGHT THE CANDLE!

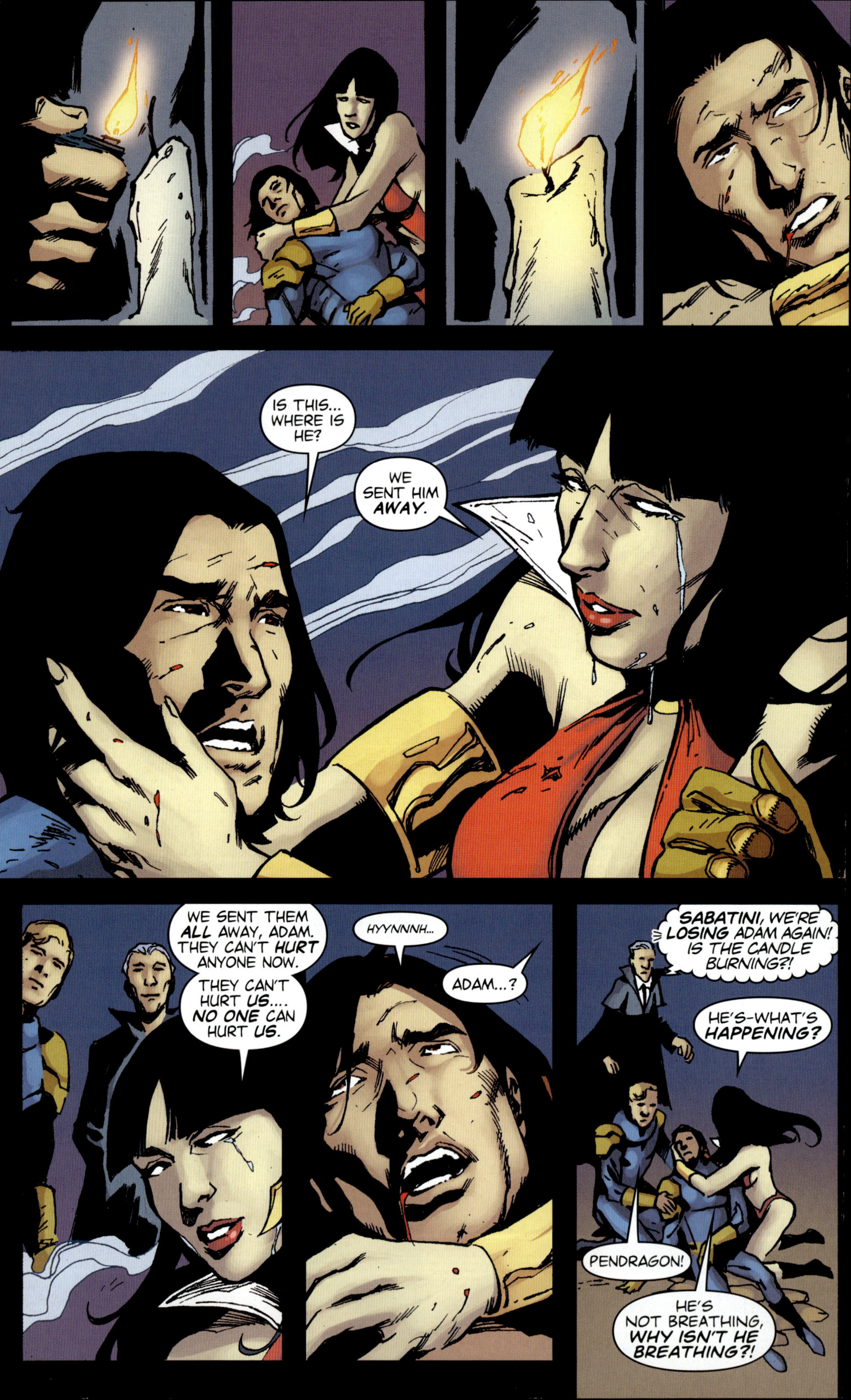
IS THIS... WHERE IS HE?
WE SENT HIM **AWAY**.
WE SENT THEM **ALL** AWAY, ADAM. THEY CAN'T **HURT** ANYONE NOW.
THEY CAN'T HURT **US**.... **NO ONE** CAN HURT **US**.
HYYNNNH...
ADAM...?
SABATINI, WE'RE **LOSING** ADAM AGAIN! IS THE CANDLE BURNING?!
HE'S-WHAT'S **HAPPENING**?
PENDRAGON!
HE'S NOT BREATHING, **WHY ISN'T HE BREATHING?!**

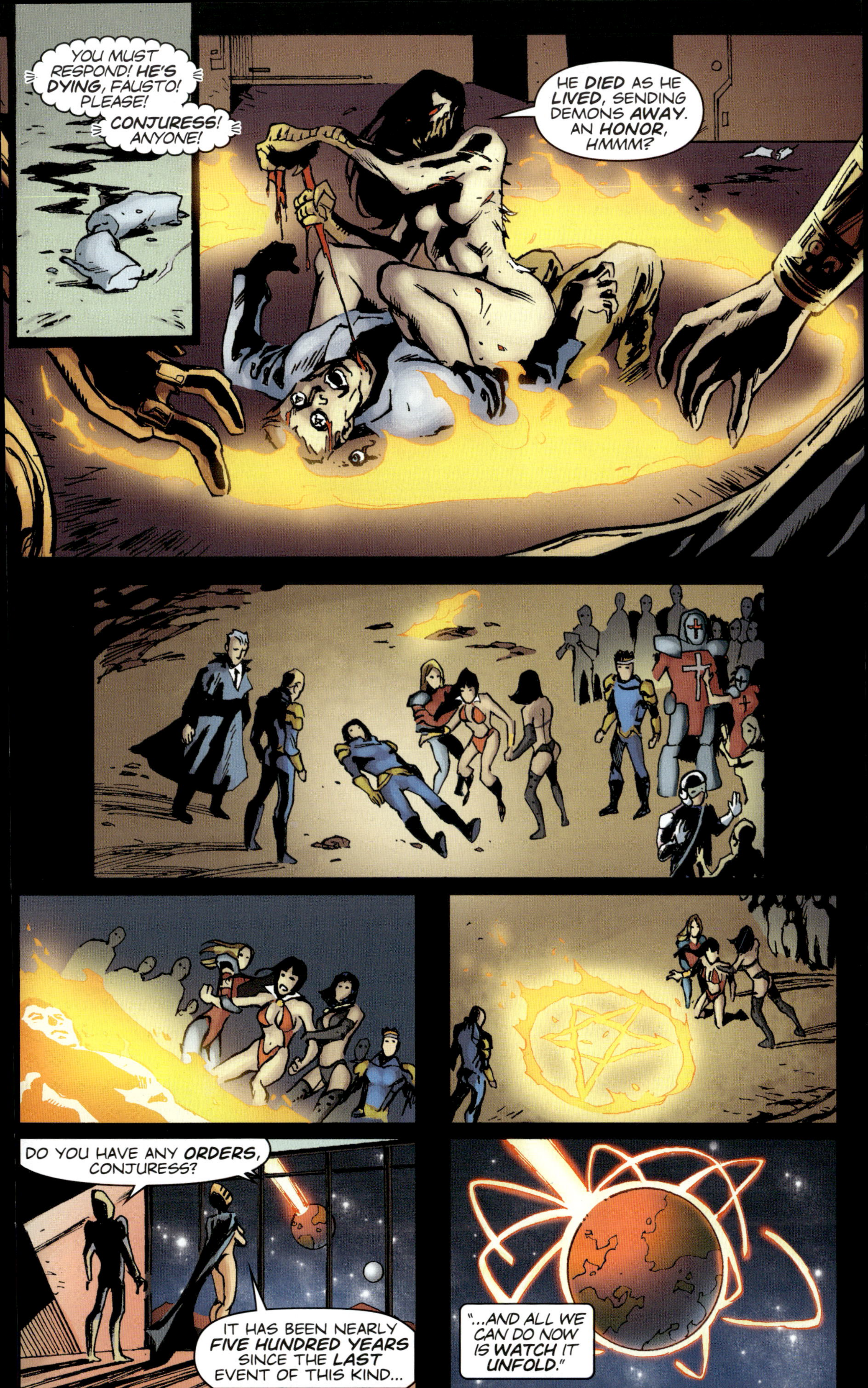
YOU MUST RESPOND! HE'S DYING, FAUSTO! PLEASE!
CONJURESS! ANYONE!
HE DIED AS HE LIVED, SENDING DEMONS AWAY. AN HONOR, HMMM?
DO YOU HAVE ANY ORDERS, CONJURESS?
IT HAS BEEN NEARLY FIVE HUNDRED YEARS SINCE THE LAST EVENT OF THIS KIND...
"...AND ALL WE CAN DO NOW IS WATCH IT UNFOLD."

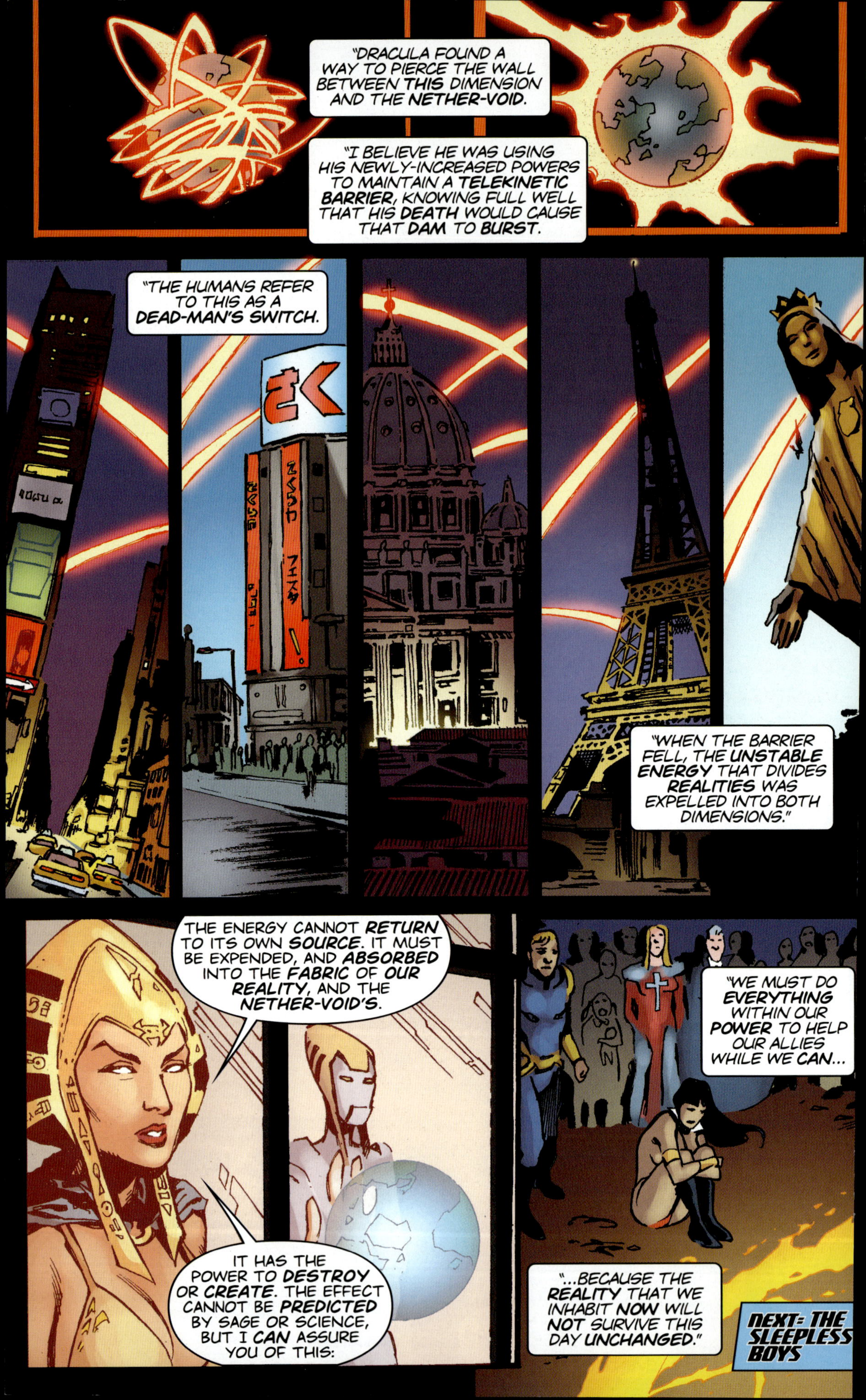
"DRACULA FOUND A WAY TO PIERCE THE WALL BETWEEN THIS DIMENSION AND THE NETHER-VOID.
"I BELIEVE HE WAS USING HIS NEWLY-INCREASED POWERS TO MAINTAIN A TELEKINETIC BARRIER, KNOWING FULL WELL THAT HIS DEATH WOULD CAUSE THAT DAM TO BURST.
"THE HUMANS REFER TO THIS AS A DEAD-MAN'S SWITCH.
さく
"WHEN THE BARRIER FELL, THE UNSTABLE ENERGY THAT DIVIDES REALITIES WAS EXPELLED INTO BOTH DIMENSIONS."
THE ENERGY CANNOT RETURN TO ITS OWN SOURCE. IT MUST BE EXPENDED, AND ABSORBED INTO THE FABRIC OF OUR REALITY, AND THE NETHER-VOID'S.
IT HAS THE POWER TO DESTROY OR CREATE. THE EFFECT CANNOT BE PREDICTED BY SAGE OR SCIENCE, BUT I CAN ASSURE YOU OF THIS:
"WE MUST DO EVERYTHING WITHIN OUR POWER TO HELP OUR ALLIES WHILE WE CAN...
"...BECAUSE THE REALITY THAT WE INHABIT NOW WILL NOT SURVIVE THIS DAY UNCHANGED."
NEXT: THE SLEEPLESS BOYS

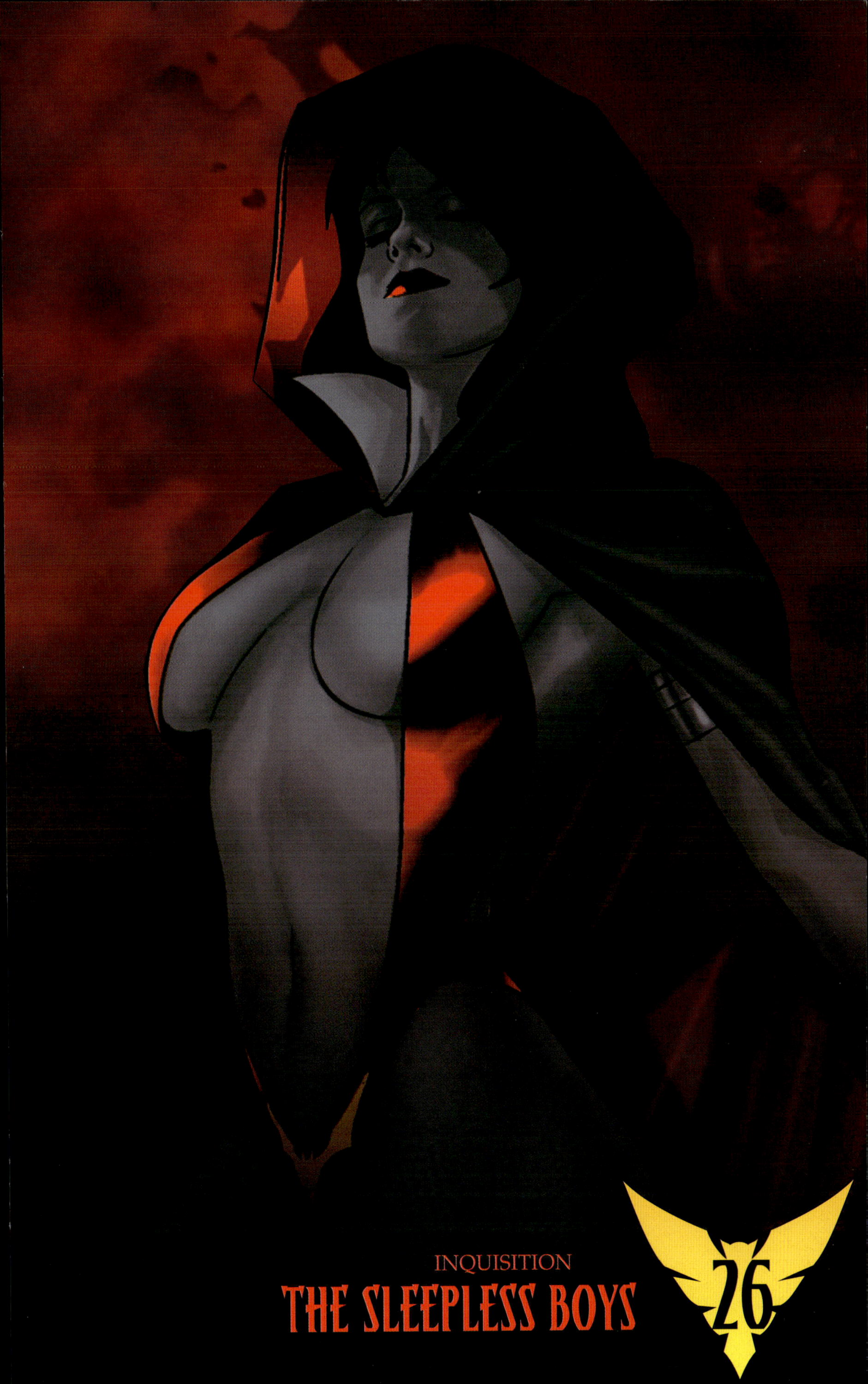
INQUISITION
THE SLEEPLESS BOYS
26

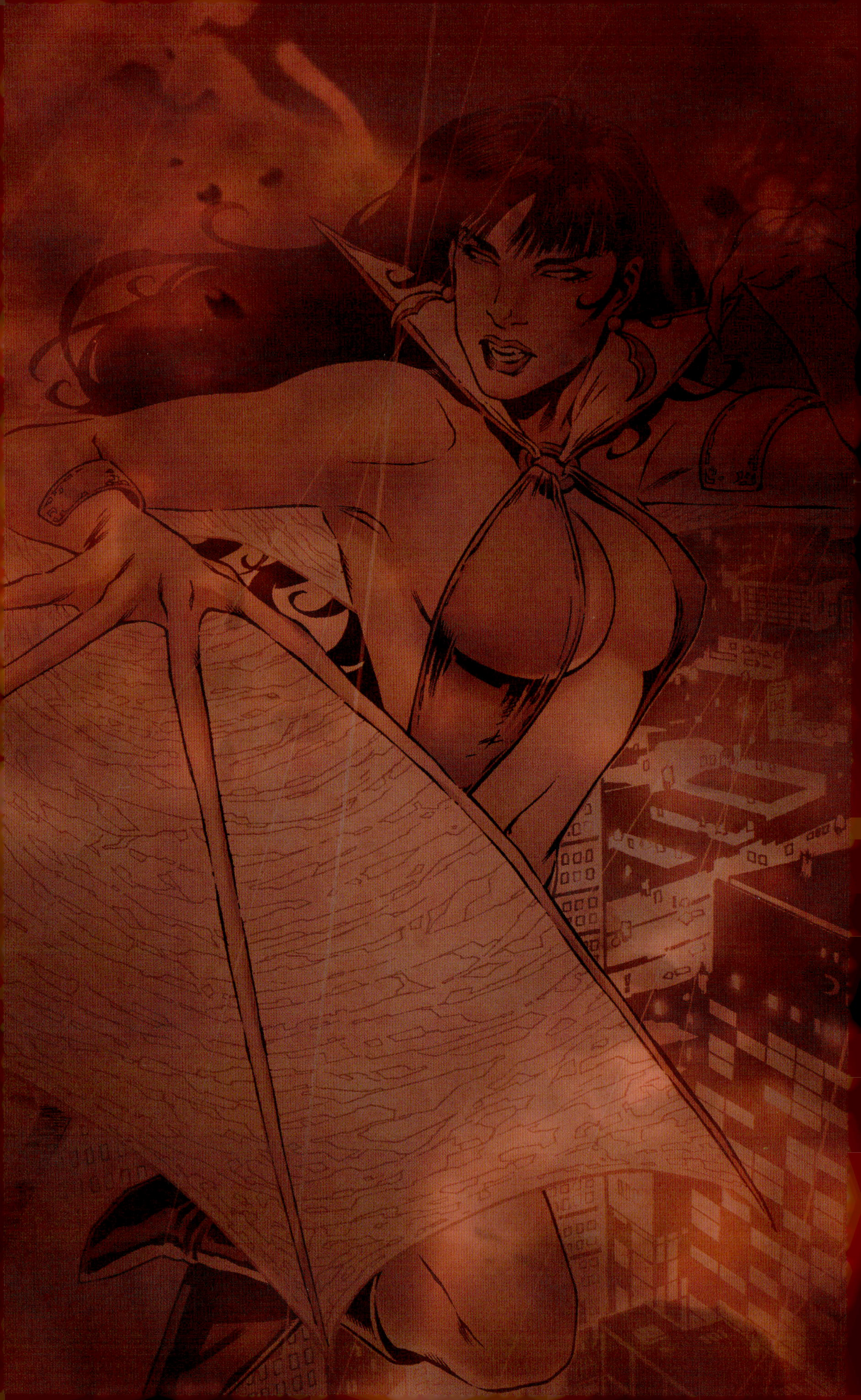

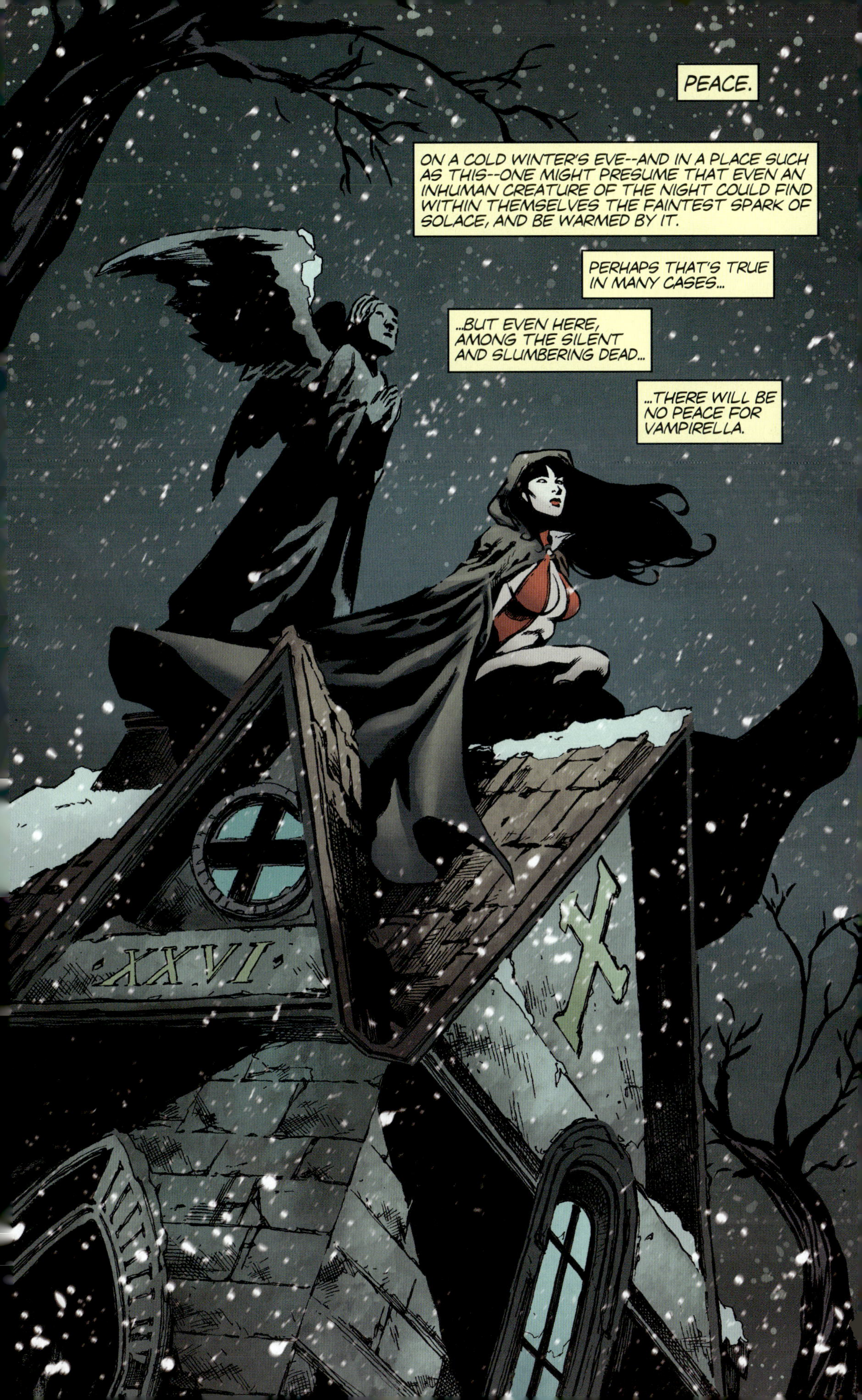

PEACE.
ON A COLD WINTER'S EVE--AND IN A PLACE SUCH AS THIS--ONE MIGHT PRESUME THAT EVEN AN INHUMAN CREATURE OF THE NIGHT COULD FIND WITHIN THEMSELVES THE FAINTEST SPARK OF SOLACE, AND BE WARMED BY IT.
PERHAPS THAT'S TRUE IN MANY CASES...
...BUT EVEN HERE, AMONG THE SILENT AND SLUMBERING DEAD...
...THERE WILL BE NO PEACE FOR VAMPIRELLA.
XXVI

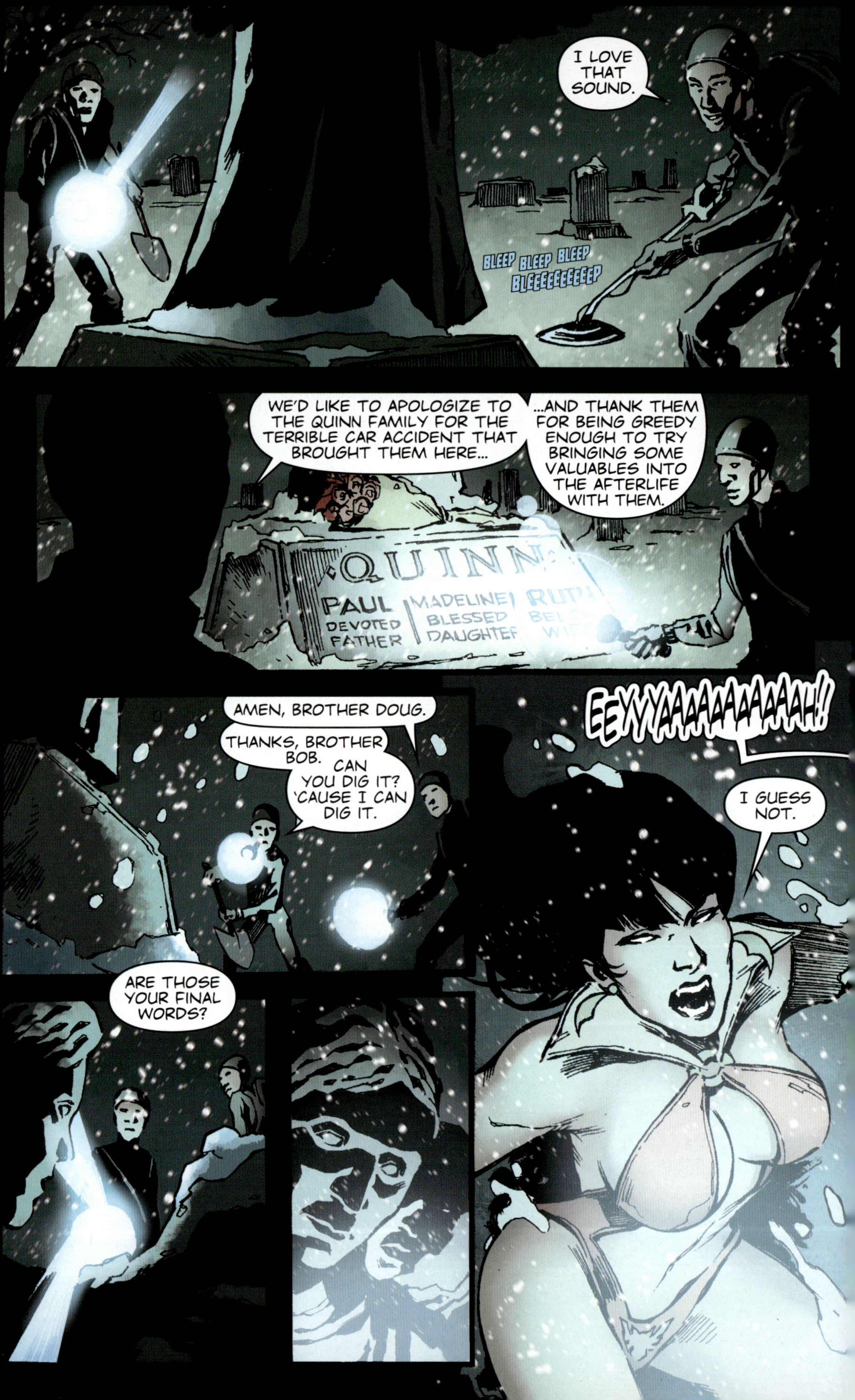
I LOVE THAT SOUND.
BLEEP BLEEP BLEEP BLEEEEEEEEEEP
WE'D LIKE TO APOLOGIZE TO THE QUINN FAMILY FOR THE TERRIBLE CAR ACCIDENT THAT BROUGHT THEM HERE...
...AND THANK THEM FOR BEING GREEDY ENOUGH TO TRY BRINGING SOME VALUABLES INTO THE AFTERLIFE WITH THEM.
QUINN
PAUL DEVOTED FATHER
MADELINE BLESSED DAUGHTER
AMEN, BROTHER DOUG.
THANKS, BROTHER BOB.
CAN YOU DIG IT? 'CAUSE I CAN DIG IT.
ARE THOSE YOUR FINAL WORDS?
EEYYYAAAAAAAAAAH!!
I GUESS NOT.

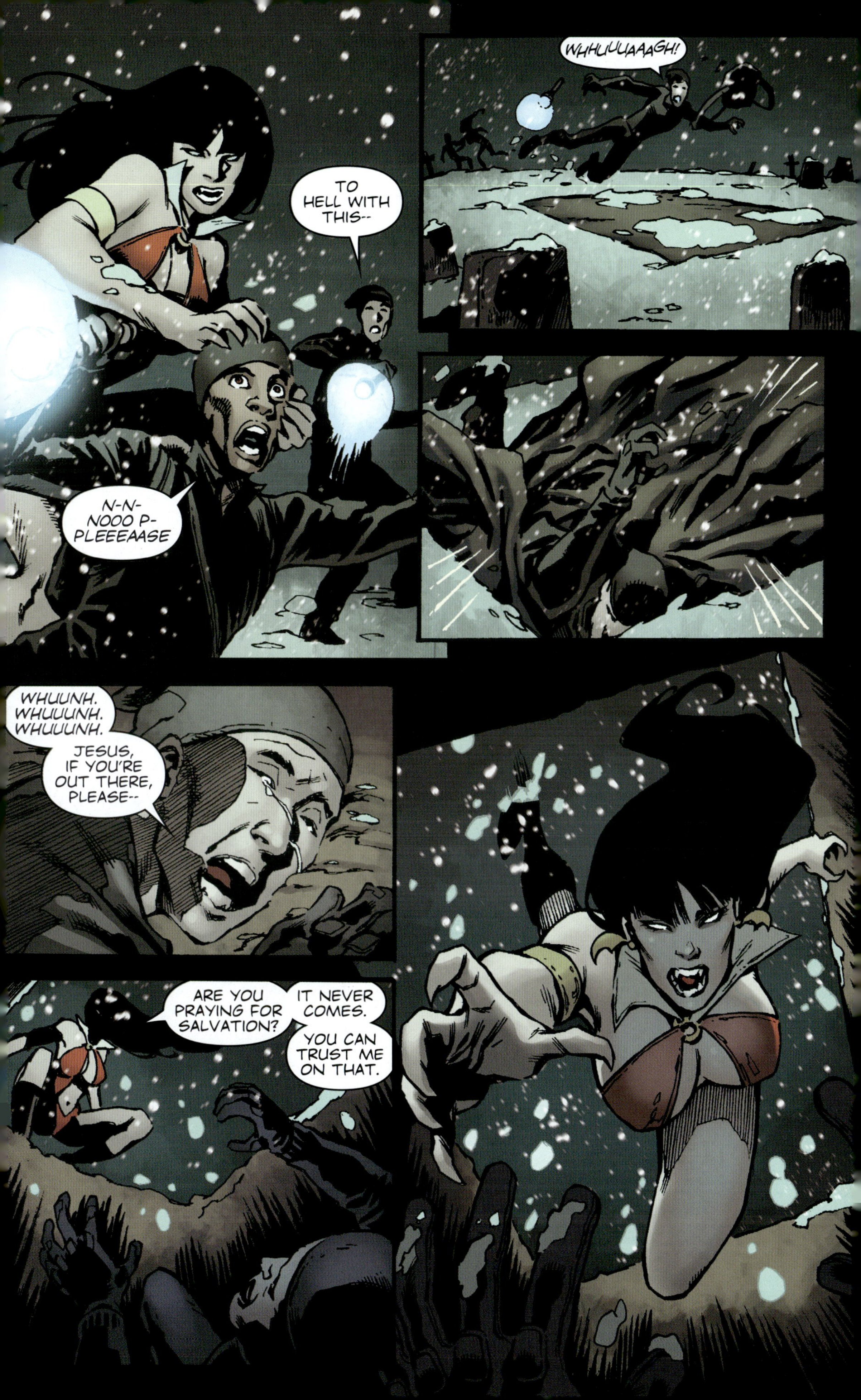
TO HELL WITH THIS--
N-N-NOOO P-PLEEEAASE
WHHUUUAAAGH!
WHUUNH. WHUUUNH. WHUUUNH.
JESUS, IF YOU'RE OUT THERE, PLEASE--
ARE YOU PRAYING FOR SALVATION?
IT NEVER COMES.
YOU CAN TRUST ME ON THAT.

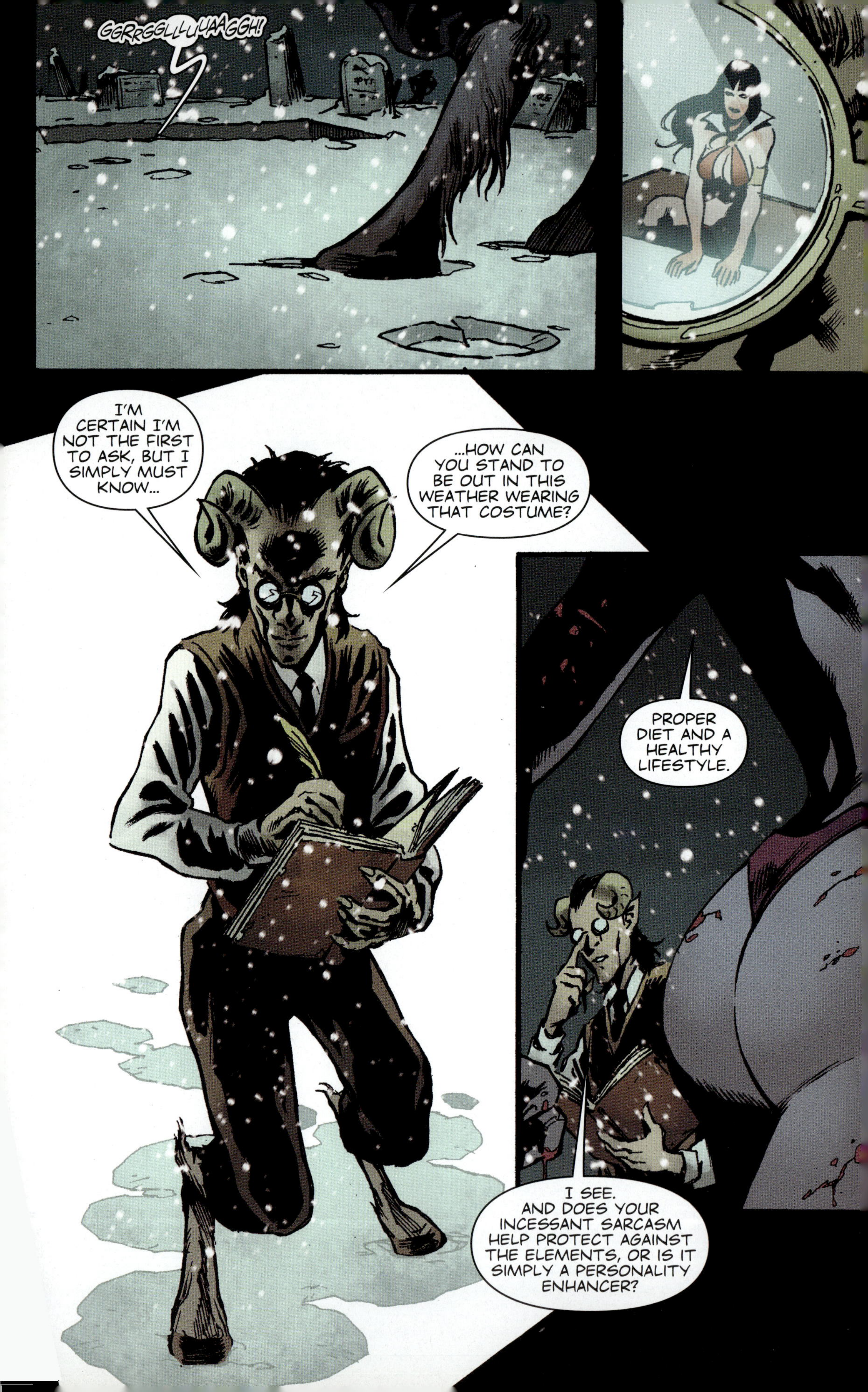
GGRRGGLLLUUAAGGH!
I'M CERTAIN I'M NOT THE FIRST TO ASK, BUT I SIMPLY MUST KNOW...
...HOW CAN YOU STAND TO BE OUT IN THIS WEATHER WEARING THAT COSTUME?
PROPER DIET AND A HEALTHY LIFESTYLE.
I SEE. AND DOES YOUR INCESSANT SARCASM HELP PROTECT AGAINST THE ELEMENTS, OR IS IT SIMPLY A PERSONALITY ENHANCER?

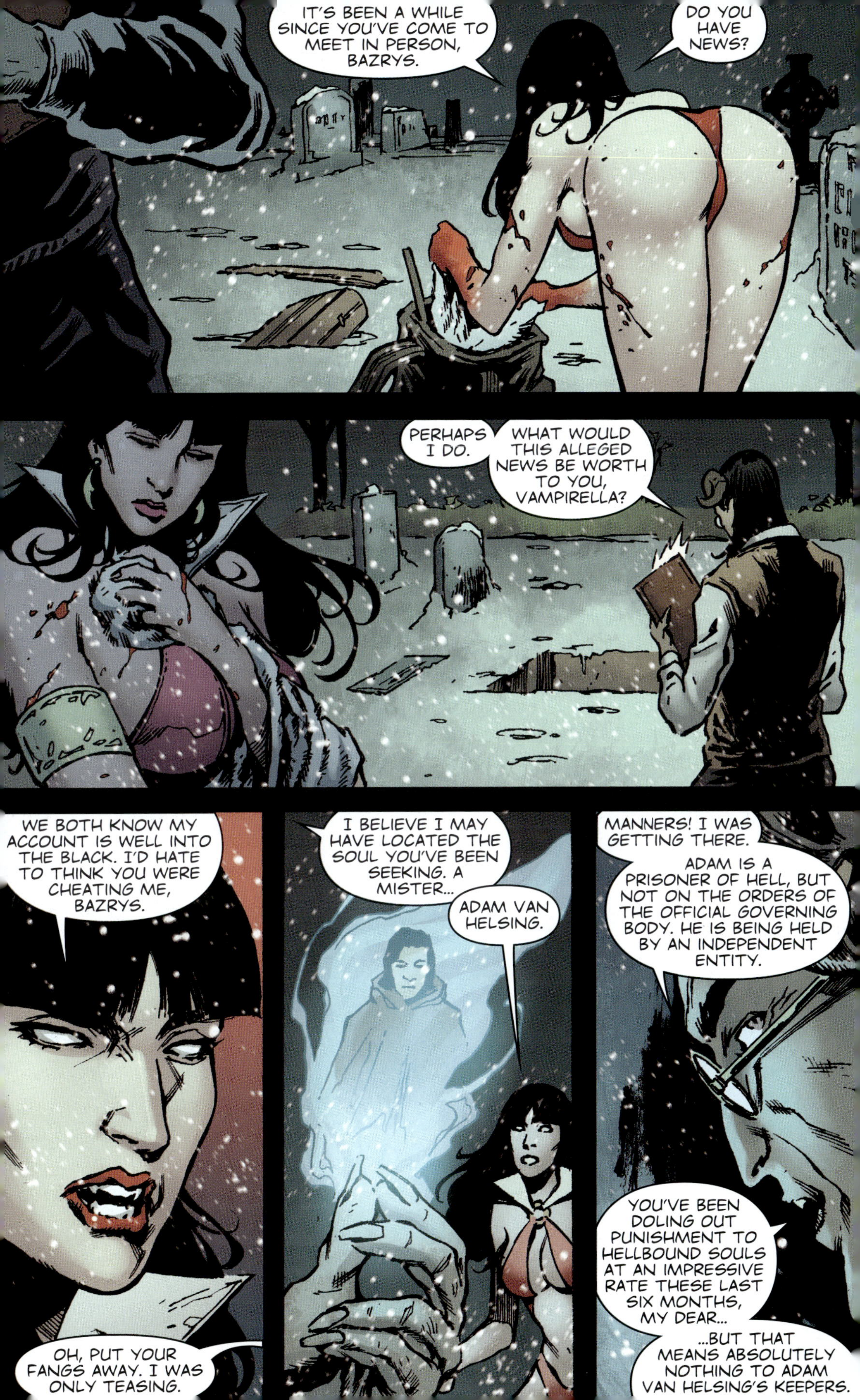
IT'S BEEN A WHILE SINCE YOU'VE COME TO MEET IN PERSON, BAZRYS.
DO YOU HAVE NEWS?
PERHAPS I DO.
WHAT WOULD THIS ALLEGED NEWS BE WORTH TO YOU, VAMPIRELLA?
WE BOTH KNOW MY ACCOUNT IS WELL INTO THE BLACK. I'D HATE TO THINK YOU WERE CHEATING ME, BAZRYS.
OH, PUT YOUR FANGS AWAY. I WAS ONLY TEASING.
I BELIEVE I MAY HAVE LOCATED THE SOUL YOU'VE BEEN SEEKING. A MISTER...
ADAM VAN HELSING.
MANNERS! I WAS GETTING THERE.
ADAM IS A PRISONER OF HELL, BUT NOT ON THE ORDERS OF THE OFFICIAL GOVERNING BODY. HE IS BEING HELD BY AN INDEPENDENT ENTITY.
YOU'VE BEEN DOLING OUT PUNISHMENT TO HELLBOUND SOULS AT AN IMPRESSIVE RATE THESE LAST SIX MONTHS, MY DEAR...
...BUT THAT MEANS ABSOLUTELY NOTHING TO ADAM VAN HELSING'S KEEPERS.

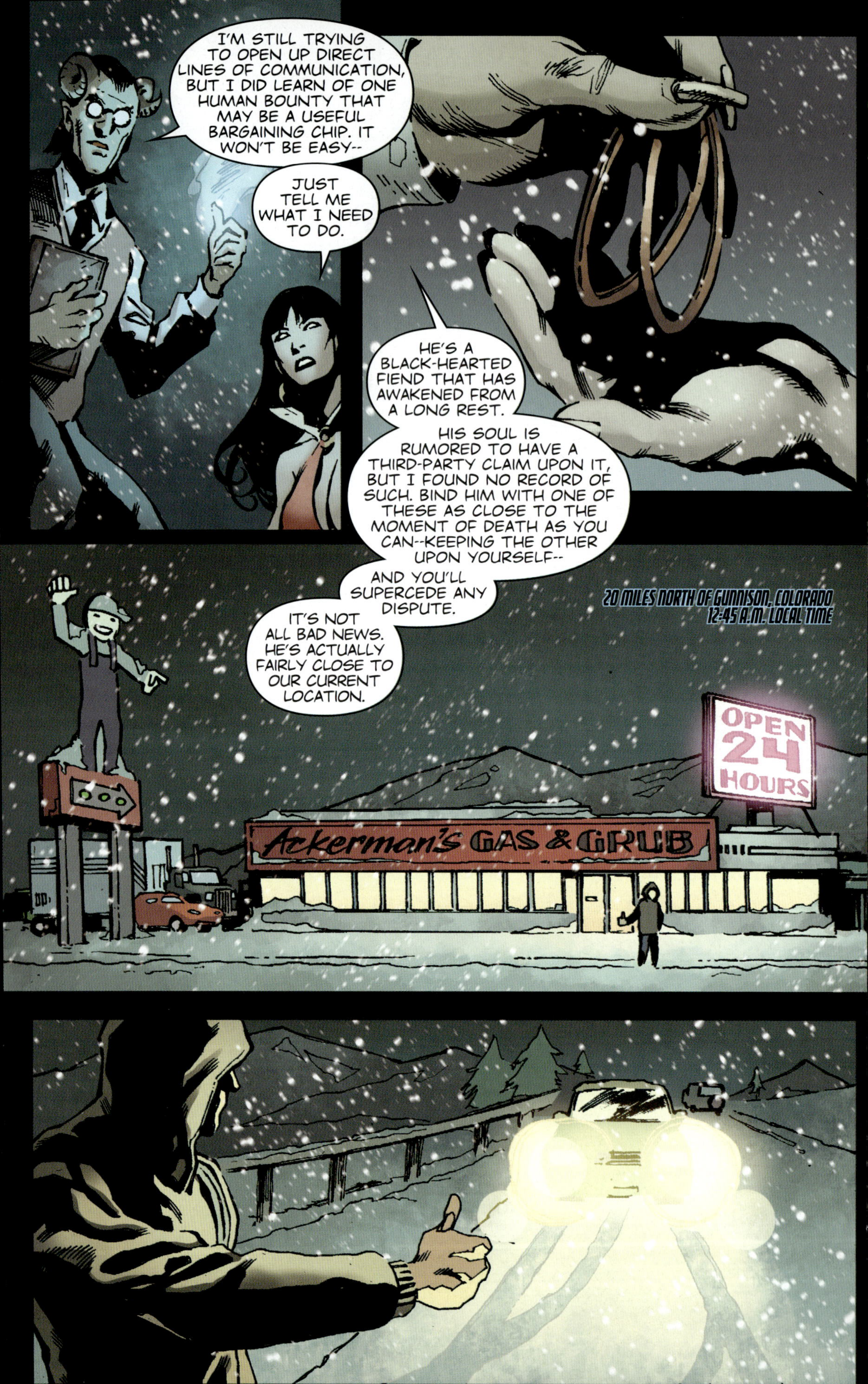

I'M STILL TRYING TO OPEN UP DIRECT LINES OF COMMUNICATION, BUT I DID LEARN OF ONE HUMAN BOUNTY THAT MAY BE A USEFUL BARGAINING CHIP. IT WON'T BE EASY--
JUST TELL ME WHAT I NEED TO DO.
HE'S A BLACK-HEARTED FIEND THAT HAS AWAKENED FROM A LONG REST.
HIS SOUL IS RUMORED TO HAVE A THIRD-PARTY CLAIM UPON IT, BUT I FOUND NO RECORD OF SUCH. BIND HIM WITH ONE OF THESE AS CLOSE TO THE MOMENT OF DEATH AS YOU CAN--KEEPING THE OTHER UPON YOURSELF--
AND YOU'LL SUPERCEDE ANY DISPUTE.
20 MILES NORTH OF GUNNISON, COLORADO
12:45 A.M. LOCAL TIME
IT'S NOT ALL BAD NEWS. HE'S ACTUALLY FAIRLY CLOSE TO OUR CURRENT LOCATION.
OPEN 24 HOURS
Ackerman's GAS & GRUB

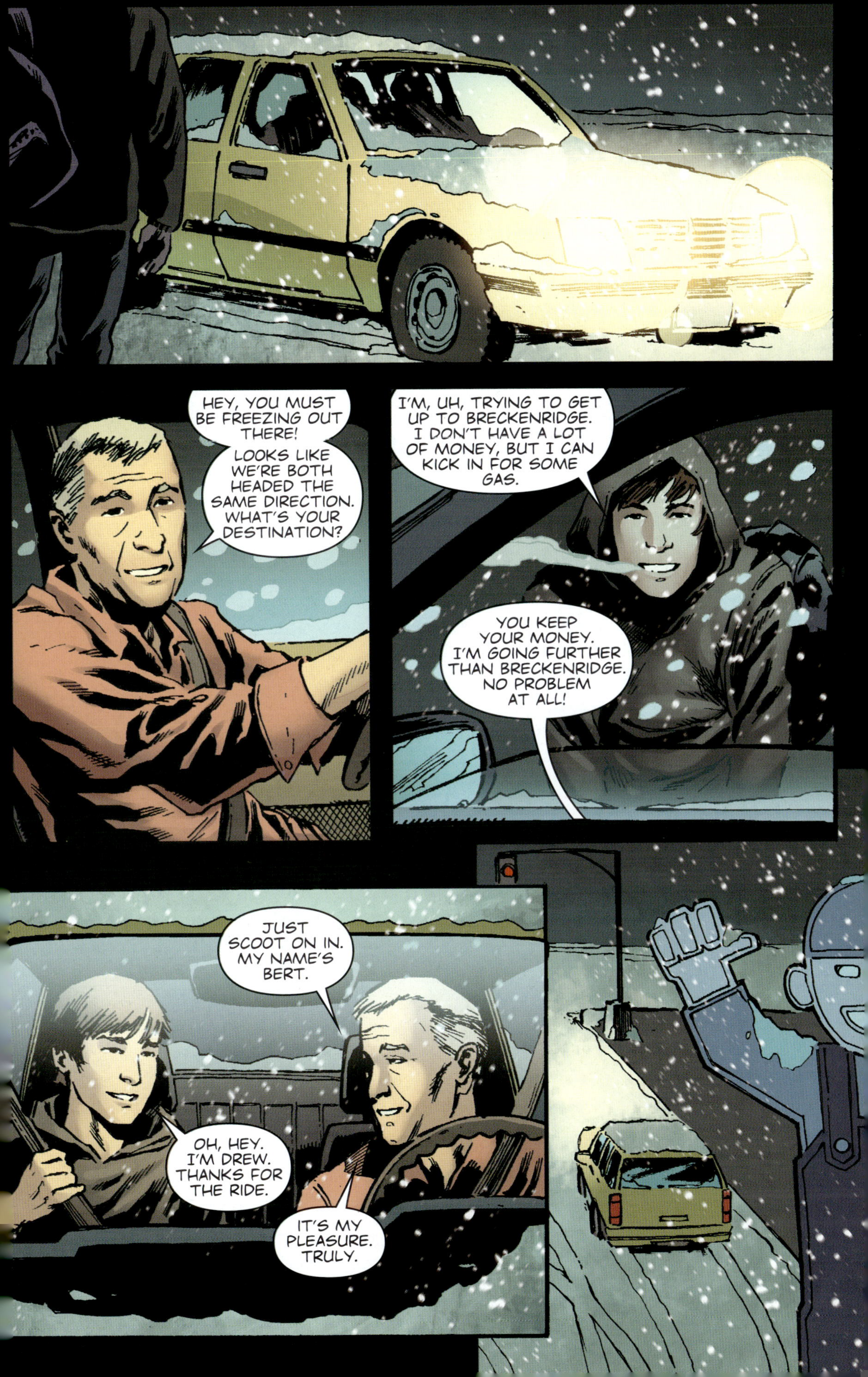
HEY, YOU MUST BE FREEZING OUT THERE!
LOOKS LIKE WE'RE BOTH HEADED THE SAME DIRECTION. WHAT'S YOUR DESTINATION?
I'M, UH, TRYING TO GET UP TO BRECKENRIDGE. I DON'T HAVE A LOT OF MONEY, BUT I CAN KICK IN FOR SOME GAS.
YOU KEEP YOUR MONEY. I'M GOING FURTHER THAN BRECKENRIDGE. NO PROBLEM AT ALL!
JUST SCOOT ON IN. MY NAME'S BERT.
OH, HEY. I'M DREW. THANKS FOR THE RIDE.
IT'S MY PLEASURE. TRULY.

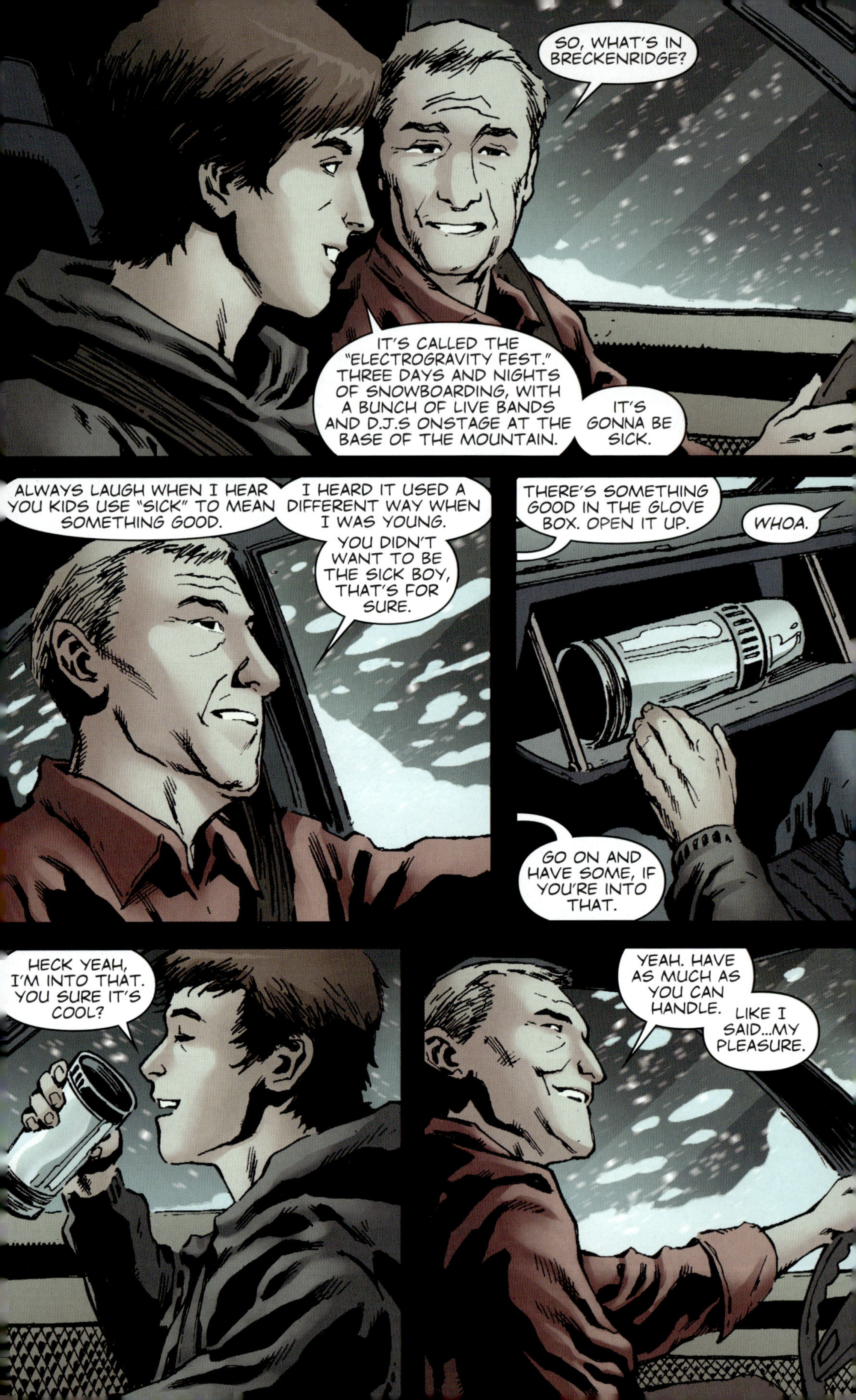
SO, WHAT'S IN BRECKENRIDGE?
IT'S CALLED THE "ELECTROGRAVITY FEST." THREE DAYS AND NIGHTS OF SNOWBOARDING, WITH A BUNCH OF LIVE BANDS AND D.J.S ONSTAGE AT THE BASE OF THE MOUNTAIN.
IT'S GONNA BE SICK.
ALWAYS LAUGH WHEN I HEAR YOU KIDS USE "SICK" TO MEAN SOMETHING GOOD.
I HEARD IT USED A DIFFERENT WAY WHEN I WAS YOUNG.
YOU DIDN'T WANT TO BE THE SICK BOY, THAT'S FOR SURE.
THERE'S SOMETHING GOOD IN THE GLOVE BOX. OPEN IT UP.
WHOA.
GO ON AND HAVE SOME, IF YOU'RE INTO THAT.
HECK YEAH, I'M INTO THAT. YOU SURE IT'S COOL?
YEAH. HAVE AS MUCH AS YOU CAN HANDLE.
LIKE I SAID...MY PLEASURE.

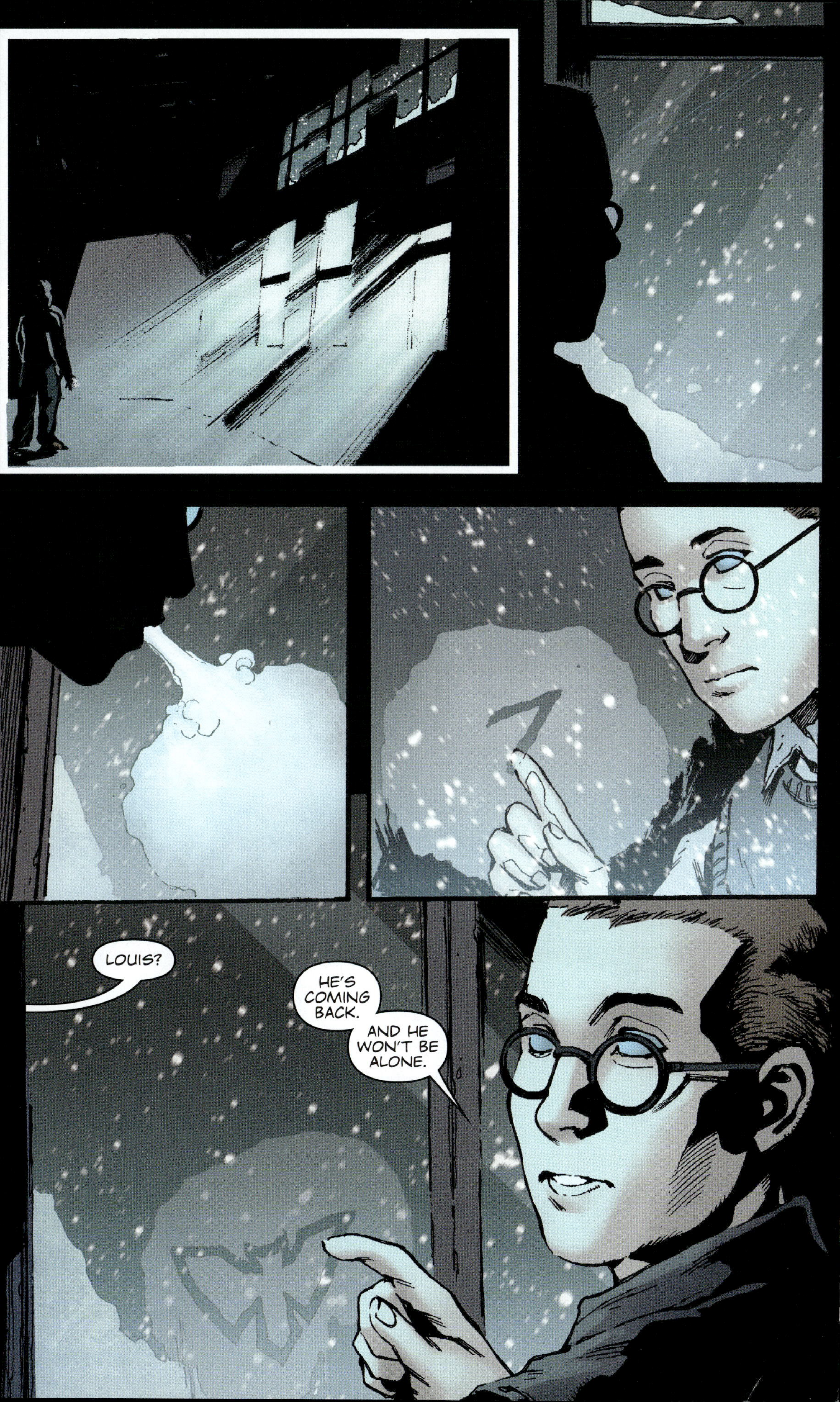
LOUIS?
HE'S COMING BACK.
AND HE WON'T BE ALONE.

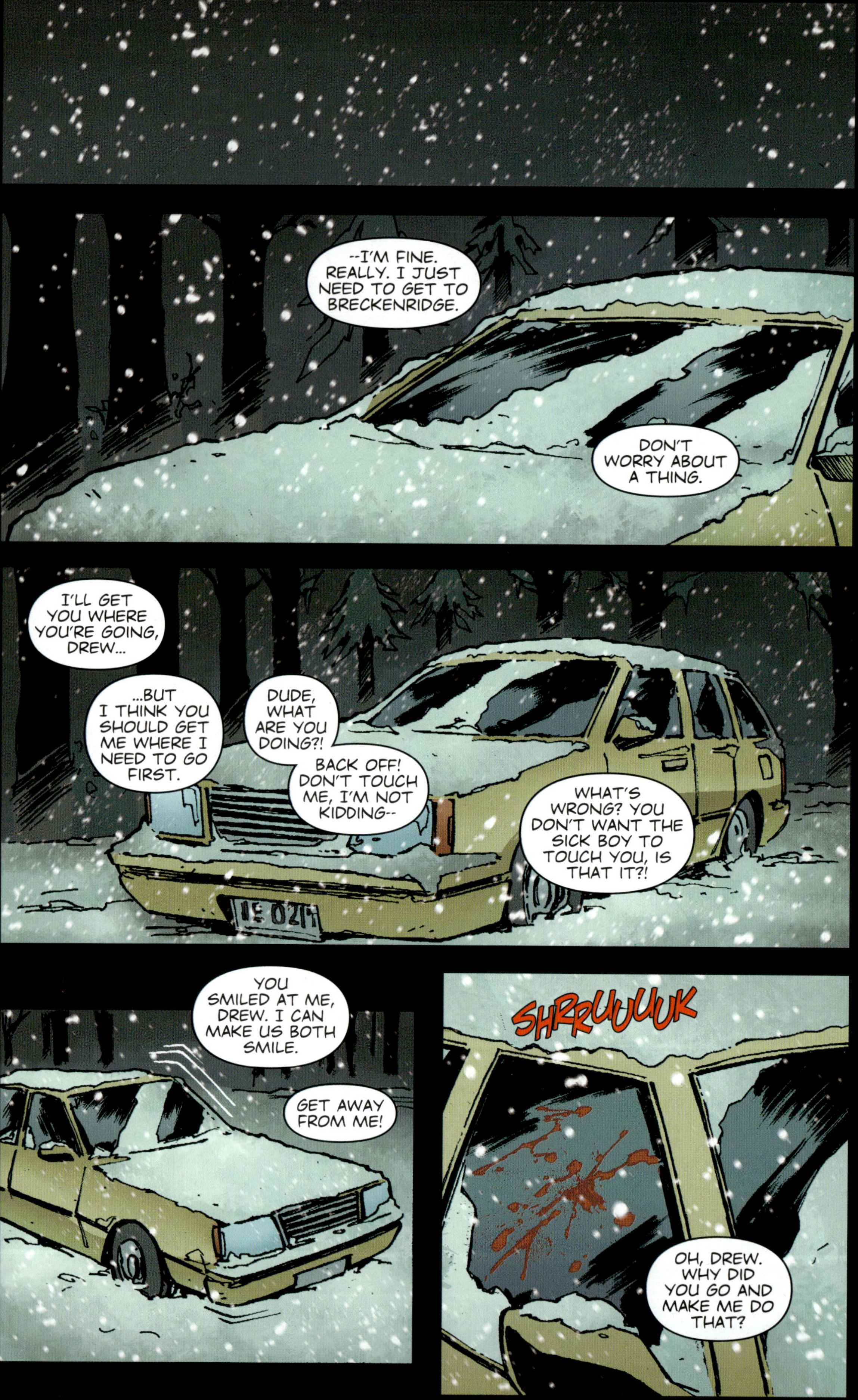
--I'M FINE. REALLY. I JUST NEED TO GET TO BRECKENRIDGE.
DON'T WORRY ABOUT A THING.
I'LL GET YOU WHERE YOU'RE GOING, DREW...
...BUT I THINK YOU SHOULD GET ME WHERE I NEED TO GO FIRST.
DUDE, WHAT ARE YOU DOING?!
BACK OFF! DON'T TOUCH ME, I'M NOT KIDDING--
WHAT'S WRONG? YOU DON'T WANT THE SICK BOY TO TOUCH YOU, IS THAT IT?!
YOU SMILED AT ME, DREW. I CAN MAKE US BOTH SMILE.
GET AWAY FROM ME!
SHRRUUUUK
OH, DREW. WHY DID YOU GO AND MAKE ME DO THAT?

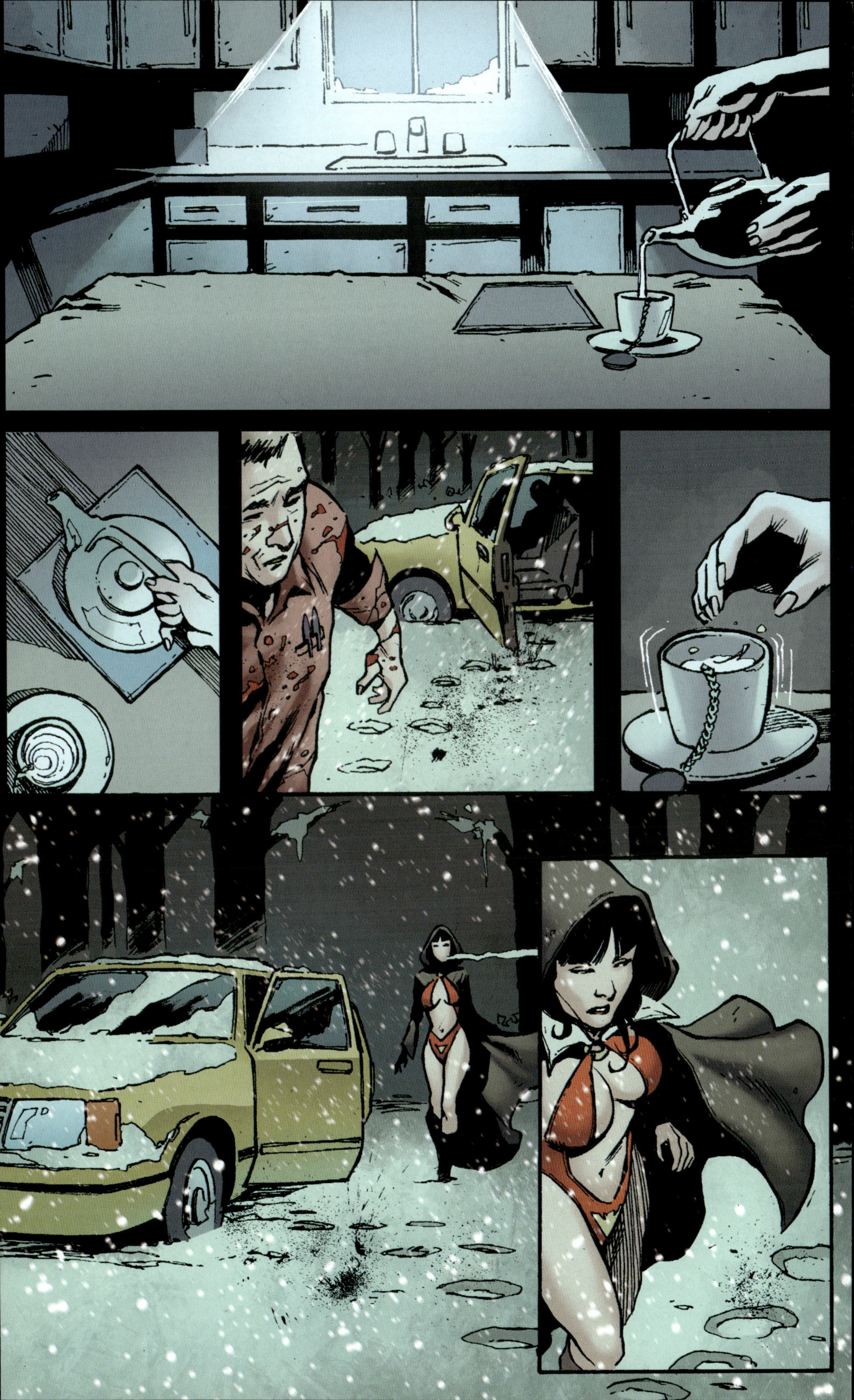

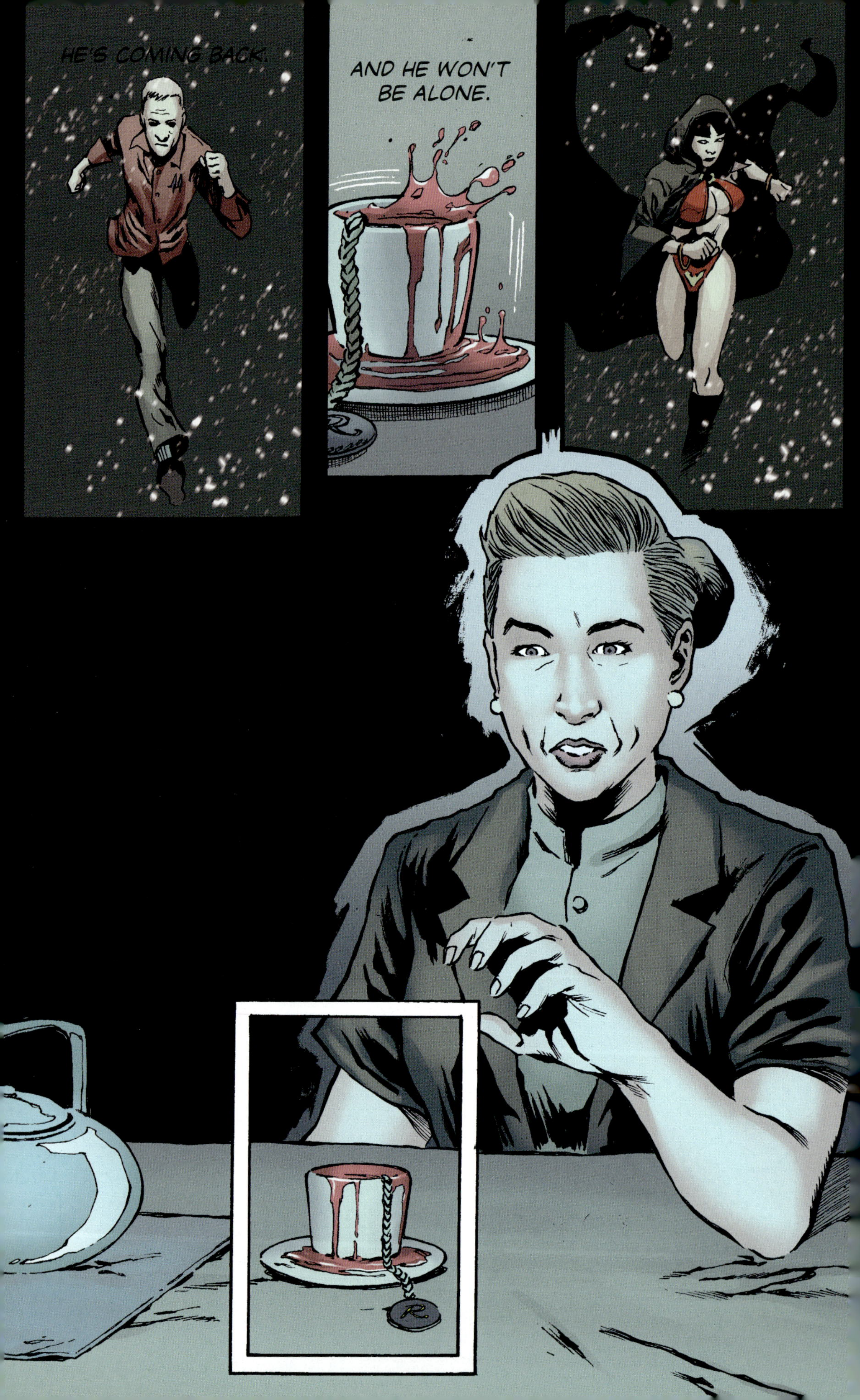
HE'S COMING BACK.
AND HE WON'T BE ALONE.

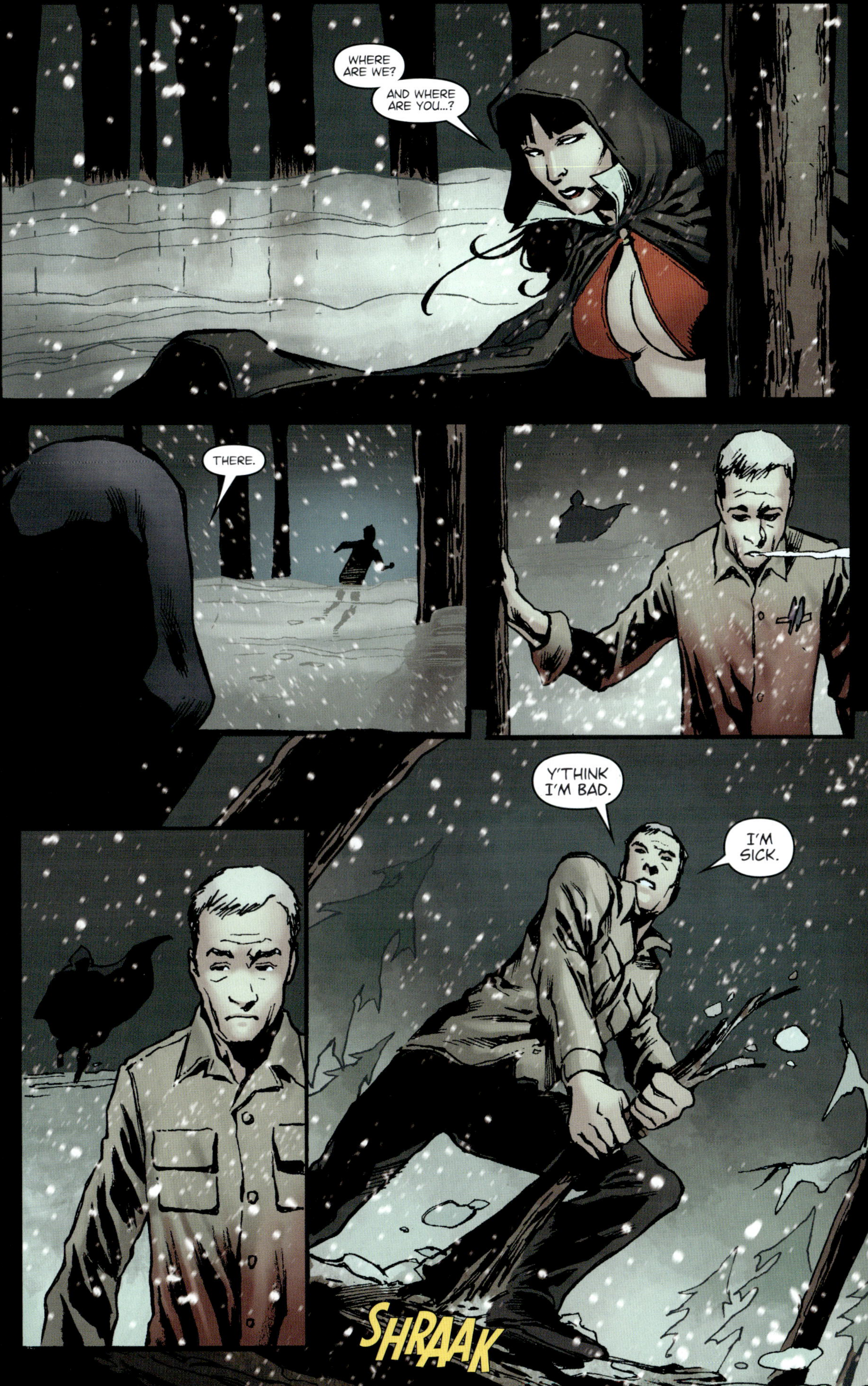
WHERE ARE WE?
AND WHERE ARE YOU...?
THERE.
Y'THINK I'M BAD.
I'M SICK.
SHRAAK

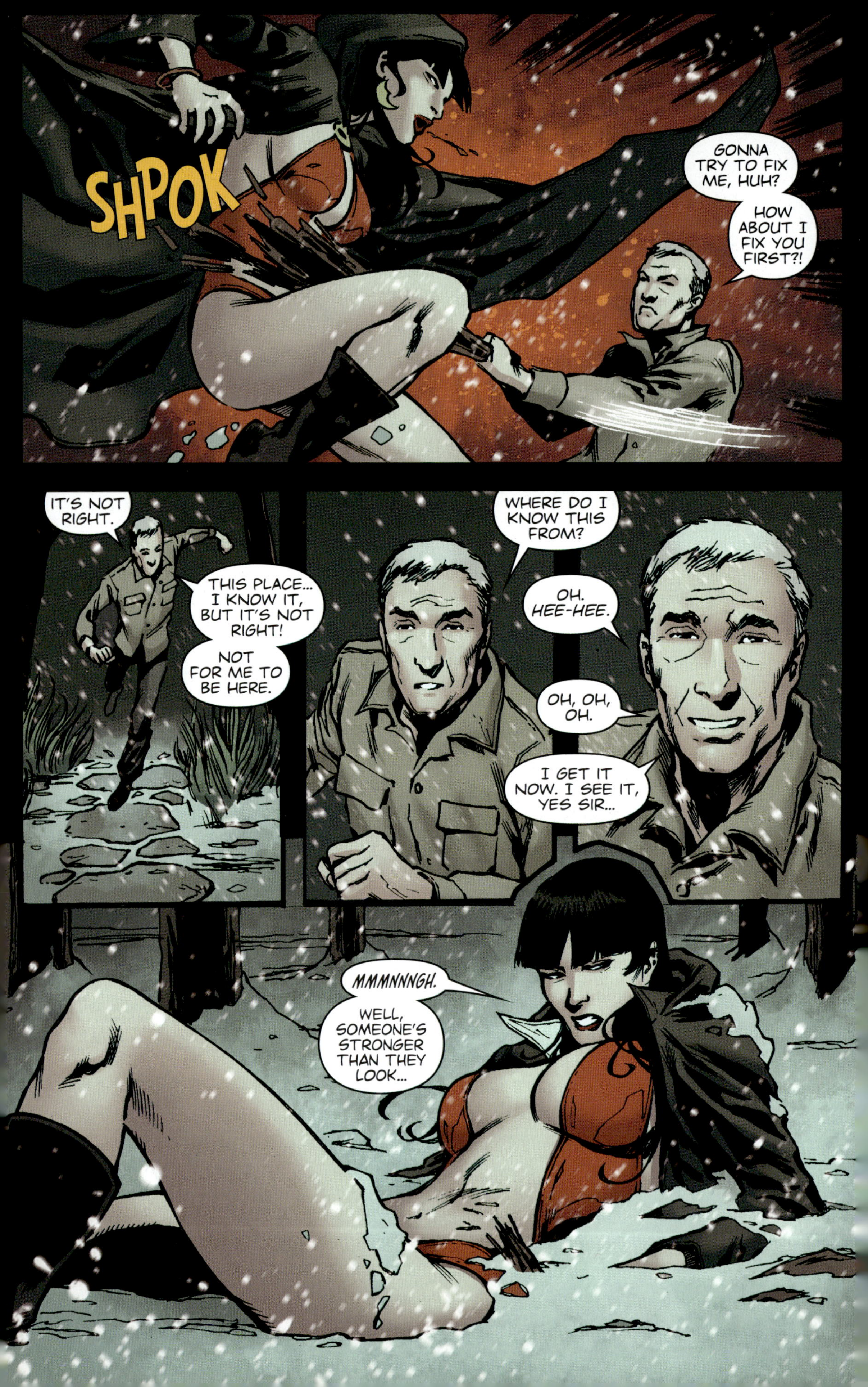
SHPOK
GONNA TRY TO FIX ME, HUH?
HOW ABOUT I FIX YOU FIRST?!
IT'S NOT RIGHT.
THIS PLACE... I KNOW IT, BUT IT'S NOT RIGHT!
NOT FOR ME TO BE HERE.
WHERE DO I KNOW THIS FROM?
OH. HEE-HEE.
OH, OH, OH.
I GET IT NOW. I SEE IT, YES SIR...
MMMNNNGH.
WELL, SOMEONE'S STRONGER THAN THEY LOOK...

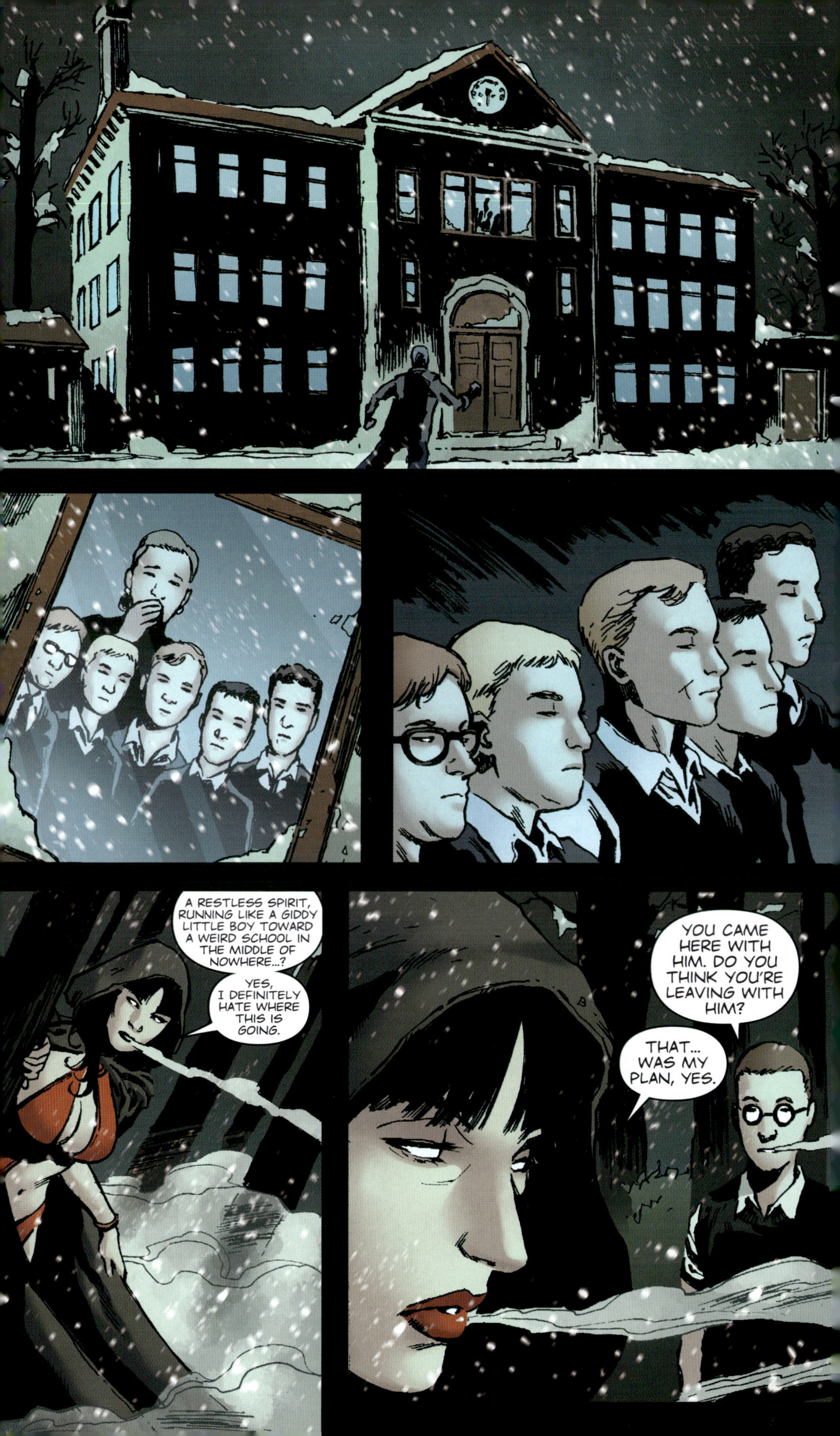
A RESTLESS SPIRIT, RUNNING LIKE A GIDDY LITTLE BOY TOWARD A WEIRD SCHOOL IN THE MIDDLE OF NOWHERE...?
YES, I DEFINITELY HATE WHERE THIS IS GOING.
YOU CAME HERE WITH HIM. DO YOU THINK YOU'RE LEAVING WITH HIM?
THAT... WAS MY PLAN, YES.

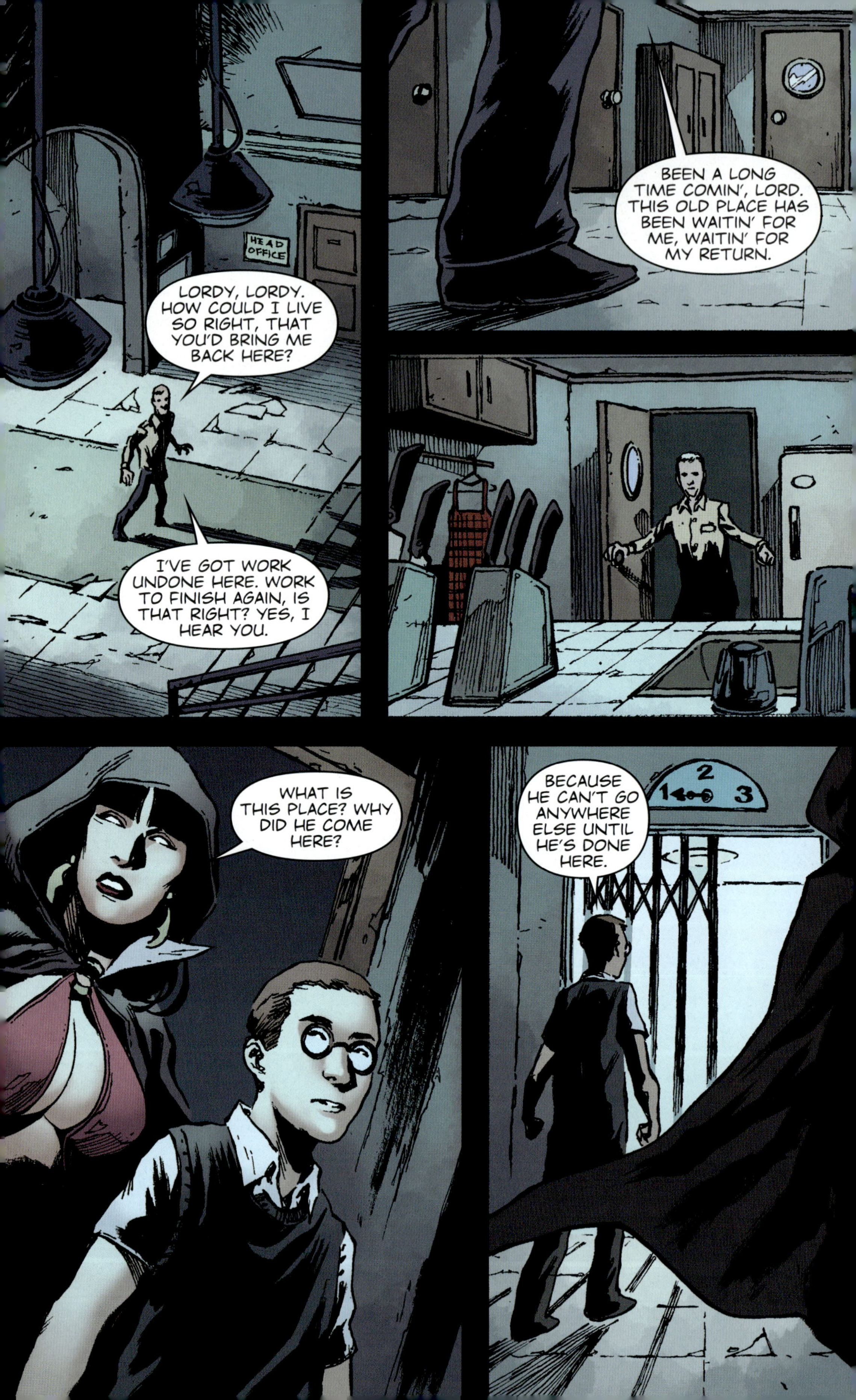
HEAD OFFICE
LORDY, LORDY. HOW COULD I LIVE SO RIGHT, THAT YOU'D BRING ME BACK HERE?
I'VE GOT WORK UNDONE HERE. WORK TO FINISH AGAIN, IS THAT RIGHT? YES, I HEAR YOU.
BEEN A LONG TIME COMIN', LORD. THIS OLD PLACE HAS BEEN WAITIN' FOR ME, WAITIN' FOR MY RETURN.
WHAT IS THIS PLACE? WHY DID HE COME HERE?
BECAUSE HE CAN'T GO ANYWHERE ELSE UNTIL HE'S DONE HERE.
1 2 3

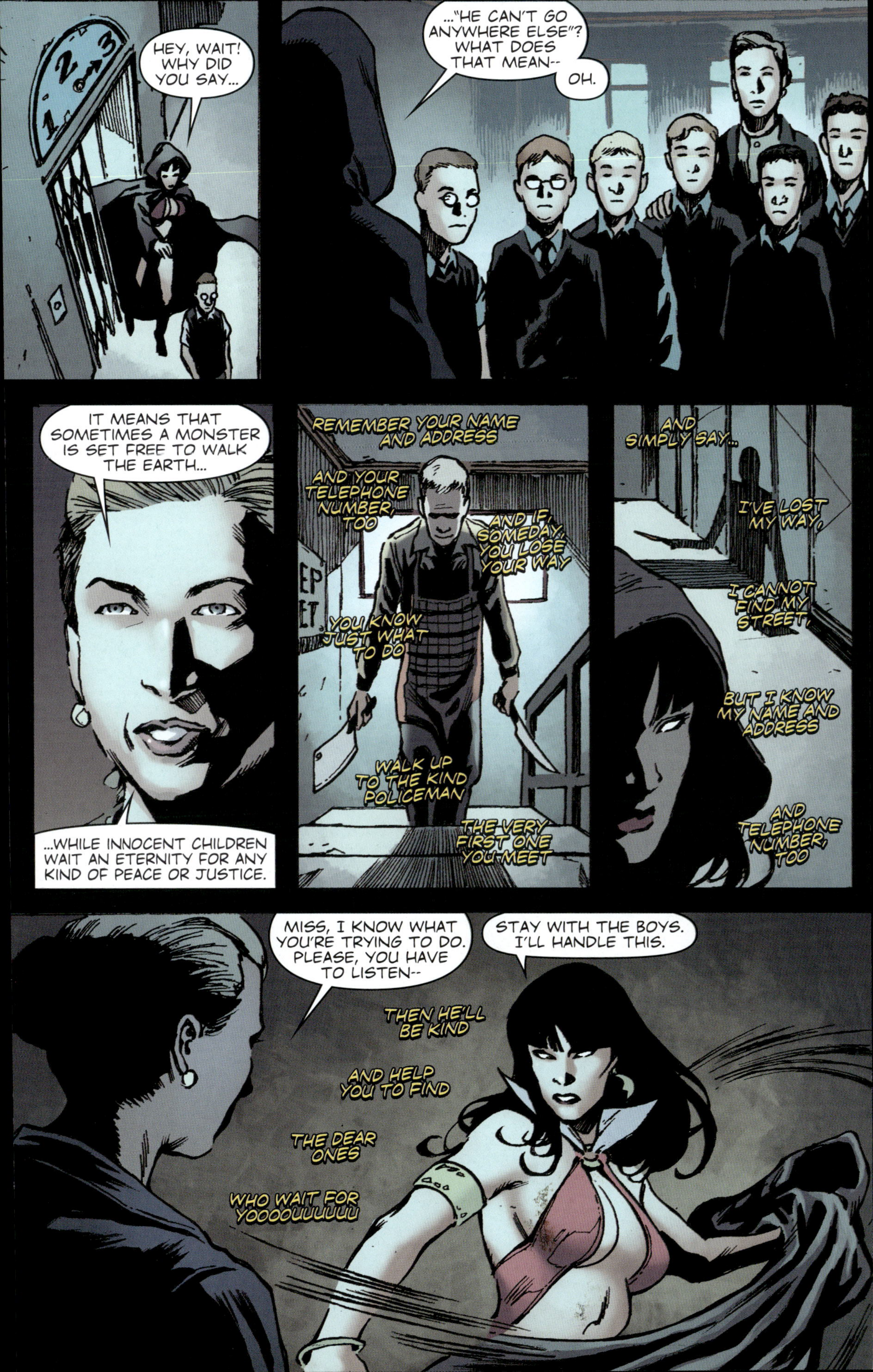
HEY, WAIT! WHY DID YOU SAY...
..."HE CAN'T GO ANYWHERE ELSE"? WHAT DOES THAT MEAN--
OH.
IT MEANS THAT SOMETIMES A MONSTER IS SET FREE TO WALK THE EARTH...
...WHILE INNOCENT CHILDREN WAIT AN ETERNITY FOR ANY KIND OF PEACE OR JUSTICE.
REMEMBER YOUR NAME AND ADDRESS
AND YOUR TELEPHONE NUMBER, TOO
AND IF, SOMEDAY, YOU LOSE YOUR WAY
YOU KNOW JUST WHAT TO DO
WALK UP TO THE KIND POLICEMAN
THE VERY FIRST ONE YOU MEET
AND SIMPLY SAY...
I'VE LOST MY WAY,
I CANNOT FIND MY STREET,
BUT I KNOW MY NAME AND ADDRESS
AND TELEPHONE NUMBER, TOO
MISS, I KNOW WHAT YOU'RE TRYING TO DO. PLEASE, YOU HAVE TO LISTEN--
STAY WITH THE BOYS. I'LL HANDLE THIS.
THEN HE'LL BE KIND
AND HELP YOU TO FIND
THE DEAR ONES
WHO WAIT FOR YOOOOUUUUUU

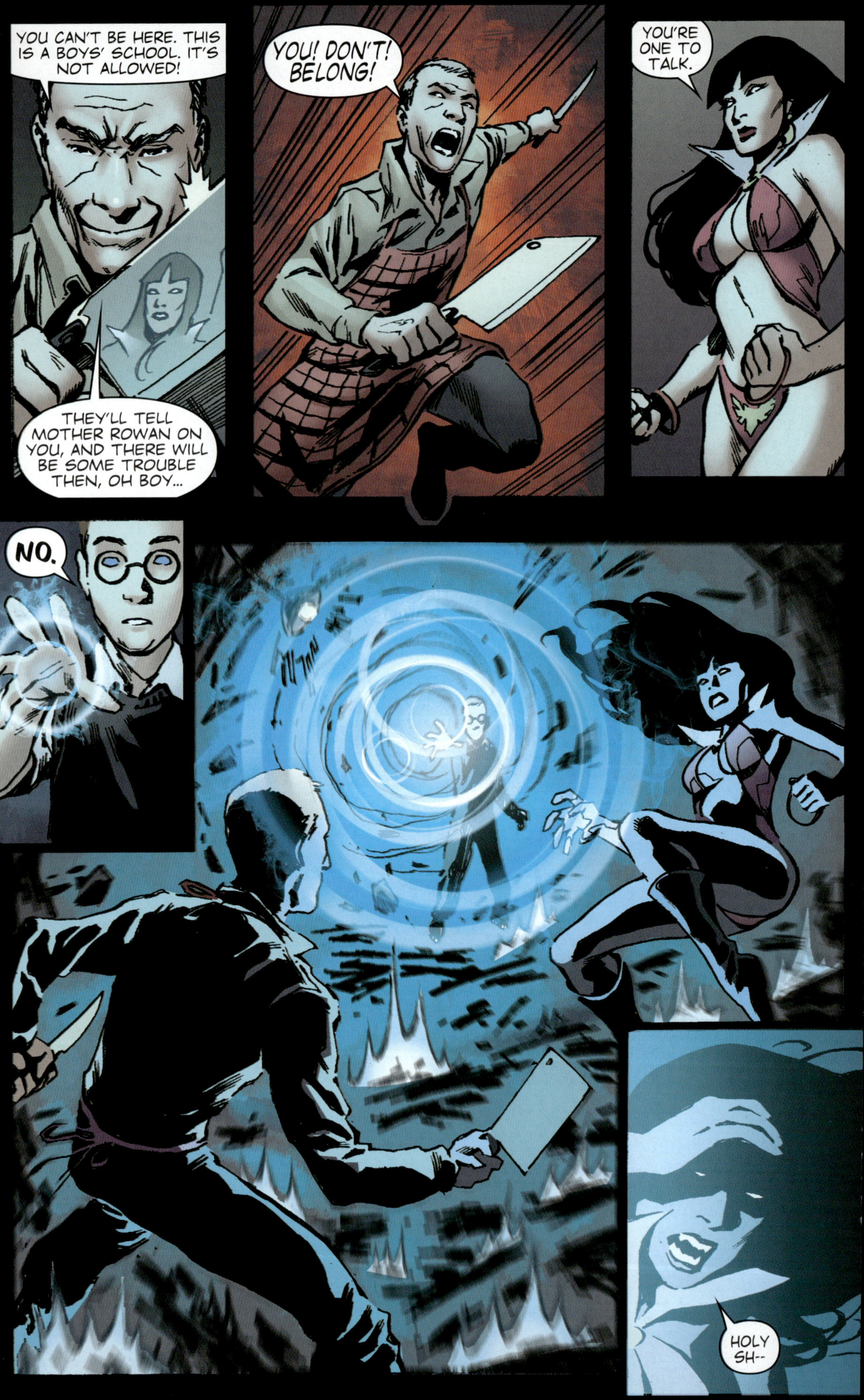
YOU CAN'T BE HERE. THIS IS A BOYS' SCHOOL. IT'S NOT ALLOWED!
THEY'LL TELL MOTHER ROWAN ON YOU, AND THERE WILL BE SOME TROUBLE THEN, OH BOY...
YOU! DON'T! BELONG!
YOU'RE ONE TO TALK.
NO.
HOLY SH--

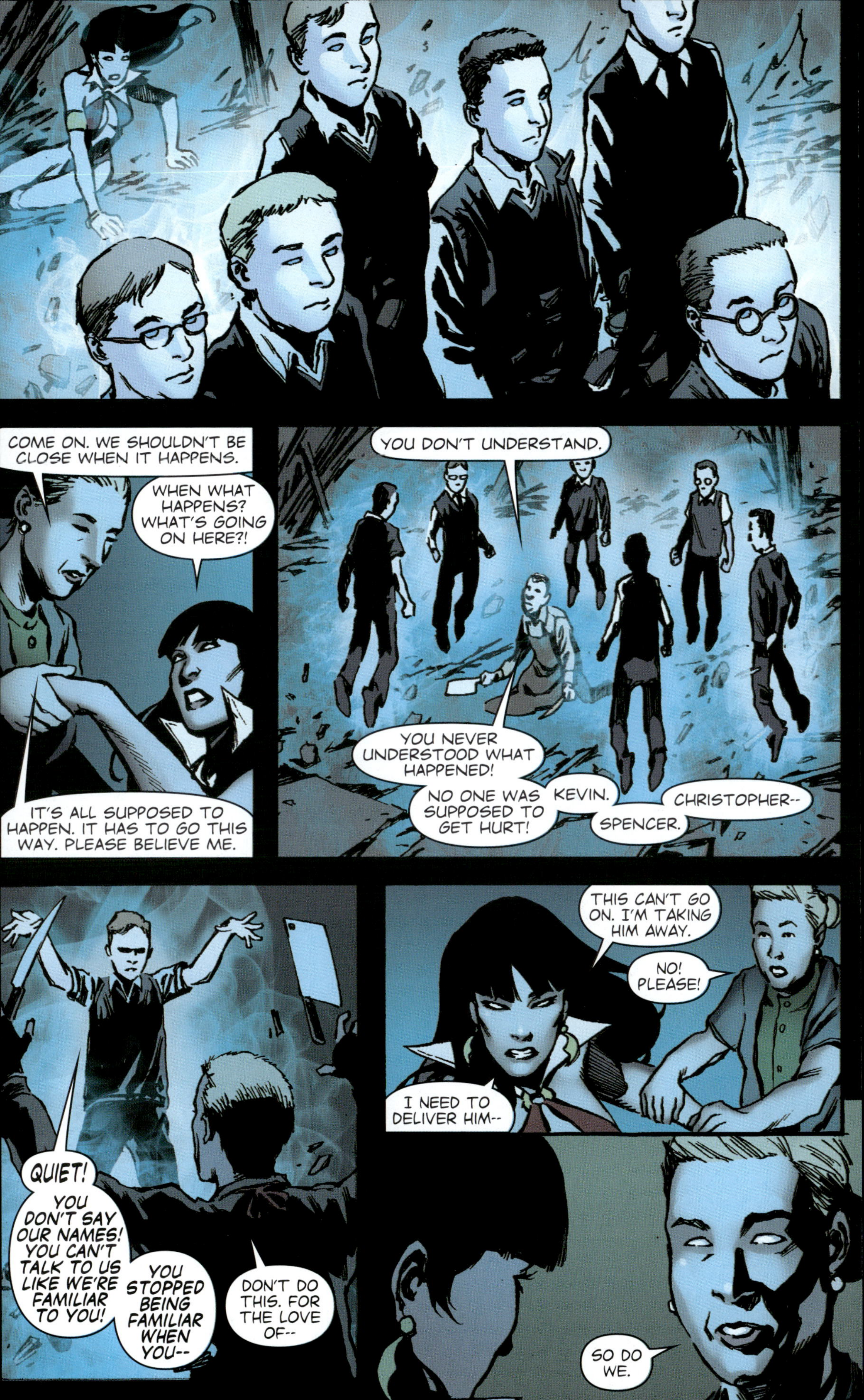
COME ON. WE SHOULDN'T BE CLOSE WHEN IT HAPPENS.
WHEN WHAT HAPPENS? WHAT'S GOING ON HERE?!
IT'S ALL SUPPOSED TO HAPPEN. IT HAS TO GO THIS WAY. PLEASE BELIEVE ME.
YOU DON'T UNDERSTAND.
YOU NEVER UNDERSTOOD WHAT HAPPENED!
NO ONE WAS SUPPOSED TO GET HURT!
KEVIN.
SPENCER.
CHRISTOPHER--
QUIET!
YOU DON'T SAY OUR NAMES! YOU CAN'T TALK TO US LIKE WE'RE FAMILIAR TO YOU!
YOU STOPPED BEING FAMILIAR WHEN YOU--
DON'T DO THIS. FOR THE LOVE OF--
THIS CAN'T GO ON. I'M TAKING HIM AWAY.
NO! PLEASE!
I NEED TO DELIVER HIM--
SO DO WE.

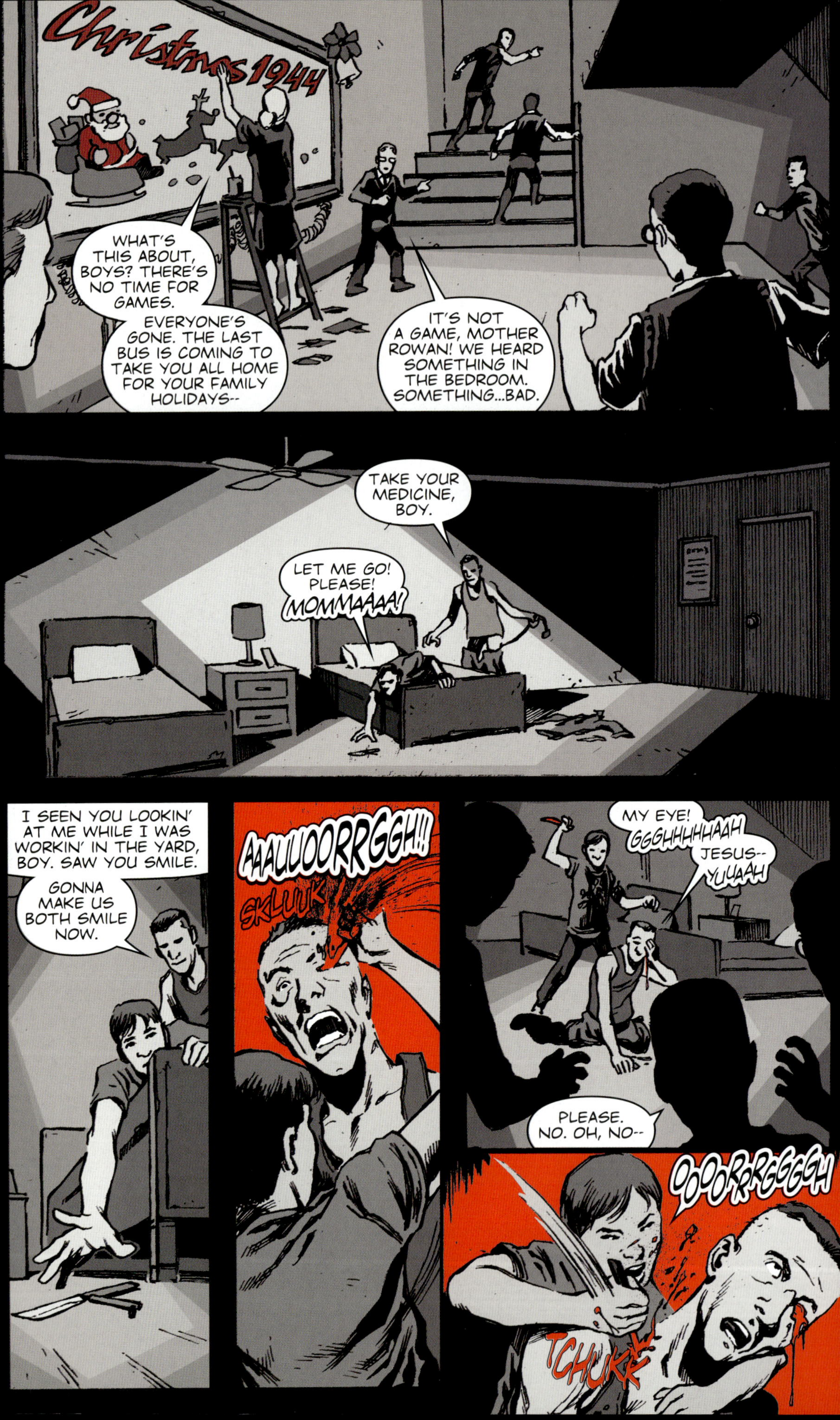
Christmas 1944
WHAT'S THIS ABOUT, BOYS? THERE'S NO TIME FOR GAMES.
EVERYONE'S GONE. THE LAST BUS IS COMING TO TAKE YOU ALL HOME FOR YOUR FAMILY HOLIDAYS--
IT'S NOT A GAME, MOTHER ROWAN! WE HEARD SOMETHING IN THE BEDROOM. SOMETHING...BAD.
TAKE YOUR MEDICINE, BOY.
LET ME GO! PLEASE! MOMMAAAA!
I SEEN YOU LOOKIN' AT ME WHILE I WAS WORKIN' IN THE YARD, BOY. SAW YOU SMILE.
GONNA MAKE US BOTH SMILE NOW.
AAAUUOORRGGH!!
SKLUUK
MY EYE! GGGHHHHAAH
JESUS-- YUUAAH
PLEASE. NO. OH, NO--
OOOORRRGGGGH
TCHUKK

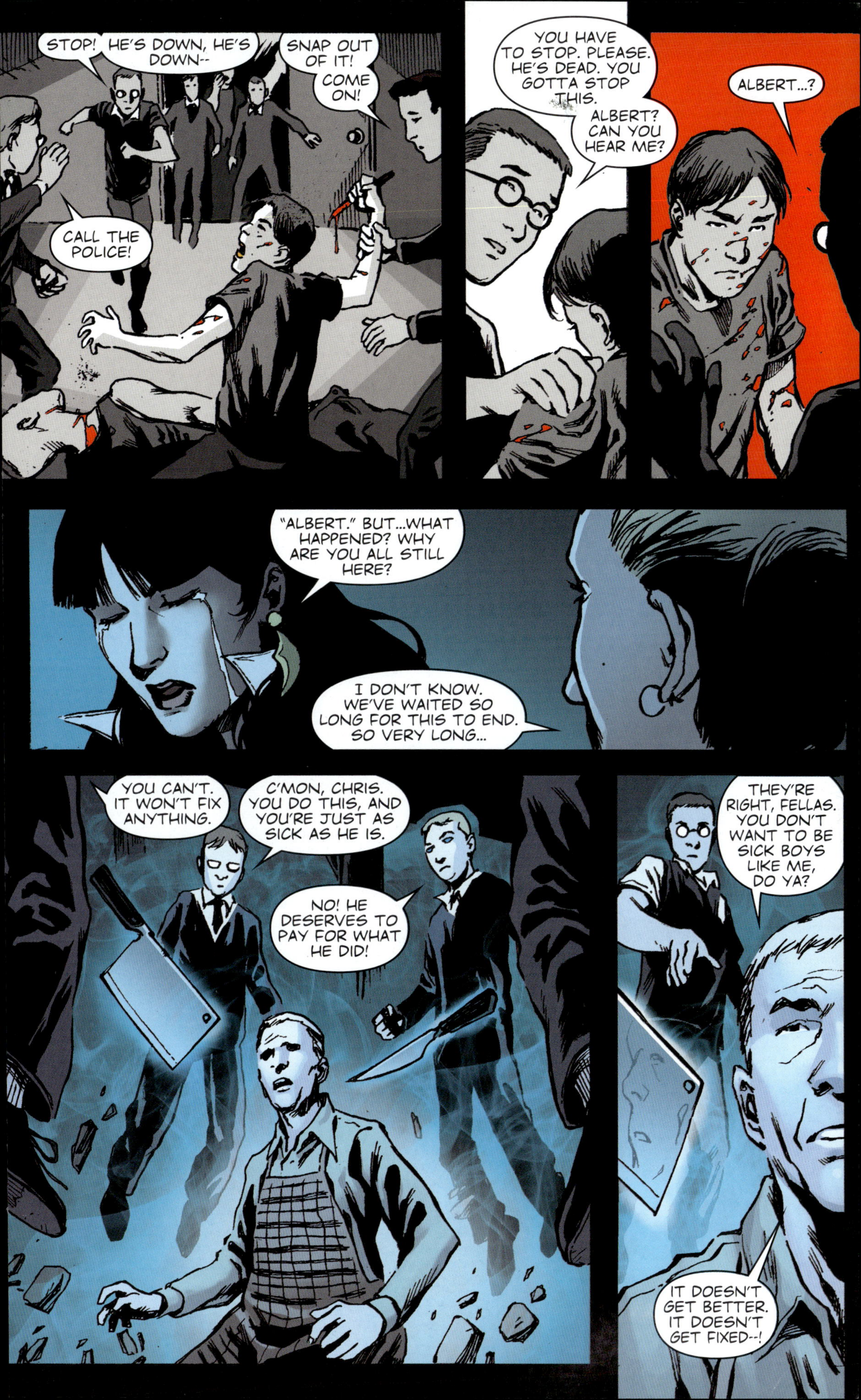
STOP!
HE'S DOWN, HE'S DOWN--
SNAP OUT OF IT!
COME ON!
CALL THE POLICE!
YOU HAVE TO STOP. PLEASE. HE'S DEAD. YOU GOTTA STOP THIS.
ALBERT? CAN YOU HEAR ME?
ALBERT...?
"ALBERT." BUT...WHAT HAPPENED? WHY ARE YOU ALL STILL HERE?
I DON'T KNOW. WE'VE WAITED SO LONG FOR THIS TO END. SO VERY LONG...
YOU CAN'T. IT WON'T FIX ANYTHING.
C'MON, CHRIS. YOU DO THIS, AND YOU'RE JUST AS SICK AS HE IS.
NO! HE DESERVES TO PAY FOR WHAT HE DID!
THEY'RE RIGHT, FELLAS. YOU DON'T WANT TO BE SICK BOYS LIKE ME, DO YA?
IT DOESN'T GET BETTER. IT DOESN'T GET FIXED--!

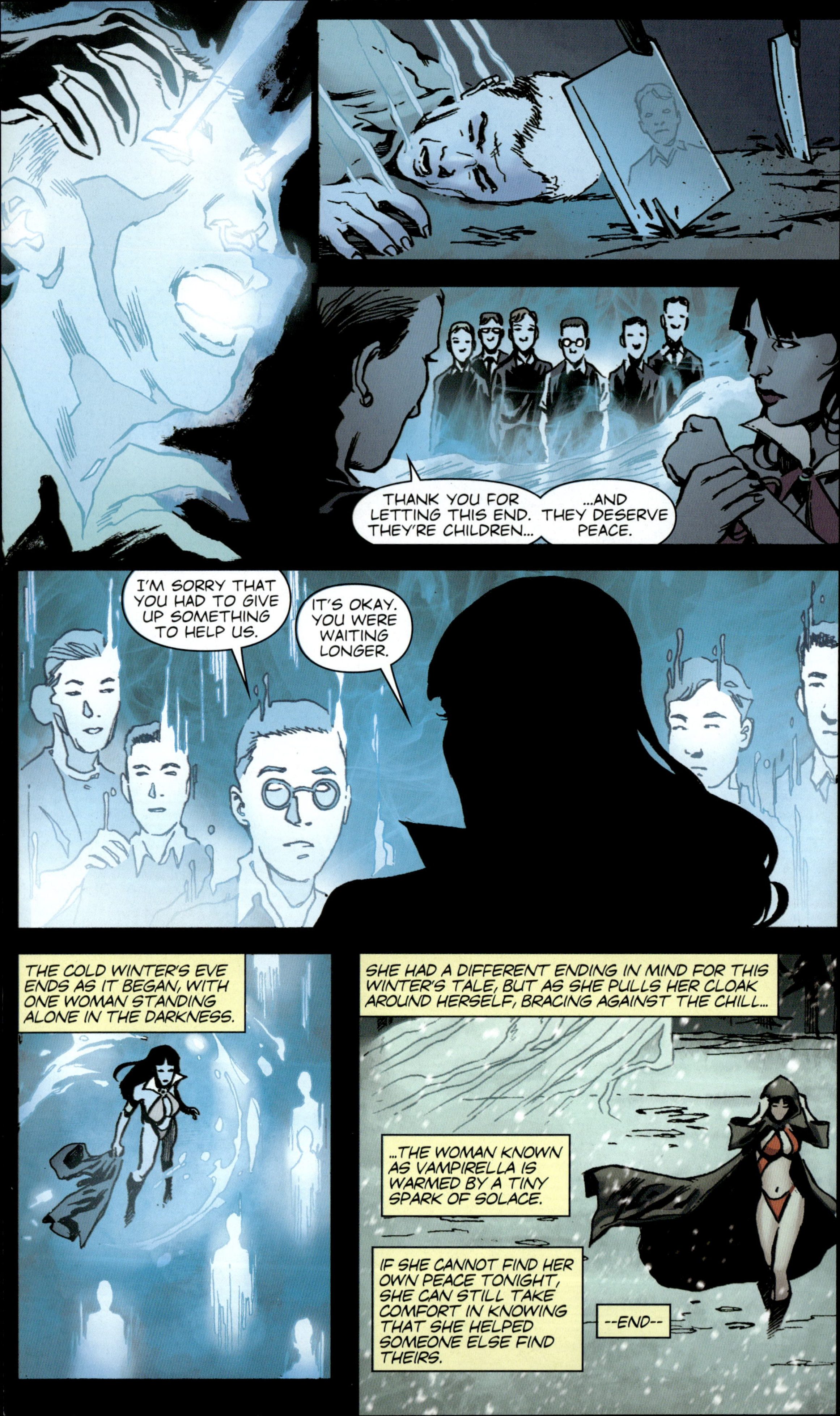
THANK YOU FOR LETTING THIS END. THEY'RE CHILDREN...
...AND THEY DESERVE PEACE.
I'M SORRY THAT YOU HAD TO GIVE UP SOMETHING TO HELP US.
IT'S OKAY. YOU WERE WAITING LONGER.
THE COLD WINTER'S EVE ENDS AS IT BEGAN, WITH ONE WOMAN STANDING ALONE IN THE DARKNESS.
SHE HAD A DIFFERENT ENDING IN MIND FOR THIS WINTER'S TALE, BUT AS SHE PULLS HER CLOAK AROUND HERSELF, BRACING AGAINST THE CHILL...
...THE WOMAN KNOWN AS VAMPIRELLA IS WARMED BY A TINY SPARK OF SOLACE.
IF SHE CANNOT FIND HER OWN PEACE TONIGHT, SHE CAN STILL TAKE COMFORT IN KNOWING THAT SHE HELPED SOMEONE ELSE FIND THEIRS.
--END--

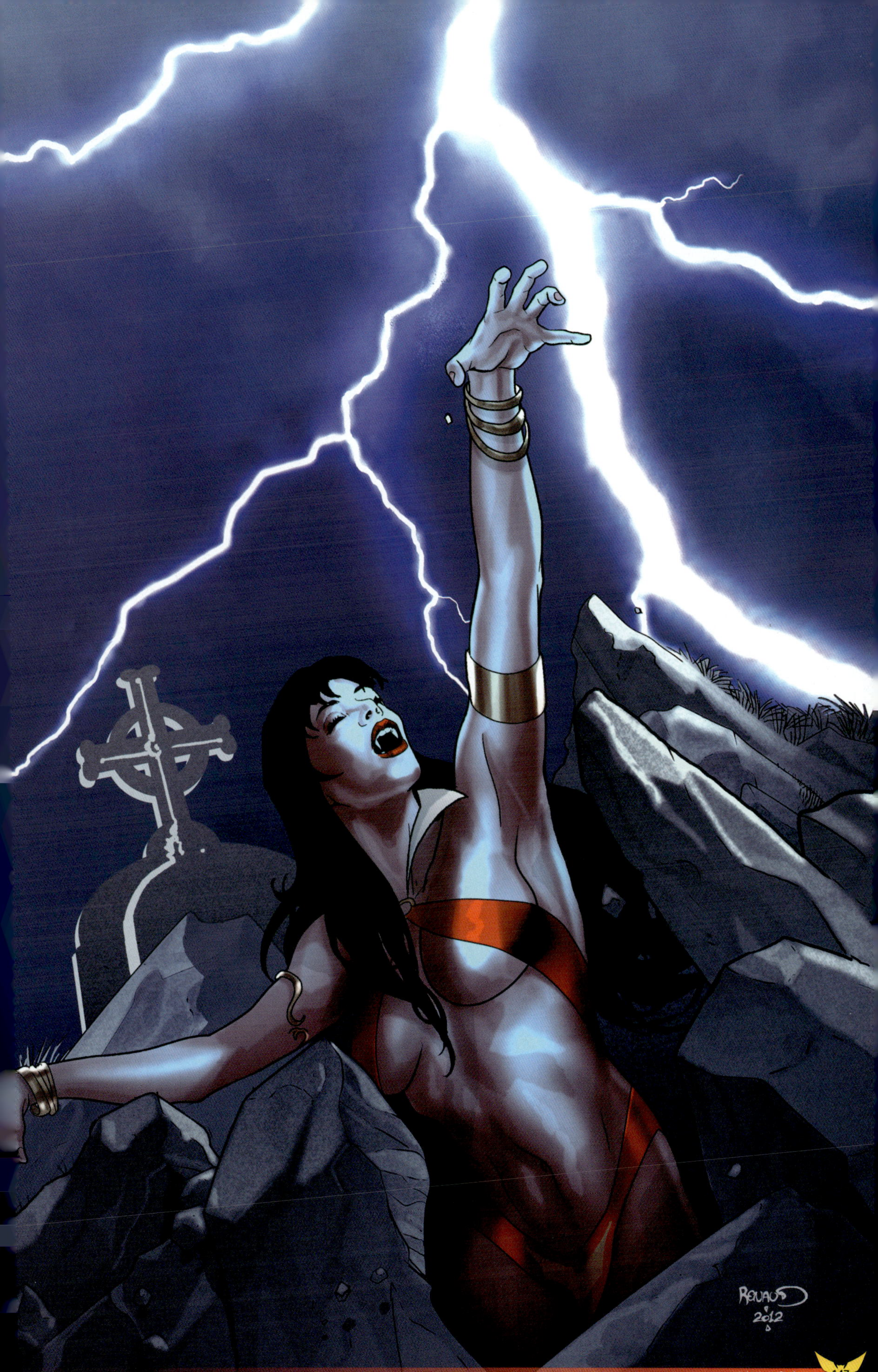
RENAUD
2012

issue #21 cover by **PAUL RENAUD**

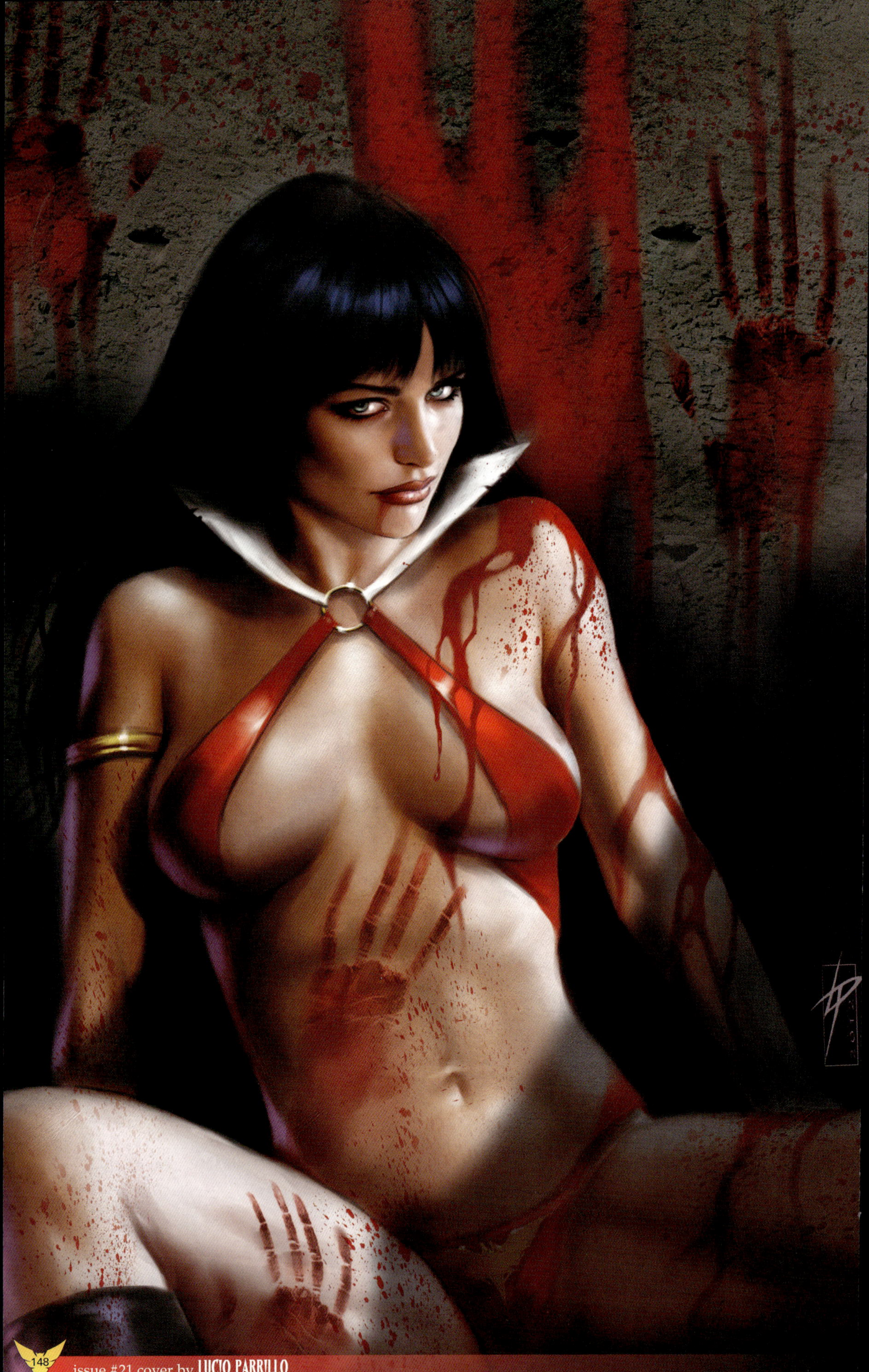

issue #21 cover by LUCIO PARRILLO

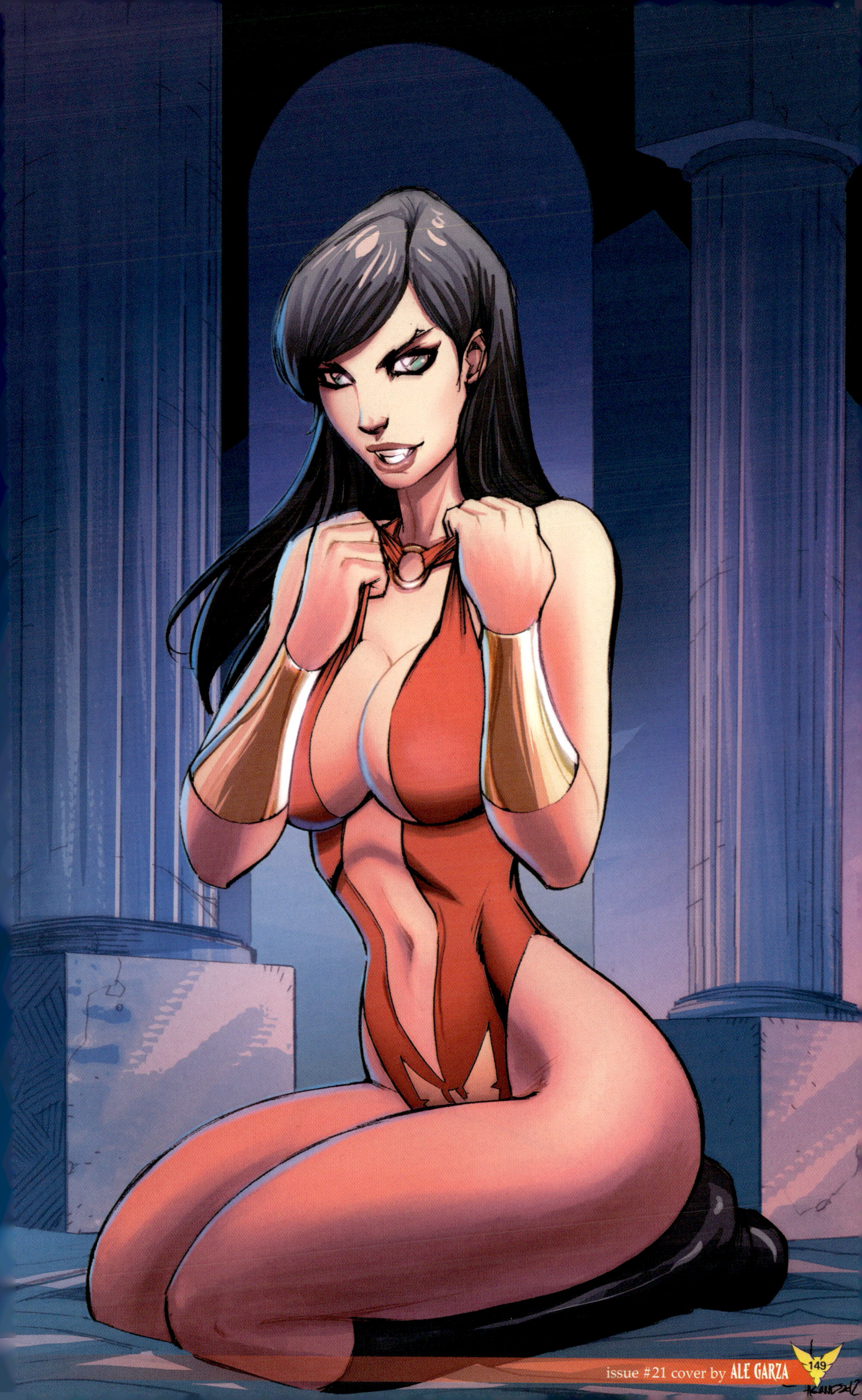

issue #21 cover by **ALE GARZA**

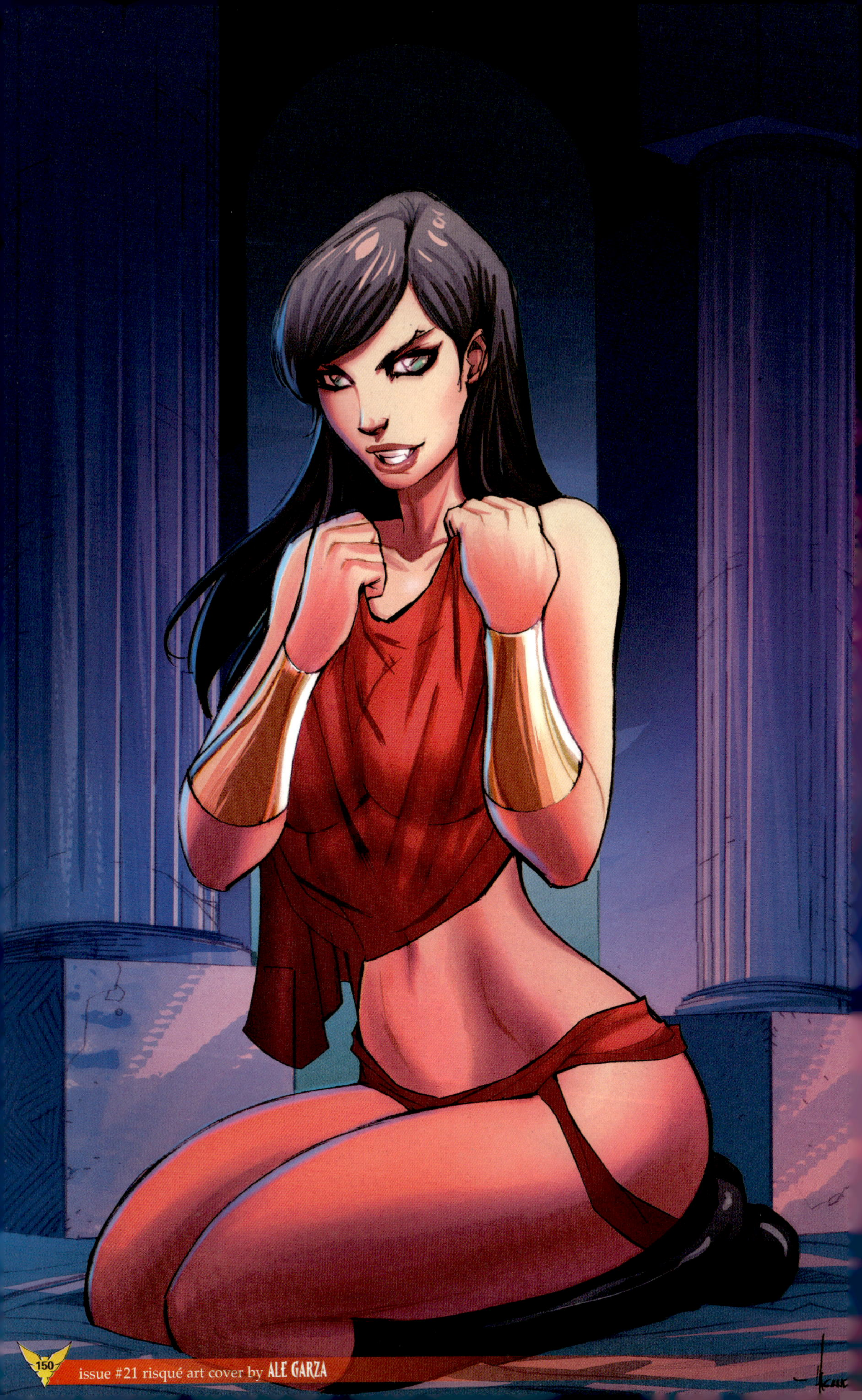

issue #21 risqué art cover by **ALE GARZA**

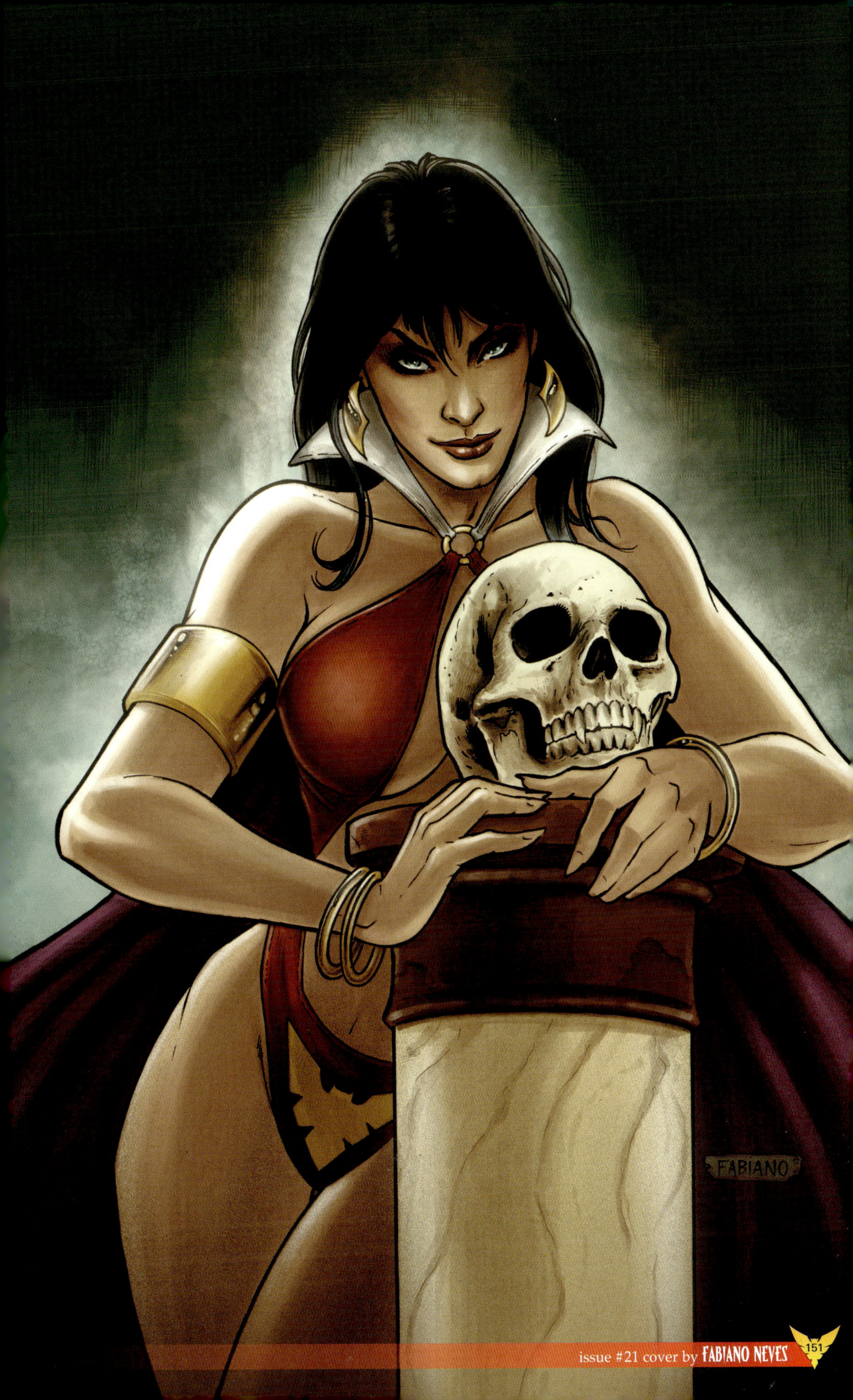
FABIANO

issue #21 cover by FABIANO NEVES

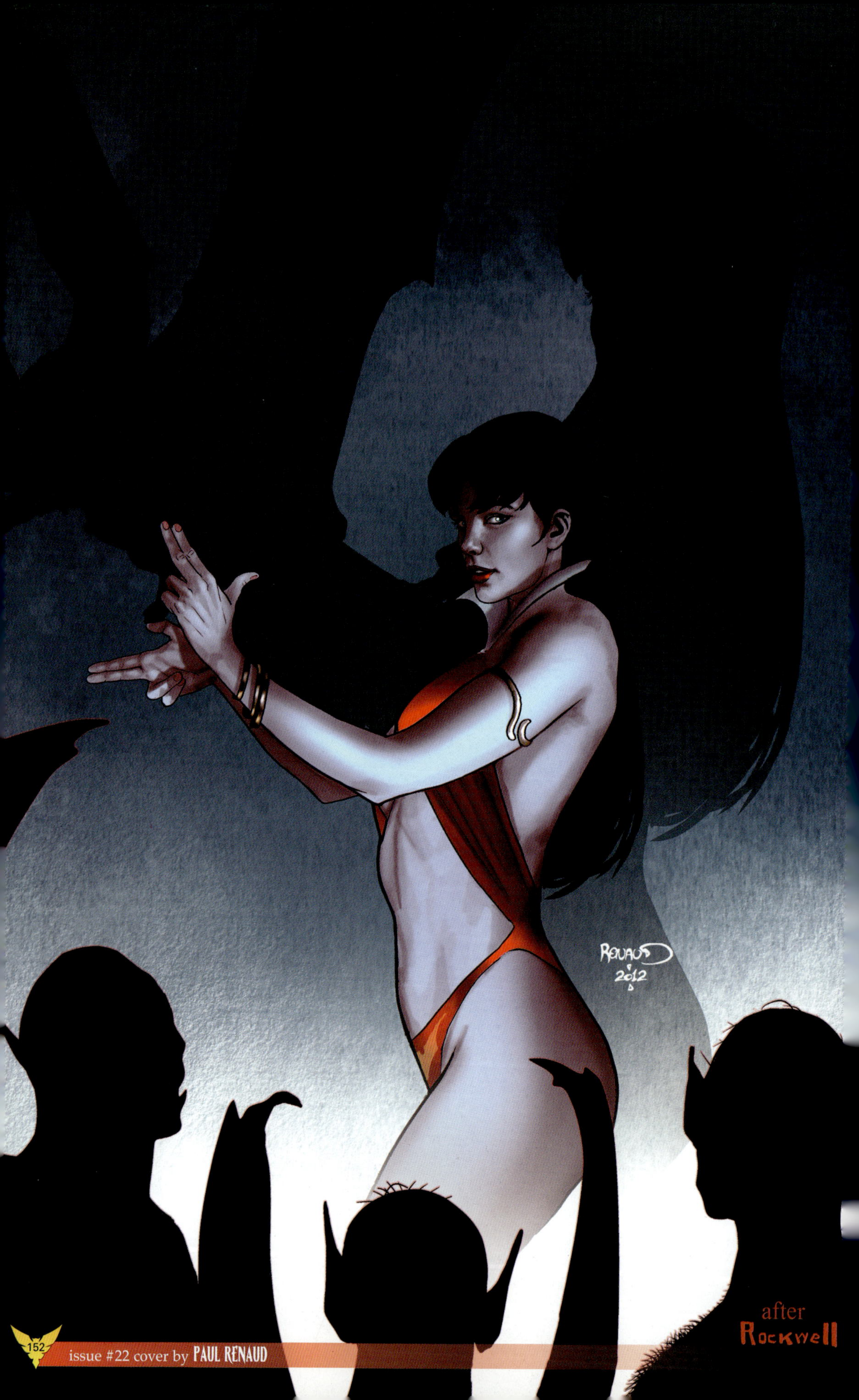
RENAUD 2012
after Rockwell

issue #22 cover by PAUL RENAUD

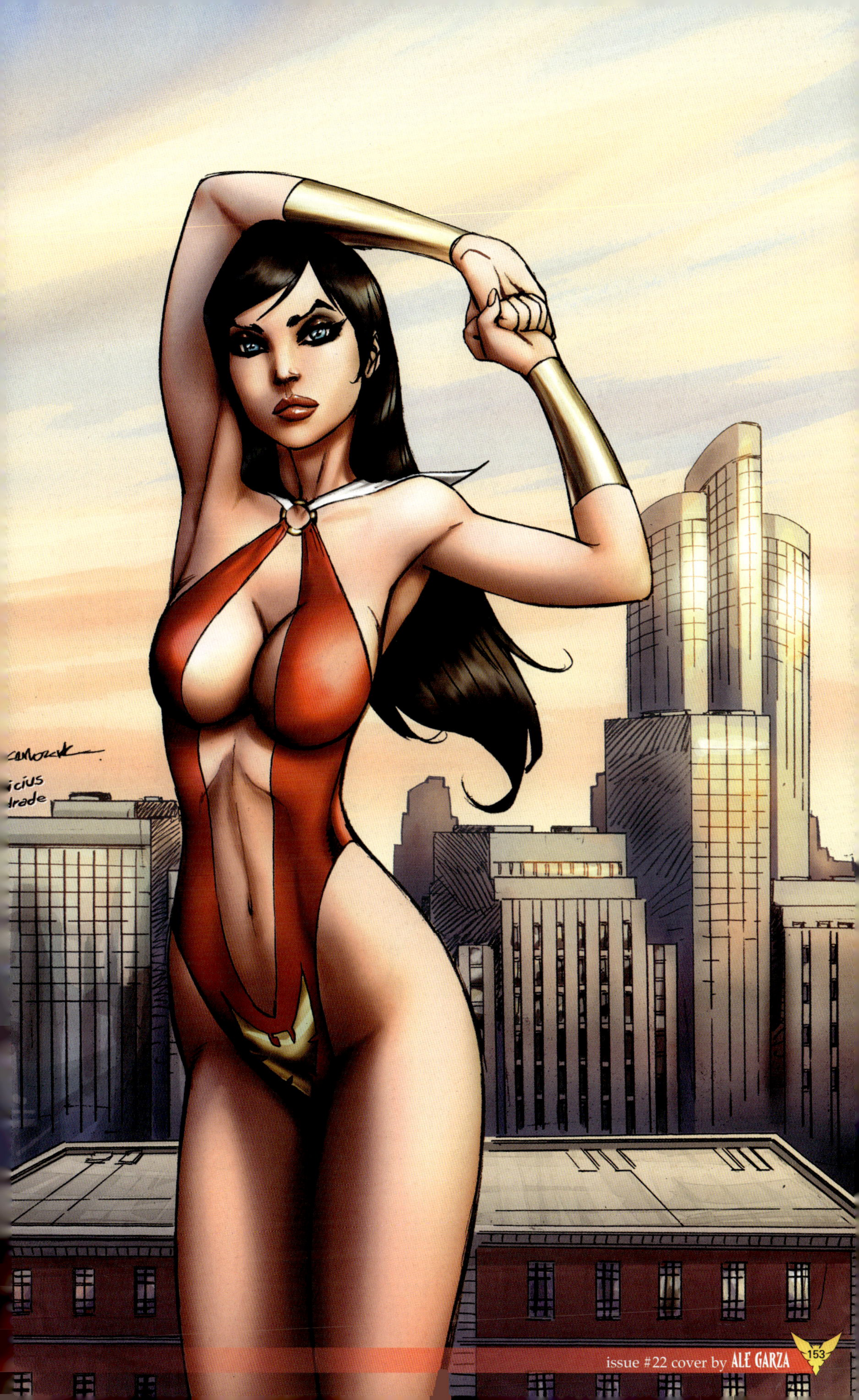

issue #22 cover by **ALE GARZA**

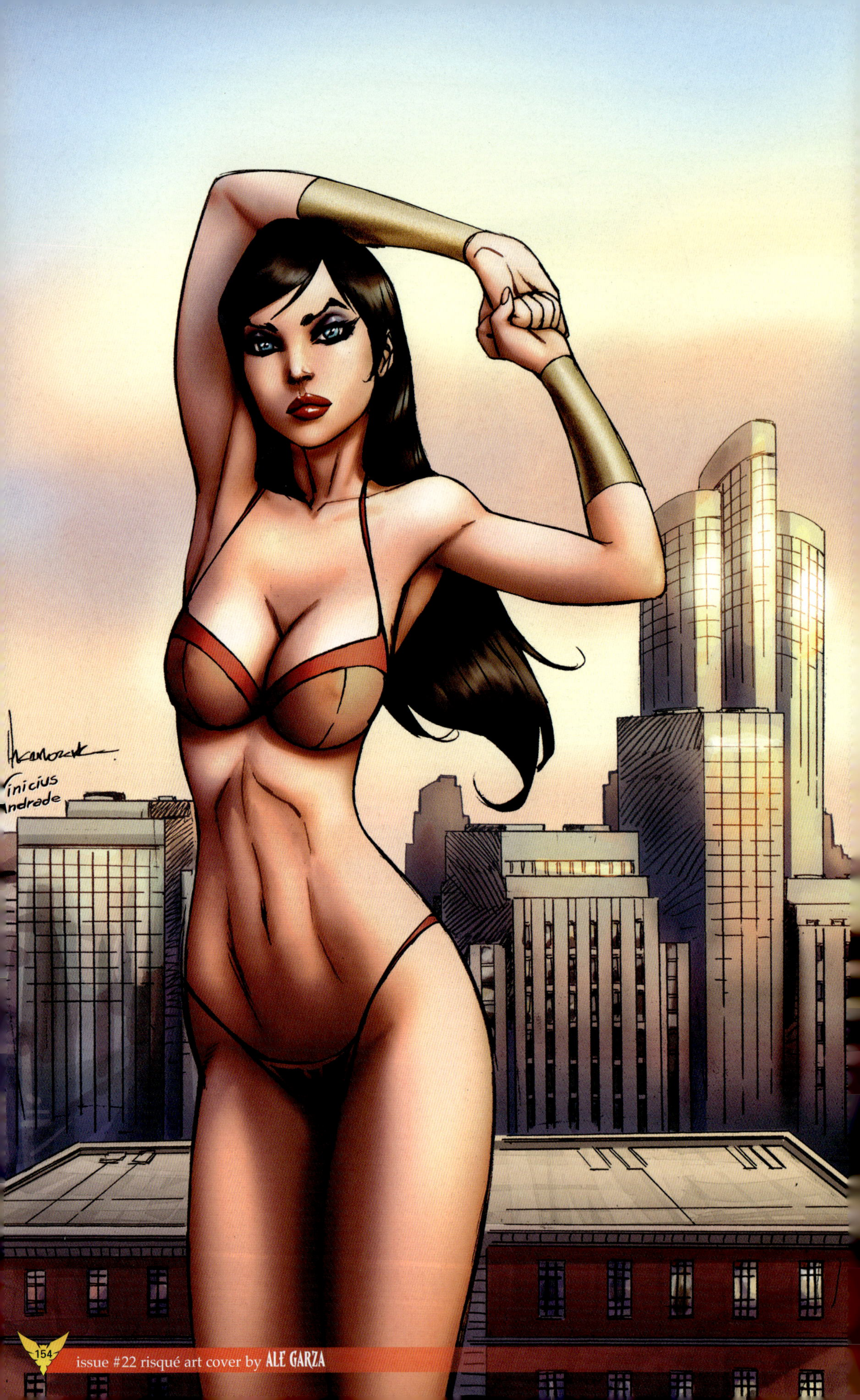
Vinicius
Andrade

issue #22 risqué art cover by ALE GARZA

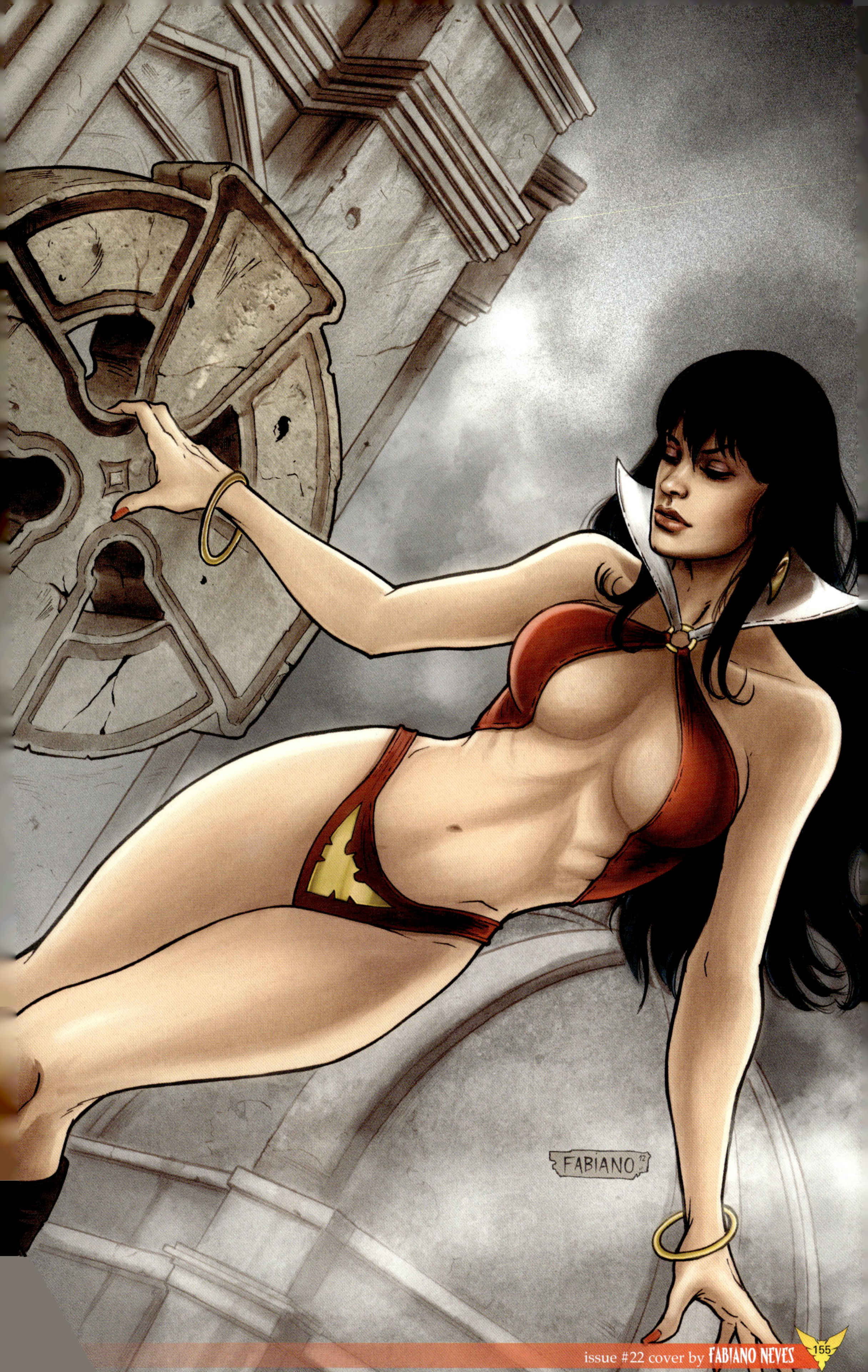
FABIANO 12

issue #22 cover by FABIANO NEVES

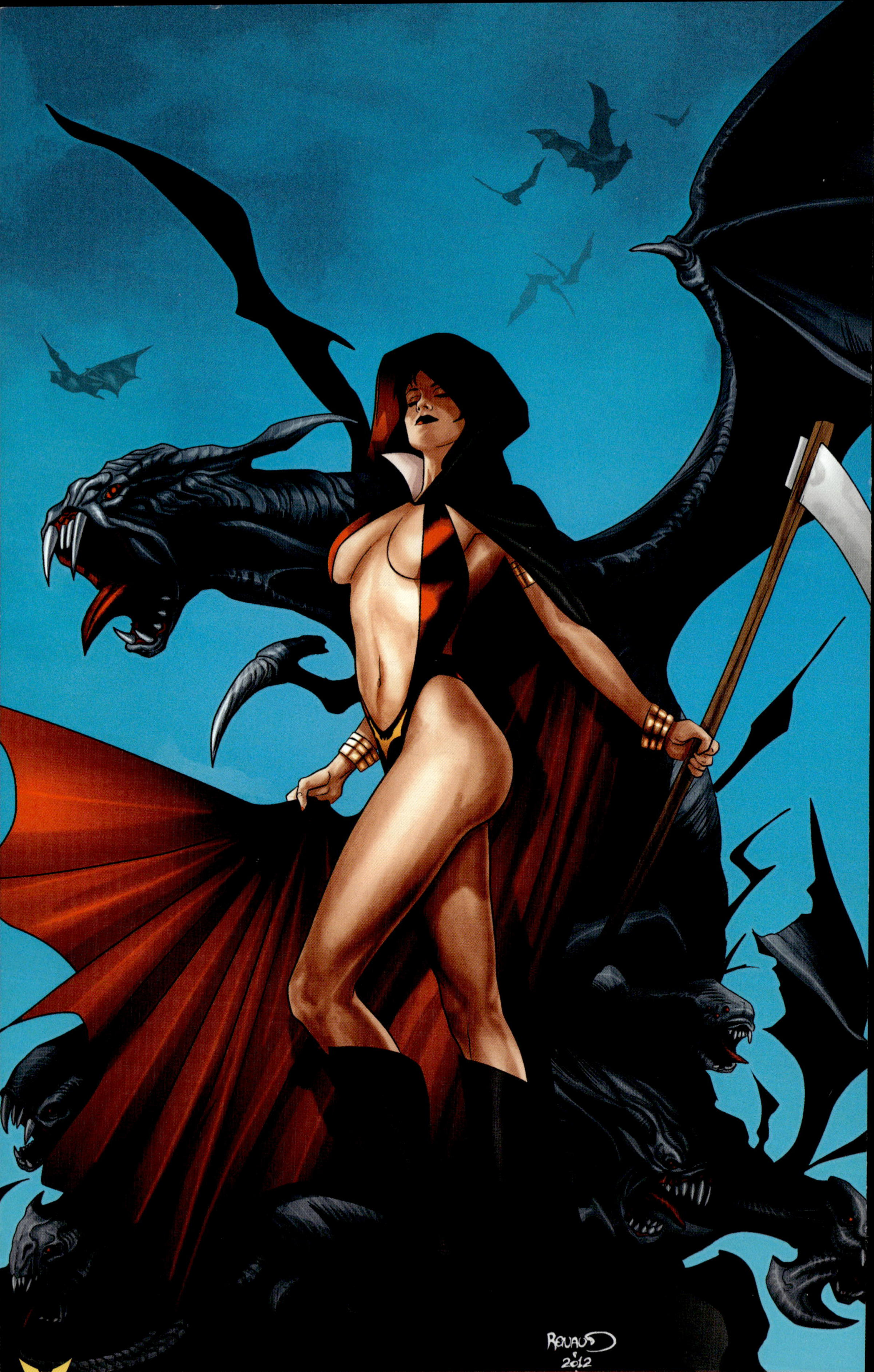
RENAUD
2012

issue #23 cover by PAUL RENAUD

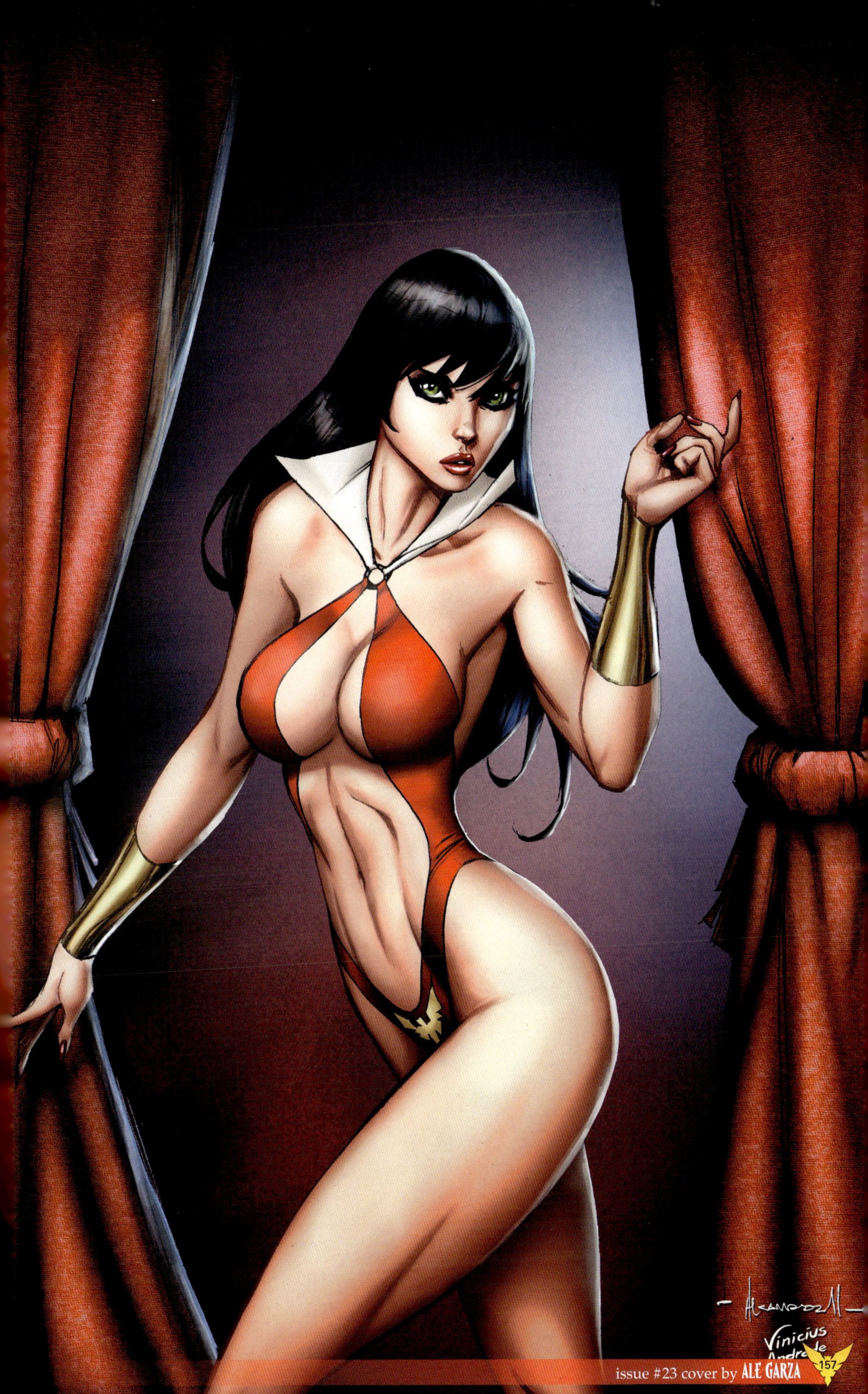

issue #23 cover by **ALE GARZA**

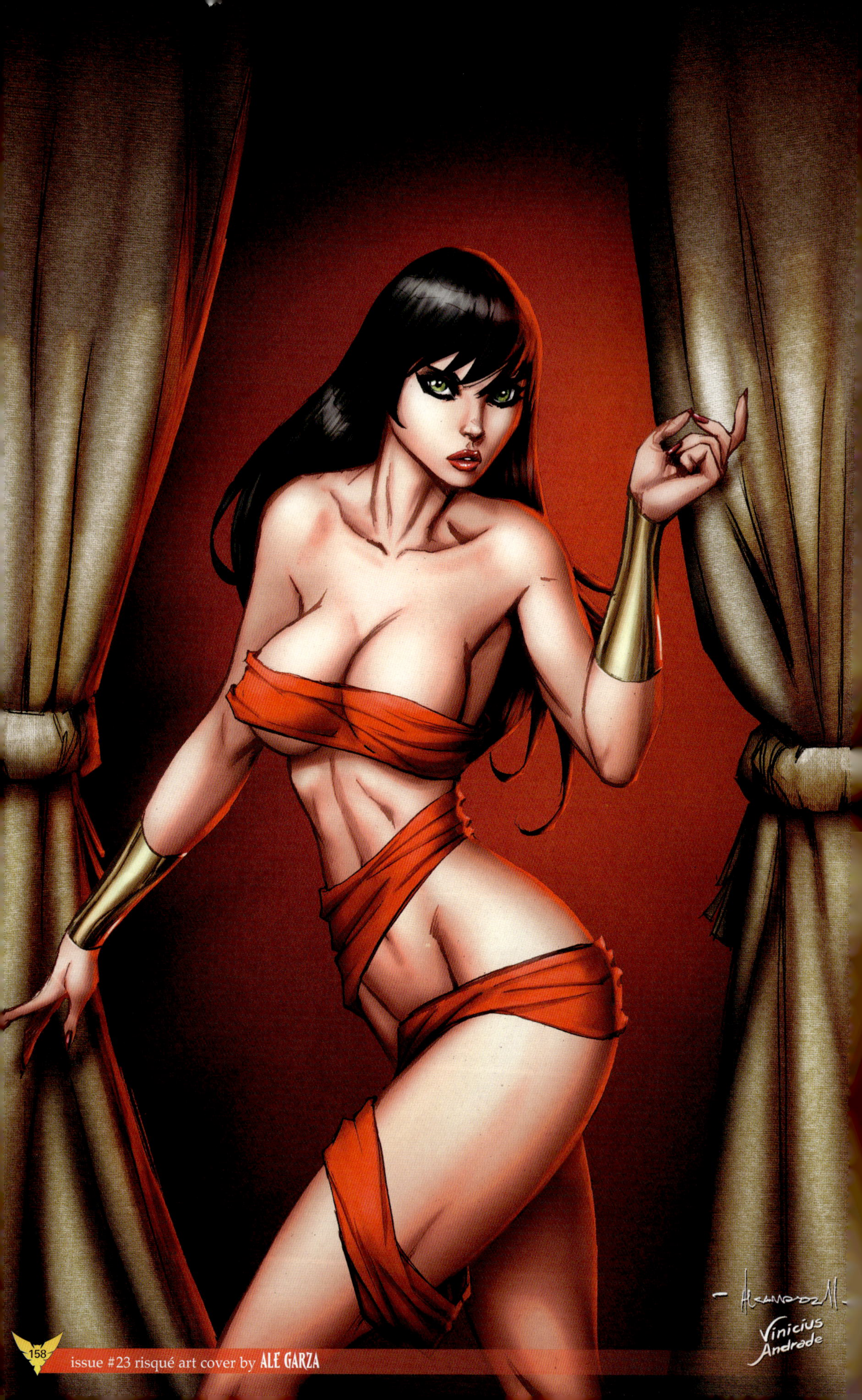
Vinicius
Andrade

issue #23 risqué art cover by **ALE GARZA**

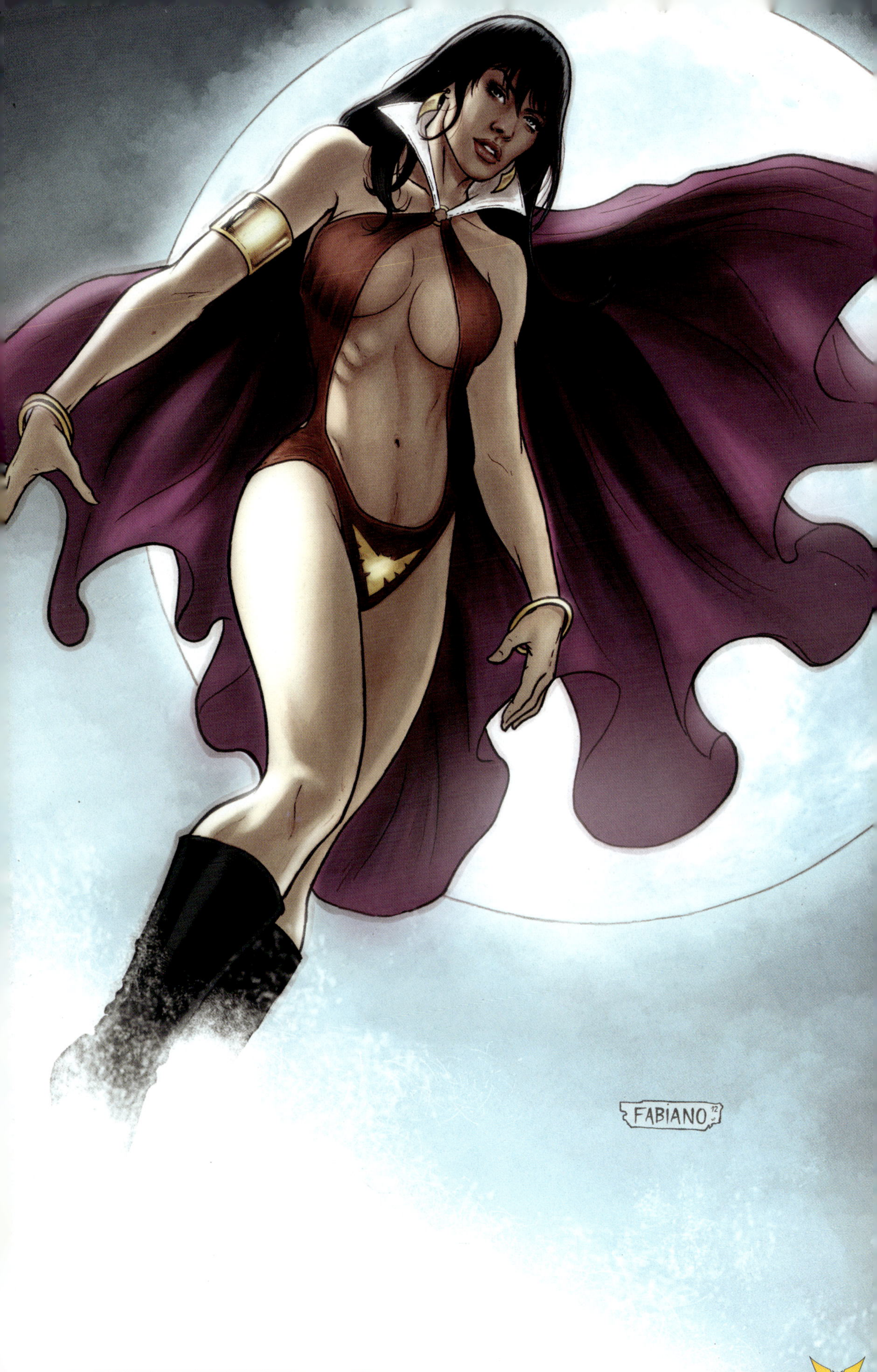
FABIANO 12

issue #23 cover by FABIANO NEVES

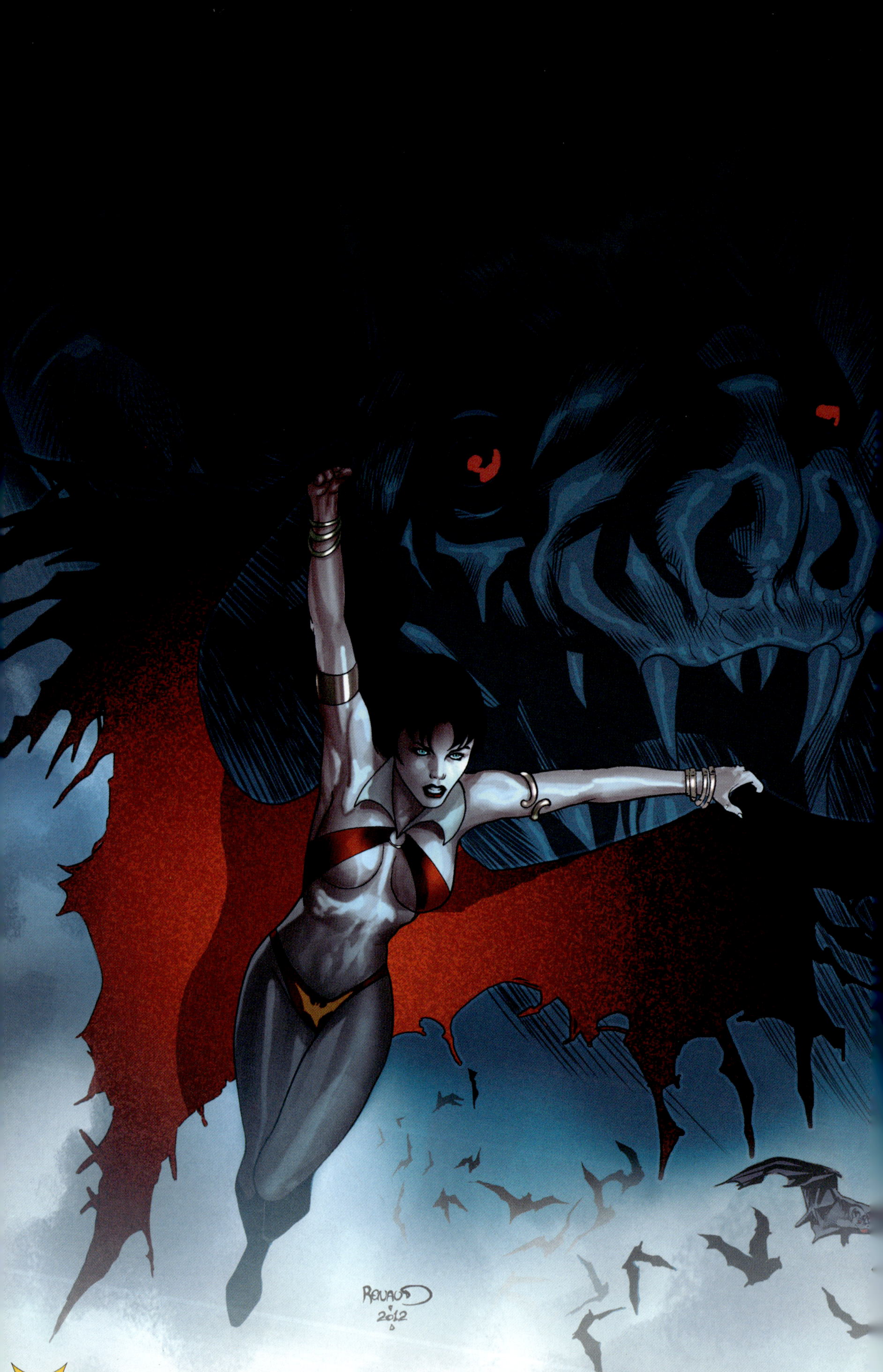
RENAUD
2012

issue #24 cover by **PAUL RENAUD**

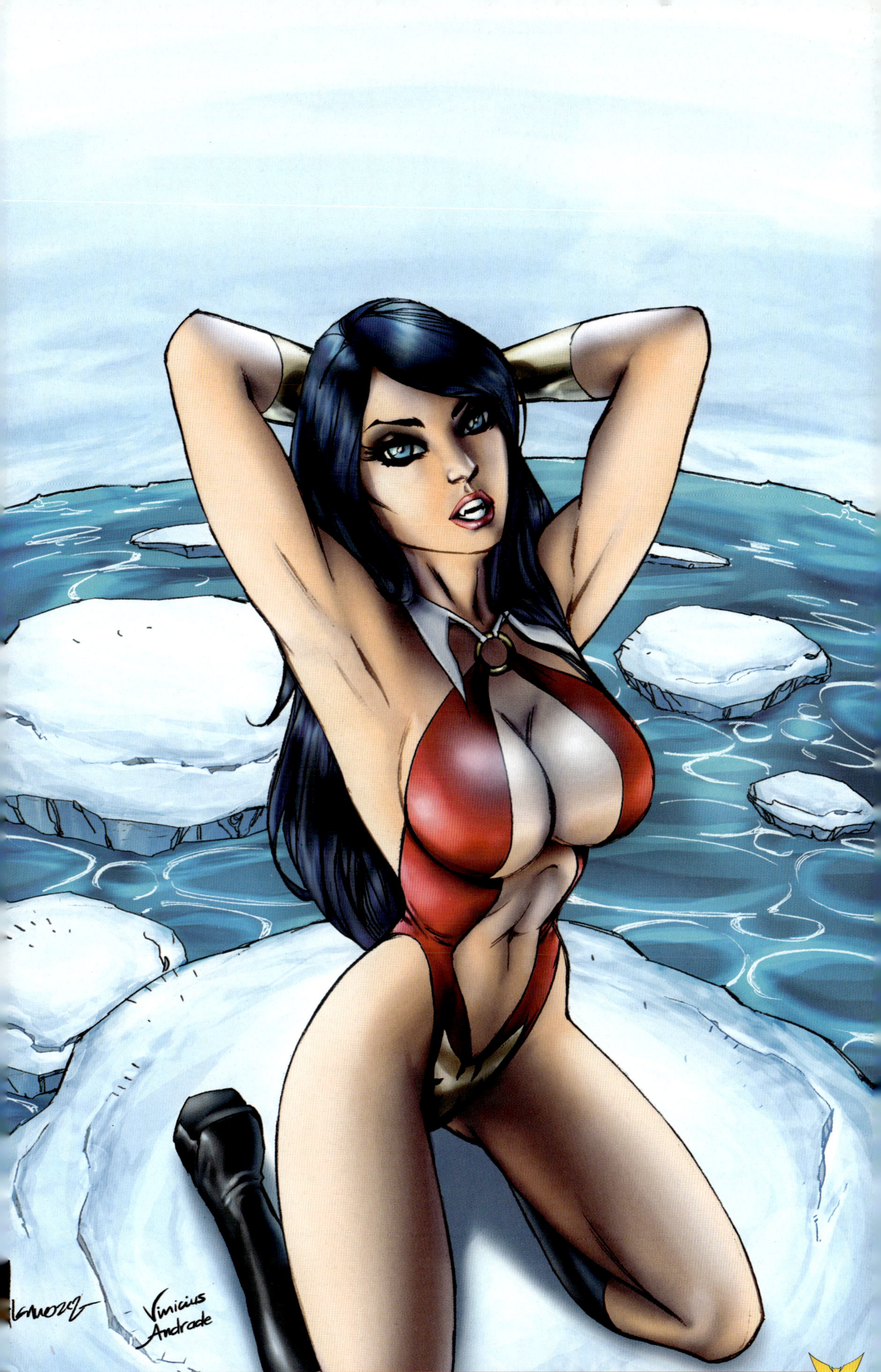
Vinicius Andrade

issue #24 cover by ALE GARZA

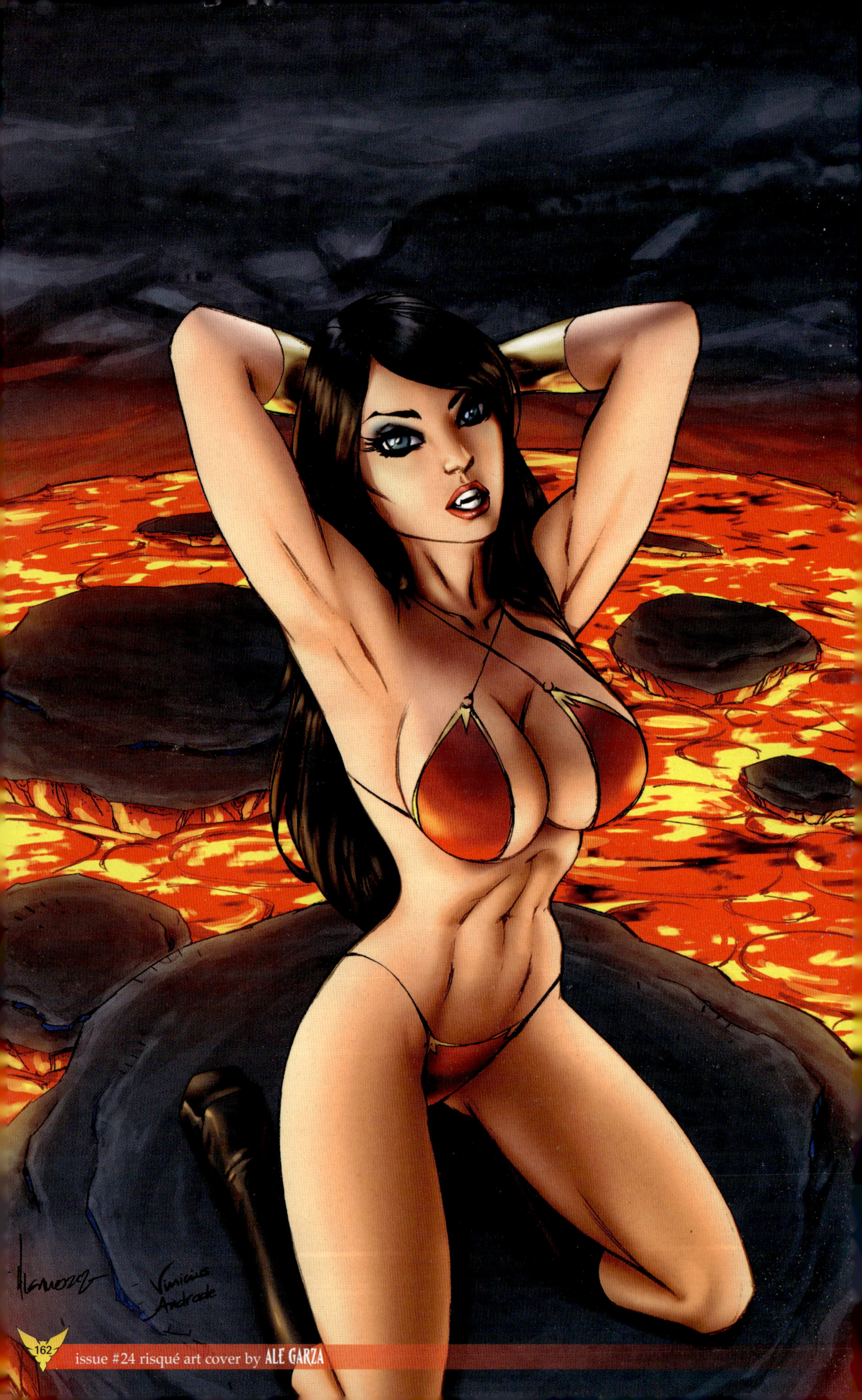

issue #24 risqué art cover by ALE GARZA

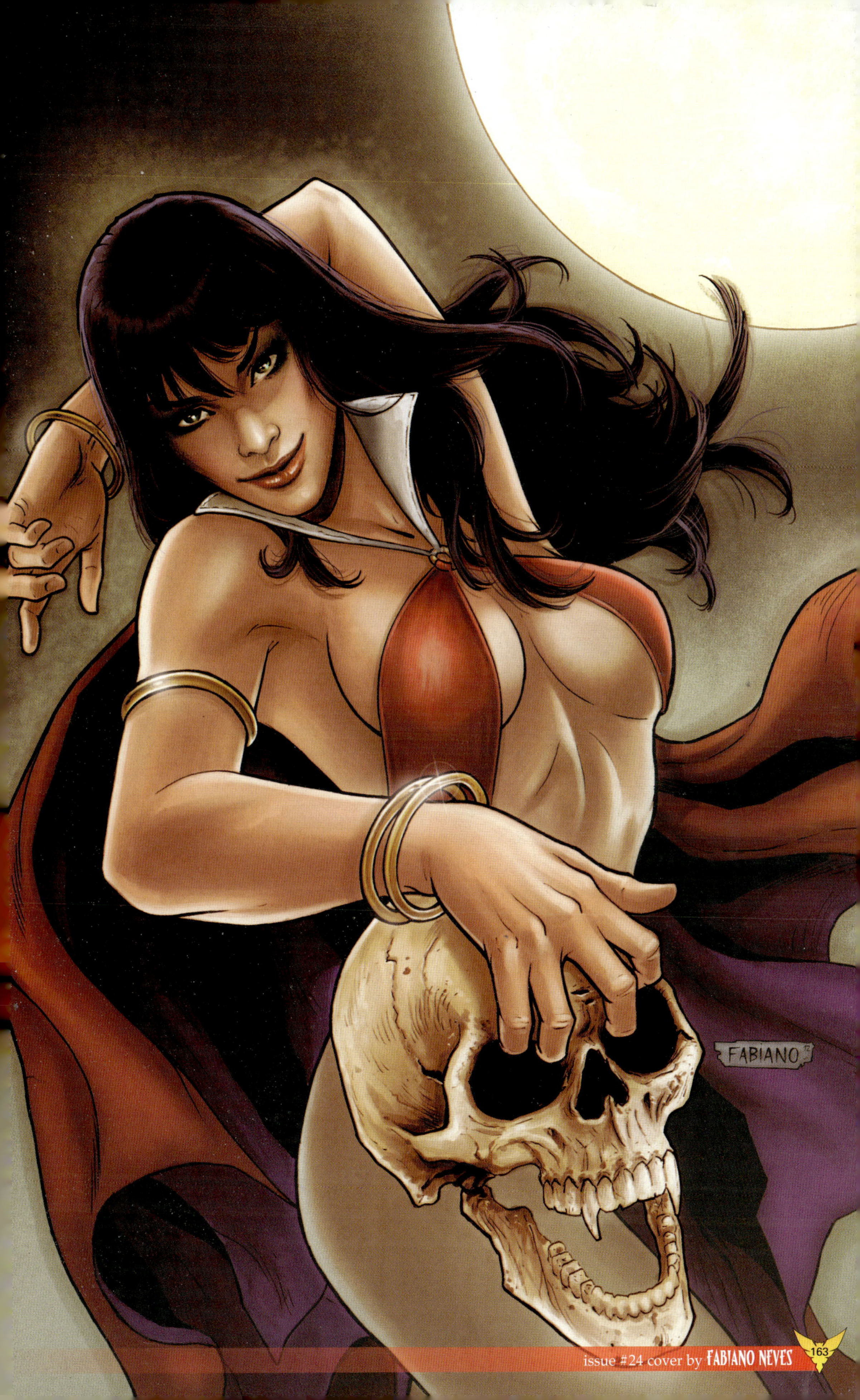
FABIANO

issue #24 cover by FABIANO NEVES

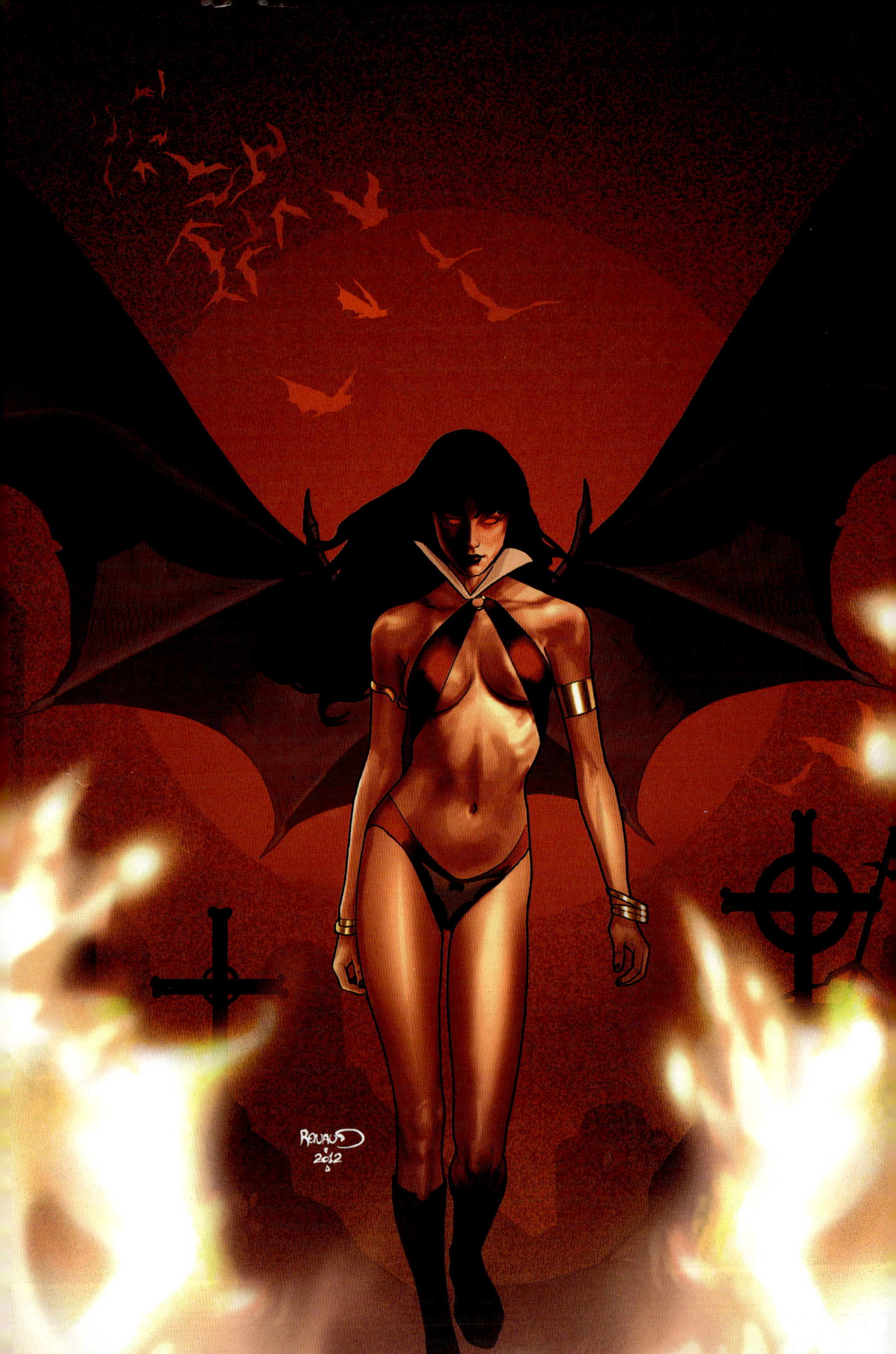
RENAUD
2012

issue #25 cover by **PAUL RENAUD**

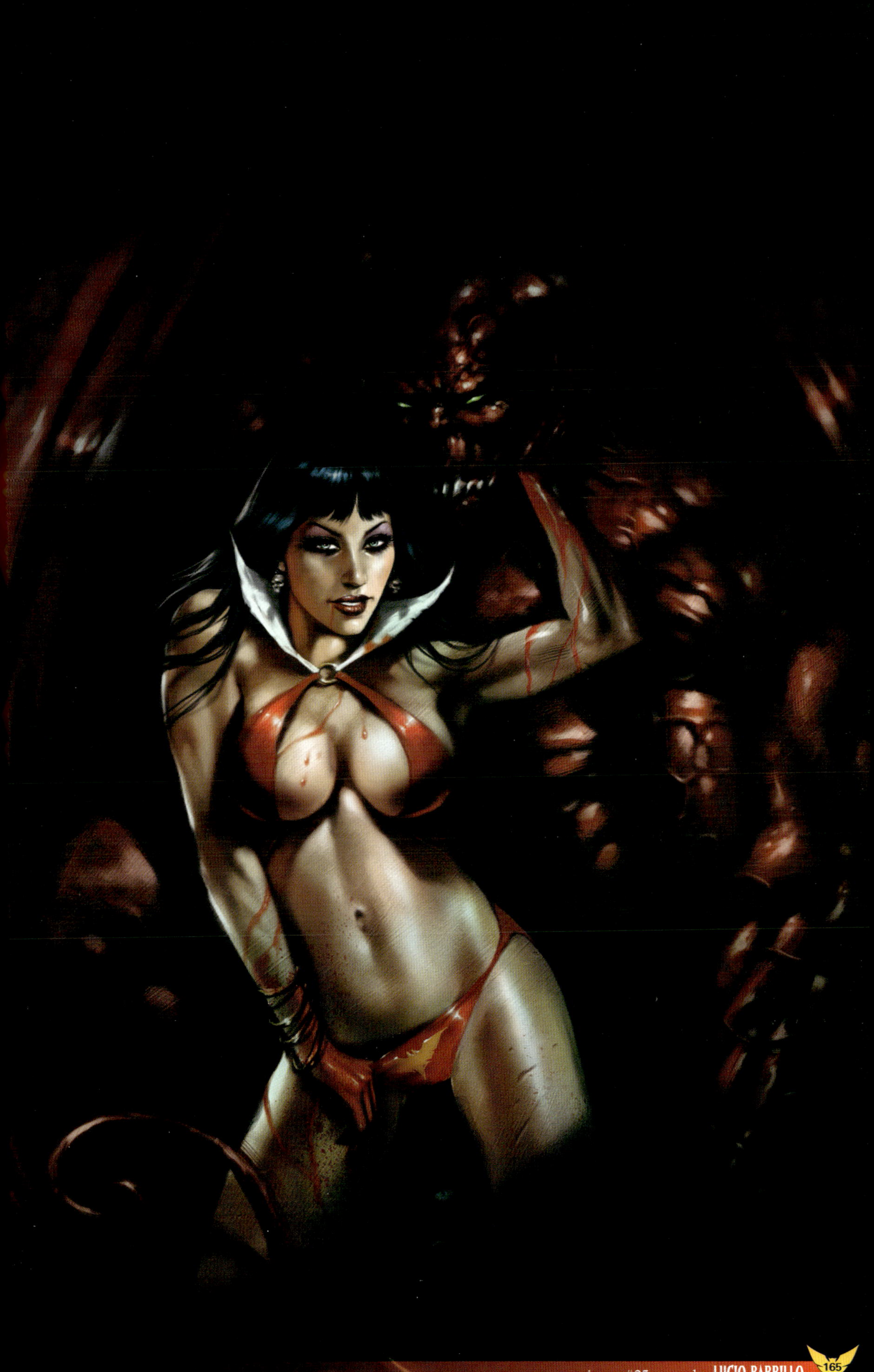

issue #25 cover by LUCIO PARRILLO

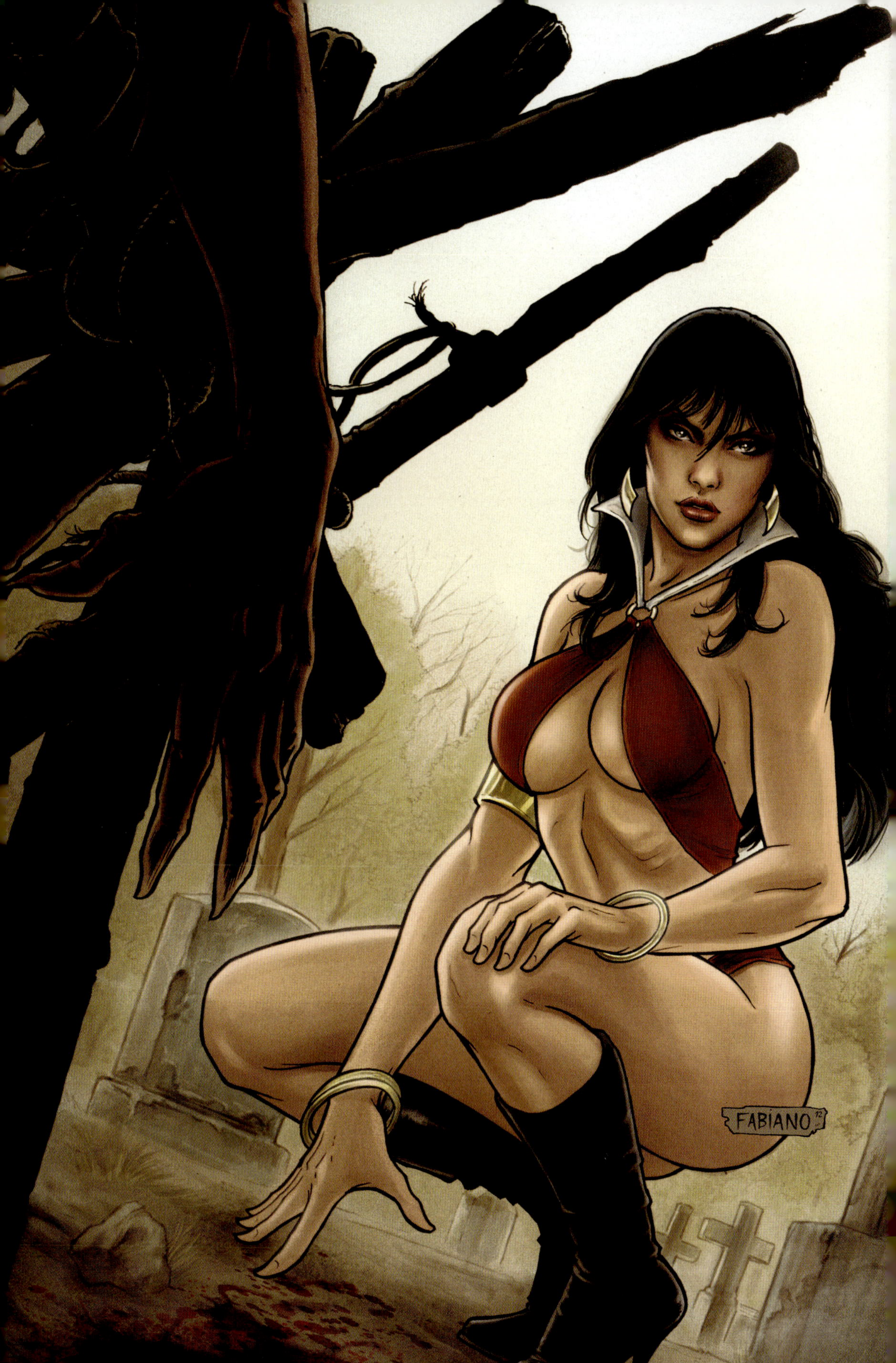
FABIANO '12

issue #25 cover by FABIANO NEVES

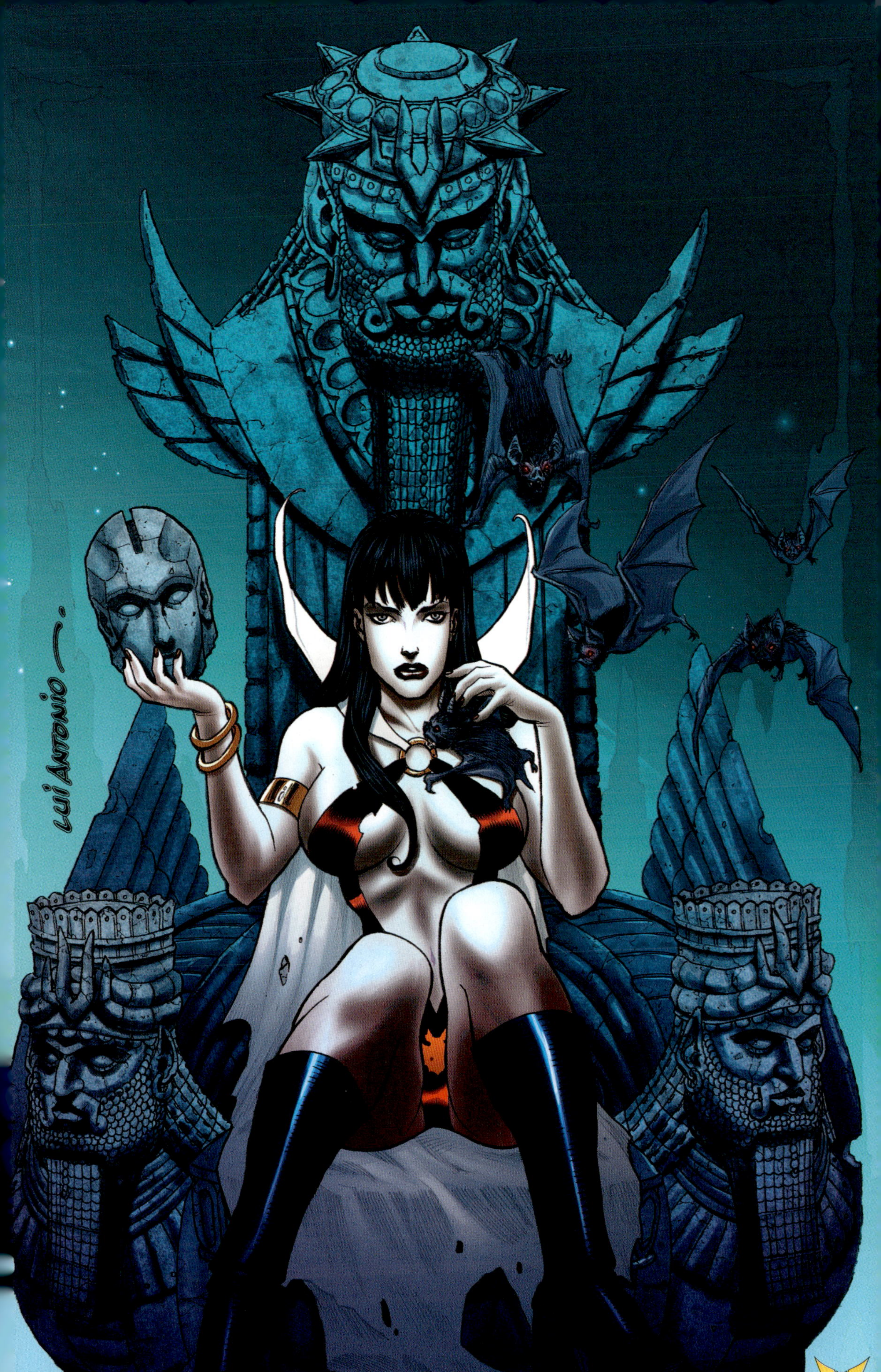
LUI ANTONIO

issue #25 cover by LUI ANTONIO

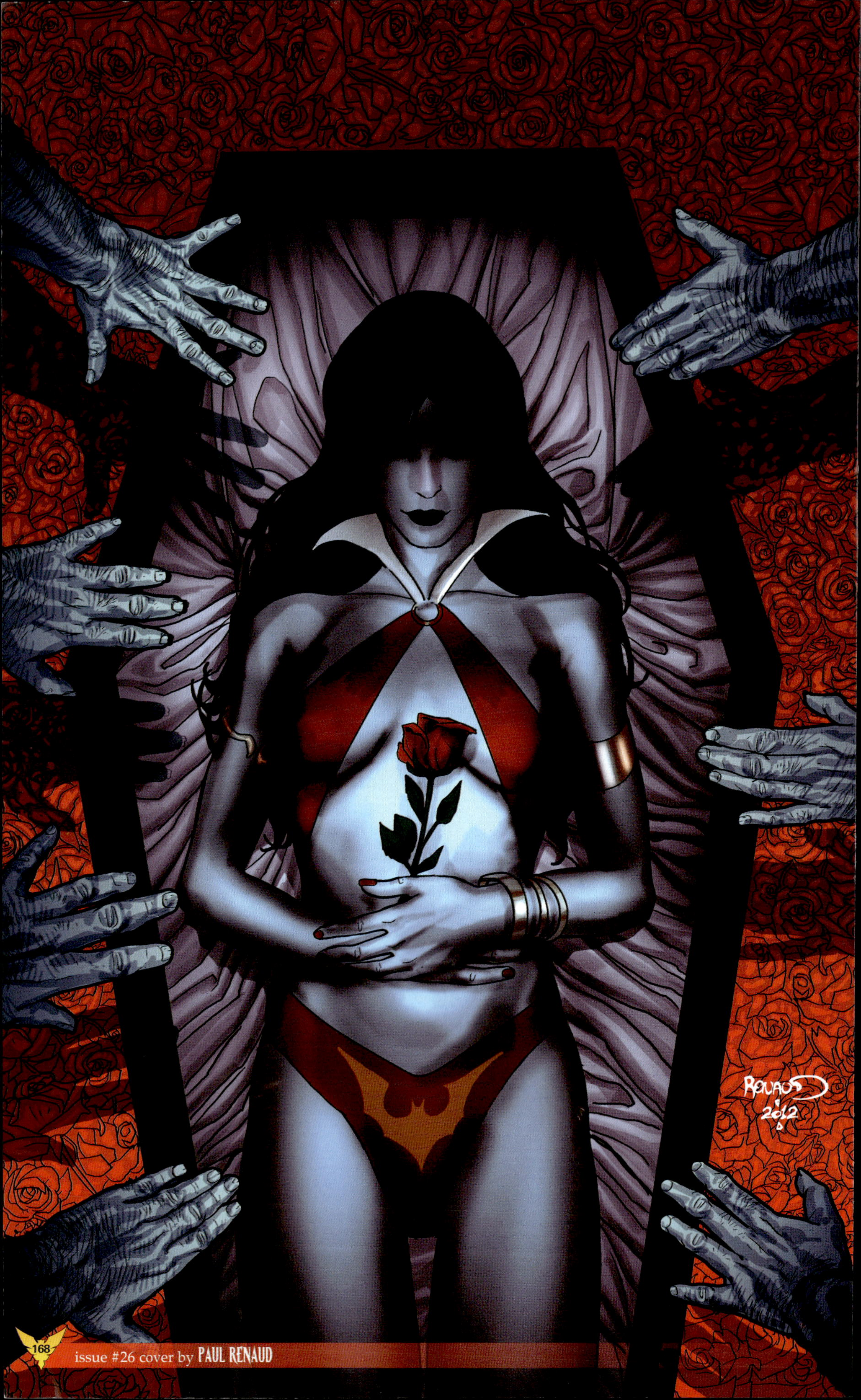
RENAUD
2012

issue #26 cover by PAUL RENAUD

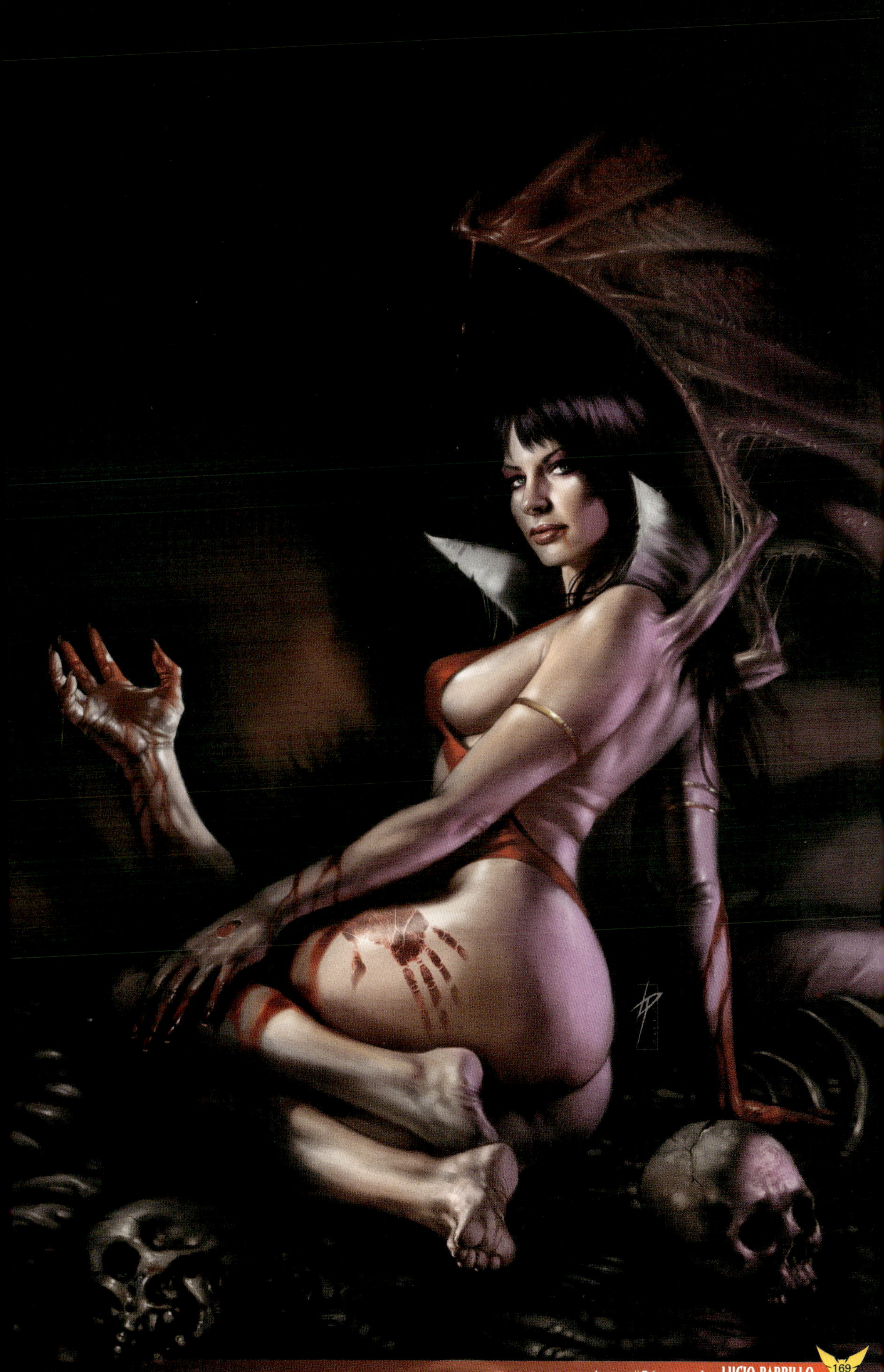

issue #26 cover by LUCIO PARRILLO

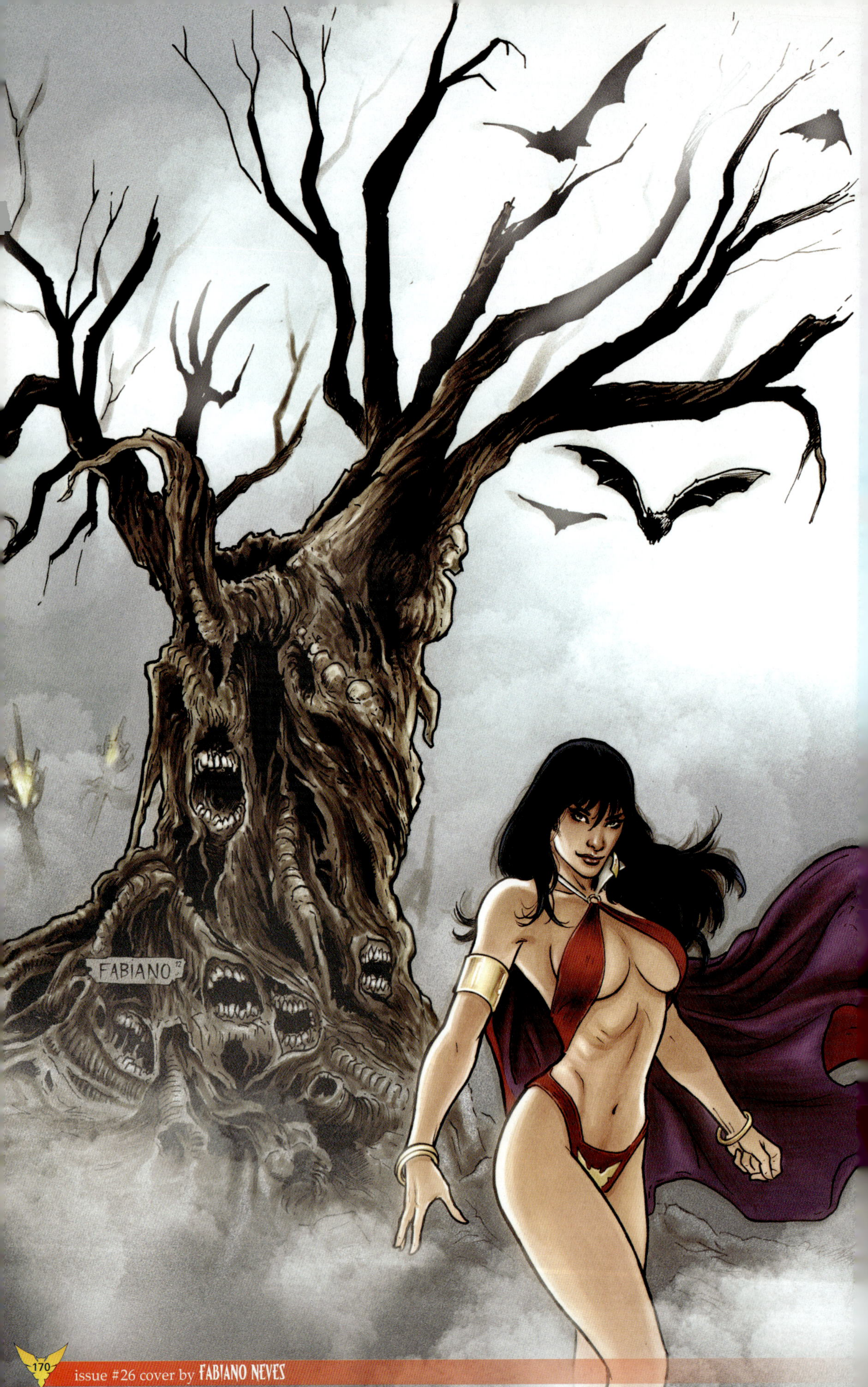
FABIANO '12

issue #26 cover by FABIANO NEVES

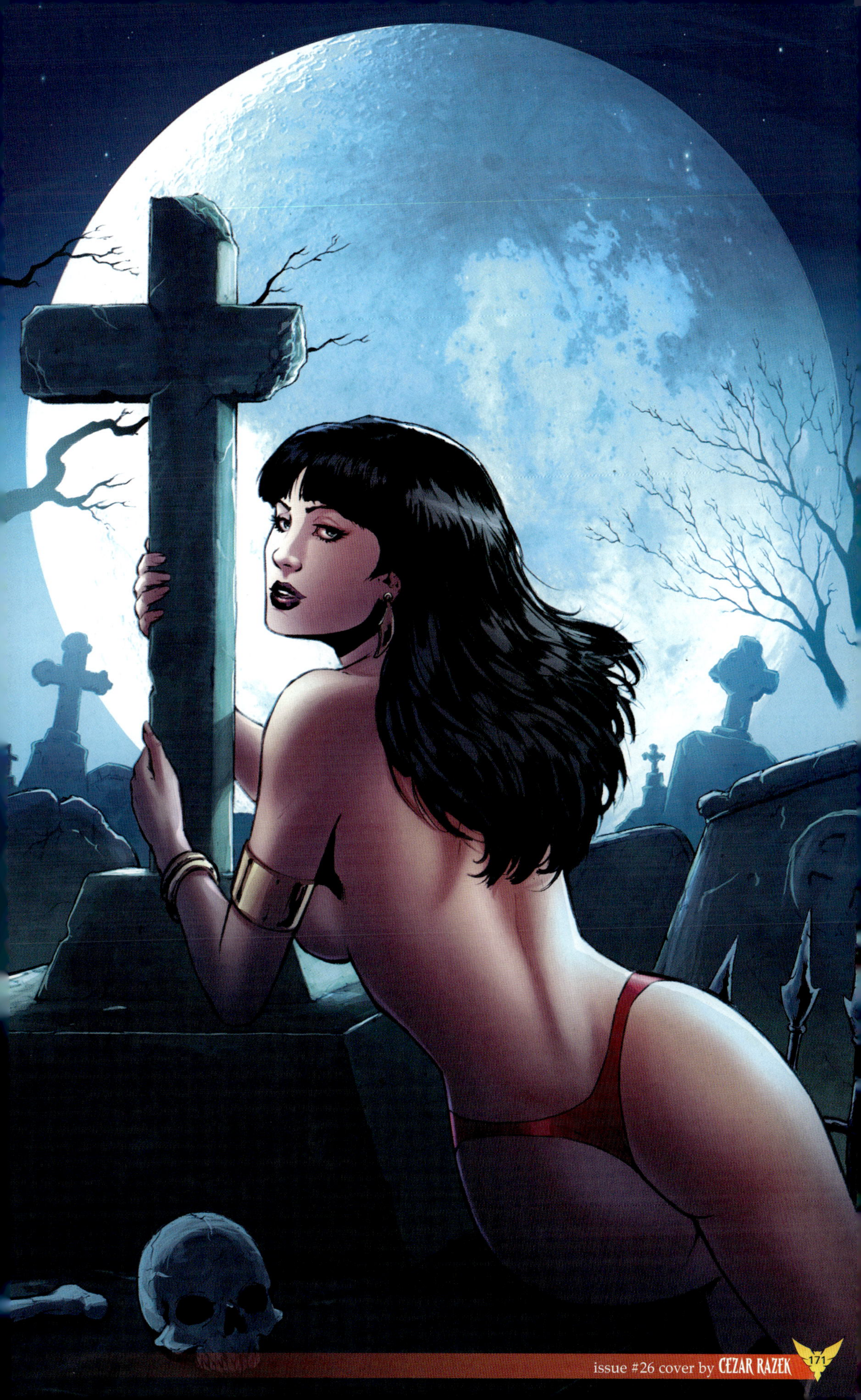

issue #26 cover by CEZAR RAZEK

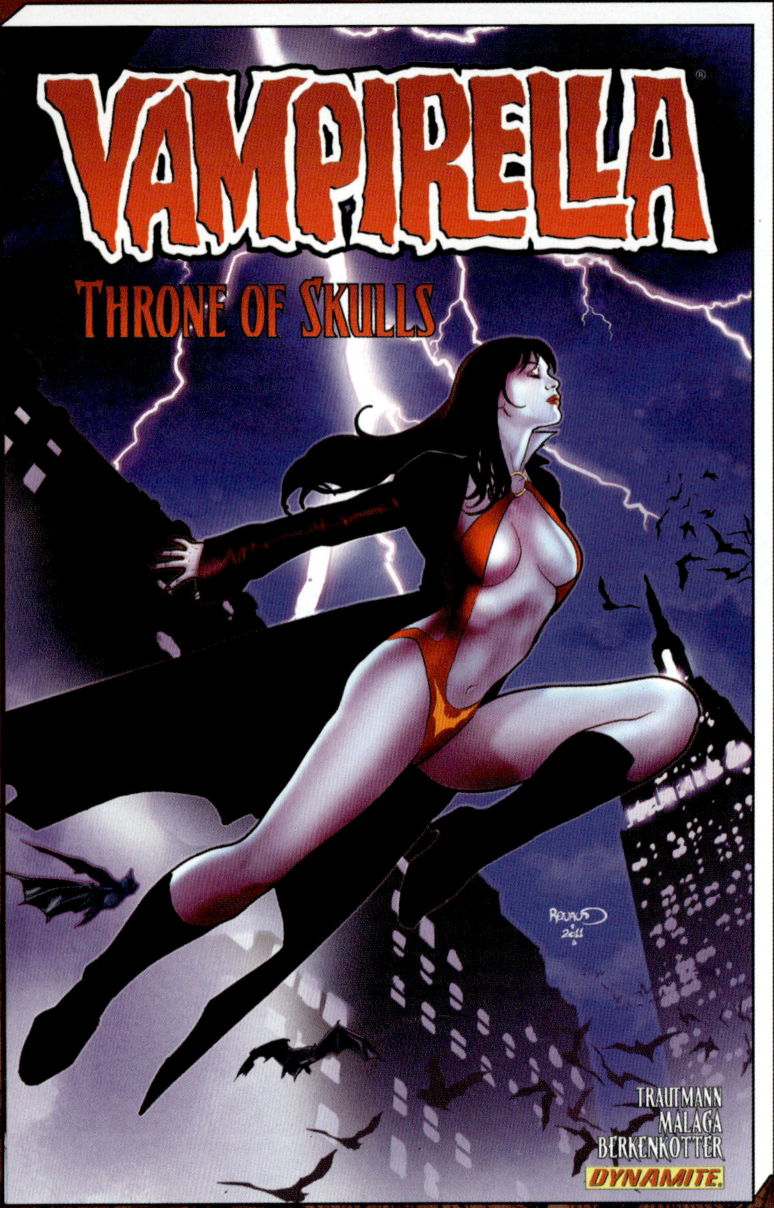
VAMPIRELLA
THRONE OF SKULLS
TRAUTMANN
MALAGA
BERKENKOTTER
DYNAMITE

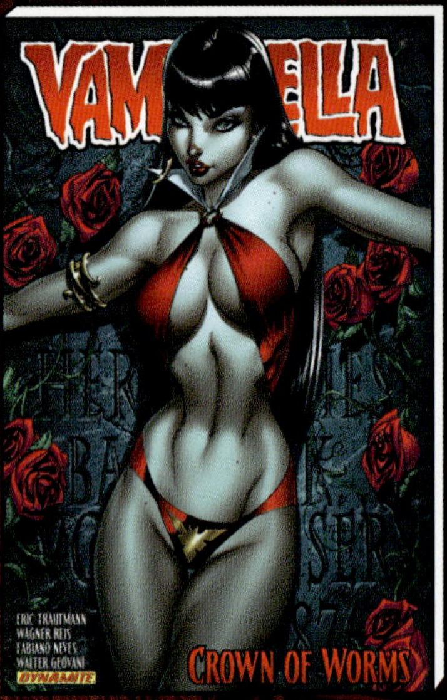
VAMPIRELLA
ERIC TRAUTMANN
WAGNER REIS
FABIANO NEVES
WALTER GEOVANI
DYNAMITE
CROWN OF WORMS

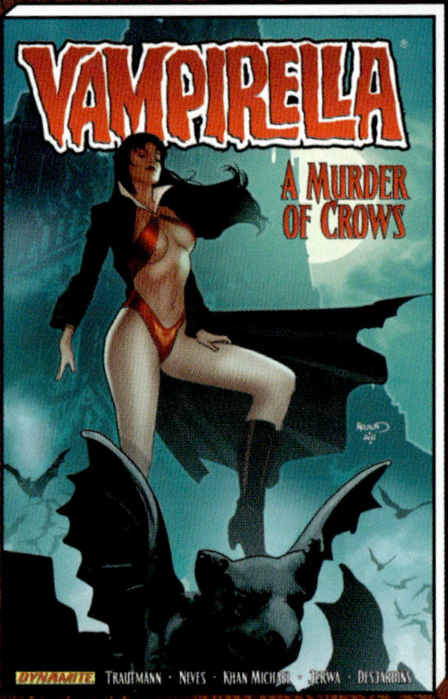
VAMPIRELLA
A MURDER OF CROWS
DYNAMITE TRAUTMANN · NEVES · KHAN MICHAEL · JERWA · DESJARDINS

In Stores Now From Dynamite!

VAMPIRELLA VOL. ONE: "CROWN OF WORMS"

written by ERIC TRAUTMANN art by WAGNER REIS & WALTER GEOVANI cover by J. SCOTT CAMPBELL

Collects issues 1-7

VAMPIRELLA VOL. TWO: "A MURDER OF CROWS"

written by ERIC TRAUTMANN & BRANDON JERWA

art by FABIANO NEVES, HEUBERT KHAN MICHAEL & JOHNNY DESJARDINS cover by PAUL RENAUD

Collects issues 8-11

VAMPIRELLA VOL. THREE: "THRONE OF SKULLS"

written by ERIC TRAUTMANN art by JOSE MALAGA & PATRICK BERKENKOTTER cover by PAUL RENAUD

Collects issues 12 through 20 of the hit series!

WWW.DYNAMITE.COM FOLLOW US ON TWITTER: @DYNAMITECOMICS LIKE US ON FACEBOOK: /DYNAMITECOMICS

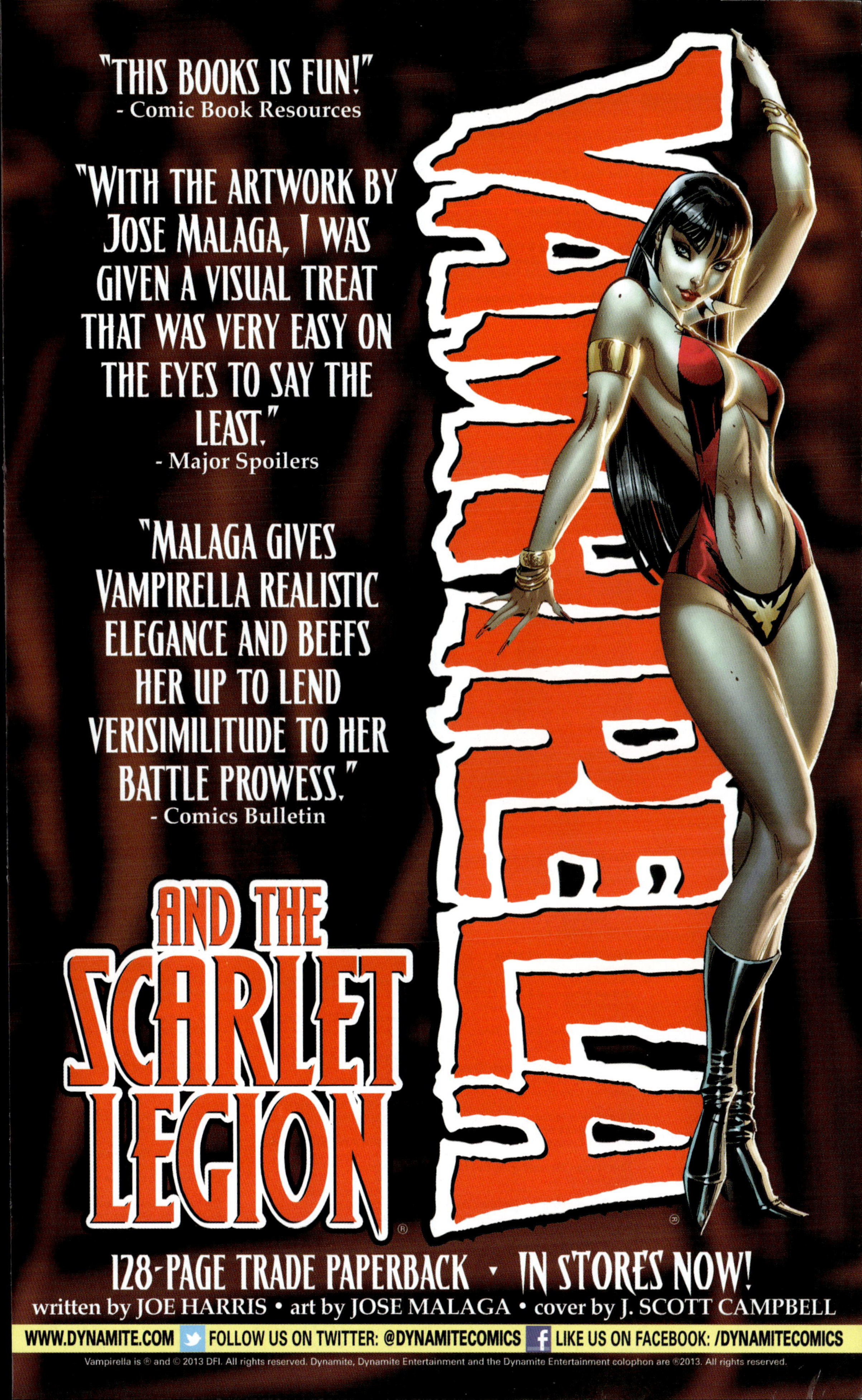
"THIS BOOKS IS FUN!"
- Comic Book Resources
"WITH THE ARTWORK BY JOSE MALAGA, I WAS GIVEN A VISUAL TREAT THAT WAS VERY EASY ON THE EYES TO SAY THE LEAST."
- Major Spoilers
"MALAGA GIVES VAMPIRELLA REALISTIC ELEGANCE AND BEEFS HER UP TO LEND VERISIMILITUDE TO HER BATTLE PROWESS."
- Comics Bulletin
VAMPIRELLA®
AND THE SCARLET LEGION®
128-PAGE TRADE PAPERBACK • IN STORES NOW!
written by JOE HARRIS • art by JOSE MALAGA • cover by J. SCOTT CAMPBELL
WWW.DYNAMITE.COM
FOLLOW US ON TWITTER: @DYNAMITECOMICS
LIKE US ON FACEBOOK: /DYNAMITECOMICS
Vampirella is ® and © 2013 DFI. All rights reserved. Dynamite, Dynamite Entertainment and the Dynamite Entertainment colophon are ®2013. All rights reserved.

LOOK FOR THESE DYNAMITE GREATEST HITS!

THE CONCLUSION TO THE NEW YORK TIMES BEST-SELLING SERIES!
Garth Ennis Russ Braun Darick Robertson
The BOYS
volume twelve: THE BLOODY DOORS OFF
DYNAMITE

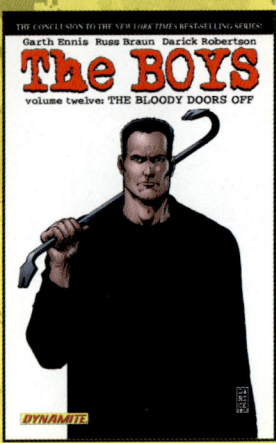

GARTH ENNIS
THE BOYS & MORE!

(Garth Ennis') Battlefields V1: The Night Witches
Ennis, Braun

(Garth Ennis') Battlefields V2: Dear Billy
Ennis, Snejbjerg

(Garth Ennis') Battlefields V3: The Tankies
Ennis, Ezquerra

(Garth Ennis') The Complete Battlefields V1
Ennis, Braun, Ezquerra, more

(Garth Ennis') Battlefields V4: Happy Valley
Ennis, Holden

(Garth Ennis') Battlefields V5: The Firefly and His Majesty
Ennis, Ezquerra

(Garth Ennis') Battlefields V6: Motherland
Ennis, Braun

(Garth Ennis') The Complete Battlefields V2
Ennis, Braun, Holden, more

The Boys V1 The Name of the Game
Ennis, Robertson

The Boys V2 Get Some
Ennis, Robertson, Snejbjerg

The Boys V3 Good For The Soul
Ennis, Robertson

The Boys V4 We Gotta Go Now
Ennis, Robertson

The Boys V5 Herogasm
Ennis, McCrea

The Boys V6 The Self-Preservation Society
Ennis, Robertson, Ezquerra

The Boys V7 The Innocents
Ennis, Robertson, Braun

The Boys V8 Highland Laddie
Ennis, McCrea

The Boys V9 The Big Ride
Ennis, Braun

The Boys V10: Butcher, Baker, Candlestickmaker
Ennis, Robertson

The Boys V11 Over the Hill With the Swords of a Thousand Men
Ennis, Braun

The Boys Definitive Edition V1
Ennis, Robertson

The Boys Definitive Edition V2
Ennis, Robertson

The Boys Definitive Edition V3
Ennis, Robertson, more

The Boys Definitive Edition V4
Ennis, Robertson, more

Dan Dare Omnibus
Ennis, Erskine

Jennifer Blood V1 A Woman's Work Is Never Done
Ennis, Batista, Baal, more

Jennifer Blood V2 Beautiful People
Ewing, Baal, more

Just A Pilgrim
Ennis, Ezquerra

The Ninjettes
Ewing, Casallos

Seven Brothers Omnibus
Ennis, Diggle, Kang, more

The Shadow V1 The Fire of Creation
Ennis, Campbell

KEVIN SMITH
GREEN HORNET
DYNAMITE
volume one: SINS OF THE FATHER

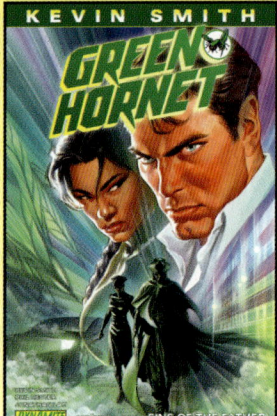

GREEN HORNET
KEVIN SMITH & MORE!

(Kevin Smith's) Green Hornet V1 Sins of the Father
Smith, Hester, Lau

(Kevin Smith's) Green Hornet V2 Wearing 'o the Green
Smith, Hester, Lau

Green Hornet V3 Idols
Hester, Lau

Green Hornet V4 Red Hand
Hester, Smith, Vitorino, more

Green Hornet: Blood Ties
Parks, Desjardins

The Green Hornet: Year One V1 The Sting of Justice
Wagner, Campbell

The Green Hornet: Year One V2 The Biggest of All Game
Wagner, Campbell

The Green Hornet Parallel Lives
Nitz, Raynor

The Green Hornet Golden Age Re-Mastered
Various

Kato V1 Not My Father's Daughter
Parks, Garza, Bernard

Kato V2 Living in America
Parks, Bernard

Kato Origins V1 Way of the Ninja
Nitz, Worley

Kato Origins V2 The Hellfire Club
Nitz, Worley

CROWN OF WORMS
DYNAMITE

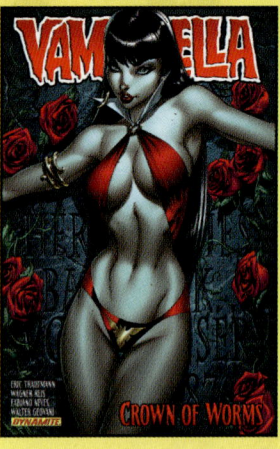

VAMPIRELLA!

Vampirella Masters Series V1 Grant Morrison & Mark Millar
Morrison, Millar, more

Vampirella Masters Series V2 Warren Ellis
Ellis, Conner Palmiotti, more

Vampi Omnibus V1
Conway, Lau

Vampirella Masters Series V3 Mark Millar
Millar, Mayhew

Vampirella Masters Series V4 Visionaries
Moore, Busiek, Loeb, more

Vampirella Masters Series V5 Kurt Busiek
Busiek, Sniegoski, more

Vampirella Masters Series V6 James Robinson
Robinson, Jusko, more

Vampirella Archives V1
Various

Vampirella Archives V2
Various

Vampirella Archives V3
Various

Vampirella Archives V4
Various

Vampirella Archives V5
Various

Vampirella V1 Crown of Worms
Trautman, Reis, Geovani

Vampirella V2 A Murder of Crows
Trautman, Neves, more

Vampirella V3 Throne of Skulls
Trautman, Malaga, more

Vampirella And The Scarlet Legion
Harris, Malaga

Vampirella vs. Dracula
Harris, Rodriguez

RED SONJA!

Adventures of Red Sonja V1
Thomas, Thorne, More

Adventures of Red Sonja V2
Thomas, Thorne, More

Adventures of Red Sonja V3
Thomas, Thorne, More

Queen Sonja V1
Ortega, Rubi

Queen Sonja V2 The Red Queen
Nelson, Herbert

Queen Sonja V3 Coming of Age
Lieberman, Rubi

Queen Sonja V4 Son of Set
Nelson, Salazar

Red Sonja She-Devil With a Sword V1
Oeming, Carey, Rubi

Red Sonja She-Devil With a Sword V2: Arrowsmiths
Oeming, Rubi, more

Red Sonja She-Devil With a Sword V3: The Rise of Kulan Gath
Oeming, Rubi, more

Red Sonja She-Devil With a Sword V4: Animals & More
Oeming, Homs, more

Red Sonja She-Devil With a Sword V5: World On Fire
Oeming, Reed, Homs

Red Sonja She-Devil With a Sword V6: Death
Marz, Ortega, Reed, more

Red Sonja She-Devil With a Sword V7: Born Again
Reed, Geovani

Red Sonja She-Devil With a Sword V8: Blood Dynasty
Reed, Geovani

Red Sonja She-Devil With a Sword V9: War Season
Trautmann, Geovani, more

Red Sonja She-Devil With a Sword V10: Machines of Empire
Trautmann, Geovani, more

Red Sonja She-Devil With a Sword Omnibus V1
Oeming, Carey, Rubi, more

Red Sonja She-Devil With a Sword Omnibus V2
Oeming, Reed, Homs, more

Red Sonja She-Devil With a Sword Omnibus V3
Reed, Geovani

Red Sonja vs. Thulsa Doom V1
David, Lieberman, Conrad

Savage Red Sonja: Queen of the Frozen Wastes
Cho, Murray, Homs

Red Sonja: Travels
Marz, Ortega, Thomas, more

Sword of Red Sonja: Doom of the Gods (Red Sonja vs. Thulsa Doom 2)
Lieberman, Antonio

Red Sonja: Wrath of the Gods
Lieberman, Geovani

Red Sonja: Revenge of the Gods
Lieberman, Sampere

Savage Tales of Red Sonja
Marz, Gage, Ortega, more

ART BOOKS!

The Art of Howard Chaykin
The Art of Painted Comics
The Art of Ramona Fradon
The Art of Red Sonja
The Art of Vampirella
The Dynamite Art of Alex Ross
George Pérez: Storyteller
The Romita Legacy

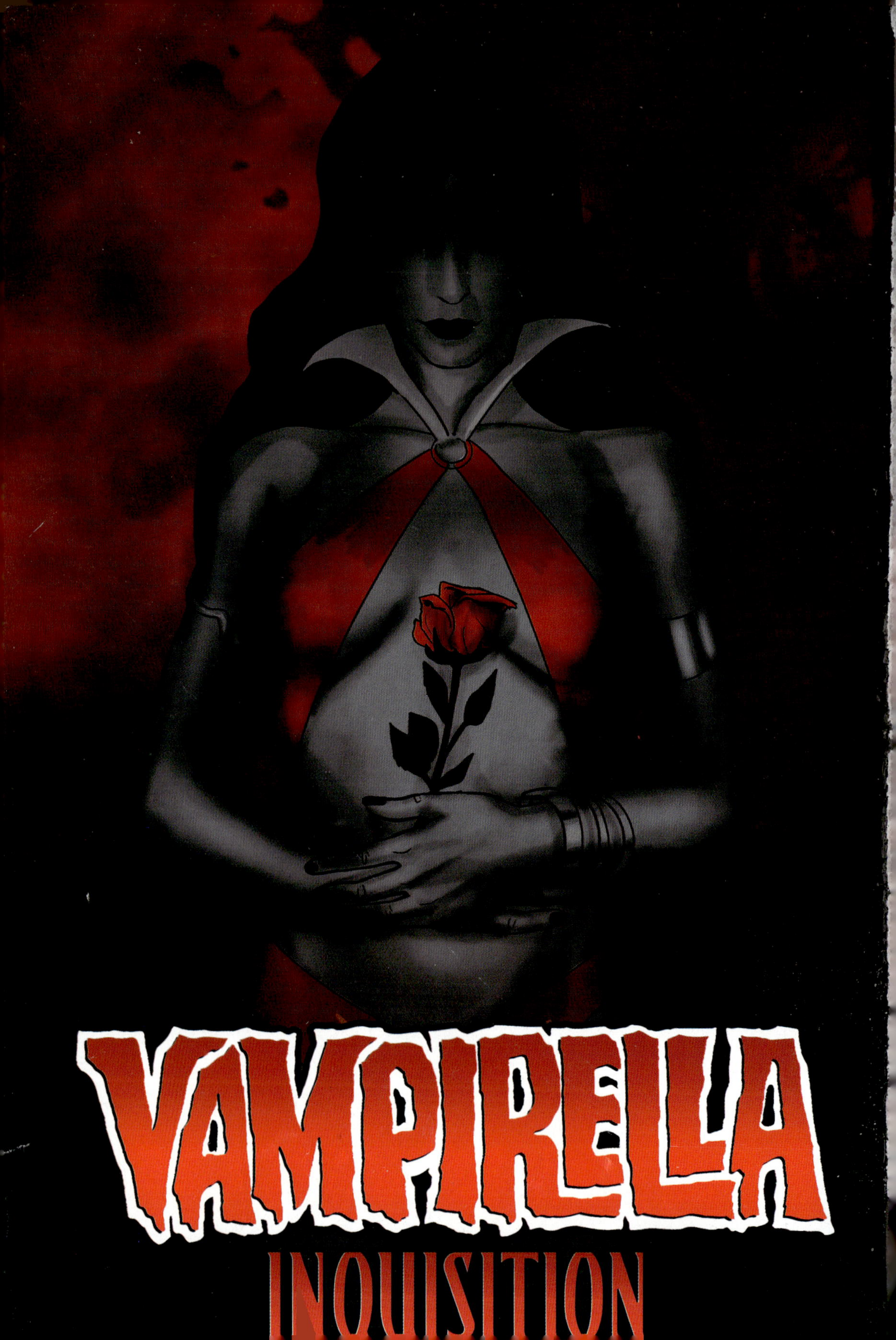
VAMPIRELLA
INQUISITION